SHEARCLIFF
AND COMPANY

ALBERT G MILLER

authorHOUSE®

AuthorHouse™
1663 Liberty Drive
Bloomington, IN 47403
www.authorhouse.com
Phone: 1 (800) 839-8640

Published by AuthorHouse   07/29/2017

ISBN: 978-1-5462-0211-0 (sc)
ISBN: 978-1-5462-0210-3 (e)

Library of Congress Control Number: 2017911824

Print information available on the last page.

Hey Gary, what's Cassy?

Spring, 1523 years post crisis

CHAPTER ONE

Christian Shearcliff awoke an hour before dawn as he did each morning in a small room in Mr. Cogwell's house. As with every day he was greeted by the sounds of the awakening town drifting in through his small single window; the sounds of business owners heading to their shops, farmers heading towards their fields, and the gentle chatter that came with people moving towards their destinations early on that spring morning. Chris knew that soon he would have to be joining them on his way to work but for the moment he simply lay in his bed soaking in the familiar sounds of his home.

The village of Shearcliff was a quiet place located in the northwestern region of Targoth. Nestled at the foot of a large mountain and surrounded by a deep forest the village rarely saw travelers, save for the occasional adventurer heading to the nearby ruins of Algeminia. Large enough to appear on most maps of Targoth, yet small enough to avoid having a permanent garrison, Shearcliff sat directly against a mountain where a large portion of rock had fallen away creating a clearing in the forest as well as giving the village its name. Originally founded as a base camp by adventures to explore the ruins it rapidly evolved into a proper settlement as the families of the adventures migrated to the small village; however as less and less treasure was pulled from the ruins fewer and fewer people came to Shearcliff until it was all but forgotten in the wilderness. These days nobody ventured to the ruins anymore as it had been widely accepted that they had been picked clean of treasure. Those who had descended from adventurers now lived the quiet lives of farmers and shopkeepers.

Eventually Chris slipped out of bed and looked around at his meager possessions seeing everything was as it should be. His knife hung in its sheath from his bed post. It was a simple thing with a wooden hilt and a steel blade slightly shorter than Chris's own forearm, serrated along its bottom half. Chris had purchased the knife seven years ago using all of his savings from a traveling merchant and valued it immensely. The bow he had fashioned just the summer before from a sapling sat propped against the trunk at the foot of his bed that contained his only two sets of clothing. Slowly he walked over to the foot of his bed and proceeded to open his trunk, pulling out the cleaner of his two sets of clothes and set it aside revealing his treasure.

Hidden at the bottom of his trunk was the shard of a mirror he had found in a nearby creek three years prior. He had absolutely no idea what such a thing was doing in a creek in the middle of nowhere but that wasn't what was important to him. What mattered to him was that so far as he knew it was the only mirror in all of Shearcliff, even if it was just a fragment. He gazed into the mirror, looking at himself. He saw the same thing he saw each morning; a dirty narrow face with high cheekbones, an angular nose, and brown eyes so dark they were nearly black. Running a hand though his shaggy black hair he thought idly that perhaps he should get it cut seeing as it hung nearly to his shoulders.

Once his treasure was once again safely stowed in his trunk he finished dressing himself in his plain wool clothes, strapped his knife to his hip, pulled on his leather boots, and proceeded to leave his room. As he walked through his small home he passed his sisters old room. On a whim he peeked inside, only to have his hopes dashed to see it just as empty as the last time he looked. Slightly smaller than his room it looked as it always did, the bed neatly made, the shelves empty, with a fine layer of dust coating everything. Seeing inside brought back memories of her, like him she had no knowledge of her parents and had been taken in by Mr. Cogwell from a young age.

Chris recalled the day they met.

He was five at the time and had discovered the delight of exploring the woods around the mountain much to Mr. Cogwell's displeasure. Despite this, on any given day he could be found wandering the forest exploring its secluded reaches. It was on one such expedition at the base of the mountain that he had heard the sound of crying and followed it to her, finding her pinned beneath a pile of fallen rocks.

"Are you alright?" he had asked her.

She had only growled in reply and struggled harder to escape from under the rubble.

Chris saw blood pooling around her, spreading from under the rocks where her legs were trapped. Realizing she was hurt he raced back and grabbed Mr. Cogwell, babbling about a little girl trapped under the rocks. Mr. Cogwell wasted no time and hobbled after young Chris as fast as his false leg would allow. Despite his age, Mr. Cogwell managed to free her from the rubble, even with her constant struggling.

Once they had safely returned to Mr. Cogwell's small home it became apparent she had been wandering the woods alone for some time. She was terribly thin, feral, and afraid of most everything. Nevertheless, they put her in Chris's bed and nursed her back to health. It was days before Chris would leave her side. As time wore on she grew less timid and with the kind care of Chris and Mr. Cogwell she became indistinguishable from the other children her age, appearing herself to be no older than Chris. Over the next few years she played with Chris, ate with Chris, fought with Chris, and slept in the same bed as Chris. They became best friends and loved each other as brother and sister. When it became apparent that the room they shared was far too small for the both of them, Mr. Cogwell even converted their store room into a bedroom of her very own, a difficult feat in the tiny house. They gave her the name Cassy, and she took the last name Shearcliff, as it is the custom for those who don't know their parentage and bastards to take the name of their home as their family name seeing as they have no other.

As the years passed however it became painfully apparent that Cassy was not normal. The other villagers became wary of her and she had fewer friends than the other girls her age. Her abnormality didn't bother Chris however and they continued to spend their childhood playing together while trying to avoid Mr. Cogwell's ever-present wrath. Still, as she approached womanhood her physical differences became unavoidable in the eyes of the villagers. She was openly shunned by all but a few friends, and even they kept their distance to avoid association with her. As such, on their sixteenth birthday, as neither Chris nor Cassy knew their birthday they celebrated together on the first day of summer, the Targothian new year, she announced to Chris and Mr. Cogwell that she was leaving the village.

Chris had begged her to stay while Mr. Cogwell remained silent and unreadable. Chris and Cassy argued deep into the night. Finally, he had turned to Mr. Cogwell.

"Say something!" Chris had demanded.

Mr. Cogwell simply looked at Cassy.

"Are you sure about this?" he had asked her quietly. "Once you leave they'll never allow you to return."

"I am," Cassy had replied, more serious than Chris had ever seen her.

"Very well," he said and rose from his chair with a groan.

He crossed the room slowly and grabbed the lockbox that stored the family's little money. Carefully he reached inside his shirt and pulled out a key he wore around his neck and proceeded to open the small box. From inside he withdrew the small purse that held their meager gold.

"Take this," he had said. "May you find happiness in your travels."

She left that same night without looking back.

That had been almost two years ago now yet Chris still checked her room from time to time with the fleeting hope she may have returned.

"It's not like I'm worried about her," Chris said to himself. "Even when we were kids she had a knack for getting out of trouble and she's quite good with her bow," he mused.

He recalled several hunting trips in specific where she had felled far more game than him.

"I must remember to ask about her again when the supply merchant comes next week, perhaps this time he's seen her," he muttered hopefully.

In the years since her departure Chris had come to understand why she chose to leave and beyond that recently he had begun to envy her. As a man nearing the age of eighteen he yearned to see the world beyond Shearcliff. He had heard tell of great cities ruled by rich kings, recalled stories of massive dragons that flew in the sky, and of mighty gods that walked among men. He imagined that Cassy must have seen something at *least* that fantastic in the years she had been away.

It helped matters little that since his sister's departure the family had no money to spare with Mr. Cogwell and himself making only enough to cover their basic needs. It also didn't help matters any that Mr. Cogwell seemed to drink far more than he used to before Cassy's departure. Chris had a plan however; a way he believed would ensure that he could get the money he needed. Enough gold that he could visit the distant lands of his dreams and that Mr. Cogwell could live out the rest of his days in a drunken stupor, though to be honest Chris thought that wasn't much different from how he spent his days now.

All he had to do was go to the ruins and find the treasure. This plan had sprung up directly after an oddity had arrived in Shearcliff two days prior, a fast rider from the nearby city of Draclige. He had come bearing news of a squad of heavy knights traveling under the orders of Governor Sorros to the ruins of Algeminia. On their way to the ruins they would be stopping at Shearcliff for rest and supplies and the village was to make all necessary arrangements before they arrive or face the Governor's wrath.

Because Shearcliff fell under the jurisdiction of Draclige they were forced to pay taxes to the city in exchange for protection of the city's troops. Being as remote as it is however Shearcliff rarely saw troops of any kind, Draclige or otherwise. This has not stopped the tax rates from steadily marching up each year however causing many within the village to become quite displeased with the current administration. Chris felt as if he rarely heard the people talk about anything other than taxes anymore, and he heard the people talk quite a bit as the serving boy at the Silver Stallion; the only tavern in all of Shearcliff. That was why when the inn was abuzz with the rider's news Chris was especially interested. For the Governor to send troops to the ruins he must have a good reason. For years the ruins had been considered picked clean and the only explanation Chris could come up with as to why Sorros would send his men was that he must have learned of something valuable hidden away within Algeminia, something the adventurers had missed. If something that valuable was in the ruins he was sure that the Governor would pay well for it so all Chris had to do was get to it first.

The night he thought of his plan he made the mistake of sharing it with Mr. Cogwell. Over the course of his life Chris believed he had made many mistakes. Wondering what would happen if he tried to domesticate the raccoon he had snared while hunting, drinking an entire bottle of Mr. Cogwell's strongest whisky, or anything involving Cassy that ended in the words *bet you won't*.

None of these things according to Chris were to be considered wise life choices, but not even the fury of an enraged raccoon compared to Mr. Cogwell's wrath when Chris told him he was planning to go to the ruins.

"All I've got to do is grab the treasure before the knights," Chris said with blissful enthusiasm. "I'll be in and out before they know I was there."

Once Chris finished sharing the details of his plan he began rambling about how good things would be for them once he got the gold from selling the treasure and failed to notice the flames of rage in the old man's eyes.

"Listen here child," Mr. Cogwell snapped suddenly cutting off Chris's excited rambling. "I don't wanna hear one more word about the ruins, you stay far away from them you hear me? Not one more word!"

"What's wrong with the ruins?" Chris asked with genuine curiosity. "It's just a bunch of old crumbling buildings. What's so bad about them?"

Mr. Cogwell rose suddenly from his chair taking Chris by surprise.

"What did I say!? What was it I just said!?" Mr. Cogwell bellowed.

Chris having lived with the man for his entire life was used to such outbursts but they were usually reserved to when Mr. Cogwell was drunk. So while surprised at this particular outburst Chris knew from experience the safest place for him was now outside the house. By the time Chris reached the door Mr. Cogwell already had his belt in hand and was hobbling after him as fast as could move his wooden leg.

"Get back here, get back here and let me teach you how to listen you ungrateful brat!" Chris heard him scream behind him as he ran as fast as he could away from the old man.

Chris had never been the fastest one in his village, that title belonged to his sister, but at that moment it was as he had traded his legs for wings. Chris credited this to the memories of all the times he had been caught by Mr. Cogwell after such an outburst and the sound that belt made as it whistled towards his backside. Chris headed to the woods where he had stashed a blanket as well as some food for an occasion such as this. This was by no means Chris's first time being chased from his home and he knew it paid to be prepared. Upon arriving at his stash Chris saw the scattered remains of the food he had left and the shreds of his blanket, courtesy of the forest creatures.

Chris sighed.

"Looks like it's going to be a long night," he grumbled doing his best to make himself comfortable on the forest floor.

The next day Chris decided to stop by at the Stallion to ask Mr. Darfew why Mr. Cogwell acted as he did. Mr. Darfew was the owner of the Silver Stallion and Chris's boss. He was also one of the few people in the village Chris felt he could openly share his ambitions with without ridicule. Over the years Mr. Darfew had often given the tavern's extra food to Chris and Cassy when Mr. Cogwell was unable to provide for them himself.

Chris caught Mr. Darfew up to speed on the events of the previous evening including his plans to loot the ruins. Mr. Darfew quietly sat and listened until Chris had finished.

"Old man Sam hates those ruins with a passion he does," Mr. Darfew said simply before falling quiet.

"I gathered that as he was chasing me last night," Chris said slightly annoyed that that was all Mr. Darfew had to say on the matter. "What I want to know is what reason does he have to be so vehement about this?"

"I doubt the old man ever spoke of it to you, I myself was only a lad when it happened," Darfew said slowly.

When he spoke again he seemed to choose his words carefully.

"You see Sam wasn't always the drunk you know now. Many years ago he was an adventurer who came to Shearcliff with his companions to seek his fortune within the ruins. Needless to say he never found it and it cost him his leg as well as the lives of his friends. He fell into despair after that and tried drowning his sorrows in a bottle."

Darfew paused here to take a long sip from his own bottle for dramatic effect.

"A few years after that he took you in when you were found abandoned on the road side, then later Cassy, and his drinking lessened significantly," Mr. Darfew said.

Chris found this hard to believe having firsthand experience with how much the old man drank on a nightly basis.

"Anyhow he never spoke a word of what happened in the ruins all those years ago and most of us know by now it's safer not to ask. You'd be wise to steer clear of anything related to those ruins else you run the risk of him flying off the handle like he does," Mr. Darfew warned

"Duly noted. Thanks Mr. Darfew," Chris said as he rose from the table. "Have a nice night sir."

"You as well my boy, always happy to talk I am!" Mr. Darfew called after him.

As Chris walked down the road to his shared home he thought about what Mr. Darfew had said. Try as he might he could not picture Mr. Cogwell, a man who drank himself to sleep nearly every evening before the sun had set, who Chris had never seen do an honest day's work in his life, the man who had raised him, as an adventurer. Yet nothing else Chris could think of would explain his reaction from the night before.

When he entered his house the first thing he noticed was Mr. Cogwell had already passed out for the evening. The door to his room was ajar and the faint snores and scent of cheap ale drifting from within told Chris all he needed to know. Chris retired to his room for the night, watching the last rays of the day's sun streaming through his small window. On a regular evening he would still be working at the tavern, however tonight was one of the few nights he had off and he planned to get all the rest he could before the knights arrived. The rider had said the knights were due to arrive in four days, which put them getting there the day after tomorrow. Chris planned to make the needed arrangements for a trip tomorrow and set out after the knights the next day. His plan was to tail them secretly to the ruins, allow them to deal with whatever dangers they may find, then quickly find the treasure before they realized he was there. Then once he had the treasure he was only a three day's ride to Draclige away from becoming very, very rich.

Chris's last thought before falling asleep was:

"What could possibly go wrong?"

CHAPTER TWO

The next morning Chris awoke to unfamiliar sounds. Rather than the usual quiet bustling and hushed discussions he was used to, this morning was filled with the shouts of men and the indignant neighs of horses. Chris leaped out of bed and raced to the window, and was shocked to see men in armor riding slowly down the street. The knights had arrived early.

"Damn them they couldn't have been on time could they?" Chris muttered.

Continuing to curse his foul luck he dressed as quickly as he could, strapped his knife to his hip, and set about stringing his bow. He then pulled his quiver from out under his bed and rushed to ensure he had enough arrows. They were simple things he had fashioned himself, lacking fletching with only small stone tips. Nevertheless they could bring down a deer so long as his aim was true. Chris had no plans of fighting within the ruins but he felt better having his bow, just in case.

As he exited his room he shut the door as quietly as he could manage and began to sneak through his house in fear of waking Mr. Cogwell. They had not spoken since the night of their argument and Chris was sure if he saw him leaving there would be a repeat of the previous fiasco. Chris let out a sigh of relief however when he saw Mr. Cogwell sprawled across his bed, door wide open, still snoring loudly.

"He'll be a lot less mad when he's rich enough to drown in booze,"

Chris whispered to himself as he crept away from the sleeping man's room.

Once on the street Chris saw that the knights had already passed through the town on the way to the ruins. Rather than take the road Chris opted to cut through the forest he knew so well. There he decided he would have far less risk of being discovered by the knights who Chris was sure would not take kindly to being followed. He had heard from travelers at the Stallion that the type of men Sorros tended to hire were not the type you wanted to cross. As such he kept a healthy distance from the road as he headed towards the ruins. It was evening when he first saw it.

Despite having lived in the area his entire life he had never made the trip to the ruins before. He was expecting a few broken down buildings scattered across the hills, but what he saw far exceeded his expectations. As Chris cleared the tree line he let out an involuntary gasp.

The ruins of Algeminia spread for miles below him. Rather than a few scattered piles of rubble what he saw was tightly packed buildings and narrow streets. In an instant it became clear to Chris that this was once a massive city. With this in mind Chris decided that the large pile of rubble towards the center of the ruins must have been the castle. He saw the knights then riding towards the ruins. At this distance he could make out no details about the riders themselves but he was at least able to count their number which was seven. Chris began to run towards the ruins. If he had any hope of finding the mysterious treasure he had to work quickly. As the ruins grew closer he once again marveled at their size.

He had a moment of doubt as the walls of the crumbling city rose around him, thinking of the fate of Mr. Cogwell's companions, but this fled from his mind as he heard a voice. Faint at first, impossible to make out, it grew clearer as Chris snuck towards it. When he grew close enough to make out words he heard a man's voice say:

"…Once we find them we must make haste to return to Draclige. Governor Sorros is not a patient man and wants the artifacts recovered as fast as possible…"

Chris drew closer, and peeked around the street corner. Now he was able to put a face to the man speaking.

"This brute can't possibly be human," was the first thought that passed through his mind.

Standing at almost seven feet tall he towered over the men around him. If Chris himself had stood by his side he doubted he would reach to the man's broad shoulders. The giant stood addressing five other men who stood in a half circle around him.

"Five men sitting, plus the leader which makes six," Chris whispered to himself. "Where's the seventh man?" No sooner had the inquiry passed his lips than he felt himself being grabbed from behind by a pair of strong hands.

"Well well we's have us a sneaking spy do we's?" came a nasally voice from behind him.

He attempted to free himself from his assailant by kicking behind him and striking at him with his elbows all the while yelling at the top of his lungs:

"Let me go you bastard! You filthy son of a whore! Gods help me I swear I'll…" His torrent of verbal abuse was cut short as an armored glove clamped over his mouth.

"Easy there kiddo, we's don't want you to hurt yourself now do we's?" asked the voice behind him and Chris felt the sharp point of a dagger digging into his back.

Chris quickly stopped his struggles and the man behind him yelled out to the knights in front of him:

"Hey Captain! I's finished scoutin! Looks what I's caught us!"

Chris suddenly found himself looking at the sky as he was unceremoniously dragged towards the knights by the back of his shirt. Without the threat of a dagger in his back he resumed his struggling but it was to no avail. As they reached the edge of the circle Chris was tossed through the air into the center. Chris sat up and finally got a good look at his captor.

He was a weasely looking man with a small mouth and a large hooked nose that looked to have been broken at one point and never healed properly. His dark eyes had a hungry edge to them and refused to look at any one thing for longer than two seconds as they darted about behind his lanky brown hair. The brutish man whom Weasel, as Chris began thinking of him, had referred to as Captain before gazed down at Chris. His face was much like the rest of him, brutish without any hint of softness or compassion. His lower jaw protruded beyond his upper, leading Chris to believe that one of his ancestors must have been an orc, or perhaps a giant. Much of his face was taken up by a long scar that ran from his chin up and across his left eye. Chris took little notice of this man's face however; his attention was focused on the man's eyes. Unlike the eyes of Weasel these eyes were steady and piercing. There was a savage intelligence in his eyes and from the way he looked at him Chris knew that he wouldn't hesitate for a moment before killing him. For nearly a minute no one spoke. It was the brute who broke the silence.

"Would you care to explain why you are here?" he asked.

"Me?" Chris said as he thought as fast as he could. "I come here all the time. I've always explored the ruins. I was about to ask what you were doing here myself," he lied. "Why are you here by the way? Are you looking for something?" Chris asked hastily.

The brute merely shook his head.

"For you to frequent the ruins you must live in Shearcliff," he said with a sinister smile. "How fortunate. Did you hear that men? This young man just volunteered to be our guide!"

This was met with a round of laughter from behind Chris. Silently he cursed himself for telling the lie he did; now he could think of no excuse to escape these men. If they arrived at the treasure at the same time as Chris, he knew he had no hope of seizing it before the knights. For his plan to succeed he had to find a way to escape.

"Time enough for that later," Chris thought. "For now I have to focus of not angering the heavily armed men around me more than I have. If only they hadn't found me so fast then I might have an idea of what they are looking for. If I follow them however I may get a clue as to what this treasure is. Perhaps I can turn this to my advantage."

Chris smiled up at his captor.

"Why of course I'll help you! What might it be you are looking for?"

he asked with as much enthusiasm as he could muster as he rose to his feet, but immediately regretted it as the brute's face morphed from the cruel mocking smile it had held up to this point into a look of suspicion.

It was Weasel who spoke next to Chris's surprise.

"You's haven't seen a tomb around then have you's? Because we's are looking for something called the tomb of the…" whatever Weasel was about to say Chris never learned because the brute sent him flying with a backhand to the face.

"Fool!" he bellowed. "Sorros gave us specific orders to tell no one of our mission! And here you are blabbing to some nosy kid, you incompetent buffoon!" the brute ranted, however the words fell upon deaf ears.

Chris could see that the blow from the brute's armored hand had sent the man flying several yards backwards into the wall of a building behind them. Weasel now sat slumped against the wall with blood trickling from the corner of his mouth, his neck bent at an unnatural angle. Chris had seen death before in the village, having attended several funerals for older villagers; still there was something about the way that this man had killed his companion without a second thought that chilled Chris to his core.

"As for you boy, I don't buy that lie you spun earlier at all," the brute said as he turned back to Chris. "Nobody frequents the ruins, least of all village boys equipped like you are. I think you you're here to steal what we're after. For that I have to thank you," he said as the cruel smile crept back onto his face. "You see, Governor Sorros was very specific with his orders, and that included what we should do if the village was to interfere with our mission. I believe his exact choice of words was *exterminate*," the brute said as his face was engulfed by a savage smile.

Chris recoiled in horror as visions of his village in flames flashed before his eyes.

"You can't! They had nothing to do with this! Do what you will with me but leave the others out of this!" Chris cried out and the knights behind him roared with laughter.

"You're in no position to be making demands boy!" the brute laughed.

It was then that one of the men spoke from behind Chris. Not having gotten a good look at the others yet Chris was surprised to see the speaker dressed differently than the other knights. While the others were equipped similar to the brute with dark grey steel plate armor over a suit of chain mail and carrying an assortment of swords and axes, this man wore the robes of a priest that had been modified to sit under his breast plate. He also wore gauntlets and greaves but no other armor was present. He carried no visible weapon. The man was quite youthful when compared to the other knights, looking only to be perhaps a couple years older than Chris. His eyes were startlingly blue and his close cropped hair was a shade of blonde so light it that was nearing white. By contrast his face was quite plain with the most noticeable feature being his short beard. At that moment his face was contorted in rage.

"Exterminate? Exterminate! How dare you Droga! What right do you have to decide those people's fates!? Leave them and this man alone," he yelled at Droga, as Chris now knew him to be called, as he marched forward.

"I have the right as a Knight of Draclige!" Droga yelled back, though Chris noticed he looked far less confident as this strange man approached him, and actually took a step back.

What could possibly make Droga, a man who Chris had just seen kill a subordinate with a single swing and without a second thought fear this strange short man. For this man was indeed quite short, nearly six inches shorter than Chris who himself only stood around five nine. Yet as he stood there staring up at Droga, Droga looked quite uncomfortable.

"Listen here cleric; I am in charge of this mission! We merely hired you to disarm any magic traps we may find," Droga stammered and suddenly it became clear to Chris why he feared this small man so much.

Clerics needed no weapons; they wielded the will of gods as their swords. They could call down fire with a word, reverse death with a prayer. They were immensely powerful and only a fool would dare anger one. At that moment the cleric seemed very angry indeed. Droga proved then he was either incredibly stupid or incredibly brave.

"You will stand down or else you shall share the same fate as the villagers! So? What will it be!?" Droga bellowed.

Chris waited eagerly for the cleric to smite Droga with holy magic while simultaneously hoping that he would survive the resulting shockwave. The seconds drew out and neither man showed signs of moving until without warning the clerics hand shot outward, but not at Droga.

"Luminita!" he yelled as his hand shot toward the sky.

Suddenly Chris's world was filled with blinding light. Around him he could hear the outraged cries of the other knights and the sound of weapons being drawn. Chris felt a hand grab his shoulder and the clerics voice next to him said:

"Hurry and follow me, the spell won't last long."

Without any idea what was happening or a better plan of action himself he allowed the cleric to guide him through the light. Without giving any indication of letting up, the light suddenly vanished around him. Glancing over his shoulder Chris saw what appeared to be a miniature sun sitting on the ground.

"It's a light spell," the cleric explained. "At that size I can't maintain it for long though. We have to hurry if we are to escape."

"Who are you?" Chris asked.

"Time enough for that later. Unless you want to get killed by those thugs I suggest that we run," the cleric told him.

So Chris and the cleric ran, away from the knights, deeper into the ruins. They had made it no more than ten steps when Chris heard a loud pop behind them and Droga yelling:

"Don't let those two escape! Catch them and end their miserable lives!"

They pelted down the street as fast as they were able, thankful that the heavy armor the knights behind them wore was slowing them down. Chris knew it was only a matter of time though. Eventually they would make a wrong turn, run down some dead end. When that happened Chris doubted that the he and the cleric would be able to stave off five very angry knights with light spells and his bow. Having managed to put a few yards ahead of their pursuers the duo rounded a corner.

"Quick lets hide in here," Chris gasped as he pointed towards a massive building that appeared to be mostly intact.

"Not like we have a better option," the cleric replied breathlessly as the two ducked into the ancient building.

As they sat panting in the shadows of the room they had chosen to hide in they heard the knights race past them.

"They must have gone down one of the side streets, they can't be far!" they heard Droga yell.

They waited in silence catching their breath as the footsteps of the knights faded away. Once they were sure the knights were gone they turned to each other.

"So," Chris began "Who might you be?"

"My name is Matthew Bleakstar. You can just call me Matt though," Matt replied. "Those monsters hired me to disable any magical traps they may have found here in the ruins. At the time I thought nothing of it and the gold was good so I tagged along. Had I known what type of men they were I never would have gotten involved. As I'm sure you've figured out by now I'm a cleric. What's your name?"

"My name is Christian, Christian Shearcliff. You can just call me Chris; everyone does," he told him.

"Glad to make your acquaintance Chris, though I wish the circumstances were better," Matt said.

"Likewise. Had you not stepped forward I'm sure they would have killed me. That was quite a cool spell you cast back there. What god do you serve?" Chris asked.

Matt's face darkened at Chris's words.

"Always the same," he grumbled to himself. "It's always whose your god? Which of the ten do you serve?" he said in a mocking voice. "Never do they ask about me, *oh no*. If you must know I don't serve any one god," Matt said grudgingly.

"I didn't mean to…" whatever Chris didn't mean to do Matt never found out because at that moment the old wooden floorboards under Chris gave way and he plunged down into darkness.

Chris landed hard with a cry of pain. As he became aware of

his surroundings he realized he must have fallen into the building's basement, faint light streaming in through the hole he had created. Looking up through the hole he saw Matt's face peaking down.

"Are you alright Chris?" he asked in alarm.

"Yeah I'm fine" Chris called back feeling like one may expect after falling through a floor.

"Are you sure? That looked like it hurt," Matt said with concern.

"How very perceptive of you. I don't feel like anything's broken so I think I'll live," Chris groaned as he stood up.

"That's good at least! Do you see any way back up?" Matt asked.

Chris looked around and saw nothing resembling a staircase, or any other way of climbing back up for that matter. What he did see was a stone doorframe set into the far wall its door having long ago rotted away.

"I see a doorway!" Chris called. "Perhaps the stairs are in another room?"

"Be careful Chris, you have no idea what's down there," Matt warned.

"Don't worry I have my bow with me, I'll be fine," Chris said dismissively.

"You may want to check that Chris," Matt said with slight amusement.

It was then that Chris noticed the condition of his bow. It had been slung over his shoulder when he had fallen and Chris saw it had been reduced to splinters by his impact. Chris felt a wave of disappointment wash over him. It had taken him days to find the perfect sapling and fashion it into a usable bow. In terms of craftsmanship the bow had never been perfect but it had put dinner on his table more times than he could count. He had been immensely proud of it and now it was reduced to little more than kindling.

"Damn," Chris cursed. "Looks like I'll have to be extra careful then."

He decided that there would be time to mourn the loss of his bow later.

"Right now, I have to focus on the situation at hand," Chris thought to himself. "I'll find a way up you wait there," he told Matt.

"Understood," Matt called in reply.

With that Chris set off through the doorway into a dark hall. He walked through the shadows for what he thought was a very long time until he came to an intersection, with the hall splitting left and right. Despite the fact that the right hand path sloped toward the surface Chris felt an unexplainable urge to go left, as if something was calling to him. He walked slowly to the left, deeper into the ruins.

Despite being underground Chris found himself able to see, courtesy of a dim grey light coming from somewhere out of sight. Almost too faint to make out, the light proved to be just enough to stop him from tripping. He thought little of it; the force calling to him dominated his attention. As he progressed down this new path it grew stronger, like he was growing closer like he was on the edge of a conversation and was straining to make out the words. He quickened his pace to a jog and barely took the time to notice that the hall began sloping downwards away from the surface. It mattered little to him; he was getting close to something, something important. It washed over him like a wave this mysterious power, driving all other thought from his mind.

Just when Chris thought it would consume him it stopped completely. He became aware of how far he had run; noticing the sweat that dripped down his face was growing cold.

"I must be pretty far underground," he muttered to himself.

Rising before him were a pair of large oak doors banded with iron. Unlike the rest of the tunnel the doors showed no signs of age or rot. Curiosity getting the better of him, he gave the doors a push and found they swung open easily without the slightest sound. The room before him was brightly lit, without any noticeable light source. Aside from three large stone slabs protruding from the room's center it appeared empty. As he walked into the room he was able to examine the slabs better. They were nearly identical. Each was roughly seven feet long and four feet wide with rounded tops. They each featured a different glyph engraved on the top of the grey stone but were otherwise unmarked. He drew closer to the one on his left and noticed another detail. There was a thin seam in the stone near the top, as if the slab could be opened.

His curiosity once again triumphing over caution he managed to push the lid of the slab off onto the floor. It landed with a deafening boom. Chris looked inside and recoiled in horror. Suddenly the slabs made sense. This room was a crypt.

Mustering his courage Chris peeked into the tomb once again. He saw an ancient skeleton grinning at him, lying on its back with its hands clasping a sheathed sword to its chest. The sword transfixed Chris, calling to every fiber of his being.

As if moved by an invisible puppeteer Chris reached into the tomb and pulled the sword free from the skeleton's grasp. It was a beautiful weapon. Its hilt was fashioned at such a length so that it could be wielded with either one hand or two at the wielders preference and appeared to be made of some type of mysterious wood. Somehow it showed no signs of having rotted during its time in the tomb. At the base of the hilt was a steel pommel carved with an intricate design which captured his eye. The pattern seemed to have no beginning or end; it simply flowed into itself over and over again, an infinite series of overlapping squares. The sword's cross guard was just as beautiful, extending down towards the blade forming a V. It was also carved with the same pattern as the hilt, and set on either side was a large ruby. It was the gems that truly fascinated Chris. They were identical to one another each roughly the size of his thumb. They were perfectly smooth and as Chris looked into them they seemed to glow with burning inner light like their cores were somehow made of molten metal. Chris felt the urge to draw the sword from its scabbard, which itself was made from soft leather capped on both ends with steel. Interestingly enough it featured straps that indicated it was to be worn across the back rather than at the hip like most swords of this size. After so many years the leather should have been dried and brittle but it was still as supple as the day it was made. Chris withdrew the blade with a faint hiss and held it before him. The blade itself was three feet long and featured a continuation of the earlier pattern running down its center. The edge was razor sharp, sharper than anything he had ever seen. Chris had never held a sword before, but still felt that this sword was well balanced as if made just for him. It seemed to hum with a faint power and if Chris didn't know any better he would have said it seemed alive in his hands. Returning the sword to its sheath he decided to investigate the two other tombs hoping to find other fantastic treasures.

After successfully strapping the sword across his back through a process of trial and error he approached the center tomb. Expecting another weapon or perhaps armor he was slightly disappointed to see that this tomb contained a book. The book was clutched to the chest of this tombs owner much in the same manner as the first though Chris noticed there was also a leather belt case to store the book in, lying at the skeletons feet. Chris carefully removed the book from the grasp of the skeleton and inspected it with caution. He feared that the book would be in a poor state after so long in the tomb but it seemed to be perfectly fine.

The book itself was bound in leather with two sapphires set into its cover, one on the front and one on the back. They closely resembled the rubies on the sword except these gems seemed to have been fashioned from ice with their cores sparkling like a clear lake. The book itself seemed to have relatively few pages yet when Chris opened it he could not reach the ending. Each time he turned a page it was as if another took its place. He also found himself incapable of opening the book to any other page than the first. It was in this fashion he realized that the book wouldn't show him the same thing twice.

"Magic!" he whispered with excitement and wondered if perhaps the sword across his back had some hidden ability too.

After toying with the book for a while, looking at the strange things it would show him, many of which were written in languages he could not understand, he stowed it in the belt pouch and strapped it to his hip. Chris now turned his gaze upon the final tomb. He made haste to open it greedily looking for more treasure and was shocked to see only a cloak folded neatly inside with no trace of an occupant. Chris pulled it out and saw a small scrap of parchment fall from within it. On it was written runes Chris could not read, but there was a small hand drawn picture of a man sleeping beneath a tree at the base. Greatly confused by this Chris slipped the paper into his pocket for further study. He turned his attention to the cloak itself.

It was a simple thing, dark grey, made from a material Chris didn't recognize. The cloak also featured a deep hood and Chris imagined it would be quite warm to wear. The most noticeable feature of the cloak was its large clasps which seemed to be made of silver. Sure enough each one was studded with a large emerald. Not surprisingly the emeralds closely resembled the other gems Chris had acquired but unlike the others of the set they did not seem to glow, rather these gems seemed hungry, drinking up the light around them. On a whim Chris donned the cloak, fashioning its clasps to his shirt and pulled the hood up over his head. It was surprisingly light contrasting his original impression and the material was remarkably soft. A sudden thought flew into Chris's mind.

"Weasel said something about a tomb before Droga had killed him…could this have been what the knights were looking for? The knights! I've been down here playing tomb raider while Matt's in danger! He must think I got lost. I've got to hurry back and find a way out of this place," Chris thought in horror.

He raced back the way he had come, and this time when he reached the intersection he continued straight down the path he had yet to explore toward the surface. Thankfully this hall proved far shorter than the others and at the end of it he found a room with a stone stair well. The stairs led up to what Chris assumed to once be a feast hall featuring a large rotting table with several doors leading out. Slowly Chris worked his way through the maze that was this building and returned to the room that he had fallen from.

He was sure it was the same room, the hole was still in the floor, but there was no sign of Matt. Chris carefully peaked onto the street through the doorway and groaned.

There was Matt, bruised and bloody, held aloft by Droga's knights. To make matters worse Droga himself was standing beside them, looking straight at him.

CHAPTER THREE

"Hello there boy," Droga said with a sweet smile upon his cruel face. "Why don't you come over here and give me those dusty old artifacts and we'll forget this whole thing ever happened. You can go home and we'll be on our way."

"Don't listen to them Chris!" Matt moaned from the arms of the knights. "They'll kill you once they have what they want! Run!"

"Quiet you backstabbing little shit!" yelled one of the knights holding Matt.

Chris watched in horror as he delivered a savage kick to Matt's ribs forcing him to cough up a large mouthful of blood.

Looking at Matt, slumped in the hands of the knights Chris felt rage unlike anything he had ever known.

"Matt helped me because he thought it was the right thing to do. How dare they hurt him?" Chris thought to himself, and as he did it was as if a hidden voice was cheering him along, fanning the flames of his anger.

The rage consumed him, the desire for vengeance against those who would harm someone like Matt, someone with a good heart. He let out a scream of rage and lost himself, his mind burned away by this alien fury.

Chris, who before that day had never touched a sword in his life, screamed words he didn't understand in a language long forgotten, drew the sword, and charged.

Matt could feel his ribs break as the knight kicked him. He truly hoped Chris would be smart enough to run. Droga and his knights were very skilled fighters and Matt prayed Chris wasn't foolish enough to try to fight them alone. That was when he heard it. It was a scream, a primal challenge, a wordless declaration of fury and it sounded like it was coming from Chris. Matt forced his swollen eyes open and saw an incredible sight.

It looked to be Chris, but nothing about the man he saw now resembled the villager he had seen moments ago. *This* Chris's eyes blazed with rage as he sprinted toward the knights, sword drawn, screaming a battle cry in a language Matt recognized only from the oldest holy books. The knights, taken by surprise by this sudden attack, dropped Matt in a heap and drew their weapons. From the ground Matt saw Chris reach the first of the knights and faster than his eye could follow Chris's sword cut the man down, slicing through his armor as easily as Matt could cut butter. Before the other knights had time to process what was happening Chris was upon them, his sword a dancing blur of steel as it scythed them down spraying crimson into the air.

It was then Matt decided that he was hallucinating. The knights must have hit his head harder than he thought, because nothing else Matt could think of would explain why as Chris approached Droga the sword's blade seemed to be on fire. Yet as Chris attacked his sword cut a blazing halo through the air, striking the large knight over and over again spraying sparks with each exchange. Droga, who was far more skilled than the other knights, was driven back before the flurry of blows, barely able to fend them off with his own sword as he retreated. Then suddenly it was over; Droga went to block Chris's strike with his sword but Chris's blade sheared straight through it, splitting it cleanly in two, biting deep into Droga's shoulder. Droga sank slowly to his knees and Chris pulled his sword free with a small jerk.

The entire fight had lasted less than a minute. Chris turned to Matt and Matt saw the fury that had possessed him had drained from his eyes leaving him looking empty by comparison. Managing to prop himself into a sitting position Matt smiled but saw that Chris looked confused and was glancing around at the fallen knights with amazement.

He turned to look at Matt with questions on his lips when he lurched forward without warning. Droga, who had not yet died as Matt had originally thought, had pulled out a small crossbow he had concealed and fired it at Chris. Wounded as he was, his aim was true and the bolt leapt toward him with a crack and struck the side of Chris's head. With only the hood of the cloak to protect him Matt was sure Chris's skull would be split but to his amazement the bolt seemed to glance off and merely knocked Chris to the ground.

Droga never saw if the bolt landed; he collapsed right after he fired never to move again.

"Chris!" Matt yelled as he scrambled to reach him. "Chris please talk to me! Come on man wake up! Chris!"

Chris was very confused. He had vague memories of fighting then suddenly he was here, the problem was he wasn't sure where here was. It was as if he was nowhere. He stood on perfectly flat grey ground, which stretched out forever in every direction around him. The sky, if it was the sky, was stark white and unchanging. He looked all around him and saw the same nothingness everywhere. Overall it was a very boring place and Chris hoped he could find a way to escape soon.

"Hello there," said a voice from behind him.

Chris spun and saw a man who hadn't been there moments ago.

"Where am I, who are you, and why are we here?" Chris asked rapid fire. "Am I dead?" he added after a moment of consideration.

"No, you're not dead," said a second man who Chris knew hadn't been there before.

It was as if he had blinked and suddenly he appeared.

"To answer your other questions friend, this is your mind, that fellow who rudely surprised you is Al, and that last bit is what philosophers have been asking themselves endlessly," laughed a third man who appeared as suddenly as the first two.

"My mind? What is going on here? Who are you people?" Chris asked, deeply disturbed by the answers he received.

"I am truly sorry about my brother's response," the man Chris knew to be Al said. "Let me try to explain what has happened."

"That would be nice," Chris said thoroughly overwhelmed by this turn of events.

"My name as you know is Al. The man next to me is my younger brother Ge and the man who so rudely answered you is our youngest brother Mi. Together we ruled the city of Algeminia until the event you know to be the crisis occurred. Unlike you we have been dead for many years. You are now in possession of our soul gems which bind our spirits to yours," Al said then fell silent.

"That's it?" Chris said angrily. "*Oh, hello you found our stuff now we live in your head,*" he said in a mocking impersonation of Al's voice.

"That sums up our situation accurately, yes," Ge told him.

"That was sarcasm asshole! Get out of my head!" Chris screamed.

"I'm sorry about those two Chris, Al's a bit stiff and Ge really has no idea how to talk to people. I get your probably not too happy with us taking up residence in your place, I get it, but this does come with benefits," Mi said as he slipped an arm around Chris's shoulder. "The items you found were our most prized possessions and with us around you'll be able to use their abilities. If that's not enough look in the pockets of the cloak, I hid a little something to sweeten the deal."

"What that little piece of paper with the guy under the tree?" Chris asked now interested in what Mi was saying.

"What that? No that just said I was going to leave my cloak in the tomb and find a nicer place to die," Mi said dismissively.

"You what?!" Al bellowed.

"Relax brother I put the cloak in the tomb like I promised and made sure that you and Ge were buried exactly like you asked. I just didn't want to spend eternity in some dusty crypt," Mi replied lazily.

"You idiot we were supposed to be buried together!" Al yelled.

"Seriously relax, no harm done! The artifacts were recovered like you intended and I got to be buried some place nice. Everyone wins!" Mi said trying to calm Al down.

"I swear brother if we weren't already dead I would kill you," Al said darkly.

"It's a shame you haven't managed to loosen up in a thousand years, I swear, you need to…" Mi began but Chris cut him off.

"Hey! Guys! Focus here, we were talking about these artifacts remember?" Chris scolded.

Al and Mi had the grace to look sheepish; shuffling their feet like children caught stealing candy.

"Yes, of course, the artifacts," Al began regaining his composure. "Each of us left behind a powerful tool before we died and now our purpose is to assist you in their use. My artifact is the sword you now wield. Allow me to apologize for earlier, I was forced to influence you so that you would attack the knights. If I hadn't you may not have used the sword and thus wouldn't realize what it was capable of and ran the risk of being wounded. I shall refrain from such actions in the future, I swear. My, now your, sword shall allow you to possess my swordsmanship in battle. Over time you will learn how to fight on you own but for now it will keep you alive. The sword is able to sense wickedness within a person and seeks to smite evil. When wielded against someone whom the sword dubs wicked the sword shall burst into flames and become light as a feather. However if you attempt to use the sword against one possessing a pure heart the blade shall become as heavy as lead in an attempt to stop you. This shall ensure you use my gift for good, and walk a righteous path," Al told him as he finished his speech, looking quite imposing.

The entire effect was ruined however as soon as Mi opened his mouth.

"He's been practicing that little spiel for almost a thousand years!" Mi laughed. "Every time I hear it I crack up."

He gasped for air as he descended into a fit of giggling.

"This is nothing to laugh about Mi! This is important!" Al said angrily but Chris thought he saw a small smile creep into the corner of his mouth, though actually it was quite hard to tell.

As Chris looked at them he found it was difficult to focus on any one part of them for long, and quickly found himself forgetting details about them. It was as if they were fuzzy, obscured by a fog. Chris decided that because they were dead that he wasn't supposed to be able to see them. It was then Ge stepped forward to speak.

"My gift to you is the book you now possess. Within its pages you can find everything ever written. I myself will do my best to show you what I deem important to the situation which is why I must ask why in the tomb you ignored my message about the proper care for magical artifacts?" Ge asked.

"Whatever language that was written in I couldn't read. I only speak common," Chris replied.

"How unfortunate," Ge said in the same flat voice he had used thus far. "Though this limits the usefulness of the book greatly I will do my best to show you only things you can comprehend."

"Ge be nice…" Al warned.

"I am being nice; I just told him that I would help him," Ge said sincerely.

"It's not what you said it's the way you said it, Ge how many times do I…" Al began.

Chris cut him off.

"Come on guys please focus! Ge, is there anything else I should know about your book?" Chris asked.

"As a matter of fact there is and it pertains to all of the artifacts. I placed an enchantment on them that prevents them from being lost, stolen, or sold. This way you are sure not to accidently misplace them," Ge told him.

"So you're telling me I'm stuck with you three in my head until I die? Wow thanks friend! I always wanted three bickering brothers in my head I can't escape from," Chris said his voice dripping sarcasm.

"You are very welcome Chris," Ge replied with a smile.

"It's not as bad as it sounds, we'll only talk to you when your asleep so don't go worrying about us butting in on your day to day life. On top of that you've got my cloak which I'm sure you'll love. It's lightweight and warm all at the same time plus it's got a ton of pockets on the inside. Like I said before I left you a little something in there. As my brothers also failed to mention the artifacts are nearly indestructible so don't worry about breaking them. The cloak also has a fun magic ability; so long as you're wearing it you'll be able to hide from anyone you like. The catch is you have to want to stay hidden more than they want to find you. Thought I'd add that just to keep things interesting, can't have things be too easy for you, can we?" Mi said and began to laugh again while Chris looked mortified.

"I still don't understand," Chris said. "Why have you given me these gifts, and why do they seem to have intentional drawbacks?"

"The book's drawback is your own fault," Ge said but Chris ignored him and looked to Al expectantly.

"The drawbacks serve to ensure that you use the artifacts as we intended, and limit you so that you don't influence the world too much. In the past when people gain too much power too fast we've noticed they end up getting killed in their sleep so we tried to avoid that with you," Al said with a small shrug.

"And for what purpose do you intend for me to use these things?" Chris asked and all three brothers replied at the same time.

"To protect the innocent!" said Al with enthusiasm.

"To expand your knowledge," said Ge in the same flat voice he had used thus far.

"To have fun," said Mi with a sly smile.

Chris was thoroughly overwhelmed by all this.

"You mean to tell me that you don't have an actual reason for giving me these things? There's nothing you want me to do?" Chris asked, disbelief evident in his voice.

"Who said there has to be some grandiose quest or something?" Mi laughed. "So long as you follow our guidelines we're happy. Go, explore the world, have fun. I don't recommend you go back to that little village of yours though. Whoever was in charge of those knights will surely come after you for this and I don't think you want to drag them into this. It's not like you ever felt like you belonged there Chris, and you did want to leave. Don't make things complicated with goodbyes," Mi told him.

"How do you know any of that stuff?!" Chris shouted.

It was Ge who answered him.

"We know everything about you Christian Shearcliff. We know your past and will share your future. From this point forward, we are one. We look forward to living with you," Ge told him.

"There will be plenty of time for us to talk later," Mi said suddenly.

"It looks like your friend the cleric is about to wake you up. Have fun Chris, don't die!" and with those words of advice Chris saw the blurry figures before him start to fade away.

Before he had a chance to tell them to wait, his eyes fluttered open and he found himself staring up at the night sky.

Matt's initial response to Chris's wound had been one of panic, but upon closer examination it wasn't nearly as serious as he had thought. The cloak he wore had protected his head as well as a steel helm and as such Matt decided that he wouldn't have any lasting injuries. Nevertheless Matt thought it would be best if he could cast a proper healing spell on him so he wasted no time in dragging Chris's unconscious body out of the ruins. The ruins were no place to spend the night if one wished to live a long and happy life.

It was slow going with Matt's own injuries hindering them considerably. It was nearly nightfall when Matt decided they were far enough from the ruins to be safe from whatever horrors hid within their crumbling walls. Gently laying Chris on the ground he began to look over his own injuries.

"A few cracked ribs, some internal bleeding, nothing a little heal spell won't fix up," Matt coughed.

He chanted the needed words and placed his hands on his chest, letting the magic flow through him. Despite the number of times he had cast this spell he never got used to the feeling of his insides shifting as the damage was repaired. He recalled his training as a cleric; when his instructors would break various parts of their bodies then have them heal each other. Matt smiled. Compared to his days in training his injuries today were trivial. After a few minutes of uncomfortable spell craft he turned his attention to Chris. He cast a simplified version of the spell upon him to aid him in his recovery.

He seemed to rest more peacefully after that so Matt went about making camp. They were close enough to the tree line that finding firewood was no issue and in a few minutes he had a cheery blaze crackling. With no tent and no food Matt simply sat and prepared for an uncomfortable night. As he was about to doze off he heard a groan coming from Chris. Matt sprung up and ran over to him, seeing that he had already sat up.

"Easy there friend, you were very lucky back there," he said to his dazed companion.

"Matt," Chris replied. "I need to talk to you."

Chris told Matt everything, from his plans to get rich, to how he found the artifacts, and ended with his strange conversation with the brothers. He talked long into the night and by the time he finished his tale the fire had been reduced to embers.

"I don't know what I should do Matt," Chris told him when he had finished.

"Well if you want my advice Chris your plan worked. If I understand your situation correctly you now possess considerable power, and there's nothing stopping you from seeing the world now. The only problem that I see is a lack of gold, because like you said you can't exactly sell these things. Hey, what was that gift Mi was talking about by the way, perhaps it's valuable?" Matt asked.

"I had nearly forgotten about that!" Chris exclaimed as he went about furiously digging through the cloaks many inner pockets.

After a moment of searching he let out an exclamation of victory. Slowly from within the cloak he withdrew a necklace, and what a necklace it was. The band was a thick chain made of solid gold, and from it hung a diamond pendant. The diamond itself was quite large, nearly the half the size of Chris's fist. Their eyes swelled as they looked upon it.

"If you sold that you would have enough gold to go anywhere you like!" Matt said breathlessly.

"We'll split it," Chris told him. "You saved my life twice back there, this will at least let me pay back some of that. On that note why did you stick up for me? If you hadn't opened your mouth you wouldn't have gotten wrapped up in all this."

Matt gazed into the fire's embers.

"I told you back there that I had no idea what type of men they were. That wasn't exactly true. Everyone in Draclige knows what type of men the Governor hires. The truth is I needed the gold desperately. Droga and his men approached me with a job, and against my better judgment I took it but as we traveled I regretted it more and more. When I heard him say he was going to attack your village I couldn't stand it anymore. So I helped you escape and here we are. I've been living off small jobs like that for most of my life, when word gets out about how I botched this one I doubt I'll ever get hired again." He sighed. "Such is the fate of a godless cleric."

"That's the second time you've said that, how can you be a godless cleric? I thought clerics drew power directly from the gods?" Chris asked.

"We do, and for simple spells like you've seen me cast I can just pray to the gods in general. The problem arises when I try to cast a more powerful spell. Without a proper god I can't," Matt told him.

"Why don't you go to one of the temples then and pledge yourself to whichever god you prefer?" Chris asked.

"It doesn't work like that. Once a cleric completes their basic training they can go to whatever temple they like and try to join, you were right about that, but it's not that simple. What most people don't know is that the temple also has to choose you. They hold a ceremony and the basis of it is you cast a token into the gods offering brazier. Depending on the color of the smoke depends on the gods answer. Green smoke means that the god has accepted you into their temple and you can begin practicing as a cleric of that order. Red smoke means that you are unfit to be a cleric period, that the gods have rejected you. That's pretty rare, and people like that usually don't make it through the training. There is a third option however, and that's blue smoke. Blue smoke means that you are fit to be a cleric, the gods have accepted you, just not the god you are applying to. Lots of clerics get blue smoke their first few times applying, however I am a special case. I have applied at the temple of every major god on Targoth and most of the minor ones. The same thing every time, blue smoke, meaning that somewhere there's a god who has decided to put a claim on me, or more likely, the gods are laughing at me as I race from temple to temple begging for work," Matt explained.

"Well it can't be that bad," Chris said. "This means you're free to travel the world as you please without being confined to any one temple."

"What it means is I can't find any decent jobs," Matt grumbled. "Any big jobs needing clerics get grabbed up by the temples leaving jack shit for me to do. You distracted me though Chris. Earlier you said you were in my debt for me saving your life, but you forget that you saved my life back there too, we're even."

The two sat in silence after that for a while, each lost in their own thoughts. It was Chris who finally broke it.

"Hey Matt," he began slowly.

"Yeah Chris?" Matt asked.

"I was just thinking, if you're not planning on going anywhere specific that is, how would you feel about traveling with me?" Chris asked.

Matt was quiet for a long time before he answered.

"Why the hell not? I've wasted the last three years of my life running from temple to temple getting rejected. I'm tired of it, I'm already nineteen and as of now don't have a single coin to my name. If there really is a god looking for me let them come find me. We'll split everything fifty-fifty starting with that necklace, that sound good Chris?" Matt asked.

"Absolutely! We'll head to Draclige first, we should be able to sell the necklace there and if we hurry Sorros won't have gotten word about the knights yet!" Chris said.

"Good plan, though I don't advise we spend too much time in the city. Sorros will eventually find out about what happened here and when he does he will come after you. What are you plans for once we leave the city?" Matt asked.

"I was thinking I might try to track down my sister. It's been a few years since I've seen her and I wanna know how she's doing. Would you be interested in helping me find her?" Chris asked.

Matt could barely contain his excitement as he replied.

"You have a sister! I would love to help! What's her name? Is she single?" Matt asked.

Chris only laughed.

"Calm down Matt," Chris said still laughing "I have no idea if she's single, it's been years since I've seen her, and I don't think you're her type."

"You don't know that!" Matt exclaimed, still visibly excited. "It's been years like you said, her type could have changed!"

Chris continued to laugh.

"Sure friend, whatever you say. In any event we should probably get some rest before our trip to Draclige. We still have to try to find the knight's horses tomorrow or it's gonna be a long walk," Chris told him.

"Yeah, you're right, we should try to sleep," Matt said. "Goodnight Chris."

"Goodnight Matt," Chris replied.

CHAPTER FOUR

Chris wished that he could have slept peacefully. As he drifted off to sleep rather than a dream he saw the flat grey world form around him. He turned around expecting to see the three brothers but was mildly surprised to only see a single figure standing before him.

"Who might you be?" Chris asked.

"Come now, can't you recognize a friend?" replied the voice of Mi.

"Sorry but I have trouble telling you three apart, you look all blurry," Chris admitted.

"That's because we're dead. The living and the dead aren't supposed to mix and it's your mind's way of trying to separate us. Don't let it bother you too much Chris. If it makes you feel any better I can see you just fine," Mi said cheerfully.

"Thanks," Chris said dryly. "So where are your brothers? I thought I had three of you in my head."

Mi posed as if he was putting deep thought into his answer.

"They're probably with their families tonight. We may be dead Chris but we do have our afterlives to live. Do you think we've just been sitting around waiting for someone to find our stuff all these years? Gods that would have been boring, having nobody to talk to except those idiots. No, you probably won't talk to more than one or two of us at a time; we've got stuff to do. Anyway, I see you found my little present. Al's wife gave me an earful about that let me tell you. That necklace used to be her mothers, and she was not pleased that I hid it."

"Thanks, I guess," Chris said unsure of how to take this information.

"Don't mention it. By the way, that Matt fellow seems like a good guy. I'm glad you found a companion for your travels. I'm sure he'll help keep things interesting. Anyway, I should probably get going. Despite what you may think our intentions aren't to ruin your sleep cycle for the rest of your life. I'll let you get some rest Chris, you'll see us again when we have something important to tell you, or whenever we get bored," Mi added with a wink.

"Hey wait I still have questions for you!" Chris called but Mi had already disappeared from sight.

"What an asshole," Chris muttered as the world around him faded away and he fell into a dreamless sleep.

Chris awoke early the next morning, a residual habit from his days in the village. He had only been away from home for a day yet it seemed a lifetime ago now with all that had happened. He turned and saw Matt curled up into a small ball, covered in the morning dew. Chris himself was grateful for his cloak which had kept him quite warm through the night as well as protected him from being soaked by the dew. He rose and stretched, loosening his muscles after a night spent on the hard ground.

"Hey Matt rise and shine. We should probably go find the horses," Chris said through a loud yawn.

Matt let out a long groan.

"I really hope you slept better than I did, because somehow I feel more tired than I did yesterday," he complained.

"At least you didn't have to deal with dead men in your dreams," Chris replied dryly.

"Fair enough," Matt yawned as he sat up and shook the dew from his blonde hair. "Seeing as we have no food we may as well set out. The sooner we get to the horses the sooner we can get a hot meal in Draclige."

"You're absolutely right about that, lets head off," Chris agreed.

Without further delay the two set off towards the ruins of Algeminia. It was far quicker returning to the ruins than it was fleeing from them, and they reached the crumbling city as the sun was cresting the horizon. Matt took the lead as he was the only one between the two of them who had been conscious when they had last traveled this way. Despite numerous times turning down dead ends and retracing their steps they eventually rounded a corner and came upon the site of the previous day's battle. They were not the first to arrive at the scene however.

"What are they?" Chris whispered as he looked out at the monsters.

At first glance they appeared to be wolves, with thick shaggy grey fur and canine features. The resemblance ended there however. Each of the three beasts was the size of a pony, and heavily muscled. Rather than being covered in fur their heads seemed to be made up of large boney plates with multiple sets of gleaming red eyes glaring out from under them. Jagged spikes of bone protruded from under their shaggy coats and ran down the length of their bodies, and along the backs of their limbs, which seemed far longer and more powerful than that of a normal wolf. Those same limbs ended in three fingered paws capped with dagger like claws that were currently holding down the corpses of the knights as the creatures tore off ragged strips of flesh. As of that moment they had yet to notice the two friends but they doubted their luck would hold.

"We should turn back," Matt whispered. "They haven't seen us yet and we can probably avoid detection if we leave now."

"But the horses are that way! Unless you want to walk all the way to Draclige we have to get to them," Chris whispered angrily.

"Those things probably ate the horses already Chris, we shouldn't risk it," Matt said quietly.

"What if I hid you under my cloak? So long as both of us don't want to be found those things shouldn't notice us," Chris proposed.

"Is that how that thing works?" Matt asked apprehensively.

"I think so," Chris said trying to sound sure of himself and failing.

"Gods damn it Chris!" Matt exclaimed quietly. "Now is not the time to be testing that thing!"

"Relax it'll be fine, they won't ever know we were here," Chris replied in a hushed voice. "That is unless you have a better plan that doesn't involve walking all the way to the city."

Matt muttered something under his breath that Chris couldn't quite make out.

"Unless that was the sound of your better plan hurry up and get under the cloak!" Chris urged him.

Matt glared at him for a moment, but eventually slipped behind him and draped the cloak over himself.

"All good back there?" Chris whispered over his shoulder.

"I can't see anything, and when was the last time you had a bath?" was Matt's muffled reply.

"I'll take that as a yes then. Hold on to me so you stay under the cloak, I'm going to start moving," Chris whispered.

And so, Chris began to creep forward slowly, with Matt following blindly behind him. As they walked Chris muttered to himself:

"Please don't see me... please don't see me..." over and over again and it seemed that it was working.

The duo had reached mid-way across the street and the monsters were still focused on the bodies of the knights.

"Please don't see me... please don't see me..." Chris muttered.

They were now passed the monsters and moving away down the street.

"Please don't see me... please don't see me..." Chris pleaded.

They neared the end of the street; if they could just make it around the corner they would be home free.

"Please don't see me... please don't see me..." Chris prayed.

One of the creatures sat up. It stared directly at them, and let out a long growl. The other beasts looked up from their feeding and turned their red eyes towards them. Chris froze, hoping that the monsters had simply seen something else, but they began to creep forward, snarls escaping their jaws. From under the cloak he heard Matt ask:

"What happened? Why did we stop? Are we clear?"

"Matt," Chris began slowly.

"What is it?" Matt whispered

"You were right, this plan sucks" Chris said, still frozen in place.

The leading creature let out a bloodcurdling howl and they began to race forward, their long legs giving them a strange lopping gait.

"I hate it when I'm right" Matt cursed as he darted out from under the cloak.

"Got any ideas?" Chris asked nervously as the beasts closed in.

"You're the one with the magic sword!" Matt yelled. "Try using it instead of looking at me! I'm just a cleric!"

"Thanks for the help buddy!" Chris snapped as he drew his sword.

As it leapt from its sheath it burst into flames in his hands.

"Any time!" Matt called as he edged further away from the monsters.

"Apparently, monsters count as evil in the eyes of the sword, lucky me," Chris thought.

With the beasts closing in Chris hoped that the blade would somehow aid him as it had the day before. As the first beast drew into reach he didn't think, he simply swung the sword. It felt natural, as if he had done it his entire life. Time seemed to slow around him as he saw the blade descend towards the creature's neck and he knew it would be a killing blow.

"Incredible," Matt thought as he watched with awe as Chris leapt into action.

He stepped forward and almost faster than he could follow swung towards the monster's neck, however to Matt's surprise rather than take the creatures head off the blade bounced off its fur, casting sparks around Chris and sending him reeling.

"Something is very wrong," Chris thought as he was sent stumbling backwards.

Rather than cut the beasts head off as he had expected the sword had only knocked it off its feet. Somehow the blade that had sheared through plate armor the day before as if it was paper had failed to pierce this monsters fur. The creature Chris hit managed to regain its footing as the other beasts caught up. After seeing how he had dealt with the first attack they began to circle him cautiously. Chris turned in an attempt to keep them all in his field of view but as he would gain sight of two the third would dart behind him. They seemed wary of his sword still but were growing bolder by the second.

"Watch out!" Matt yelled as the beast currently behind him lunged at his back, slashing with its claws.

Had it not been for Chris's cloak it would have been the end for him but as it was the attack only served to knock him to the dirt, sending his book skidding across the ground and forcing the wind out of him as the snarling mass crashed atop him. Chris struggled trying to free himself from under the creature as it in turn attempted to snap at his neck. Managing to role to his back, the creature's claws became tangled up within the folds of his cloak and it fell across his chest. Holding back the creatures snapping jaws with his left hand he realized that the monsters belly and neck were bare, without the thick fur that covered its top. Managing to position his sword under the beast, he thrust toward the monster's chest.

This time the blazing blade met no resistance and it sunk halfway up its length between the monster's ribs, spraying Chris's face with dark blood. As the sword slid into the beast the creature let out a high-pitched scream, which rent through the morning air. The other two beasts that had circled the thrashing mass of man and monster let out sad whimpers and whines. Chris shoved the corpse of the creature off of him and rolled to his feet. He reached down and with a jerk he pulled his sword free from the now still form and it burst back into flames in his hands.

"Well? Come on!" he screamed at the two remaining beasts, and to his amazement they turned their tails between their legs and fled down the street.

Chris turned to face Matt.

"Are you hurt?" he asked.

"I'm fine," Matt replied. "What about you? Is any of that blood yours?" he asked.

"I don't think so. Other than a few bruises I'm alright," Chris said as he looked himself over.

"Good then I don't feel bad about doing this," Matt said with a smirk.

"What are you talking abo..." Chris's words were cut off abruptly.

"Satrafi!" Matt yelled and thrust his hands toward Chris.

It was if some invisible person had dumped a large bucket of ice water over his head.

"Gods above that's cold!" Chris cursed. "What the hell Matt?"

Matt could only laugh.

"I did…say…you needed a bath!" he choked out between peals of laughter. "Besides you were covered in blood, you should be thanking me," Matt said before once again descending into a fit of giggling.

"You, my useless friend, are a massive asshole" Chris said, but he was unable to hide the smile that had crept onto his face.

Chris did his best to shake off as much water as he could from himself, a task made easier by his waterproof cloak. He walked a few feet away from Matt to where his book lie opened. As he picked it he noticed the writing on the page. It read:

> Dire wolves pose a threat to those who travel the less populated reaches of Targoth. They possess sharp teeth and claws, and are known to hunt in packs. The most notable feature the dire wolf has is its fur, which is nearly impossible to cut and is highly resistant to magic of all kinds. This makes fighting a dire wolf difficult, though thankfully the nature of the dire wolf makes it quite cowardly, and it is as likely to flee from danger as it is to fight. As such when confronting a pack of dire wolves one should attempt to intimidate them by shouting and waving weapons.

Chris closed the book in disgust.

"Big help Ge," he muttered under his breath as he slipped the book back into its case.

"Ready to go?" Matt asked. Chris glanced down the street and to his relief saw no sign of the dire wolves.

"Yeah let's go find the horses," Chris replied.

They retraced their path from the day before as the knights had chased them. After only two wrong turns they saw the spot where the day before the knights had tethered their horses. Of the seven from the previous day only three remained, one being Matt's own horse, a young white gelding. The other two were a brown mare and a large black stallion. The others seemed to have pulled their stakes from the ground and fled sometime during the night.

"I recommend you take the mare!" Matt called from his horse's side. "The stallion belonged to Droga and it had a temper similar to his if I remember correctly."

"Thanks for the tip," Chris called in reply. "Would you happen to know her name?"

"I believe the knight riding her called her Sal," Matt said and upon hearing the name the horse gave a toss of her mane.

"Sal huh," Chris said. "Mind if I mount up Sal?"

The horse merely looked at him with its large liquid eyes.

It seemed the knights hadn't had time to unsaddle them before they had run into Chris thus the horses still had equipment tied to the back of the saddles. Matt had already mounted and gestured for Chris to hurry up. Without waiting any longer Chris slipped his foot into the stirrup and climbed into the saddle.

"I probably should have asked sooner but you know how to ride right Chris?" Matt asked.

"Yeah I'm a fair rider," Chris replied.

"Good, then let's get going. It's a three-day ride to Draclige and I wanna make it there fast," Matt told him, and so the two set off on their journey to the city.

Their first day on the road was spent riding hard, with only brief breaks to rest the horses. Both men were eager to reach the city. They saw not a single soul during their ride. As the sun sank low they found a clearing off to the side of the road in which to make camp. To their delight, they found trail rations within the saddlebags. Once the horses were tethered and camp was set up they chowed down. Neither of the men had eaten in over a day so though the meal consisted only of hard bread and strips of dried meat, Chris thought it was the best thing he could remember tasting.

They had made it quite far that day, and the mountain that Chris had spent his entire life living beside was now looming on the horizon.

They had no tents but did have bed roles which marked tonight as a huge improvement over the previous night. Having eaten and tended to the horses the two men lay beside their fire and relaxed.

"We made it pretty far today," Chris remarked as he leafed through his book.

Tonight Ge had elected to show him a passage that detailed the history of Draclige, which Chris found quite interesting.

"Yeah we got further than I expected. If we can keep this pace we should arrive a half day early," Matt told him.

"That's great news," Chris said looking up from the book. "I can't wait to see the city."

"It's honestly not that great," Matt sighed. "Draclige is roughly the same size as Algeminia and it's full of shops and fancy things…but it's crawling with soldiers and the Governor is a cruel man. Anyone who catches his displeasure won't last long, and as soon as he learns what happened in the ruins we'll be on his list. We can't stay more than a day or so before we have to press on."

Chris was quiet for a while after this, reading his book. After a few minutes, he spoke up.

"This passage must be older, it says Draclige is run by a man named Regar, do you know who that is?" Chris asked.

"It's not that old then," Matt replied. "Hal Regar was the Governor before Sorros. Sorros ran him out of the city about thirty years ago."

"Wouldn't the King not like it if someone attacked his Governor?" Chris asked.

Matt gave a snort.

"The King doesn't care at all so long as the taxes keep coming in, and under Sorros the taxes are higher than ever. The King will let anyone run a city these days so long as he gets his cut," Matt told him.

"That doesn't seem like a good way to run a kingdom," Chris commented.

"Nobody said it was a good way, but it's the way things are. So long as the money keeps flowing everyone stays happy and nobody asks questions," Matt said with a sigh.

"What was it like under Regar?" Chris asked after a minute.

"Better, I suppose. It was before my time but from the way people talk I gather he was a just ruler, and he ruled for some time too. The man was in his sixties when Sorros took over. Doesn't matter now though, nobody has seen him in years and most think he got picked off by Sorros's assassins. It's either that or he's bedded down somewhere remote and is lying low. It doesn't matter to me though, because regardless we're still stuck with Governor Sorros," Matt yawned and laid back on his bedroll. "Either way why are you so interested in this? You didn't strike me as the political type," Matt remarked tiredly.

"I wouldn't say I am" Chris replied. "It's just…It's just I've never been this far from Shearcliff before, and I wanna learn as much about the world around me as I can. It's different for you Matt. You've traveled, been exotic places, and met exciting people. I've spent my life serving drinks in a tiny town in the middle of nowhere. I'm ready to see the world, to do great things; I wanna see something nobody's ever seen before. This is my chance to do that, and it starts in Draclige."

Matt was silent.

"Matt?" Chris asked.

His only reply was a low snore. Chris smiled.

"Good night friend," Chris said as he rolled his cloak around himself and drifted off to sleep.

CHAPTER FIVE

The men awoke early the next morning.

"Any otherworldly guests last night?" Matt asked as they broke camp.

"Yeah I talked to Al for a bit. Mostly just recounting the previous day's fight and discussing tips for next time. How about you, sleep well?" Chris asked.

"Like a log," Matt said cheerfully. "I was thinking Chris, there's another village not too far from here, we could reach it by this afternoon. If we made a slight detour we could get some more food before we reach the city, and possibly sleep in a real bed if they have an inn. How about it, are you willing to postpone our trip to the city by a day? It probably won't make a difference to whether or not Sorros knows we're coming, no other riders passed us yesterday so they couldn't possibly know about the knights yet."

"Yeah, I know about the village, I think it's called Dewbank. It sits along the river east of here. It's even smaller than Shearcliff but they get some traffic because of the river," Chris told him.

He felt his stomach growl and dimly remembered in their joy of finding their rations the previous night they had eaten them all.

"I don't think that one day will make a difference either way," Chris said as he smiled, imagining a hot meal and a real bed.

"So it's decided then!" Matt exclaimed. "We're off to Dewbank!"

"Let's hurry up and get going!" Chris said sharing Matt's enthusiasm.

The two hurried to finish breaking camp and saddled the horses. Without further discussion, they set a quick pace down the road. About a mile down they came to a crossroads and rather than continue south to Draclige they turned east towards Dewbank. They pushed their horses hard, and as the sun reached its highest point they could see the river in the distance, and saw the smoke from the town. Roughly an hour past noon the two men rode into the town.

As they rode through the village they noticed something was wrong. In a small town such as this, travelers were usually greeted quickly in order to get news from the outside world, Chris knew this well because this village was much like Shearcliff in both size and feel. Despite this as they rode down the street nobody ran out to greet them, rather they saw worried faces peeking out from behind windows and doorways.

"What happened here?" Chris wondered aloud.

"Let's ask at the inn, perhaps someone there will tell us what's going on," Matt replied.

They found the inn easily enough; it was the only two storied building in the town. As they approached they saw a faded sign hanging above the door depicting a clam with a large crack running down its shell. They tethered their horses outside and walked in. The first floor of the inn they saw was a dimly lit bar, with roughly hewn tables scattered throughout the room. A single staircase ran along the right-hand wall leading up to what Chris assumed were the rooms. The bar ran along the left-hand wall and a large fireplace was located along the back wall. Aside from them and the barkeeper the inn was empty. As they approached the bar the innkeeper eyed them warily. He was a stout man, standing somewhere between Chris and Matt in height. His gut protruded slightly past his chest and his cheeks seemed to sag on his face. He had small watery eyes and a long thick drooping brown mustache that ran past his double chin. Chris also noticed that his arms were heavily layered with muscled however, and he had no doubt that there was a sturdy club hidden behind the bar somewhere.

"Afternoon," the innkeeper muttered as they neared and begun to wipe out a glass he pulled from beneath the counter.

"Good afternoon sir," Matt began as he pulled up at stool at the bar. Chris followed suit as Matt continued.

"Would you happen to have any rooms available?" he enquired.

"Yeah, all of them," the innkeeper grunted without looking up from the glass he was washing.

Chris and Matt looked at each other. While remote it was shocking that this inn would have no guests. This confirmed their suspicions that something was very wrong in Dewbank. Rather than dance around the issue Chris decided to be direct with the man.

"Sir what's happened to this village?" Chris asked.

The innkeeper sighed and set down the glass he had been wiping.

"A few months ago, we started having trouble with a bandit. It's not the first time, as remote as we are we occasionally get robbers preying on the roads around here, but this time's different. It seems the bandits are less bandits, and more of a singular person. They haven't killed anyone yet, but they've been targeting our supply merchants and taking food and valuables. They got the people of the town scared; nobody wants to venture out from their homes in fear of being robbed," he said.

"How do you know it's only one person?" Matt asked.

"The survivors say they only ever see one woman armed with a bow. Other than that, nobody knows what she looks like because she has clothes that cover her entire body, even her face. She's dangerous. So far she hasn't killed anybody but she's scary good with her bow from what I hear. She's also much faster than a normal person, and the last group of people she robbed said she had weird legs, like a cross between a bird and a human. That's how the people round here are though, they spook easy. Give it a few more months and they'll all be saying she can spit fire and flies. If you ask me it's just some woman who's good with a bow, not that it matters. The fact remains she's been robbing us blind and we haven't been able to catch her."

The innkeeper gave a sigh.

"That's why people were so afraid of you when you rode into town, they're not the most trusting of strangers at the moment," he told them.

Chris barely heard him finish, his mind was still mulling over the comment about the mysterious woman's legs.

"Where has this woman been robbing people? Chris asked quickly, a look of interest plain on his face.

"Along the south road, between here and Draclige, why, do you fancy yourself as a bounty hunter?" the innkeeper asked eyeing Chris's sword.

Chris and Matt exchanged a quick look and both gave a small nod.

"We've been known to take a bounty or two from time to time," Matt lied.

The innkeeper looked over the two men with an appraising eye. They appeared to him well equipped, if young. The tall one wore no armor under his cloak but carried his sword comfortably, without trying to draw undo attention to the fact he had it, unlike many his age would try to do. The shorter of the two had no weapon he could see but wore some armor over his robe. The innkeeper had lived long enough to recognize him for what he was; a cleric, but he could discern no visible holy signs on him. The two formed a strange duo thought the innkeeper but then again much of his business came from such strange people.

He looked at them warily.

"We haven't the money for a proper reward you know. What would you want for taking the bandit down?" the innkeeper asked.

"Well it's only one bandit," Chris replied. "What would you say about a hot meal and a free night in the inn?"

The innkeeper was taken back with surprise.

"That's all you guys want? That hardly seems fair for you," he said with suspicion in his voice.

"You haven't seen us eat yet," Chris replied with a smile. "We'll set out first thing tomorrow, but for now would you mind if we headed up to our rooms?"

"Sure, go on ahead. I'll have the serving girl tend to your horses so you can head on up now. Take the room at the end of the hall, it's got two beds so you two should be able to rest easy. Dinner will be ready around sunset," the innkeeper told them.

"Thanks sir. We'll see you then. Come on Matt, let's get some rest," Chris said and the two headed up the stairs to their room.

The room itself was clean enough to be serviceable. As promised it was furnished with a pair of beds each with a small nightstand. They saw a large wardrobe in the corner of the room that they could store their extra clothes in, if they had any. The room also had a small table and a pair of chairs in its center, but was otherwise bare. As they sat on their beds Matt turned to Chris.

"You seemed awfully interested in that woman down there, any particular reason?" he asked.

Chris was quiet for a moment before he finally replied.

"It's probably nothing, but his comment about her legs reminded me of my sister. I have no idea where she ran off to after she left and I wouldn't put it past her to turn to a life of crime. She was never one to follow the rules exactly," Chris said sheepishly.

"Your sister had misshapen legs?" Matt asked slightly surprised. "But they said this bandit is really fast, how could she run with legs like that?"

"Usually I'd agree with you but my sister was always quick on her feet. We found her when she was very young, trapped under a pile of rubble. When we dug her out we saw her legs were deformed. We thought it was a result of the accident when she was young but as she grew older we realized it was something different entirely. The other villagers saw what she was and shunned her, that's why she left," Chris explained.

"What was wrong with her?" Matt asked.

"We weren't exactly sure, and it didn't bother me at all but not all the villagers thought the same way. Despite having lived with us for most of her life they had become so hostile to her she left on our sixteenth birthday. That would have been two years ago now once summer starts," Chris told him.

"That's awful," Matt said. "I definitely hope we can find her."

"Thanks," Chris said looking gratefully at Matt.

A sly smile crept onto Chris's face.

"I'll even put in a good word for you when we meet her," he added and watched with delight as Matt's face lit up.

"Really! You'd really do that for me?" Matt asked excitedly.

Chris laughed and envisioned his sister beating Matt over the head with her bow.

"Of course Matt, we're friends aren't we?" Chris said with the sincerest grin he could muster.

"Thanks buddy!" Matt exclaimed "You're a true friend!" he added and Chris felt a twinge of guilt.

"I only said I'd introduce him," Chris thought to himself. "It's not my fault when she rejects him."

Despite trying to convince himself of this he felt as if Al was standing beside him shaking his head in disapproval.

"Anyway, Matt I'm gonna get some rest before dinner, mind waking me up when it's time to eat?" Chris asked

"Sure thing. Hey, do you mind if I borrow your book for a little bit?" Matt asked.

"Go ahead," Chris said as he tossed the book over to Matt.

Chris unstrapped his sword and leaned it beside his bed, and hung his cloak and knife from his bedpost. He decided against taking off his shirt and collapsed atop his covers, thoroughly exhausted after a day and a half of hard riding and practically no food. As he drifted off to sleep he saw the grey world that he spoke with the brothers in form around him.

He turned around and saw that both Al and Mi were standing before him today.

"No Ge today?" Chris asked.

"At the moment, Ge is showing your friend a passage on spellcraft I believe," Al replied.

"Ah. I see," Chris replied and turned to Mi. "We made a slight detour away from Draclige. I think I found a lead on my sister and I wanna check it out."

Mi only shrugged.

"We know that Chris, we hear your thoughts remember?" Mi told him.

"Then why are you here? If you already know what I'm doing what's the point of having me update you? Chris asked slightly irritated.

"We're here to tell you that you're doing well," Al replied. "So far you've proven that you're capable of thinking quickly and are able to utilize the artifacts."

"Though the cloak only works for one person at a time," Mi cut in. "That bit with the dire wolves was priceless may I add."

Mi's mirth died as both Chris and Al shot him withering looks.

"As I was saying, you've proven yourself and because of this we no longer feel the need to hold your hand. From now on you may not see us quite as regularly, though if you seek our council we shall appear to give it. Other than that, we'll only really come around if we have something important to tell you," Al said.

"Don't worry, we'll be watching still," Mi added. "Ge set up something in our homes so we can see what you see whenever we want. My wife loves it, says it's the most entertaining thing she's seen in a thousand years."

"Thanks, I think," Chris replied slightly confused.

Al gave Mi another look.

"In any event, we'll let you get some sleep. Good luck with your travels, and remember, we'll be watching," Al said as the grey world faded to black around them.

The last thing Chris heard before he drifted into the darkness was Mi yelling:

"Have fun!"

Chris slept for the remainder of the afternoon while Matt was engrossed within the pages of the book. As promised around sunset the smell of roasting meat drifted up to the two men, and pulled Chris from his slumber. With a moan of:

"Foooooood," he rose from his bed like a zombie as Matt laughed.

Matt placed the book back within its case as Chris strapped his knife back to his hip. He decided to leave the artifacts in his room, seeing no need for them at dinner. Matt himself had opted to forgo his armor and wore only his plain robe.

As the friends walked down the hall they heard the din of the tavern below them, voices rising and falling in conversation or laughter, and the sound of a lute being played. As they entered the tavern the conversation died slightly and many sets of eyes turned towards them. Rather than the hostile gazes they had received that morning however these were more curious looks. Word of the duo had spread and the villagers had high hopes that they could remove the mysterious bandit woman.

Matt spotted an open table near the fireplace and he and Chris sat themselves, and then noticed that the innkeeper was making his way towards them.

"I should be thanking you boys!" he said with a grin. "Word that you were here to kill the bandit got around and the people flocked to the inn to see you!" he said happily.

"Word no doubt spread by you," Chris remarked.

"Trading information is part of the innkeeper's business!" the man laughed. "And I've seen more business tonight than I've had all month!"

"Congratulations," Matt said. "Could we perhaps get a few mugs of ale?"

"Of course, I'll have the serving girl bring some over, and as much food as you can eat!" he said still excited.

"Challenge accepted," Matt said with a grin.

With a laugh the innkeeper walked back towards the bar and the conversations of the room returned to normal a few moments later. Chris and Matt sat quietly as they waited for their food, enjoying the sounds of the people around them and the warmth of the fire, as well as the song being played by the musician in the far corner. After two days on the road the men felt quite content, enjoying this moment of rest.

This contentment quickly became overt joy as they spied the serving girl, a curvy young woman in her twenties with short brown hair and a wide smile, making her way through the crowded room toward them, arms filled with their food and drink.

"Here we are!" she said cheerfully as she set their food on the table. "We slaughtered a couple of chickens for you two, and we have had a side of beef roasting with some potatoes since this morning. Hope you two like it!"

She slid a steaming platter of roast beef, chicken, and chunks of potato toward each of the men. The entire affair had been covered with a generous amount of gravy and each man had received a hunk of freshly baked bread. The duo hardly noticed as she set down their mugs of ale, as they were already busy tearing into their plates with the enthusiasm of starving men. The serving girl giggled as she watched them eat.

"I take it you two like it?" she asked still laughing.

Matt, already halfway through his plate, looked up.

"It's the best thing I can remember eating!" he said before taking a deep drink of his ale.

From across the table Chris mumbled his agreement from behind a mouthful of food.

"I'll be sure to bring more then," she managed to say through her peals of mirth as she walked away.

The men wasted no time talking; the next few minutes were spent attacking the contents of their plates pausing only to take the occasional sip of ale or a quick breath. Just as it seemed they would finish the food before them their server reappeared.

"I'm back!" she chimed, arms once again laden with food.

They looked at her and at that moment that curvy girl with brown hair and arms full of food was the most beautiful thing either of the two men could remember seeing. Their admiration must have shown plainly on their faces because the serving girl blushed as she set their food down.

"Enjoy yourself blondie," she said with a wink as she slid Matt his food.

Matt's face turned beat red and the serving girl giggled as she walked off.

"Did you hear her Chris? She was flirting with me! I could get used to this hero business," Matt said excitedly.

"Ne mavn't gun baythin' mt," Chris mumbled through a mouthful of food.

"Food," Matt replied curtly.

Chris swallowed his food and took a gasp of air.

"I said we haven't done anything yet," he repeated.

"All that means is we gotta be sure to take down that bandit tomorrow," Matt told him.

"Yeah then it's off to Draclige though, we don't have the luxury of hanging around," Chris reminded him.

Matt sighed.

"Yeah I know. Still it would be nice to spend a few days here," Matt said thinking of a certain waitress with brown hair.

"Don't worry Matt, there'll be plenty of other taverns with pretty girls once we make it to Draclige, I'm sure of it," Chris assured him.

"Yeah but how many of them are interested in flirting with me? Let me answer from experience, zero," Matt replied, his voice dull.

"Don't worry about it," Chris said as he used a hunk or bread to mop up the last of his gravy. "There'll be other waitress in other cities. It's a big world and we'll see as much of it as we can."

Matt sighed and sipped his ale.

"I guess you're right. Plenty of time ahead of us, no need to rush," he conceded.

"For now, let's focus on taking down this bandit. We should get back to our room and get some rest. We need our sleep if we wanna be able to function tomorrow," Chris said.

"Your right," Matt agreed. "Let's head back up."

The two finished the last bites of their meals and drank the final sips of their ales before rising from the table. Chris waved goodnight to the innkeeper as they walked up the stairs back to their rooms.

Later that night as they lay in their beds Matt spoke.

"Hey Chris," Matt began.

Chris was quiet for a minute before he spoke.

"Yeah what is it Matt?" Chris asked.

"What will you do if by off chance it is your sister we find tomorrow," Matt asked.

Chris was silent again.

"I'm not sure," he said after a long while. "I guess it depends what she does. I definitely won't fight her. If it comes to that we will just leave her be. If she's willing I might ask her to join us, if you're ok with that."

"It really depends," Matt replied. "Tell me Chris, what type of person is your sister. How is she really?"

"She's brave," Chris replied. "When we were kids she was always getting into trouble, but she has a good heart. Part of the reason I think this may be her is the fact that nobody's been killed yet. Cassy isn't the type of person who would kill somebody just to make a little gold."

After a moment's consideration, he added:

"Maybe she would for a lot of gold though, it really depends who the person in question is."

Matt chuckled from his bed.

"For a lot of gold we would probably do the same," he said and Chris laughed quietly. "Do you think she'd even want to join us?" Matt asked.

"She wants to explore the world even more than I do, I can't imagine why she would refuse," Chris said.

"Alright then, if you think it's a good decision I'll go along with it. I guess it doesn't really matter if we split the necklace two or three ways. That's all I wanted to talk about Chris, I'll let you get to sleep," Matt said.

"Alright Matt, I'll see you in the morning" Chris said as he rolled onto his side.

A few minutes later he heard light snoring coming from Matt's bed but still he could not fall asleep. He thought about his discussion with Matt. It had been nearly two years since he had seen Cassy, could he honestly say she was still the same person? In the end, he decided it didn't matter. She was his sister and he knew that he could always find a friend in her. He just had to find her first.

No spirits troubled him that night, and Chris rose just before dawn, as he usually did. Seeing that Matt was still asleep he decided to look at his book before waking him. Chris pulled the tome from its case and ran his hand over its leather cover, feeling the smoothness of the sapphires beneath his hand. He opened the book to the first page and saw in flowing handwriting a brief poem. It read:

> Kingdoms may rise and fall,
> Friends may come and go,
> Family is eternal.

Taking this as a good sign Chris closed the book and slipped it back into its case, and strapped it to his hip. He then proceeded to do the same with his sword, ensuring it was securely on his back and within easy reach. His knife followed. Forgoing the cloak for the moment he strode over to where Matt still lay snoring. Seeing the peaceful look on the clerics face a savage smile snuck its way onto Chris's own. With a swift movement, he reached down and flipped Matt's mattress up as high as he could, spilling Matt onto the floor of the room.

"Gaaahh!" Matt cried in surprise as he rolled to his feet. "What was that for Chris?" he asked.

"Payback from when you soaked me in the ruins," Chris laughed. "Hurry up and get dressed. We'll eat and head off to catch our bandit."

Muttering things under his breath that Chris decided he would be better off not hearing, Matt began to pull on his robes and strap on his armor. When they were ready to go, Chris donned his cloak and together they walked down to the tavern.

"Morning boys!" the innkeeper called, still cheerful after the previous night's business. "Sit yourselves anywhere and I'll have some food right out."

The duo decided to seat themselves in the same place as the night before, and a few minutes later the innkeeper had brought them two mugs of water as well as a few slices of cold roast beef from the night before and a thick slab of bread.

"Is the serving girl not working today?" Matt inquired as the innkeeper set their food down.

"No, after such a busy night yesterday I gave her the day off, I think she's spending it down by the river with her boyfriend," the innkeeper replied before he walked back to the bar.

"Oh, thanks," Matt said to no one in particular.

Chris did his best to stop from laughing and failed miserably. Matt scowled at him and Chris quickly filled his mouth with food to stop his mirth. The brief conversation with the innkeeper put Matt in no mood for conversation and they spent the rest of their meal intent on their food. When they had finished, they thanked the innkeeper and went around the back of the inn to get their horses. They found them well fed and freshly groomed.

"These people take this hero business seriously don't they?" Chris remarked.

"Don't get too used to it, nobody will care who we are once we reach Draclige," Matt said as they saddled the horses.

"I think Sorros might care," Chris commented as he mounted up.

"All the more reason not to draw attention to ourselves once we arrive," Matt agreed.

With this in mind, the men began to ride south toward Draclige.

Along the way they watched the road for signs of ambush by their mysterious bandit. About an hour before noon they arrived at a bend in the road. The bend was caused by the road curving around a small cliff on the left-hand side of the trail that looked to be caused by erosion. The top of the cliff was covered with trees and brush, this combined with the surrounding forest completely stopped the two from seeing around the bend.

"Looks to be the perfect place for an ambush," Chris said.

"We should be careful," Matt agreed. Chris dismounted, unsheathed his sword and walked slowly toward the corner, Matt following closely behind.

"Stay here Matt and let me scout it out, I can hide with the cloak," Chris said.

"Good idea, stay safe," Matt replied.

Chris pulled up his hood and crept forward alone. As he rounded the corner he saw nothing. Trusting the cloak, he walked forward briskly, scanning the cliffside and the woods for signs of any would be attacker, yet he saw nothing out of the ordinary.

He was about to signal for Matt to bring the horses around when he saw a flicker of movement from the tree line. It was faint, and could have been mistaken for the wind except there was no breeze that day. Chris scanned the trees closely trying to pinpoint where the movement had come from. After looking for nearly a minute he saw the movement again, and this time was able to pinpoint it to its location. He saw her, crouching in the brush with a bow lying across her lap. It was as the villagers had said; she was covered from head to toe in black cloth, with only a slit for her eyes exposed. At the moment, he saw those eyes were scanning the road looking for travelers.

Chris walked straight toward her, determined to not be seen. Her eyes never once focused on him as he approached, he seemed invisible to her. He strode ever closer, ending up directly in front of her. He crouched low and looked at her eyes, and saw they were a vivid shade of green. Chris smiled and stepped behind her, and placed the blade of his sword against her neck.

"Don't move a muscle," he said from behind her.

It was as if she had been freed from a trance, she jerked back to reality and tensed up, but noticing the razor-sharp blade pressed against her neck she stayed still.

"Who are you, and how did you sneak up on me?" she asked, and Chris noticed her voice had a slight hiss to it, drawing out her S's.

"Stand up very slowly and walk toward the road. I don't recommend you try to run, I can take your head off before you take a step," Chris warned.

The masked woman complied, standing very slowly with her hands held above her head, still clutching the bow. Chris marched her slowly to the road and noticed the way she walked. She seemed to strut slightly as she took each step, and he saw that she did in fact have strange legs, like those of a raptor. When they reached the road, he said to her:

"Drop your bow on the ground, and turn around slowly."

She reluctantly complied. He looked at her eyes for a moment, and made up his mind. Still keeping her at sword point he used his free hand to toss back the hood of his cloak, still watching her eyes. As she saw his face he saw her eyes widen in surprise, and Chris asked her:

"Do you know me?"

Very slowly, she reached up to the wrap that covered her face and pulled it away. Two years had changed her face little. Cassy's bright green eyes gazed in shock at his familiar face.

"Chris?" she asked in disbelief.

"It's good to see you Cas," Chris said with joy in his voice.

He quickly sheathed his sword and ran to embrace his sister. The siblings stood there for nearly a minute, laughing, overjoyed to be reunited. At the end of the minute Cassy broke the silence.

"Hey Chris?" she said still hugging him.

"Yeah Cas?" he replied.

"What the hell!" she yelled as she drove her knee savagely into his gut.

Chris fell to the ground and she planted her foot, which Chris noted was also wrapped in black cloth rather than a boot, on his chest. Chris felt several sharp points dig into his skin.

"Why the hell did you march me out here at sword point! What were you thinking!?" Cassy demanded.

"Cas I didn't know it was you! You're all wrapped up in that cloth. Why are you wearing that shit anyway?" Chris argued.

"I guess that's fair," she said and suddenly stepped off him, once again seeming happy. "As for the cloth; it's to help me hide what I am, the people around here don't take to kindly to my type."

"Did you ever consider they don't like you because you rob them?" Chris asked his voice dripping sarcasm.

"I rob them because they weren't willing to treat me like a person. If they want to make me a monster I'll act like a monster," Cassy told him.

"I'm not exactly sure I agree with that sentiment," Chris said with disapproval written on his face.

"What about you!" Cassy chimed suddenly changing the subject. "When did you get a sword, and since when can you sneak up on me?"

"It's a long story Cas, I'll explain later. For now, could you take off those black rags? I can't take you seriously looking like that," Chris asked.

"Oh, sure thing, my camp is right down the hill a little, give me a moment to change and grab my things, I'll be right back," Cassy said quickly.

"Grab your things? Why?" Chris asked puzzled.

"Well I'm assuming your traveling somewhere dummy, why else would you be all the way out here? I'm gonna come with you! It's getting boring here and I think I've overstayed my welcome anyway. So if I wanna learn how you got a sword I'll have to tag along. Wait right here!" and with that she streaked away into the forest, leaving Chris standing alone in the road.

Chris stood dumbfounded for a moment as he tried to figure out how holding his sister at sword point translated to an invitation to travel with him, not that he was unhappy with this turn of events. With a shrug he turned and jogged back down the path to fetch Matt. He reached the corner and called:

"Hey Matt bring up the horses! I found our mystery bandit, turns out it was my sister after all!"

Matt walked around the bend leading the horses.

"Where is she then?" he asked looking past Chris.

"She ran back to her camp to get her things to travel with us," Chris replied.

"You convinced her that fast? I'm impressed, you were only gone like five minutes," Matt said somewhat surprised.

"Truth be told I didn't even offer, she just told me she was coming along. Cas's like that, you'll get used to it," Chris admitted.

"Got it," Matt replied with a small laugh. "So how long do you think she'll be? I'd like to meet this sister of yours finally," he said running his hand through his short hair.

"Yeah about that," Chris said somewhat nervously. "Before you meet her there's one last thing I should tell you about her. I didn't bring it up before because I didn't wanna say anything until I was sure this was her, but my sister and I look very different. We're both adopted you see and..." Matt cut him off.

"Don't worry Chris I won't be affected by how she looks, I'm just eager to meet her," he assured him.

"No, it's not that, it's just she's not..." Chris was cut off yet again because at that moment Cassy burst from the tree line with a backpack slung over her shoulder.

She skidded to a halt in front of them and Matt was caught gaping at her. For her part, she gave him a funny look as well.

"Human," Chris finished meekly.

"Who's the dwarf?" Cassy asked giving Chris a puzzled look.

Cassy's comment snapped Matt back to reality.

"Dwarf! Chris, *this* is your sister?!" he exclaimed in shock.

Matt had good reason to be shocked, for Cassy was not what he was expecting at all.

She stood far taller than either of them at around six and a half feet, and was most certainly not human. Her body appeared normal enough, lithe and curvy with caramel colored skin and striking green eyes. Her jet-black hair was longer than Chris's own, hanging just past her shoulders in a silken sheet. She wore a much more revealing outfit than when Chris had found her, having traded the black body wraps for a short skirt cut at a sharp angle, hanging to her lower thigh on the right, and stopping a few inches before her hip on the left, under which she wore leather leggings that stopped at the knee. Aside from that she only wore a cloth wrapped several times around her chest and tied in the back. The clothes seemed to have been fashioned by Cassy herself, as they appeared to be made from the same bolt of bright red cloth. Despite this they were very well put together Chris noted. She also wore a leather harness from which hung her bow and quiver. Had she been a normal human Matt thought she would have been quite beautiful, however her human resemblance ended here. The further from her main body he looked the more reptilian she appeared. Starting around her elbows emerald green scales became apparent, thickening as you approached her hands, which resembled those of a lizard complete with inch long talons. Her legs were equally shocking. From the knee up she looked normal, but below that her skin became rougher and as you neared her ankle her leg seemed to bend backward like a bird's leg, and was completely covered in scales. She wore no boots, and had no need to. Her feet ended with four short thick toes each capped with a dagger like claw, with a thickly scaled heel for support. Matt also noticed as she opened her mouth to speak that rather than human teeth her mouth was filled with short, sharp fangs.

"You didn't say anything about anyone else Chris," Cassy said ignoring Matt's outburst. "Who is he?"

"That's because you ran off without letting me talk!" Chris said slightly annoyed. "Had you let me speak I would have told you I'm traveling with a friend. This is Matt, and he's a cleric."

"Oooooh a cleric! How exciting! What god do you serve?" she asked with excitement, all trace of her former distain gone.

Matt only looked frustrated and threw his hands in the air.

"Every time! I tell you *every damn time* Chris!" he ranted.

Chris did his best to look sympathetic to his plight while Cassy looked very confused.

Once Chris had managed to calm Matt down they gathered by the horses, to discuss their plan.

"Cas the short version of our story is that we're traveling to Draclige to sell this necklace," Chris said as he showed her the item in question. "You said you're willing to travel with us and we already talked amongst ourselves and decided to give you a share of the necklace, if you're willing to join our band."

"Your band?" Cassy asked with a snort that sounded more like a hiss.

"Yes, we've decided to travel together and explore Targoth," Matt told her. "Chris spoke highly of you and I agreed that you could come along if we found you, which we have. Seeing that you agreed to join us before we even asked we should get going, every moment we waste is another moment that Sorros will figure out what we did and decide to stick our heads on a pike."

"Wait, hold up, what did you two do exactly?" she asked with suspicion in her voice.

"It's a rather long story," Chris told her. "I'll fill you in as we ride. For now, you can ride with me because we only have two horses," Chris told her.

Cassy only shrugged. She was happy to do whatever so long as it was interesting, and she was sure this would prove far more interesting than hanging around here.

So, the three of them set off to Draclige and Chris began to tell his tale.

CHAPTER SIX

They rode through the day, and by nightfall they had left the forest and could see Draclige on the horizon, surrounded by farmland. The city's stone walls seemed to spring from the earth itself and they could see the distant glow of lanterns from within. Standing in the center of the city was the castle, looming over the rest of the city as if it was keeping watch, equipped with several tall towers. To Chris it was an impressive sight and he yearned to explore its streets, but seeing as none of them had any money they decided to camp outside the walls and explore the city in the morning.

They found a spot to make camp at the forest's edge as Chris finished telling his story, and to his shock Cassy was quiet. As he had told his tale she had plagued him with questions and he had expected more now. Eventually she spoke.

"Let me sum up, you ditched Mr. Cogwell, ran off to the ruins, met this weirdo," she said gesturing to Matt. "Found some crazy magic stuff that you can't get rid of and in the process, you managed to kill five of Sorros's knights?"

"Don't forget the bit where he gets the spirits of three dead Kings stuck in his head," Matt chimed as he worked on pitching their single tent which Cassy had brought with her.

It was slightly cramped but the three of them could fit inside without too much trouble.

"Yeah that's about it," Chris said. "Now we're at Draclige to sell the necklace and resupply before we head further south."

"What's the plan once you make it south?" Cassy asked.

"We really don't have one yet," Matt called from the tent, which he had succeeded in pitching.

"Well the gold from the necklace won't last forever; we should come up with a more permanent plan," Cassy said.

"Do you have any suggestions?" Chris asked her as he staked the horses down for the night.

"Well I'm all for traveling together and exploring with you guys, but I think we should come up with a more permanent arrangement. We should form a proper adventuring company," Cassy told them.

Chris and Matt paused what they were doing to consider her proposal.

"That idea's not half bad," Matt said after a moment's consideration.

Often explorers and mercenaries across Targoth will band together and form adventuring companies. These companies are recognized by most cities and guilds and are often hired to deal with monsters, retrieve rare items, act as security or do any number of other tasks. The longer Chris and Matt thought about it the better the idea sounded. They looked at each other and saw that they both were in agreement.

"I think that's a great idea Cas," Chris said with a smile and Matt nodded his approval.

"Well then all that's left to do is come up with a name," Cassy replied.

"A name?" Chris asked puzzled.

"Of course, all adventuring companies have names. We need one too if we wanna look official," Cassy told him.

"Well do you have any suggestions?" Matt asked her, furiously thinking of names himself.

"As a matter of fact, I do," she said proudly. "I propose that we become Shearcliff and Company, sounds pretty official doesn't it?"

Chris smiled and nodded eagerly.

"I like it, it's got a nice ring to it," he said.

"Well of course you like it, she named it after you!" Matt said annoyed. "Why should the company be named after Chris? That hardly seems fair."

"The companies not named after Chris, it's named after us, my name's Shearcliff too if you would remember," Cassy scolded. "Besides I included you in it too! You're the Company part. Seems fair considering there's two of us and one you, don't it?"

Matt only gave her a dark look.

"Unless you have a better idea," she said after a moment, rolling her eyes.

Matt dropped his gaze.

"Well then I say we put it to a vote then. All those in favor of the name Shearcliff and Company raise their hands. All those named Matt sit there and suck it. Ready? Let's vote," Chris said.

Cassy's hand and his own went into the air while Matt scowled at him.

"You really are an ass, you know that?" Matt said to him.

"I try," Chris replied with a small grin while Cassy giggled.

Matt sighed.

"I'll go draw up the contract," he said as he stepped into the small tent.

Chris and Cassy smiled at each other and went back to setting up camp.

Within the tent, Matt withdrew a small bottle of ink and a quill along with paper from his own supplies. He began to write.

Later that evening after they had all shared a meal of dried fruit and nuts that Cassy had brought they sat within the small tent and shared the light of a single lantern. They were preparing to go to sleep when Matt cleared his throat.

"I have completed the contracts," he announced as he withdrew three sheets of paper with a small flourish and began to read the first one.

It said:

> By signing this document, I agree to join Shearcliff and Company. In doing so I agree to all the rules and regulations of the company as listed below.

1. I will protect the other members of Shearcliff and Company and will not do anything to intentionally endanger the other members of the company without just cause.
2. I agree to remain loyal to the Company as a whole, will protect its best interests, and will not attempt to destroy or destabilize it.
3. In regarded to treasure I agree to an equal portion of any gold found, or received as payment. Any items found or received will either be sold or given to a company member who could make appropriate use of them, if they desire the item. The items worth will be subtracted from their pay from that mission.
4. I agree that fifteen percent of the all gold earned will be reinvested into the company for use of supplies, lodging, and other expenses. Any personal gear will be purchased with my own funds.

I _____ hereby agree to the above rules and pledge myself to Shearcliff and Company. I agree that any violation of the above rules may result in forfeit of my payment and possibly expulsion form the company.

"Sound good to you guys?" Matt asked.

Chris nodded, impressed, while Cassy quietly applauded.

"I made a copy for each of us," Matt told them as he handed the contracts around.

They took turns signing with the quill and passed the contracts to Matt, who stowed them carefully in his bag, muttering a short spell to ensure they wouldn't become accidently damaged.

"As of now, we are officially Shearcliff and Company," Chris said excitedly. "Congratulations everyone!"

"Hurray!" Cassy cheered. "Anyone have anything to drink? We should celebrate this!"

"Afraid not Cas," Chris said glumly.

"Sorry," Matt said with a shrug. "Besides with us heading into the city tomorrow we should keep a clear head. We can celebrate once Draclige is far behind us."

"You're no fun," Cassy pouted but Chris noted that she complained no further.

"Let's get to sleep then," Chris told them. "We'll head into the city at first light."

The others nodded their agreement and Matt blew out the lantern.

The guard yawned and leaned on his spear. He had the misfortune of drawing gate duty this morning with his partner. He hated gate duty at this hour, it was early enough to force him to awaken much sooner than he would like, and on top of that it was boring. He had spent most of his shift so far on this cloudy morning watching farmers head off to their fields while trying not to fall asleep at his post. He was failing at the second part when he heard his partner call out.

Looking up quickly he saw something far from ordinary that morning approaching them. It appeared to be three people riding two horses. As they grew closer he saw the first rider was a young man wearing the robes of a cleric, albeit slightly tattered. He looked familiar but he turned his attention to the second horse. It carried another young man who wore a gray cloak with a sword strapped across his back. He also wore plain woolen clothes that had seen better days. The guard was far more interested in the other passenger however. She wasn't human, that became clear almost immediately. Though he had never seen one before the guard thought she might be a naga, one of the snake people rumored to live to the far east. Draclige had its share of nonhumans, but most were orcs or dwarves. It was rare to see a member of another race travel to the city and as such the guard took note. As they reached the gate the guard held out his hand.

"What's your reason for entering the city?" he asked the travelers.

"Business," the cloaked man replied.

"How long do you plan on staying?" the guard asked warily.

"We should be out of the city by tomorrow," the cleric said.

"Very well, who should I put down as entering the city, for the official record." the guard asked.

He saw the cloaked man smile.

"Shearcliff and Company," was his reply.

"Oh, adventurers are you? Alright then, head on in," the guard said.

The cloaked man nodded his thanks and he and his companions rode through the gate. Once they had passed, the guard realized why the cleric looked familiar, he had seen him leave with the expedition knights a few days ago. He turned to his partner and said:

"Run and tell the Captain that a group of adventures arrived under the banner of Shearcliff and Company. The cleric that accompanied Droga is with them. She'll want to hear about this."

His companion nodded and jogged through the gate on his way to the barracks. The guard returned to watching the road and thought that today may not be as boring as he had first thought.

"Do you think that was wise?" Matt asked Chris as they road down the city street.

Chris, who was busy gawking at everything in sight, didn't heard him. Having never been to a city before Chris was overwhelmed by everything around him. The streets seemed alive, with a constant flow of people, some of which Chris recognized as nonhumans. He saw one person who he swore was a half giant strolling down the road, for they stood at least nine feet tall. The road they traveled down was paved in large flat stones and was wide enough that six horses could ride abreast easily and there were shops and vendors everywhere. The air was heavy with loud voices and strange sounds, and Chris could smell a thousand new smells all at once, for better or worse.

"I love it here!" Chris yelled to his companions as he looked back at them.

"Hey, I asked if that was wise," Matt replied slightly irritated.

"Was what wise?" Chris replied slightly confused.

"Telling that guard the name of our company, we aren't supposed to draw attention to ourselves while we're here," Matt said worried.

"Relax Matt, they have no idea who we are, to them we're just another passing group of adventurers. They have no reason to have suspicion of us," Cassy called to him.

"Very well, but we should still hurry. Every moment we are in this city is another one we'll be recognized," Matt reminded them, seeing that the number of guards posted on every street corner had not lessened since his last visit.

"Calm down friend, we'll be out of the city before you know it," Chris chided. "Look! There's a jeweler's shop over here! I bet we can sell the necklace there!" he called suddenly, pointing to a shop featuring a sign of gems on a scale.

Sarah Morgson was not in a good mood that morning. The day had started poorly when she had to deal with an incident of soldiers harassing a vender in the market, and after confirming the report to be true having to try to find their Captain. To her displeasure, but not surprise, she found that they were Droga's men. Droga himself had yet to return from the ruins and because these men weren't under her direct command she was unable to properly discipline them. Over the last few days she had been forced to deal with several such incidents, all involving Droga's men. She decided she would have a long talk with Sorros about the type of men Droga had been hiring of late, but doubted it would make a difference. Droga was Sorros's favorite pet.

Once she had finished apologizing to the vender she returned to the barracks to finish filing reports from the day before. This was interrupted, however, when one of her men who had been guarding the gate rushed in with an unsettling report. According to the man, he had sited the cleric, Matthew Bleakstar as she remembered his name, who had been hired by Droga to accompany him to the ruins. He said that the cleric was traveling in a band of adventures under the banner of Shearcliff and Company, without any sign of Droga or his other men. Sarah wasn't sure the reason for the cleric's sudden return but doubted it was a good sign. Rather than send her men to investigate his return, and likely fail, she decided to head out herself.

She walked down to the armory and began strapping on her armor, cursing that she had to do everything herself.

"I still think we could have sold it for more," Cassy complained as they rode down the busy street.

"I don't know," Chris replied. "I think six hundred gold pieces was a ton, that's a hundred and seventy gold each after we deduct the Company's share."

"Yeah, I don't think we did too badly," Matt agreed. "What should we do now?"

"I don't know about you guys but I need some new clothes" Chris said. "We should try to find a tailor because I've been wearing these since I left Shearcliff," he said gesturing to the filthy woolen clothes he still wore.

"Not a bad idea," Cassy agreed wrinkling her nose. "I could probably use a spare set or two myself, how about you Matt?"

"You're right, my robes seen better days, let's find a tailor," Matt agreed

Sarah rode down the street in full armor, and watched as the crowd parted around her like the sea breaking around a rock. The guard had said that the adventurers were heading toward the business district, so that's where she started her search. As she proceeded down the street she scanned the crowd for a swordsman with a gray cloak accompanying a naga woman. When they entered the city, they had been on horseback but they could have since dismounted, making her job harder. She wanted to question them as to why they were traveling with the cleric who at that moment was supposed to be exploring the ruins. She had been searching for nearly an hour and had seen no sign of them, however she was determined. She continued to scan the crowd.

Chris stood in front of the large mirror and admired his new clothes. He had traded out his tattered woolen clothes for three brand new sets. The entire purchase set him back fifteen gold pieces but he considered it worth it. He now wore a white long sleeved cotton shirt and forest green pants which featured reinforced pieces of leather sewn over the knees. Over his shirt, he had also purchased a leather vest and wore studded leather bracers on his wrists. Of his original outfit he had kept only his boots and cloak, which he wore as well.

"Looking good brother!" Cassy said as she walked down the stairs with the tailor.

The tailor, a frail looking old man with a pointed face and sharp eyes wearing a fine midnight blue robe tied with a white sash, had led her upstairs after they had walked in to show her their women's selections while the *fine gentlemen* as he had called them browsed the racks of clothing in the men's selections below.

"You as well Cas," Chris replied.

She had opted to keep her old clothes as they were of fine make and still in good repair. She did however buy several new sets of clothes of her own, and currently wore almost the exact same outfit as before, this time in sky blue rather than red and having added a small dark vest.

"I picked up a sewing kit as well," Cassy told him. "That way I can repair the various tears and rips we get without having to buy new clothes all the time."

"Good call," Matt said as he walked over from where he had been changing.

While the others had seen it fit to change their outfits Matt had simply picked up a few spare white robes in addition to the one he had already been wearing.

"Not looking to change up your style at all Matt?" Cassy asked him noticing his lack of variety.

"I may not have a god but I am a cleric. I gotta look the part," he replied.

Cassy shrugged.

"Suit yourself," she replied.

"In any event, we should pick up the supplies we need and be on our way. We could also see about finding Cas a horse of her own. If we are going to be traveling a long way we would definitely benefit from that," Chris said.

"And a tent of my own!" Cassy piped in. "I really don't want to be stuck in the same tent as you two idiots for the entire journey."

"Hey that's hardly fair we…" Matt began protesting but Chris cut him off.

"Sure thing Cas," he said to her ignoring Matt completely. "I'll pick one up when I'm buying the company supplies."

"Why should she get a tent all to herself?" Matt asked Chris. "If nothing else she should have to pay for it."

Chris sighed.

"Matt, have you considered the tent we are already cramming into is her tent?" he asked.

Matt looked at his feet. Truthfully, he hadn't considered it and was slightly embarrassed that Chris had to remind him. Chris wasn't finished however.

"Secondly it makes sense that Cas would get a tent to herself, or have you also forgotten that she's a woman, and may prefer a little privacy?" Chris asked and Matt turned scarlet while Cassy descended into peals of laughter.

Matt mumbled something unintelligible under his breath and Chris decided the matter was closed and was preparing to leave when the tailor approached them.

"Apologies my good sirs, my good lady," he said nodding to them in turn. "I couldn't help overhearing that you were in need of supplies and a good horse. May I recommend the general store on the southwest corner of the business district? It's called Bart's Basic Goods; the owner is a kind man who I'm sure will give you a good deal. As for a horse as I am aware the owner of the general store recently bought several fine horses he was planning to sell to the stable master up in the castle. I'm sure you could persuade him to let go of one."

"You seem to know quite a bit about this shopkeeper," Matt said slightly suspicious.

The old man only laughed.

"I should most certainly hope so. The shop is owned by my brother Bart. Tell him I sent you, he'll make sure you're well taken care of," the tailor replied and the small amount of suspicion Matt had melted away.

"Very well then, we'll be sure to check out what he has on offer,"

Chris told the old man. "Let's go guys; we have a bit of shopping left to do."

After two hours of futile searching Sarah finally had a stroke of luck involving the whereabouts of the cleric and his companions. Having found nothing combing the streets on her own she had turned to asking the guards stationed around the district if they had seen any people matching the descriptions of those she sought. Two guards who had been patrolling the district reported seeing a naga woman entering a tailor's shop in the company of two men. After getting the shop's address she rode as fast as she could toward it but to her dismay the tailor told her they had left a while ago. He had however told her where they were heading, mostly because he could see the rage building in her eyes and wanted the armored woman nowhere near his shop when she finally snapped. So, Sarah now headed to a shop on the southwest corner of the business district, Bart's Basic Goods, furious for having wasted so much time already, and intent on finding the cleric.

Chris and his companions had just finished purchasing their supplies, as well as a new horse for Cassy, a young black mare, and were walking down the alleyway behind the shop where the horses were tied carrying the last few pieces of gear when they heard a large crash followed by loud voices on the street behind them.

"I wonder what all that's about?" Chris asked as they proceeded down the alley.

"Whatever it is we had best be far from it as soon as possible. We're wanted men, even if they don't know it yet. The guards will be here soon," Matt replied.

Sarah stepped toward the shopkeeper who was scrambling on his back in the street. As it turned out this shopkeeper was far less cooperative than the previous one, and had denied any knowledge of the ones she sought. Having no patience for this sort of thing today she had decided that the best course of action was to throw the man through his shop window into the street so that the sunlight may refresh his memory. While not one to usually abuse the citizens, Sarah had reached the end of her patience, and amazingly this seemed to do the trick, because as the short aging shopkeeper saw the angry armored woman walking purposely toward him he decided it would be for the best if he told her where these people were. It was in this fashion, with one steel clad boot pressing on the chest of the babbling shopkeeper, that Sarah learned that her quarry was only a few yards away. She smiled a savage smile behind her helmet and moved quickly to the alley.

"Halt!" Sarah yelled from the entrance of the alleyway, her voice sounding metallic and harsh coming from inside her helmet.

She saw the three she sought clearly for the first time. The cleric was the one she had remembered, Matthew. He stood between the other two. The naga woman stood furthest away from her and she took note that she had a bow strung and slung over her shoulder. The man standing closest to her drew special interest as well. He stood an inch or two shorter than her and wore no armor she could see, not counting the small bracers on his wrists, and a long gray cloak. He was handsome enough, in a rustic sort of way, with shaggy black hair and a narrow face. Of the three he was the only one with a weapon suited for close quarters fighting with an impressive sword on his back and a knife at his hip. Of the three he would be the one to dispatch first she decided, then the naga. The cleric she would take alive for questioning. As she began to step forward she was surprised to hear the swordsman speak. Most usually ran when she approached yet he showed no sign of fleeing.

"What can I do for you miss?" Chris asked her.

He saw she hesitated for a half step but continued to approach him.

She cut an imposing figure, wearing a suit of armor unlike any he had seen before. It was both bulky and slim at the same time, with the midriff, arms, and legs covered with hard molded leather while the chest, thighs, and greaves were dark grey steel, accompanied by a chain skirt. The shoulders, gauntlets, and helmet were also dark steel but stood apart from the rest of the set. Each shoulder pauldron had three large spikes running from chest to back that stood nearly four inches each. The gauntlets were also spiked with two long barbed spines, resembling daggers, protruding from the front reaching past her gloved fists, with another long spine extending past her elbow. Her helmet was like that of the other knights, shaped like a cylinder with a slit removed for sight, but rather than a flat top her helmet was rounded and adorned with a short crest of spikes running from front to the back. She carried a short sword and a small kite shield, but her shield bore no crest, rather it as well was adorned with spines. Each of the shields three top points and its bottom point had been extended into sharp spikes with a row of spines running down the shields center.

Seeing her stride toward him with measured steps Chris decided those spikes weren't for decoration, this wasn't a person to waste time with something so trivial. Chris drew his sword.

"That's far enough miss, what do you want?" he asked.

To his surprise, she stopped a few paces from him.

"What I want is to know why the cleric we paid to explore the ruins is currently standing behind you," she said pointing at Matt.

"You must have me mistaken for somebody else…" Matt began.

"There's no mistake Matthew!" she yelled drawing her sword. "You're all coming with me for questioning!"

Behind him Chris heard Cassy ready her bow and Matt muttering the words of a spell.

Chris decided to make the first move, but as soon as the thought entered his mind he sensed something was wrong. It was as if his sword that only moments ago felt perfectly balanced in his hands had suddenly turned to stone. He felt the blade lurch toward the ground and he stumbled forward, pulled by this new weight. Sarah, seeing a perfect opening, lunged forward only to be sent flying backward out of the alleyway and into the front of the shop across the street with a booming crash, as if swatted by a giant's hand as Matt yelled:

"Ecra!" and thrust his fist at her.

He turned to look at Chris.

"What's wrong with you? Use your sword! Fight or we'll all be rotting in Sorros's dungeon this time tomorrow!" Matt yelled.

"It's the sword!" Chris replied as he gave it a test swing.

Now that the knight had left the alley the weight felt normal again.

"It must be the enchantment!" he said thinking quickly. "For whatever reason the blade has decided that this knight must be a good person or something, it won't let me wield it against her!"

"Just our luck, we find the one decent knight in all of Draclige! What do we do now?" Cassy asked.

"Get to the horses and flee the city. We got what we came for so why stay?" Chris replied.

"We run away?" Matt asked.

"Got any better ideas?" Chris replied.

Matt looked down the alleyway and saw that the spiky knight had freed herself from the shop she had landed in and was running towards them again.

"Come on, to the horses!" Matt yelled as he raced down the alley away from the knight, with the others close behind him.

Cassy reached her horse first and leapt into the saddle, readying her bow. As Chris and Matt ran, her bow string sounded like music to them, like a harp, and they saw arrows flashing over their heads toward the approaching knight.

If Sarah had started off angry, now she was furious. That impertinent little cleric had used magic against her! The crash had embarrassed her more than it had hurt but nevertheless it was beyond forgiveness. There was also the matter of the false swordsman who couldn't even wield his blade. What type of idiot carries a sword for show? She decided in her rage that it would be a waste of time to interrogate the little man; she would end him here and now. She hurried toward them as they raced for their horses, so intent on catching them that she almost failed to notice the arrow streaking toward her. She quickly raised her shield and felt the arrow smash against it, forcing her to halt her advance. It was as if it had begun raining arrows around her, as fast as she could deflect them with her shield or sword they came, and despite her best efforts she felt several smash off her armor. For the moment, all thoughts of advance was forgotten, and Sarah found herself doing everything in her power to survive this deadly hail. As quickly as it had begun the storm of arrows stopped, and Sarah looked up to see her quarry riding fast away from her. She would not let them escape so easily, she decided, and she sprinted to where her own horse was tethered.

"Why didn't you kill her?!" Chris yelled to Cassy as they galloped through the streets of Draclige, heading for the south gate.

"It wasn't from lack of trying!" she yelled in response.

"What do you mean by that? I've seen you make shots most archers would only dream of, are you telling me that knight can move faster than your arrow can fly?" Chris yelled.

"That's exactly what I'm saying, she's fast!" Cassy replied. "If Matt hadn't cast that spell we would have been in trouble!"

"Where did you learn that anyway?" Chris yelled over to Matt who rode beside him.

"From your book!" he replied. "When you loaned it to me the other day it showed me a bunch of new spells!"

"Lucky for us!" Chris laughed as they streaked closer to freedom. "Look there's the gate!" he yelled suddenly as the city's wall loomed into view.

"Chris, we have a problem!" Cassy yelled to him.

He looked at her and saw her pointing behind them, and to his dismay he recognized a certain spiked silhouette upon an armored battle horse galloping behind them.

"You have got to be kidding me!" Chris cried and turned to Matt. "What did you do to piss her off so much?!"

"Gods only know! Maybe she was a friend of Droga's?" he replied angrily.

"You pushing her through the front of a shop probably didn't help the matter any," Cassy yelled at him.

"Thanks for the advice! Next time I'll just let her gut your brother!" Matt shouted and shot her a foul look.

"I'm just saying, it probably didn't improve her mood is all!" Cassy replied.

"Guys please focus, she's gaining on us!" Chris bellowed breaking apart their argument.

"We're almost through the gate though; do you think she'll follow us?" Matt asked.

"Let's find out!" Cassy yelled as her horse shot through the gate, startling the two guards posted there, with Chris and Matt right behind her.

Sarah pulled her horse to a stop as she reached the gates. As she saw the three rapidly distancing themselves from the city she made up her mind. She dismounted and walked up to the two confused guards.

"You two, run and report directly to Fenir. Tell him Captain Morgson sent you on an urgent matter if he tries to send you away. Tell him than I am heading after a group of dangerous rebels fleeing south under the banner of Shearcliff and Company. I will return once I have captured them. Do you understand?" she asked angrily.

"Yes Captain!" the guards yelled in reply.

"Good, now go!" she said and remounted her horse.

The adventures had too much of a lead for her to catch them outright. She decided she would wait until they made camp and strike them then, and finally put an end to this nonsense.

CHAPTER SEVEN

The morning's clouds transformed into rolling thunderheads above them, flickering with lightning as they road hard, until the sun had sunk below the horizon. When they finally stopped to rest their horses were frothing at the mouth and drenched with sweat. It began to drizzle rain. They decided to make camp ways from the road, in a small clearing within the forest, next to a small creek. They made sure the horses were well cared for after such a hard ride and set about making a small camp.

"We can't risk a fire," Chris told Matt as he saw Matt starting to gather kindling while the wood was still dry.

"Do you think that we were followed?" Cassy asked from by the tents.

"I'm not sure but until we put another day's ride between us and Draclige I wouldn't let our guard down," Chris told her. "We should also sleep in shifts so that nobody sneaks up on us in the night. I'll take the first shift so you two get your rest; we have a long day in the saddle tomorrow."

"Sounds good buddy, I'll take the second watch around midnight. Cassy, are you good with three till six? That's when we'll be hitting the road tomorrow," Matt asked her.

"That's fine, I'll get to sleep now then. See you two in the morning," Cassy said and with that she retreated within her tent.

"I think I'll follow her example, see you at midnight Chris," Matt said as he walked toward their tent.

Chris pulled the hood of his cloak up and walked over to a nearby tree. He leaned back against it and had a good view of the tree line on the road side of camp. He settled in and sighed. By his calculation, it was about nine in the evening, he had a long three hour watch ahead of him.

Sarah had followed the adventurer's trail down the road without much difficulty; they had been riding fast and made no effort to disguise their tracks. She rode quickly herself, intent on not losing her prey's trail. By nightfall she assumed that they would have stopped to make camp and slowed her pace, scanning the tree line for signs of disturbances. Around ten a clock the rain became a storm and lightning flashed angrily above, illuminating the world in brilliant bursts of bluish light. In one such flash she saw a place where the brush had been crushed down, as if a rider had passed through. She dismounted to investigate, and saw several sets of hoof prints in the mud. With a grim smile, she crept down the trail, sword drawn. She had decided to leave her shield with her horse as it would only slow her down. She moved slowly to reduce the noise from her armor, but it was unnecessary, the storm hid any noises she made. Her thoughts burned in her head, her desire to find those who had escaped her. It consumed her, and soon all thoughts of capture had left her mind, she wanted vengeance for the way they shamed her in the city. The brush trail ended and she found herself looking out over a small clearing. She saw in a burst of light that there were two tents pitched and only a single sentry, the false swordsman from before.

"He must be as poor a sentry as he is a swordsman" she whispered to herself because he simply leaned against a tree, making no effort to conceal himself aside from the grey cloak pulled around him.

From what she could see he was bored and barely paying attention. Deciding to silence him first then deal with the other two after she rose from her crouch and sprinted silently towards him in the darkness, sword out.

Chris had been on guard for nearly an hour and was bored out of his mind. After scanning the tree line for the hundredth time he sighed and pulled his cloak tighter around himself.

"Glad you're waterproof," he grumbled to himself as he watched drops of water drip from his hood in front of him.

Between the lightning and the thunder, he couldn't hear or see anything at all, and he debated whether it was even productive to be on watch in such conditions, it wasn't making much of a difference anyway as far as he could tell.

Not long after he had thought this a large bolt of lightning forked across the sky and lit the clearing, and in that instant Chris thought he saw a glint of light, like metal, on the far side of the clearing. Before he could make out what it was however the light was gone and he was plunged back into darkness. Still, Chris took a small step forward and loosened his sword in its scabbard. He squinted into the night and tried to make out what he had seen. As he leaned forward he felt something akin to a battering ram smash into his shoulder, driving him to his knees. Chris let out a cry of pain and surprise and attempted to role away from whatever had hit him as another blast of lightning lit the clearing.

Standing before him was the knight from before, rising like some terrifying wraith in the storm. Chris scrambled backward and attempted to draw his sword as he rose to his feet but the knight had other ideas. She charged him with her spiked shoulder lowered and drove it into Chris's side, and if not for her hitting the side where his cloak still covered he would have been skewered. As it was, they collapsed in a heap in the mud, her sword flying out of reach, and Chris's pinned underneath him.

They grappled for control as Chris called desperately for help. He saw from the corner of his eye a light flare up from within Matt's tent but it was quickly blocked from view as the knight rolled atop him, pinning him with her knees. Without hesitation, she aimed a savage punch to his face with her right hand, made all the more deadly by her wrist spikes, but Chris managed to jerk his head out of the way, and her barbed spines sank deep into the mud. As she jerked her arm to free them, Chris franticly reached for his dagger on his thigh, in the hope of evening the fight somewhat, but the knight was no stranger to this type of fight.

Seeing what he was trying to do she drove her left fist into his wrist, impaling it upon her spikes. Chris screamed and his vision swam as he felt the spines slip between the bones of his arm and out the other side. Chris watched in horror as the knight raised her now freed right hand above his chest, and knew without a doubt that this time she would not miss.

The knight drove her fist into his chest hard enough to break several of his ribs, and he felt the barbed spines slip deep inside his chest. At that exact moment, Chris heard Matt's voice cry out. It was unlike anything he had ever heard before, a single word and saga, a whisper and a scream all at once. It was a dark thing, Chris felt it slither into his mind and twist around before slipping from his memory into nothingness.

The effect was immediate, the knight was violently ripped off Chris and he let out a small cry as the wrist blades ripped free from him with a spurt of blood. Chris's cry was nothing when compared to the knight's however.

She hung as if suspended by puppeteer's strings, only the puppeteer was drunk. She twisted and contorted a few feet off the ground above Chris, limbs twitching and jerking into odd angles. A strange nimbus of faint red light surrounded her and a similar glow could be seen around Matt's outstretched hands. Her screams echoed through the night. They were more than screams of pain, screams of fear, they were something deeper. She screamed as if her very soul was being torn from her, as if this was the last moment of anything. It did not rise or fall, it did not seem to change pitch, nor did she seem to draw breath. It was a single scream, drawn out for an eternity, ripped from within her. Chris felt sickened hearing it.

"Matt stop!" Chris heard Cassy scream from somewhere behind him.

Matt only stood there, hands outstretched, wreaking his terrible magic upon her. Chris stumbled to his feet and ran through the mess of blood and mud he stood in to reach Matt.

"Matt come on snap out of it! Stop!" Chris yelled at him as he shook

Matt by the shoulders but still he stood there as if in a trance and still the scream drew on through the storm, drowning out the thunder.

Not knowing what else to do Chris drew his dagger awkwardly with his good hand and smashed its hilt atop Matt's head. Matt fell slumped into the mud unconscious and the tortured knight fell with a crash of metal onto the ground, where she lay twitching every now and again.

Chris stood in shock for a moment, looking at the chaos around him. He felt a dull throb from his arm, and looked at his wound. He saw a great jagged tear through the center of his arm continuing to his wrist, large enough he could see clean through. He saw shards of bone and ragged strips of flesh within the hole, but mostly he saw blood, so much blood, pouring from it, and more still rushing from his chest.

"Strange, I can't feel it at all," Chris said dreamily as he smiled up at his sister who stood horrified at the opening of her tent.

With that, the world around Chris faded into nothingness and he collapsed face down in the mud between Matt and the knight.

No sooner had the real world faded away around him that the grey world of the brothers formed around him. Chris had departed from one scene of chaos to another it seemed, for before him stood the three brothers attempting to kill one another.

Al, who Chris only recognized because he was the largest, was busy trying to strangle Ge, the smallest, while Mi was perched on Al's shoulders pounding him over the head with both fists. The entire scene would have been quite terrifying except for the fact that they were already dead.

Chris stood there, mouth agape, unsure of how to proceed in such a situation when Al tossed Mi off and he landed at Chris's feet. Mi looked up at Chris and smiled, at least he thought, as he never did get used to the blurry faces, and hopped to his feet.

"Hello Chris! Lovely evening isn't it!" he said cheerfully as he hopped to his feet.

Al immediately released Ge and both of the brothers stepped forward to Chris.

"Mind telling me what the hell that was about?" Chris asked somewhat bemused.

"I was trying to explain to my brother why it's not ok to teach somebody dark magic without them knowing," Al said looking sheepish.

"By strangling them," Chris said flatly. "You can't kill a dead man, right?" Chris asked.

Al only shuffled his feet.

"And you," he said now looking at Mi. "What were you doing on top of Al?"

"I was trying to express why the enchantment he placed on his sword is possibly the dumbest in history. I was only putting it in a way he could easily understand," Mi said earnestly.

"While I hate to agree with you I think the swords defective. It wouldn't let me fight that knight woman, she almost killed me!" Chris said.

"There's nothing wrong with the sword!" Al proclaimed. "It's just that that knight woman must have a good heart."

"Yes, and I'm sure that her good heart was set on carving out our young friend's here, or have you forgotten she tried to kill him!" Mi yelled at Al.

"All I am saying is she can be trusted, that much is certain. It's just a matter of whose side she's on is all," Al defended.

"Al's not the only one who's enchantment nearly got me killed, or have you forgotten that she saw past the cloak without any trouble at all?" Chris said to Mi.

"Sorry but that's on you," Mi said with a shrug. "She just wanted to find you more than you wanted to hide, nothing I can do about that."

Chris just shook his head in disgust. He turned his gaze to Ge.

"And you," he said with a glare.

"Yes?" Ge asked tilting his head slightly.

"Did you really teach my friend dark magic?" he asked with a voice full of malice.

Ge tilted his head the other way.

"I don't believe any magic is good or evil. I showed him many spells he could cast that called upon many different gods. I thought it may help him find his personal god later to sample the different gods powers more. It just so happened that that specific spell happened to call upon Gith, the god of torment. In the future, I will ensure I include to which god the spells belong when he reads the book, to prevent any further... *incidents*," Ge said.

Chris buried his face in his hands.

"I have no idea what to do now," he groaned.

"I suggest you start by killing the knight when you wake up. If she makes it back to the city she will surly bring reinforcements. It's the safest option," Ge replied.

"Gotta agree with Ge here, she's too dangerous to let go and it's not like you can bring her with you," Mi said.

"Absolutely not! You cannot execute a fallen knight in such a manner, she has a pure heart, the sword showed you!" Al yelled at them.

"Good person or not Chris can't force her to follow him, and he most certainly can't her let go! We don't have any other options Al," Mi said.

Chris thought for a moment.

"Al, you said she would keep her word, not break an oath? I can trust her to do that?" Chris asked him.

"I'm sure; else the sword would have at least been usable against her," Al confirmed.

"Very well, I know what I have to do," Chris told them.

"Care to share your plan with us?" Ge asked in his flat voice.

"Nope, you'll just have to watch when I wake up," Chris said with a smirk.

"I have a feeling this will end poorly," Mi said slowly.

"I can't believe I'm saying this but I agree with Mi. If I think I know what you're planning this will end badly," Al said.

"You'll all just have to watch then. I wonder when I'll wake up?" Chris asked idly.

"Probably soon, time flows differently here. You have been asleep for some time now," Ge said.

Chris went to ask just how time worked here but the world was already fading around him, and he felt himself slipping back to reality once more.

Chris awoke with a start, staring at the roof of his tent. From the way the sun streamed through the tent flap he judged it was a little before noon, meaning he had slept far later than usual. He sat up and took stock of his surroundings. Somebody, he assumed his sister, had removed all of his clothing save his pants and laid him on his bedroll. He had been washed off after the fight and he found cloth wrappings around his wounds. Carefully, as to not injure himself further, he began unwrapping the bandages around his wrist and smiled as they fell away. The night before there had been a ragged hole going through his arm, now there was only a large dark scar on both sides of his wrist. He flexed his hand a few times and found that there was no soreness or stiffness.

"Good morning," Matt said as he poked his head into the tent. "I see the patient is doing well."

"Thanks to you I believe," Chris said as he smiled up at him.

"Sorry about the scars, if I had managed to get to your wounds faster I would have been able to prevent them but you bled for nearly an hour before I woke up. If not for your sister you would have bled to death," Matt told him.

"Its fine really, thanks again for healing me," Chris reassured him.

"Listen Chris, about last night…" Matt began.

"It's alright, you had no idea what that spell would do. I'm just glad you did something is all," Chris said but Matt shook his head.

"I know my spells Chris, and I had a general idea of what that one would do, I just couldn't think of anything. She was going to kill you and I panicked. Normally I would never use dark magic, I'm godless, not heartless," Matt said voice strained.

"I know Matt, its ok, really," Chris said gently. "What became of that knight by the way? I need to talk to her."

"Cassy is guarding her now, she's tied up outside. She wanted to kill her right away but I protested. Luckily, she prioritized treating us above seeking vengeance else you would be out of luck," Matt replied.

"It was probably a close call for her," Chris laughed and Matt smiled a little. "Anyway, I need to get moving," Chris said as he tried rising to his feet, but his vision filled with spots and he nearly collapsed.

Matt jumped forward to steady him.

"Easy Chris, my magic can heal you but it won't replace lost blood. You have to take it slow for a bit," Matt warned him.

"Good to know, I'll be sure not to do anything too rash," Chris said and took a step forward on his own.

Matt helped him remove the remaining bandages then stepped back. Chris dressed himself slowly, taking care to not fall over while Matt stood outside. Once he finished putting on his clothes, one of the new sets from the tailor, he strapped on his weapons and pulled his cloak around his shoulders. Cassy had left the book on his hip as he slept.

Finished dressing himself he stepped out of his tent and took a deep breath of the morning air, smelling fresh rain and wet earth. The storm form the night had passed while he slept and today the sky was bright and clear. Looking around the clearing he noticed an extra horse wearing armor staked with the others and recognized it as the knight's.

"Cassy scouted around to make sure the knight came alone and found her horse, and it seemed a waste to leave it so she brought it back with her," Matt said as he busied himself making a small fire.

Chris nodded and continued to look around until he saw his sister.

She was sitting on a stone beside the river and waved at him. Her bow had an arrow fitted on the string and was sitting across her lap. Beside her was a tree that had grown closer to the water than the others, and tied to it was the knight from before. It seemed that Cassy had removed her armor from the waist up, on account of the spines, and tied her hands behind the tree. The knight slumped against the tree, her chin against her chest. Her eyes were closed but she appeared to be awake.

This was the first time Chris could see what his assailant looked like. As Chris walked toward her he noticed that her wavy hair was a vivid shade of red, pinned up to fit under her helmet. She was pale, with cream colored skin showing on her face and arms. Even if he had not seen her fight already he would have been wary of her. Most girls

Chris had met had thin arms and little muscle, even his sister, who was strong enough to pull her large longbow with ease, was built slimly, her strength a testament to the naga people. This woman was different. Perhaps once she had had a slim build, but years of wearing heavy armor and wielding a sword had poured heavy muscle onto her form. Her arms were by no means large, but he could clearly see each and every muscle ripple like an iron cord as she shifted position. The rest of her body was every bit as impressive as her arms and as he stopped before her she looked up at him, her proud face held up by a strong neck. The years of fighting had striped her of almost any ounce of fat, making her cheekbones stand tall and her face appear stern. Her chest was not overly large or curvy; rather it was layered with hard muscle. Despite this Chris found her attractive though intimidating, with large pale blue eyes like twin shards of ice. She was younger than he had expected, appearing to be in her early twenties. He expected to see rage or hate burn in her eyes but instead she seemed sad, empty, as if resigned to her fate.

"She hasn't said a word all night, which is good because I would have gagged her if she started talking," Cassy called to him but Chris raised his hand signaling for silence and knelt in front of the knight.

"What's your name?" he asked her softly.

She shrugged, her short shirt lifting to revel her muscular body.

"Why does it matter? I take it I'll be killed and dumped here so why should I waste my breath talking to you?" she told him.

Chris was surprised by her voice, in the alleyway it had been harsh and imposing, but now it was soft and smooth. It was slightly unsettling that her voice didn't seem to match the rest of her at all, as if it belonged to someone else entirely.

"Because I really don't want to kill you and if you're willing to talk to me perhaps we can reach a deal," Chris replied.

"I have no interest of dealing with bandits and thieves," she spat at him.

Chris drew his sword and she flinched back slightly. He lowered himself into a cross legged position in front of her and laid the blade across his lap.

"Do you recognize this sword?" he asked her.

"Should I?" she asked

"This sword, as well as the cloak I wear and the book I carry are the artifacts Sorros sent Droga to retrieve from Algeminia. I followed the knights from my village and they caught me. Droga said he was going to kill me and destroy my village for interfering with his mission, that's what caused Matt to come to my aid. We escaped, and by random luck managed to find the artifacts Sorros wanted," Chris told her.

"What about Droga and the knights?" she asked skeptically.

"I killed them with this sword," he said and she scoffed.

"Please, in the ally you couldn't even hold up that sword, how am I supposed to believe that you killed that murderer Droga, an accomplished fighter, by yourself," she mocked

"Because this sword is magical, it, as well as the cloak and book cannot be lost, sold, or stolen. Most importantly it can sense what type of person you are and the types of people around you. It is made to smite evil, and it cannot be used against those with a pure heart, which is why I'm talking with you now. The sword decided you're a good person in that alleyway, otherwise I would have let my sister put an arrow through you already," Chris told her and she looked at him strangely for a moment.

"My name is Sarah Morgson. I am one of the guard Captains under command of Governor Sorros," she said slowly, eyes full of suspicion.

Chris smiled at her.

"My name is Christian Shearcliff; I'm the leader of this band. The woman with the bow is my sister Cassy Shearcliff, and I believe you already know our cleric, Mathew Bleakstar. Together we form Shearcliff and Company; we're traveling south looking for work," Chris told her.

"That's all well and good, but why are you telling me this? Knowing all that you can't let me go, so if you're going to kill me hurry up and get on with it already," she told him angrily.

"I already told you I don't want to kill you," Chris reminded her. "And you're right; I can't just let you go."

"What is it you want from me then? You can't let me go but you don't want to kill me, so am I to be your prisoner as you bumble across Targoth?" Sarah demanded with a sneer.

"Come on Chris, cut the crap," Cassy called to him. "Step aside and let me put an arrow through her and we can be done with this."

"You can't just kill an unarmed prisoner!" Matt yelled at her as he marched across the clearing.

"Would you idiots quit wasting my time and make up your minds already?!" Sarah bellowed cutting off their budding argument.

Matt and Cassy jumped in surprise and looked to Chris.

"It's your call," Matt told him and Cassy nodded her agreement.

The clearing was silent as everyone looked at Chris expectantly.

"There is a third option you all seem to have forgotten," Chris said after a moment.

He turned to Sarah.

"Did you swear any binding oaths to Sorros?" he asked.

She looked at him confused.

"No, he just paid me week by week. None of the guards swear any oaths; we're just sell-swords that he calls his knights. Why do you want to know anyway?" she asked.

Chris ignored her question.

"Sarah, would you break a sworn oath, or a contract?" Chris asked, already knowing the answer.

"I'm no liar," she said looking at him sternly. "I'm a mercenary, if my word can't be trusted how can I expect to be hired?"

"Good," Chris said brightly. "In that case, you have two choices. First, we kill you here and now. I promise you that you'll get a proper burial, however as I have said I really don't want to kill you, and I don't imagine that you want to be killed."

"Better than she deserves," Cassy called but Chris ignored her.

"That brings you to your second choice; signing on to Shearcliff and Company. You'll get an equal share of the treasure and get to see the world," Chris told her.

"I've already seen a good share of the world thank you. Why would I want to sign on with you three idiots?" she asked.

"Well the alternative is we kill you," Matt said and Chris smiled over to him, grateful for his support.

Cassy however was less convinced.

"You can't be serious; you want to let this woman join us, never mind the fact that last night she almost killed you?!" Cassy yelled.

"Do you have a better suggestion?" Chris asked her.

"Yes! As a matter of fact, I do! It's called pinning her to the tree with an arrow!" she yelled nearly hysterical. "Seriously you two, think for a second! She'll probably slit our throats in our sleep or something; we have absolutely no way of trusting her!"

"We can trust her," Chris said firmly and Sarah looked at him quizzically. "The sword cannot be used against those with pure hearts remember? It showed me that she's a good person. Al assured me that we could trust her to keep her word."

Cassy looked away darkly.

"Do whatever you want, but don't say I didn't warn you," Cassy hissed.

Chris returned his attention to Sarah.

"So, what will it be?" he asked her.

"Not much of a choice, is it?" Sarah said with a roll of her eyes. "Fine, I'll join your little band of misfits, just cut me loose from this tree," she added after a slight pause.

"Excellent!" Chris said excitedly as he cut her binds with his dagger. "Matt, go draw up another contract!" Chris called to him but Sarah held up her hand.

"Wait a minute there Matthew, I need to have a word with you," she said as she stretched her sore muscles.

"What is it you need?" Matt asked slightly confused as she walked toward him.

She advanced until she was only a pace away and beckoned him to lean in. Confused, Matt leaned forward to hear her and she delivered a mighty punch to his jaw, lifting him nearly a foot off the ground. Shocked, Chris readied his dagger and Cassy snatched up her bow but Sarah made no further move to attack, rather she offered him her hand and helped him to his feet.

"What the hell was that for?" Matt mumbled nursing his jaw.

"If you ever use a spell like that on me again I swear on all the gods I'll cut your balls off," Sarah told him.

Then it was over, she turned and walked casually to her horse and began stowing her remaining armor. Matt looked at Chris worried but Chris only shrugged. Cassy looked at the two men and said:

"This is going to be soooo much fun," and rolled her eyes.

They stayed in the clearing for the rest of the day. Sarah went down the creek a ways to clean up seeing that she was still covered in mud and blood from the last night's fight while Matt drew up the contract. Chris spent the afternoon sitting in the sun reading due to the fact that he still felt a bit faint. Cassy had retreated to her tent, presumably to sulk. When Sarah returned, she was wearing a different set of clothes than before, but like the previous set these looked to be plain, made to fit under armor being made of soft leather. She had put her hair into a simple braid that hung down to her mid back. It still shone from her impromptu bath but she otherwise appeared dry. She looked around the clearing and sited Chris sitting on a rock by the edge of the creek and walked over to him. She found a comfortable position on the ground leaning against his rock and sat for a moment. Chris saw her approach but decided it would be wiser to let her talk first. After some time, she spoke.

"Thank you," was all she said.

"For what?" Chris asked putting his book down.

"For not killing me," she said and he looked at her to continue. "Most wouldn't have given me the chance you did. If anyone else had captured me after that fight I would be dead now. Hell, if our positions were reversed I definitely wouldn't have given you that choice. It's a rare thing you did and I'm grateful," she said without looking up at him.

Chris smiled slightly to himself.

"Well after a few days on the road with us you may decide it would have been far more merciful if I had killed you," he said and she laughed.

Chris was surprised, she had not laughed until now, not that she had had any reason to. It was a lovely sound, soft and musical. Like her voice, it seemed out of place belonging to her rugged frame. She looked up at him and smiled and Chris decided that she was actually very pretty when she wasn't trying to kill him and he smiled back.

"That may be so but I still promise to repay you for this," she told him. "You let me keep my life, so I swear to protect yours. Seems like a fair trade wouldn't you agree?"

"There's no need for that, you're part of the company now, we all look out for each other. They'll warm up to you, just give them a chance," Chris assured her.

"Regardless Christian, I am in your debt," Sarah told him.

"Seriously you don't have to be so formal, call me Chris, everyone else does," he told her.

"Alright... Chris," Sarah said, testing out the name and deciding that she liked the sound.

They fell into a comfortable silence for a time.

"So, when will I meet the rest of your party?" she asked him suddenly.

"What do you mean?" Chris asked very confused.

"I heard you mention somebody named Al earlier, when can I meet them?" she asked and he laughed.

"What is it?" Sarah asked confused.

"Al isn't a...*person*," Chris explained to her. "He's a spirit who lives in my head. He was the one who owned the sword before me. I actually have three spirits hanging around me counting him."

Sarah groaned.

"What like voices in your head?" she asked cautiously.

"Yeah, but they only talk to me when I'm asleep," Chris explained.

Sarah stood up and walked a few paces with her hands on her head.

"I'm trapped with a godless cleric, a naga who wants me dead, and the person who saved my life can hear voices nobody else can! Gods help me," she said pacing.

"Contract's ready!" Matt yelled from the entrance of his tent.

"Come on Sarah, time to officially make you a member of Shearcliff and Company," Chris said as he stood up.

"Lucky me," Sarah replied.

CHAPTER EIGHT

"Hey Chris, I have a question," Sarah announced as the group was preparing to settle down for the night.

"What's on your mind Sarah?" Chris asked.

"Where am I going to sleep? I didn't pack a tent when I left the city," she asked.

Chris paused for a moment.

"Well I guess it would be best if you bunk with Cas. That way the men and women have separate tents," Chris said and Matt nodded in agreement.

Cassy and Sarah both began protesting immediately however.

"That naga wants me dead!" Sarah yelled while Cassy shrieked:

"You can't be serious; how can I trust her?"

Chris stumbled back a pace under this barrage of anger and held up his hands.

"Listen you two; you're going to be traveling together for a while so you should make your peace as soon as possible. Sarah's a part of the company now and that means we have to trust her. She won't do anything to endanger you Cas," Chris told her.

"Endanger *her*?" Sarah yelled. "I'm more worried that she's gonna slit my throat in my sleep," she said pointing at Cassy.

Cassy started toward her, claws at the ready but Chris stepped between them.

"Sarah, Cas is my sister; I guarantee that she won't do anything to hurt you," Chris said to Sarah.

He turned to Cassy.

"Cas, do you trust me?" he asked.

"Of course," Cassy replied, still glaring at Sarah.

"Good, because I trust Sarah. Nothing will happen between you two, I promise," Chris told her.

Both women were quiet for a moment.

"Fine," Sarah said simply as she slung her gear over her shoulder and walked towards what was now the woman's tent.

Cassy gave Chris a strange look but she followed after Sarah and disappeared into the tent. Matt, who had been silent until then gave a low whistle.

"Those two scare me," he said shaking his head slowly.

"I appreciate your help by the way," Chris said sarcastically, annoyed that Matt had let him handle the situation alone.

"Hey unlike you I value my life, I'm not about to go jumping between those two over anything. Besides, if they had tried to kill you I would have been ready to put you back together again," Matt said a little too cheerfully.

"Thanks, you're a true friend," Chris sneered.

"Best one you got," Matt laughed giving Chris a slap on the shoulder on the way back to their tent. "Come on lets got some rest, I know a village a ways south of here; if we hurry we can reach it the day after tomorrow. Keep up the good work and you may keep those two from killing each other until then."

By the time they reached the village, Purevein, as Matt had called it, Chris's nerves were on edge. There had been little conversation on the road to the village with any communication between the two women ending in shouting, and while not threatening to disembowel one another they had spent the entire time glaring at one another from horseback.

Despite Chris's best efforts to make peace between them, each seemed assured that the other was plotting against them. He tried pointing out to them that they had shared the same tent now for two nights without killing one another but neither had seemed convinced. Chris decided he had to ride between them to ensure that they wouldn't attempt to murder one another. So, after two days of preventing bloodshed Chris was worn out, which led to his enthusiasm when they spotted the village.

"Oh, thank the gods, it looks like this place has a decent inn," he said with relief as they entered the village, seeing a two-storied building with a sign depicting a small man holding a flagon.

"I could use a hot meal," Matt agreed as he rode up behind Chris. "What do you say ladies? This place look good to you?" he called up to them.

"So long as I don't have to share a room with her it's fine," Cassy said from beside Chris without as much as a glance at Sarah.

"Someone make sure I'm not dreaming because for once I agree with the naga," Sarah spat from Chris's other side.

"Separate rooms will be more expensive," Matt pointed out to her but she shrugged.

"Then I'll pay for my own room, anything to be rid of her," Sarah said before riding down to the inn.

Chris and Matt exchanged glances and rode after her, with Cassy close behind them.

"Welcome to the Drunken Dwarf!" bellowed a tiny bearded man serving drinks as they entered the inn.

He was standing behind a strange bar, which appeared to have two separate halves. The left side was normal height; with a few men sitting nursing mugs of ale, while the right was nearly a foot and a half shorter; where several dwarves wearing dusty overalls spoke quietly. The bartender himself stood on a raised platform behind the left half at the moment, seeing that he was nearly a head shorter than Matt, but he disappeared behind the bar as he jumped down to greet them. As he emerged from behind the counter it became clear he was a dwarf as well.

Chris had never seen a dwarf before up close but knew a little about them. They were a strong and hearty people who were well known for their excellent craftsmanship. While not as common as humans a few could usually be found in nearly any city or large town. This town, Chris thought looking around the inn, had an unusually large number of dwarfs.

"Pleasure to meet you," Chris said as he reached down to clasp the dwarf's hand.

The dwarf returned the greeting and beamed up at Chris giving him a good look at his face. Like many of his race he had a large flat nose and small bright eyes. Most of his face was covered by an impressive bushy red beard which was braided down to his waist. His hands were large compared to the rest of him, and Chris found he had a firm grip.

"Ay, likewise my lad. I'm so glad ye came," the dwarf said.

Chris looked at his companions quizzically but they seemed as confused as he was.

"What do you mean by that sir?" Chris asked the dwarf.

"Ye are here about the contract aren't ye?" the dwarf asked slightly confused.

"We don't know anything about a contract, we're just passing through," Sarah told the dwarf earning herself a scowl from Cassy.

"Oh," the dwarf said crestfallen. "I had ye pegged as adventures on account of ye gear. Thought ye were here to deal with our mine problem. Sorry to trouble ye."

"Wait a moment, we didn't come because of a contract, but we are indeed adventures, Shearcliff and Company, at your service," Matt said stepping forward.

The dwarf's face lit up.

"Wonderful! Are ye looking for work? As I said we have a problem that needs taking care of. We have gold too, if ye take the job," the dwarf said excitedly.

"Let's sit down and talk about it then," Chris told the dwarf and they headed to the bar.

They pulled up stools, with Sarah and Cassy sitting on opposite ends, and the dwarf climbed up on his perch behind the bar.

"So what seems to be the problem?" Chris asked.

"It's the mine," the dwarf told him sadly. "About a week ago our boys busted into a new cavern. Came back to town saying it was completely filled with ore, and that we were going to be rich. The next day when they went back in none of them came back out, and the day after that the other miners were attacked by something while they worked. Said they wouldn't go back in until whatever was in there was dealt with, and I don't blame them. They elected me as their spokesman seeing I get the most travelers in my shop and asked me to find somebody to clear out the mine. I sent out messages to the cities but hadn't heard anything until ye showed up. We're a small village, that mine is everything to us. Without it we won't have anything to trade for food, we're miners, not farmers. Will ye help us?" the dwarf asked with hope evident in his voice.

Chris couldn't believe his luck; the first village they came to already had a contract for them.

"Of course we'll help you," Chris said and the dwarf gave a sigh of relief. "We'll take the rest of the day to talk to the miners and investigate then head into the mine tomorrow."

"Thank ye greatly, I'll be sure to have rooms for all ye ready by tonight," the dwarf told him. "As for talking to miners, there's a few over there," he said pointing a thumb over this shoulder at the dusty looking dwarves behind him. "They've been coming around most every day since the mine closed. Don't think they have anywhere else to go."

Chris nodded his thanks and they walked over to the small group. The dwarves looked up as they approached, and unlike the bartender their gazes were full of suspicion and anger. They all sported impressive beards and their clothes were caked with a layer of dust no amount of washing could remove.

"What is it ye want?" one of the dwarves asked, barely glancing at Chris.

"We're here to clear out whatever's in the mine," Chris told him. "We were hoping that you could tell us a little about whatever is in there, so that we can be better prepared," Chris explained.

The dwarf gave a grunt and drank deeply from his mug.

"I don't know what good it will do ye, none of us got a proper look at the beasties. A couple of our boys called from the new cavern, said they found something. When we went inside the creatures came fast from the shadows, and snatched up half of our boys before we knew what was happening. After that we were running so fast we didn't see what they looked like. Anyone who saw them up close didn't make it out so far as we know," the dwarf told him.

"You say there's more than one of them?" Sarah asked the dwarf.

"Ay lass, there was definitely more than one. No other way they could have grabbed us up so fast," the dwarf said and the other dwarves grumbled their agreement.

Sarah turned to Chris.

"Well at least we learned something," she told him.

"Thank you for your time, we'll be sure to avenge your friends," Chris told the miners but they barely acknowledged him, with the leader only raising his mug slightly in Chris's direction.

It was clear to Chris that they would learn nothing further from talking to the miners, so he returned to the bartender for directions to the mine, which was a short ride away laying in the hills outside of town. Along the way Cassy spoke.

"You would have thought that those miners would have been a little happier to see us," she said as they rode.

No one responded at first, and as they rode it seemed her comment would go unanswered until Sarah spoke up.

"I feel like they acted appropriately," she replied.

"How?! They're sitting around moping, waiting for somebody to save them then we waltz in practically served on a silver platter! They should have been licking our boots and begging us to help them! Instead they barely gave us the time of day! Explain to me how that is appropriate?" she asked Sarah angrily.

Sarah said nothing and again it seemed the conversation would end there until she replied once more.

"Those dwarves have most likely been working in that mine their entire lives, and their fathers before them. Now the mine they've depended on is no longer safe and many of their friends are missing, presumed to be dead. I'm surprised they were willing to speak to us at all given the circumstances," Sarah said in an unusual display of calm.

"Still, they could have thanked us at least," Cassy argued.

Chris and Matt exchanged uneasy glances, this was the longest Sarah and Cassy had spoken to one another without shouting or threats since they had met, but they could feel the tension rising in the air.

"We haven't done anything yet except talk; they have no reason to thank us. Once the job is done I'm sure they'll pay us well and thank us for our time but until then they owe us nothing," Sarah explained slowly, as if speaking to a young child.

Cassy's face flushed darker than normal and she opened her mouth to reply but Chris cut her off.

"There's the mine!" he said as he pointed ahead of them, grateful for the distraction to stop the looming confrontation.

All eyes turned forward to examine their destination.

The mine opened into the side of a large hill, framed in sturdy wood. The sun shone into the mine's entrance revealing it sloped sharply into the earth. Tracks for a cart could be seen running down the center of the mine, but how far down it went they couldn't tell, because after a few yards the mine swallowed up the light and they could see only shadow. They dismounted and stood before the entrance, peering into the gloom.

"So what's the plan Chris?" Matt asked after a minute.

"Well we know where this place is now, I say we head back to the village for today, then explore the mine tomorrow," Chris said.

The others seemed to agree with this so they turned to leave, but Cassy hesitated.

"Wait a second Chris," she said softly and walked closer to the mine's entrance.

"What is it Cas?" Chris asked.

"I thought I heard something coming from the mine," Cassy replied and stepped into the mine's entrance, leaning forward and flexing her clawed hands slightly.

"What do you mean, we didn't hear anything," Matt said confused but Sarah shook her head.

"Naga have far superior senses compared to humans. It's possible she heard something we could not," Sarah said, shocking Chris that she would back Cassy on anything.

"Are you sure you heard something Cas?" Chris asked her.

"I think so. When we were kids I always thought you and the other kids were a bit dim witted, guess I've just got better senses than I thought," Cassy replied.

"You mean to tell me you don't know anything about your own people?" Matt asked shocked.

Cassy shrugged.

"I was raised human remember? I've never actually met another naga. All I know about being a naga is that I used to shed my skin when I was growing up and once a month I lay an egg," Cassy replied very seriously.

Chris burst into a fit of laughter as Matt turned scarlet, even Sarah let a small smile creep onto her face. After a moment Cassy's stern mask fell and she too joined in the laughter, prompting Matt to let out a nervous chuckle. Their mirth was cut short however as Cassy held up her hand suddenly and ran a few steps deeper into the mine.

"I heard it again!" she called up to them.

"What is it?" Chris called back.

Cassy listened for a moment before looking back up at him. All signs of their previous amusement were gone from her face.

"It's a voice, somebody's calling for help," she said quietly.

They wasted no time.

"Luminita," Matt said softly and a glowing ball of light appeared in his hand.

Sarah drew her short sword and shifted her shield from her back to her arm in a natural movement she had done a thousand times.

Chris drew his sword from its scabbard and felt its familiar weight in his hands. It was strange he thought, how he had only had the sword for a few short days yet it already felt like an extension of his body, like he had wielded it his entire life. He decided it must be part of the enchantment as he raced after Cassy, who was already running deeper into the mine with her bow at the ready.

Chris was grateful for the light Matt's spell provided because he could see no further than the edge of its glow, the rest of the mine was pitch black. Cassy seemed to have no such problem however, and raced ahead through the darkness calling directions to them as they ran. After some time Chris became aware of a voice coming from deeper within the tunnels.

"Help me, help me," it called softly, over and over again.

"It's this way!" Cassy yelled as Chris saw her disappear around the corner ahead of them off the main path into a hole in the wall.

"Cas, wait up!" Chris yelled but he had lost sight of her. "Matt can you give us more light?" Chris asked as they stepped around the corner into a large cavern.

Chris assumed it was large at least, because the light from Matt's spell was unable to reach the ceiling and he couldn't see any walls around them, save the one behind them they had just passed through. Matt did not reply, but he muttered under his breath and the glow expanded a few more yards around them, but still the cavern remained shrouded in darkness.

"Cas, where did you go?" Chris called into the darkness.

"It's this way!" Cassy's voice called from the shadows ahead of him.

Chris stepped forward a few feet.

"We can't see anything in here Cas, come back over here and lead us through," Chris said.

"It's this way! It's this way!" came her reply, only this time it came from the shadows to Chris's left rather than ahead of him.

"Cas?" Chris asked confused.

He heard a gasp from behind him.

"Chris your sword, look!" Sarah yelled.

Chris turned his attention away from his sister and looked at his sword. Soft flames licked up the blade, small enough he hadn't noticed in the light, but growing stronger by the moment.

"Matt, light the entire room, now!" Chris yelled as he stepped backward to his companions.

"I'll only be able to hold that for a moment," Matt warned.

"Just do it!" Chris yelled.

The light blinked out for a second.

"Luminita!" Matt bellowed with as much strength as he could muster and suddenly the cavern was as bright as day.

Chris recoiled in horror as he saw the hoard of creatures around them. They resembled small humans in shape standing about as tall as a child, walking on two short legs that ended in cloven hooves. They wore no clothes, nor showed no signs of gender whatsoever. Their entire body was covered in pale wrinkly skin, hanging like draped fabric over their gaunt frames. Their arms hung nearly to the ground, splitting into two fingers capped with hollow claws dripping a thick purple liquid. Their heads were roughly rectangular in shape, wide, and covered entirely by a disgusting lipless mouth filled with large flat teeth. They had no eyes or nose that Chris could see but had massive pointed ears drooping from the side of their heads. They seemed to grin as they moved towards them. From time to time one would open its wide mouth and call out:

"Help me, help me!" or "It's this way!"

Across the room Chris saw Cassy lying on the ground, her dark skin marred by a deep slash on her chest which oozed blood. She lay on a pile of small humanoid bones, which looked to be fairly fresh. The light went out once more with a small pop.

"Matt we need that light!" Chris screamed as the darkness swallowed them up once more, the only light coming from the flames on his sword which grew brighter by the moment.

"I can't hold a light that big that long! It could kill me!" Matt yelled back through the shadows.

"If you don't get the lights back up *I'll* kill you, assuming those things don't do it first! Sarah bellowed at him.

That seemed to do the trick.

"Luminita!" Matt yelled yet again dropping to a knee, holding his hands above his head.

A ball of light shot from his hands and struck the roof of the cavern, illuminating the area like a miniature sun. Matt froze in this position, face scrunched in concentration muttering words of prayer, while Chris and Sarah readied their weapons. The creatures stalked around them, as if waiting for them to move. One of the bolder ones darted forward, faster than Chris thought possible, claws outstretched toward Matt.

Chris responded instinctually, pivoting to intercept the monster with his sword cutting a blazing trail between it and his friend. With barely a sound the blade sliced through the creature's neck cleanly severing its head. Its body collapsed in a heap leaking black goo from where its head once attached. Matt didn't seem to notice, being too focused on his spell.

It was as if the creature's death gave some invisible signal to the others and like a wave they sprang forward, screaming in Cassy's voice and those of the fallen miners. Chris let the sword take over as it carved a fiery halo in its wake. It sliced through the creatures as if they were as insubstantial as shadow and they fell around him in droves. As he fought he saw one of the creatures divert from the battle and race toward Cassy, who was attempting to rise slowly on the other side of the room. He began to push forward through the crowd to reach his sister but as he did so the monsters converged on Matt. Cursing, he retreated to defend his friend.

"Sarah, Cas is in trouble!" he cried out as he sliced at the wall of moving flesh before him.

To Chris's relief she didn't hesitate.

"On it!" Sarah yelled back and took a few steps away from the crowd of monsters she was fighting.

Before he had a chance to ask what she was doing Sarah lowered her shoulder and raised her shield before her, bracing against it with her sword hilt. Sarah charged forward and smashed into the hoard like a battering ram sending small pale bodies flying through the air accompanied by the sound of crunching bone. As she raced through the crowd the spines on her armor tore into the monsters nearest to her, spraying her with their black blood. She punched free of the crowd as the creature reached Cassy, slashing her with one of its clawed hands. Cassy gave a small gasp as the claws cut into her and went stiff, falling back to the ground. The monster reached back to strike again but the blow never landed. Sarah rammed into it with her shield at full speed, impaling it on its spikes. With a wrench of her arm she shook the limp body free of her shield and marched purposefully forward toward Cassy's still form. Sarah looked down at her and saw her eyes darting around the room, but she seemed unable to move.

"Don't let them cut you, you'll be paralyzed!" Sarah yelled across the room to Chris.

"I wasn't planning on getting cut but thanks for the heads up!" Chris yelled back as he pulled his sword free of one of the creatures.

He had lost track of how many he had killed; every time one fell it was if three more jumped forward to take their place. He glanced back at Matt, and saw wisps of smoke rising from his mouth and eyes. Chris doubted he could hold the spell much longer. If this fight didn't end soon Matt would collapse, and that would mean the end for all of them.

Across the room, Sarah had positioned herself directly over top of Cassy, and was fending off wave after wave of creatures. At first she fought with her shield as well as her sword, using its spines as effectively as her blade, but it had become lodged in one of the bodies around her and she had no opportunity to recover it. She looked down at Cassy and saw she had managed to prop herself up on an elbow but was unable to rise.

"Stay down, it'll be alright," Sarah tried to reassure her over the din of battle, but she had no idea if Cassy heard because her attention was ripped away as yet another monster jumped forward skewering itself upon her sword.

The blade bit deep into one of the creatures bones, and Sarah struggled to pull it free as the creature croaked:

"This way…" and died still attached to her sword.

Cursing the fallen monster Sarah tossed the blade aside with the beast still attached as yet another creature raced forward. Sarah crouched low and readied her fists, eying the monster over the barbed spines on her gauntlets.

Chris could see the battle was going poorly. On the far side of the cavern he could see Sarah getting swarmed by the beasts. She fought like a cornered animal as she tried to protect Cassy and was covered from head to toe with black blood. She laid into them with the spines on her armor, punching them with her barbed gauntlets, skewering them on her elbow spikes, even smashing them with the spiked crest of her helmet. She was tiring. Chris could see her blows came slower and slower, and it was only a matter of time until one of the creatures scored a lucky hit. Chris himself wasn't tired courtesy of his sword's magic, but he knew that once the lights went out they were all doomed.

It was then Chris heard the voice. It came from behind him and flowed over him like a gentle breeze, calming him, reassuring him that everything would be alright. The creatures around him halted their advance to listen and even Sarah paused her slaughter to hear this mysterious voice. The voice was singing. What it sang Chris could not tell, for the words were in a beautiful language he did not recognize. He began to feel very tired, like the stress of wielding his sword had finally caught up to him. If he took a nap he would be refreshed and ready to fight again he thought. His sword began to slip from his fingers as he fell to a knee, and across the room he was vaguely aware that Sarah was struggling to stand, and many of the monsters around him had begun to sway where they stood or had simply curled up and fallen asleep.

As Chris began to nod off he became aware that the song had changed. The words became harsh and frightening, like each one was a threat. Chris's head cleared and he looked around. Sarah had also recovered and was pulling Cassy away from the hoard as fast as she could, obviously terrified of something Chris could not see. The monsters had yet to recover, with many still sleeping or standing in a trance. From behind Chris, Matt gave a low moan and slumped to the ground, and his spell broke with a pop, but the lights did not go out. Though the cavern was no longer lit by sunlight, he could still see courtesy of a red glow spreading across the cave, coming from behind him. Chris turned and saw the cause of the glow and recoiled in horror.

Floating in the air behind him was a serpent made of fire. It twisted and writhed as if trapped in an invisible bubble, growing bigger each passing second. The song ended. The singer uttered one final word, and though Chris didn't know the language the meaning was clear; it was a command to kill.

Several things happened at the same time. Chris screamed:

"Matt!" and leapt to his fallen friend covering both of them with his cloak.

As he did this Sarah pulled Cassy close to her chest and turned away from the fire serpent, trying to shield her from the spell's deadly effect.

The serpent struck, launching itself toward the swarm, mouth agape. As it flew forward its mouth opened wider and wider until it burst apart into a thousand spears of fire, blanketing the room in an inferno. Chris felt two of the spears strike his cloak, and though they did not pierce through he felt their scorching heat and cried out in pain. Sarah had managed to pull Cassy far enough away from the spell that they remained unscathed, but only barely, with several spears landing only feet short of them. The monsters were not so lucky.

Where once a massive hoard of flesh and claws had stood now only smoking ash remained; with the spears burning hot enough to melt even their bones. The room was quiet, with the only sound coming from faintly crackling fires scattered about the cavern. They cast eerie shadows on the walls, giving the place a hellish feel.

Chris rose unsteadily to his feet and saw with relief that Matt was still breathing, though only faintly. He looked across the field of death at Sarah and saw her cradling Cassy's body. Seeing him looking she gave a weak thumbs up signaling that they were alright before sinking to the ground exhausted. Chris gave a sigh of relief and turned to look at the entrance of the cavern and saw a cloaked figure standing silhouetted by the fire's glow. Seeing him stand up the figure raced to him, cloak flapping behind them.

Fearing another enemy Chris looked franticly around for his dropped sword and saw it laying a few feet away. He lunged clumsily toward it and snatched it off the ground, but screamed and dropped it as the super-heated hilt burned into his hand. He dropped slowly to his knees clutching his hand in agony, seeing that the hand the sword had touched had charred to the bone.

"Chris!" Sarah cried out from across the room as she saw the cloaked figure reach him.

The figure said something to Chris and he seemed to nod before slumping next to Matt. Sarah struggled to rise and took a few shaky steps toward them. The cloaked figure turned their attention away from Chris and sprinted toward Sarah. Sarah readied her spiked fists but the figure waved their arms toward Chris's wounded form yelling something Sarah couldn't understand as she ran.

"What?" Sarah asked, still dazed from the first spell.

The stranger reached Sarah.

"Bring her," the figure said in a heavily accented voice, a woman's voice, pointing to Cassy.

Not understanding what was happening Sarah picked up Cassy's unconscious body and stumbled after this strange woman back to Chris. When Sarah arrived the woman pointed to the ground and Sarah laid Cassy next to Matt's still form. The woman then took Matt's limp hand and placed it in Sarah's right then placed one of Cassy's hands in her left. Before Sarah could ask what she was doing the mysterious woman reached down and took Chris's uninjured hand in hers, and placed her free hand on Sarah's shoulder. The world seemed to spin around Sarah, with shapes and colors blurring together as they spun faster and faster until everything became white. Sarah felt like she was going to be sick with the spinning sensation causing her to become nauseous, and just when Sarah felt she could take it no longer there was a small bang, and she found herself standing in front of the strange bar in the Drunken Dwarf, still clutching her companion's hands.

She stumbled forward a few steps dripping black blood from her armor, tripped over Chris's sword which had been transported with them, fell to her hands and knees and barely managed to pull off her helmet before she was violently ill on the inn's floor. After nearly a full minute of horrible retching she managed to recover slightly, and was able to pull herself to her feet with the help of a nearby chair. Sarah looked around and saw a circle of curious bar patrons had formed around her, mainly dwarves but with a few scattered humans. Her companions still lay where they had arrived, with Chris having passed out from shock. Sarah watched as the woman poured a thick red liquid from a vile she procured from under her cloak into Chris's mouth and tilted his head back so that it ran down his throat. The mysterious woman turned away from Chris and now seemed to be giving orders to several of the dwarves. Sarah saw them pick up her friends and began carrying them toward the stairs. The woman turned to Sarah and walked quickly to her side.

"Are you alright?" she asked with a thick accent that Sarah didn't recognize.

Her voice seemed to rise and fall quickly, like she was singing rather than speaking.

"I'm fine, whatever that was just shook me up a bit is all," Sarah replied between deep breaths.

"My apologies, teleportation can take some getting used to," the woman told her.

"I don't care what it was, thank you. You saved our lives back in that mine," Sarah said gratefully.

The cloaked woman shrugged.

"I believe you humans say the enemy of my enemy is my friend. I had come here to take the mine contract not realizing you were already on the job. When I heard you were off at the mine investigating I headed over to speak to you, and found you fighting within. You seemed in dire straits so I decided to assist you as best as I could," the woman said.

Sarah was confused by her answer.

"You humans?" Sarah asked and let out a gasp as the cloaked woman removed her hood.

Standing before Sarah was something straight out of her childhood fairytales, something that by all accounts didn't exist. This mysterious woman was an elf.

"Yes, you humans. My name is Ditrinadoma Figinoma Rike, but most humans find it easier to call me Ditrina," she said while Sarah stood mouth agape.

Ditrina was impossible to mistake for a human without her hood. She stood about as tall as Chris, wearing pale orange robes of fine make under her long black cloak. Her body was built thin and narrow, like a reed, and Sarah thought a strong gust of wind may take Ditrina off her feet. Now that Sarah could see her properly she immediately noticed that Ditrina had long pointed ears which reached slightly past the top of her head. Her hair was perfectly straight, hanging down in front of her chest to her waist. The reason her hair caught Sarah's interest was because it was bright blue, like the color of the sky on a clear day. Her skin was also strange, seeming to be slightly translucent and having a faint green tint to it, and Sarah could see the veins standing out on her slim arms were dark green, the entire effect reminding her of a leaf. Despite this Ditrina's most striking feature was her eyes which Sarah could only describe as inverted. Ditrina's eyes were completely black, with only a thin white ring where her irises should have been. Those strange eyes seemed to look through Sarah, as if seeing into her soul. The rest of her face seemed fairly normal, with round cheeks and a sharp nose giving her a regal appearance.

"You're an elf," Sarah said in awe.

"And you are a human. Many of those around us are dwarves. Is there anything else obvious you would like to point out or do you wish to stare some more?" Ditrina asked sharply and Sarah realized that she had indeed been staring.

"I'm sorry…it's just…well…" Sarah stumbled with her words trying to explain.

She took a deep breath and tried again.

"I didn't mean to offend you; it's just that I've never seen an elf before. Many people believe the elves to be extinct so I'm just a little shocked to be talking to one is all," Sarah said and Ditrina nodded.

"It's true, my people are far less common than the other races. We never did fully recover from the crisis, but we are far from extinct I can assure you of that. As for you staring I forgive you. I remember you humans appeared strange to me when I first saw you, I can only assume I appear just as strange to you. I don't believe I know your name," Ditrina said.

"My name is Sarah Morgson. I'm a part of Shearcliff and Company, the band you just saved," Sarah told her.

"Yes, the bartender did tell me about your band. It is good to meet you," Ditrina said and shook Sarah's hand.

"Will my friends be alright?" Sarah asked nervously.

"The naga will be fine, her wounds were minor and mimic venom is fairly weak. The naga are a strong people, she should feel like herself by tomorrow. As for the one with the sword, he should be alright as well.

I gave him a potion that should heal his injuries, though it will cause him to sleep for some time. It's strange the sword was teleported also; the spell only works on things that are directly touching," Ditrina said as she crouched beside the weapon.

She reached out to pick it up but Sarah saw her hand stop a few inches from the hilt.

"I can't pick it up," she said curiously.

"The sword is enchanted, Chris told me it can't be lost, sold, or stolen," Sarah explained to her.

Ditrina grew very excited upon hearing that.

"Incredible! If I remember correctly the sword was on fire in the mines as well wasn't it?" Ditrina asked eagerly.

"Yeah, as far as I know the sword was made to smite evil. It came with a spirit that lives in his head that helps him use it. He has a couple other artifacts like that as well," Sarah explained.

Ditrina squealed in delight.

"Incredible! Magic like that hasn't been seen since before the crisis, do you have any idea how rare those things are?" she asked excitedly.

"I think I'm beginning to get one," Sarah said with a small smile.

It didn't last long however as she thought of Matt.

"Speaking of magic, what will become of our cleric, he was struggling with a spell and collapsed right around the time you arrived," Sarah told her.

The excitement drained from Ditrina's face and she became somber.

"I have no idea what could have compelled him to do what he did. Unlike elves, humans have no magical energy of their own, or mana, as we call it. Because of this you pray to the gods for power and they grant it to you in exchange for your worship, which they feed upon. This allows your race to wield magic akin to the inherently magical races like the elves. Your cleric cast a spell without borrowing the power of a god, for reasons I cannot begin to fathom. Rather than fueling the spell with mana he fueled it with his own life force and only time will tell if he will fully recover," Ditrina explained.

"Oh" Sarah said simply as she felt a wave of guilt wash over her, remembering that Matt had warned her of the consequences of casting the spell and that she had forced him to anyway.

Though she had not known Matt long she enjoyed his company, and remembered it was him who had forestalled her execution until Chris had awoken.

"Don't worry too much; you humans often overstep your boundaries when it comes to magic. If everyone who ever cast a spell above their ability died there wouldn't be any magic users left on Targoth," Ditrina said trying to comfort her.

"That's reassuring," Sarah said feeling anything but reassured.

"You should get some rest, I'm sure the battle took its toll on you as well. I'll look after your friends and try my best to speed their recovery with my magic," Ditrina said.

Sarah shook her head.

"There's nothing more you can do for them," Ditrina insisted.

"Thanks for the offer but I can't ask that of you, we only just met," Sarah told her.

"Nonsense, you and your companions cleared half of the creatures by yourself, meaning that we're partners on this contract, like it or not. I couldn't possibly abandon my partners after such an encounter. I'll stay by their side until they've properly recovered," Ditrina said firmly.

"That's very kind of you," Sarah said, taken back by her dedication.

"Thank you, now you need rest as well or you'll collapse," Ditrina chided but Sarah shook her head again.

"There's no way I could sleep knowing what state they're in. I'll stay awake until they've recovered," Sarah said seriously but Ditrina only smiled. "What is it?" Sarah asked her as Ditrina continued to smile.

Without answering Ditrina began to sing softly, the words floating around Sarah's mind, unknown but familiar.

"Why are you singing?" Sarah asked but her words slurred together.

She began to feel heavy, just like in the mine, and saw the floor rushing toward her. Ditrina caught her before she hit, slipping her arm under her shoulders and carrying her toward the stairs. As she slipped into unconsciousness Sarah's last thoughts were that Ditrina must be far stronger than she looked, and that perhaps a little sleep would be alright.

CHAPTER NINE

Chris awoke feeling like a swarm of bees had taken up residence in his head. He looked around trying to make sense of his surroundings. The last thing he remembered he was fighting for his life in the mines, then some horrible fire serpent had destroyed everything. After that things became less clear, and he wrestled with memories of a blue haired woman with strange eyes, and a strange spinning sensation. After that he remembered nothing. Now he was lying on a bed in an unfamiliar room. It seemed clean, with a small table against the far wall holding his book still in its case and an open wardrobe in which he saw his cloak hanging next to his other clothing. Sunlight shone through a window to his right, and it appeared to be morning. His scabbard hung from a bed post, along with his knife, but his sword was nowhere to be seen. Looking down he saw that somebody had removed his clothes from the waist up. His hand was wrapped in bandages, and Chris felt a sense of déjà vu, recalling the morning after his fight with Sarah he had awoken in a similar position. Curious, he unwrapped the bandages from his hand and saw the burns had completely healed, and he showed no sign of injury save a dark scar, courtesy of Sarah.

"I have got to stop ending my fights like this," Chris said to himself.

"That would probably be for the best," Sarah agreed as she stepped through the door, carrying a large bowl of soup.

Chris nearly fell out of his bed in surprise.

"Gods Sarah, don't do that," he said heart still racing.

Sarah gave a small laugh.

"Sorry, I've got used to not knocking over the past two days. It's good to see you up Chris," she told him.

"Two days? I've been sleeping for two days!?" Chris exclaimed in shock.

"Yeah, the potion Ditrina gave you healed your hand but it also made you sleep like the dead. I've been taking care of you while you recovered," Sarah said sitting on the edge of his bed.

"Thanks Sarah, I really owe you one," Chris said and he thought he saw her blush slightly.

"Think nothing of it; I owe you my life remember? I was just trying to repay you a little," Sarah mumbled.

Chris laughed.

"Let's call us even then. From here out I don't want you to feel indebted to me," Chris told her. After a moments consideration he added "If anything I should be thanking you, you saved my sister after all."

"I signed the contract, in doing so I swore to protect the other members of the company. I would never go back on an oath," Sarah said seriously. "Besides, it was Ditrina who really saved us, without her I doubt we would have escaped the mines in one piece."

"Who is this Ditrina anyway? You've mentioned her twice now," Chris asked.

"Ditrina is something of an oddity. She's powerful, you remember what she did back in the mines, but she also seems very kind even though she doesn't seem to understand humans very well," Sarah said shaking her head.

"You make it sound like she's not human herself," Chris said.

"That's because she's not, Ditrina's an elf," Sarah told him.

Chris stared blankly at her.

"I didn't know elves were real," he said simply and looked at Sarah for further explanation.

She merely shrugged.

"Don't look at me like that; until I met her I didn't think the elves existed either. Now we've got one staying with us at the inn," Sarah said.

"Why is she hanging around the inn? What is it she wants?" Chris asked confused.

"Well the last few days she and Cassy have been taking care of Matt. Ditrina said something about being responsible for her partners and wanting to help," Sarah explained.

"What do you mean taking care of Matt? Is he alright?" Chris asked sitting up quickly.

Sarah looked at the floor.

"Matt hasn't woken up since he cast that spell. Ditrina isn't sure if he'll wake up at all, he's not looking good," she said quietly.

"I want to see him," Chris said firmly and tried to stand.

Sarah stood quickly, nearly spilling the soup, and pushed him back into the bed with her free hand.

"Take it easy, the last thing we need right now is for you to go running all over the place and hurt yourself. You were sleeping for two days; don't try to do anything stupid," Sarah said with concern.

"Sarah let me go, I feel fine!" Chris said as he struggled against her but she held him firmly in place.

"Promise me you're not going to do anything stupid," Sarah said and gave him a sharp look, still holding him down.

Chris stopped his struggling.

"I swear I'll be careful, I just want to see Matt," he said solemnly.

Sarah released her grip on him.

"Fine, Matt's on the last room on the left. I think Cassy and Ditrina are in there right now with him, so they can probably answer your questions better than I can. Once you've finished head straight back here, I haven't fed you yet today," Sarah said gesturing to the bowl of soup.

Chris raised an eyebrow and said nothing.

"Well you weren't exactly in any state to feed yourself these last few days," Sarah explained quickly and this time Chris was sure he saw her blushing.

"Thanks again Sarah," Chris said with a smile as he swung his legs out of the bed and stood up, stretching his arms above his head.

As he stretched he let out a small gasp of pleasure as he felt his back crack, stiff after two days of lying in bed.

Chris became aware that Sarah was staring at his chest, specifically at the large scar that remained after their fight. When she saw he had noticed she apologized quickly.

"I'm sorry, if I could go back and undo what I did I would," she said quietly.

"It's alright Sarah, you were just doing what you thought was right at the time," he said and put his hand on her shoulder. "Besides, this way I'll always remember the day we met," he added with a grin.

Sarah gave a weak smile and stood up.

"I'll leave this here," she said and set the soup on the table. "If you need me I'll be downstairs," she said and went to depart.

"Don't you wanna go see Matt?" Chris asked.

Sarah turned and gave him a sad look.

"There's not much to see," she said softly and walked out of the room.

Chris heard her footsteps retreat down the hall and hurried to dress himself, throwing on a shirt and pulling on his boots as he rushed out of his room heading toward Matt. Chris burst into the room and crashed into Cassy, who was about to leave, causing them to fall to the floor in a heap.

"Whoa, easy there brother!" Cassy said as they untangled themselves.

She managed to rise to her feet, and offered him her hand. Chris took it, and felt the rough scales under his palm.

"Thanks Cas," Chris said as he was returned to his feet. "How's Matt?"

"See for yourself," Cassy said and stepped aside.

Chris saw him then, lying still in his bed. He walked slowly to him. Ditrina, who was currently wiping Matt's forehead with a towel, looked up at Chris.

"How do you feel?" she asked him but he ignored her question.

"What's wrong with him?" Chris demanded pointing at Matt's unconscious form.

It was obvious he was unwell. Matt lay on his back, with his hands folded across his chest. He would have looked peaceful if not for his face, which was scrunched tightly and drenched with sweat. His breath came in short ragged gasps through clenched teeth.

Ditrina sighed and stepped away from him.

"To put it as simply as I can, he cast a spell that was more than he could handle. As a result he burned away part of his life force to fuel the spell," she explained.

"Is there anything you can do for him?" Chris asked with concern. Ditrina frowned.

"In the past, those who I've seen this happen to heal naturally over time, but I've only ever seen elves treated before. With the elves they simply converted mana as they created it into life force and after a day or two were fine, but Matt is a human, and therefore has no mana of his own," she said.

"Why don't you just heal him then? Cast a healing spell, I've seen Matt cast them plenty of times," Chris said but Ditrina was already shaking her head.

"I can't cast a spell like that, I don't know how. I was trained as a pyromancer, not a healer, and even if I could cast such a spell I doubt it would help his current condition," Ditrina told him.

"Why wouldn't it help?" Chris asked angrily, frustrated he couldn't aid his friend.

"Matthew's problem isn't a physical one; his bodily wounds were minor and have already healed. His problem is one of the soul. The damage from the spell has caused his soul to become partially torn from him, and if it doesn't return to him soon his body will die," Ditrina said sadly.

"Well call it back then, shove it back inside him so he can wake up then!" Chris shouted at her.

"It's not that simple, the soul is anchored to the body by something we have yet to understand. Scholars have many names for it but little is known about it, save that it is crucial for maintaining life and nearly impossible to replicate," she said.

Chris perked up.

"You said it's nearly impossible, that means it has been done though right?" Chris asked hopefully.

Ditrina looked uncomfortable.

"Some old texts have records of soul transferring, which is to say anchoring one's soul to a physical object powerful enough to hold the soul rather than a body, but no one has been able to successfully create such an object since the crisis. I'm afraid such magic is beyond the abilities of anyone living, let alone myself. I'm sorry, but all we can do now is ensure he's comfortable. His soul may manage to return on its own after all," she said in an attempt to reassure him but Chris was thinking and barely heard her.

He remembered what the brothers had called the jewels on the artifacts, soul gems they had said. Was it possible that the items she was talking about were the ones he already possessed?

"Wait here, I'll be right back," Chris said and sprinted out of the room.

Ditrina looked at Cassy confused but Cassy only shrugged.

Chris ran back to his room and looked around for the artifacts. He saw the cloak and book from before but had no idea where his sword was. He thought perhaps Sarah may know and after fastening the book to its place on his hip, pulling on his cloak, and strapping his sheath to his back, he ran down to the inn's common room. The bar was empty except for the innkeeper who stood behind the bar polishing a glass, and Sarah. Sarah was sitting on a stool beside the bar, sharpening a pair of short swords Chris didn't recognize. They were small, with blades only half as long as his own sword's and for some reason the blades seemed to widen as they moved away from the hilt before coming to an abrupt point. She also had a long sword sitting in its sheath next to her, presumably already sharpened, and a wooden buckler reinforced with a steel edge sitting on top of the bar.

Chris ran over to her.

"You're running around an awful lot for someone trying to be careful," she said giving him a look that reminded him of the look a hawk gives a mouse.

Chris decided he had better change the subject quick.

"What do you have there?" he asked pointing at the sword she was sharpening.

"My new kit," Sarah said handing him one of the short swords proudly.

Chris examined the sword, and found the strange blade made it heavier than it looked. Seeing his surprise Sarah explained:

"The blade's extra weight gives me more power when I swing."

Chris nodded his understanding.

"Why two, and why the long sword as well?" he asked.

"Well after the experience in the mine I decided it would be better if I had more than one sword on me at a time, so now I've got the short swords for close quarters, and the long sword for more open areas. I'm planning on sharpening the edge of the shield as well. As it is, I seem to be lacking proper equipment so I decided to replace some while we're in town," Sarah told him.

"What was wrong with your old sword and shield?" Chris asked and Sarah frowned.

"Ditrina's spell melted them into slag. The dwarves reopened the mine and found what was left of them. Cassy got lucky enough that her bow survived though, it was further from the blast. Your weapons may be indestructible, but ours run the risk of breaking still," Sarah told him.

"That actually brings me to my next question, have you seen my sword anywhere? I haven't seen it since the mines," Chris asked quickly.

Sarah pointed to the middle of the room.

"It's laying right over there. It teleported back with us and nobodies been able to touch it ever since," Sarah informed him.

"Thanks Sarah, see you later!" Chris said and ran to his sword, snatching it off the ground, slipping it into its sheath, and running to the stairs without breaking his stride leaving Sarah very confused.

"Don't do anything stupid!" she called after him and the innkeeper chuckled quietly.

This earned himself a dark stare from Sarah, and he returned to washing the glasses, his smile hidden under his beard.

"I'm back," Chris said as he skidded into Matt's room.

"That's nice, but why did you run off to begin with?" Cassy asked.

"I went to grab these," Chris said gesturing to his artifacts.

Ditrina grew excited.

"Yes your artifacts, they're incredibly important. I was hoping to discuss them with you once you woke up. Do you have any idea how..." she began but Chris cut her off.

"There's time enough for that later, for now I'm more interested in these," Chris said as he slipped the book out of its case and pointed to the sapphire set in the cover.

Ditrina leaned in and stared at the gems.

"It's a beautiful gem I'll admit but I don't see what that has to do with your friend," she said puzzled.

"This gem holds the soul of an ancient king; it's how they're able to speak with me. Each of the artifacts has a spirit residing within them. Is it possible to anchor Matt's soul to one of the gems?" Chris asked hopefully.

Ditrina was silent as she considered the possibility.

"It may work..." she said after some time. "Nothing like this has been attempted in a very long time, but those gems were fashioned before the crisis, when magic was at its peak. It is possible that we could use one of the gems as an anchor point for Matt. Now say we were trying to recreate the original spell, and bind his soul completely to the gem, I would say that was impossible because the gem already has a soul residing within it, but seeing as we're only trying to hold his soul in one place it might actually work," Ditrina said, growing more excited as she thought about the possibility. "Assuming this actually works I will be the first person to successfully bind a soul since the crisis!"

"There was quite a few if's in that plan," Chris said uneasily.

"What are you talking about? I didn't say if once," Ditrina said looking at Chris strangely.

Chris looked to Cassy, confused by Ditrina's response.

"Di, what my brother meant was that that plan has many uncertainties," Cassy said coming to Chris's aid.

"Oh, thanks Cas," Ditrina said and Cassy nodded and smiled.

Chris did a double take. Her entire life Cassy had never let anyone call her Cas except him and Mr. Cogwell, growing angry if anyone tried. Despite this, here she was smiling as the elf called her by the nickname. Perhaps more had happened while he was asleep than he had thought. Chris filed this information away for future consideration and returned to the matter at hand.

"Yeah, that's about what I was trying to say. Do you think you can do it?" Chris asked Ditrina.

"I believe so; the theories have been fairly concrete for a couple hundred years now, the limiting factor has been lack of proper materials. By using one of the gems I should be able to re-anchor his soul to this world. I will warn you, if this works, he'll have to stay close to the book for the rest of his life. This will mean losing one of your artifacts," Ditrina told him.

Cassy looked at Chris nervously and he felt a moment of confliction.

"Of the three artifacts I've never been able to use the book as it was intended. Matt's a scholar, he'll be able to make better use of it than I ever could," Chris said as he walked over to Matt's sleeping form. "The brothers told me the artifacts cannot be lost, sold or stolen, but they never said anything about them being given away."

He laid the book on Matt's chest and folded his hands over it.

"I, Christian Shearcliff, hereby pass the Book of Ge, as well as any magic it holds on to Mathew Bleakstar. May he use it well and further his knowledge of the world," he announced.

Chris stepped back.

"Cas, try to take the book from him," Chris told her.

"Alright," she said as she reached for it, but her hand stopped a few inches away from the book. "I can't," she said cheerfully and stepped back.

"Good," Chris said and reached for the book himself.

As he had hoped, he was unable to pick it up.

"It seems like your plan worked," Ditrina said. "I'll begin the preparations for the spell; I shall call you when it is time. Until then you should rest, I shall require your assistance if this is to work."

"What do you need me for? I don't know any magic," Chris told her.

"I may need you to guide Matt's soul to the gem; it should be similar to when you speak to the brothers if I understand your situation correctly," Ditrina said.

"I've got a question Di; I thought you were a pyromancer, that's fire magic right?" Cassy asked.

"That's right Cas, I focus on creating and controlling fire through my magic," Ditrina said.

"Alright, then how is it you know how to do this soul trapping thingy? It seems pretty different from controlling fire to me," Cassy asked slightly confused.

Ditrina smiled at her and her black eyes seemed to be looking far into the past.

"When I was younger I spent much of my time reading in the royal library. I remember one of my favorite topics was soul transmutation, which is the practical uses for a living soul, but as I grew older I realized there had been no new research since the crisis. Determined to revive the field I studied it as much as I could, before arriving at the conclusion that it was impossible, with no vessel capable of holding a living soul existing on Targoth. Dismayed at wasting the better years of my youth studying a useless branch of magic I dedicated myself to becoming a pyromancer. It may not be the most exciting field of research, but it definitely has its practical applications," Ditrina told them.

She began to pace excitedly.

"That was in the past though; now I'm just excited that my research may not have been for nothing," Ditrina said, mostly to herself.

"How long did you spend researching soul transmutation?" Chris asked, not entirely convinced she was qualified to be casting spells on his friend that she herself said hadn't been cast in over a thousand years.

The longer he thought about it the more cautious he became. Ditrina looked to be in her early twenties, and she claimed she had only studied this type of magic in her youth, meaning at most she would have studied it for around five years considering she abandoned the field for fire magic.

"Well let's see," Ditrina said pausing her pacing to think. "I grew interested in soul transmutation when I was around fifty or so, but I didn't start any hard research until I was in my eighties. I gave up on my studies after my one hundred and fiftieth birthday; which means I studied soul transmutation for the best part of seventy years. It hardly makes me an expert I know, but I've studied it longer than any of the other scholars have so I'm probably the best chance you have at fixing your friend."

Chris and Cassy gaped at her.

"What is it?" Ditrina asked confused by their expressions.

Cassy recovered from their shock first.

"Di, how old are you exactly?" she asked quietly.

"I celebrated my two hundred and tenth birthday just a month ago, my first birthday since I left home," Ditrina said proudly.

Cassy returned to staring with Chris.

"Are you two alright?" Ditrina asked with concern.

"Yeah Di, we're good," Cassy said dully. She turned to Chris and said in the same flat voice "Come on brother, I'm sure she has a lot of work to do," and led him by the arm out of the room.

"What was that about?" Chris asked her when they reached the first floor of the inn.

Cassy ignored him and walked in a trance to the bar. She plopped herself onto a stool and buried her face in her hands. Chris stood behind her in shock; he had never seen his sister act like this before. Sarah, who was working on putting an edge on her shield, noticed what was going on and walked over.

"What seems to be the matter Cassy?" Sarah asked kindly, placing her hand on Cassy's shoulder.

Chris couldn't decide what was stranger, Cassy's sudden descent into sorrow, or the fact that Sarah seemed to be acting kindly towards his sister all of a sudden.

"Sms bo nundrt yers ol," Cassy mumbled from under her arms.

"What?" Chris asked with confusion.

"I said she's two hundred years old!" Cassy yelled at him as she sat up quickly.

Chris jumped back a pace in surprise.

"So what? I don't understand what the fuss is about," Chris asked trying to understand why his sister was suddenly lashing out at him.

Sarah gave Chris a pitying look and shook her head.

"You must be the most observant person on Targoth aren't you?" Cassy asked angrily, her voice dripping sarcasm, and stormed off back up the stairs leaving Chris baffled.

"What the hell was that all about, and since when do you two get along?" Chris asked as he turned to Sarah.

"Cassy and I have gotten along fine since the mines, she seemed ready to end our feud and I saw no reason to continue it. I think her change of heart had something to do with me saving her life," she said with a shrug. "As for what that was about, well, the best way I can put it is that Ditrina and Cassy have taken a liking to each other since they met. They've spent quite a bit of time together over the last two days."

Chris looked at her blankly.

"I mean Ditrina's probably never seen a naga before, and I know that Cas has never seen an elf before so I guess they would interest one another," Chris said, not sure he fully understood what Sarah was talking about.

Sarah gave him a pitying look.

"Gods you're dense," Sarah said and walked off, returning to her work on the shield.

Chris sat in the stool that Cassy had recently occupied and pondered what Sarah had said for a moment. He felt a light flare up inside his head.

"Oh, you mean…" Chris said looking at Sarah with surprise.

Sarah looked up and shook her head slowly before going back to her work.

"Oh," Chris said simply.

Chris heard a chuckle from behind him. Spinning quickly on his stool he saw the innkeeper's head pop up above the bar.

"When did you get here?" Chris shouted with shock almost falling off his stool.

"Been here the whole time I have. I was storing some things under the bar when ye came back," the dwarf said cheerfully.

"Oh, sorry sir, I didn't mean to snap at you, you just surprised me is all," Chris told him.

"It's fine my boy, ye did no harm, and there's no need to be so formal, call me Rolf," he said. "Your lady friend is right though. Whenever she's not treating that cleric upstairs your sister's been hanging around that elf," Rolf said. "Now that I think about it she treats the cleric with the elf too," he added.

"It makes sense, Cas has never really been interested in men if you understand what I'm trying to say, and she craves new and exotic things. I'm just annoyed I didn't notice sooner," Chris said glumly.

Rolf laughed.

"In ye defense lad, ye just woke up today," Rolf told him.

"Still, it caught me off guard a bit," Chris said.

"I don't see why, from what ye told me the elf is exactly her type, exotic, pretty, and most importantly, not a man," Rolf said with a chuckle.

"Yeah, I guess," Chris said.

He spun on his stool.

"What do you think of this Sarah?" Chris asked.

"I think who Cassy wants to spend her time with is her business, and rather than gossiping with him you should try to console your sister, who if you haven't forgotten is upset," Sarah said giving him a look that told him it was not a suggestion.

Chris looked at the innkeeper sheepishly and stood up.

"You're right Sarah; I'll go talk to her," Chris said as he walked quickly to the stairs, eager to escape Sarah's building anger.

"Her room is to the left of yours," Sarah called as he walked away.

Chris strode up to Cassy's room and saw the door was closed. He knocked quietly but Cassy did not answer. Chris knocked again, louder this time, and to his relief the door swung open.

"What is it you want?" Cassy asked sullenly.

"I came to talk to you about Ditrina," Chris said. "Do you mind if I come in?"

Cassy said nothing but she moved out of the doorway and Chris took this as her approval. He walked into the room and sat himself on the edge of her bed, and to his relief his sister followed suit and sat next to him. Neither spoke for a long time, and the silence weighed heavily upon Chris. When he felt he could take it no longer he opened his mouth to speak, but the words he heard were Cassy's, not his own.

"She's two hundred years old," Cassy said quietly.

Chris thought carefully about his words before he said them.

"I know it may seem like it's an issue but Ditrina still seems really nice, what does it matter how old she is?" Chris asked her.

"How nice she is isn't the issue Chris! She's more than ten times my age! What could someone my age offer to someone like her? What could I provide that she hasn't already seen?" Cassy asked sadly.

"You remember Ditrina said her last birthday was her first away from home, and despite her age she appears to be no older than us. Who's to say her body was the only thing to develop slowly?" Chris asked.

"You have no way of knowing that," Cassy said and they fell back into silence.

It was Chris who finally spoke.

"You're right Cas, I have no way of knowing whether or not Ditrina thinks like we do, I can't promise that she'll feel the same way you feel, and I couldn't know less about elven culture. What I do know is if you don't try you'll never know. I'm not telling you to march in there and confess your undying love or anything rash, I'm simply saying give it a chance. Over the past two days has Ditrina given any indication that she's not interested?" Chris asked.

"Well…no," Cassy said slowly.

"Then don't you think your overacting a little bit?" Chris asked kindly.

Cassy said nothing and they fell into another long silence, however this time it felt more relaxed. Without warning Cassy leaned over and hugged Chris, burying her face in his shoulder. Chris gave a small jolt of surprise, it was rare for Cassy to act like this, but he quickly returned the embrace.

"Thank you, Chris," Cassy mumbled into his shoulder.

Chris gave a small laugh.

"All I did is point out how crazy you're acting, usually you hate it when I do that," he said.

"I know, but sometimes it's what I need to hear," Cassy said breaking off their hug and giving him a wide smile, providing him a good view of her sharp teeth.

"Any time sis," Chris replied matching her smile. "Now why don't you head back and talk to Ditrina. She may not understand us very well yet but I think even she noticed you were acting a little strangely."

Cassy nodded and stood up.

"Thanks again Chris," she said and walked to the door.

Chris followed her, seeing no reason to stay in her room. They walked out together, Cassy turning towards Matt's room where Ditrina still worked, and Chris back to rejoin Sarah at the bar.

CHAPTER TEN

Chris spent the rest of his afternoon down in the inn's common room with Sarah. At her command he had eaten the soup she had brought him that morning, though it had long ago lost any trace of heat. Now he simply sat and nursed a mug of ale while Sarah put the finishing touches on her new shield's bladed edge. Rolf had left the inn some time ago heading out to buy ingredients for that evening, leaving them to their thoughts.

Chris was worried about Matt; Ditrina had been working for most of the day now and still had not called him. He feared that something had gone wrong, and that his friend would be lost forever. Chris was unsure if Sarah felt as concerned as he did; her face was a mask of calm as she ran the wet stone over the shields edge over and over again, the steady rasping lulling Chris into a state of calm despite his concern. It was Cassy who ended their wait.

"Come on you two, Di says that we're all ready now. It's time to fix Matt," she said as she poked her head down the stairs.

Chris stood with haste, hurrying to Cassy, and Sarah slung the shield across her back before joining them at the stairs. They headed up to Matt's room together and Chris was surprised to see that nothing looked changed from that morning.

"Good, you're here. It is time to begin," Ditrina told them.

"What is it you need us to do?" Chris asked looking around trying to imagine what Ditrina had been doing over the past few hours.

"I have prepared the spell needed for this endeavor, and reviewed what I know about soul transmutation. Once I begin the spell I will require someone to go to the entrance of the astral realm to lead Matthew's soul to his body," Ditrina said.

"Wait, how do we do that? What's this spirit realm place?" Sarah asked confused.

"Don't worry Sarah, you won't be needed for the spell, I only really need Chris for this to work," Ditrina explained.

"Why him?" Sarah asked still confused.

"So far as I know Chris is the only one with any experience speaking to spirits. From what he has told me he has already traveled near the astral realm on several occasions when he speaks to the brothers, though he did not realize it," Ditrina explained.

"When I visit the brothers everything appears gray, and the brothers look blurry," Chris told Ditrina.

"That is because you are in the space between our realm and the astral realm. Because you are alive you are unable to cross over into their realm, and similarly they are unable to cross into ours because they are dead. By meeting in the middle you are able to commune with the spirits and them with you. Matthew's soul is currently wandering between these two realms. You need to lead him back to our realm once more so that I may bind his soul to the gems. You cannot let him cross over into the astral realm, if you do his soul will be lost to us forever and Matthew's body will die. Do you understand?" Ditrina asked.

Chris shook his head.

"I don't know what I'm supposed to do once I find him, this place is flat and grey without any sign of direction. How do I lead him anywhere?" he asked.

"That I do not know. Remember this type of magic hasn't been done since before the crisis. What we are attempting is based on theory alone and I cannot promise we will be successful," Ditrina told him.

"We don't have any other options though," Cassy said. "If we don't try this Matt will almost certainly die."

Chris looked at Matt's still form.

"Tell me what to do," he said firmly.

"For this spell I will put you to sleep. Because of your pre-existing connection with the astral plane you should be able to enter without my assistance. Once inside look for Matthew, and bring him back with you. I cannot offer any more advice than that. Please try to remember everything about what transpires in there, your experience will prove invaluable to the field as a whole," Ditrina said.

"First things first, we save Matt. Once we do that we can worry about the science behind this," Sarah said. "We're wasting time, every moment we waste Matt gets closer to death. Let's begin."

"Very well. Chris, please lay down on the bed next to Matthew," Ditrina told him. Chris awkwardly positioned himself on the bed, which was only made to hold one, next to his friend.

"Wish me luck," Chris said with a nervous grin.

"Don't try anything reckless," Sarah warned him.

"I'm fairly sure subjecting yourself to an experimental branch of magic counts as reckless," Cassy pointed out.

"Don't worry, I've visited this place plenty of times, this time I just happen to be looking for someone is all. I'll be back before you know it," Chris reassured them.

"Bring him back safe," Sarah told him and Cassy gave him a clawed thumb up.

"Are you ready Chris?" Ditrina asked him.

"Let's do it," Chris replied.

Ditrina began to sing softly to him, and Chris felt himself quickly slipping off to sleep. The last thing he saw was the worried faces of Sarah and Cassy before he drifted into another world.

Chris saw the familiar grey nothingness expand around him. He looked around and tried to think of how to find his friend in a place with no visual distinction. On a whim he called out to the brothers.

"Al! Ge! Mi! Where are you guys?" he yelled but they made no move to show themselves.

Chris sighed and began to walk, unsure if he was heading toward anything, hoping to see some sign of his friend. Chris was unsure how far he walked. Without any land marks he couldn't be sure he wasn't just walking in circles, and as he had previously learned time flowed differently here. After a while, perhaps a few minutes, perhaps a few hours, Chris felt a presence appear behind him. He turned and to his relief saw Mi standing before him.

"Mi, thank the gods, I need your help," Chris began but Mi held up his hand.

"I know, you're looking for your friend Matt. Don't worry, we already found him, but that's not what I came to tell you. I came to warn you that Al is mad, madder than he's been in a long time. It has to do with your decision to give Matt the artifact," Mi told him.

"What do you mean; we're trying to save Matt's life!" Chris yelled at him. "It's not like I just gave the thing away for no reason, if we had another way to save him I would have gone with that."

"Easy friend, Al's the one mad, not me. I personally couldn't care less what you did with the book, it wasn't my artifact. Ge isn't mad at you either; he sees the logic in what you did," Mi explained.

"Where can I find them?" Chris asked looking around at the flat grey nothingness.

"Take my hand," Mi said and when Chris did he found himself elsewhere, not in the sense that the landscape had changed, but in the way that he was no longer alone with Mi.

Al and Ge stood in front of Chris and seemed to be in the middle of a heated debate in a language Chris couldn't understand. They spoke very fast and Chris decided that he was better off staying out of the situation for the moment. Matt sat looking bored listening to their argument, and had not noticed Chris yet. The brothers argued for several more moments before they noticed Chris and fell silent. Matt looked around confused by their sudden pause and saw Chris standing behind him.

"Thank the gods your here, these two haven't stopped arguing since I got here, wherever here is," Matt said as he hurried to Chris's side. "Where are we?"

"This is the space between our world and the astral realm. These three are the brothers I've been telling you about," Chris explained.

"Wait, I thought the brothers lived in your head, what are they doing here, or am I in your head? Chris I'm confused help me out here," Matt pleaded.

"As best I can explain you preformed too much magic in the mines and tore your soul away from your body. Ditrina, she saved us in the mines by the way, has cast a spell to bind your soul to one of my artifacts so that you don't die," Chris explained quickly.

"But if my soul was torn from my body wouldn't I just die? And how am I supposed to be bound to your artifacts, I thought you couldn't get rid of them?" Matt asked.

"Funny, that's what we were just discussing," Al said darkly as he walked closer to them.

"Wait you speak common? I've been here for hours and you haven't said a word to me! What gives?" Matt yelled but Al ignored him.

"More like two days," Mi piped in.

Matt's shocked response was cut off before it began by Al.

"We gave you three of the most powerful items ever seen on Targoth, prepared for over a thousand years to guide you and offer our council, and you just throw it away!" Al bellowed at Chris.

"I didn't throw anything away; I'm trying to save Matt's life!" Chris yelled back.

"Do you think you were the first idiot to wander past our tomb in the past fifteen hundred years? Countless adventurers and sell swords, soldiers and kings, they all came seeking the artifacts, but we waited patiently for one we thought was worthy to wield them. We waited for you Chris, but now I see we were wrong. You are unfit to exploit our gifts," Al spat.

"You forget that you used magic to lure me to the artifacts! I never asked to be cursed with three idiots haunting my dreams! Still I made the best with my situation and tried my hardest to listen to you all. When I first met you, you told me to protect the innocent; those were your exact words. Again, when I met Matt, I was praised on my choice of companions and encouraged travel with him. Now you're telling me

I should just let him die just so I can keep a dusty old book? If I really was a person who would do such a thing do you think you would have given me the artifacts to begin with?!" Chris yelled.

Al said nothing but still appeared to be furious. Chris realized he was at an advantage and decided to press it.

"Listen to me, all three of you," he said gesturing to the assembled spirits. "You may share my thoughts, you may watch my life, but don't forget that this is *my* life to live. That means that I'll do things you don't agree with from time to time and you'll just have to deal with it. *As for him*," Chris said as he pointed to Matt.

"Wait me?" Matt asked, worried he was now somehow the target of Chris's rant.

"Yes, you Matt," Chris said exasperated.

He turned back to the brothers.

"He'll be able to make far better use of the book than me; he knows the language of magic," Chris told them.

"I agree," Ge said stepping forward. "While I disagree with the idea of separating the artifacts on principle, given your situation I believe you took the best course of action. I have been trying to explain to my brother that this situation isn't as bad as he is making it out to be. The artifacts are still within close proximity of one another so long as you two are traveling together and logically Matt is a far better candidate to use the book than you," Ge said without a trace of emotion.

"Thanks Ge," Chris said dryly and looked at Al. "I understand you're angry, I don't like losing the book either, but it's not worth my friend's life."

Al didn't speak for a full minute.

"Time will tell if you are correct," he said and vanished from sight.

Chris turned to Mi and Ge.

"Well that was unpleasant," he said.

"Yeah, you'll get used to it; Al has quite the temper, that's just the first time he's turned it on you. You did well to stand your ground. Once he gets going there's no stopping him," Mi said.

"If you guys are done fighting I would really like to get back to reality," Matt cut in.

"Yes, if you linger here much longer in this state your body will most surly die," Ge said to Matt.

"You said I've been here for two days?" Matt asked Mi.

"Almost three now, time flows differently here, you get used to it," Mi said.

"Hopefully I don't have to," Matt said but Ge was shaking his head.

"I'm afraid that you'll be spending quite a bit of time here actually. Because of the way Chris passed the book to you the same magic that bound him to us now binds you. It seems that you will be joining our nightly chats from here on," Ge said.

"Wait so I have you three stuck in my head now too?" Matt asked nervously.

"No, specifically only I reside in your head now, but because my brothers and I speak together within this place it doesn't make much of a difference in the end," Ge said.

Matt turned to Chris.

"What does this living in your head stuff entail exactly?" he asked.

"It's not that bad, they just see what you see, know your past, read your thoughts, that sort of thing," Chris said with a smile.

Matt groaned.

"Hey Ge, how do I get Matt out of here?" Chris asked.

"Take his hand and wake up, it should pull his soul with yours. Physical contact creates a strong bond within this realm as you may have already noticed when Mi brought you to us," Ge replied.

Chris reached out and grabbed Matt's forearm.

"Send us back Ge," Chris said and Ge waved his hand in front of their faces slowly.

"Wait I still have questions for you!" Matt yelled but it was too late, the world was dissolving around them and they felt themselves slipping back into reality.

Chris awoke at the same time as Matt, and found that only Ditrina was still present. She was busy muttering a spell over his book and did not notice at first that they had awoken.

This did not last long because as soon as Matt saw her he jolted upright, scaring her, while yelling:

"She's green!"

"Yes, my skin has a greenish tint, how nice of you to point it out. My name is Ditrina," she said trying to regain her composure.

"Why are your ears pointed and what's wrong with your eyes?" Matt asked tactlessly.

Ditrina looked irritated.

"There is nothing wrong with my eyes, and my ears are pointed because I am an elf," she said angrily.

"Matt, Ditrina saved your life," Chris said as he slipped out of the bed.

Matt had the good grace to look embarrassed.

"I'm terribly sorry; I was just a little surprised is all," Matt said.

Ditrina shrugged.

"I'm used to it, I've noticed you humans tend to be a little rude at first but you don't seem like too bad of a lot. Chris is right however, I have spent the last three days keeping you alive," Ditrina told him.

"What time is it Ditrina?" Chris asked.

"You slept the rest of the day, and through the night. It's not yet sunrise," she told him.

"You should get some rest then; you've been up all night," Chris told her.

"I'm fine; I cast a spell so that I didn't have to sleep," Ditrina explained. "I'll gather the others, you two, stay here," Ditrina said and left them alone.

"So now what?" Matt asked Chris.

Chris shrugged and sat on the end of the bed.

"Now we get back on our feet and move on. We only stayed in this village so long because we were injured. Once you're fit to travel we'll be hitting the road again," Chris said.

"Are you sure you'll be ok without the book?" Matt asked examining it carefully.

"I'm sure; you'll be able to make *far* better use of it than I ever could, I can barely read common," Chris reassured him.

Any further conversation between the two was paused as Ditrina returned with Cassy and Sarah in tow.

"Good morning sleepyhead!" Cassy said cheerfully.

"It's good to see you awake Matt," Sarah said and walked over to Chris's side.

"I don't know what we would have done if you hadn't woken up, who would have put my brother back together again whenever he does something stupid?" Cassy asked brightly.

"Well I could always try my hand at sewing," Sarah replied and both women laughed.

"Chris," Matt whispered and tugged on his sleeve. "Are you sure we woke back up? They're getting along."

"They've been doing fine since the mines; maybe the secret to their happiness is being far away from you," Chris said with a chuckle.

"The secret to all women's happiness is being far away from him," Cassy said and everyone laughed except Ditrina and Matt, looking confused and annoyed respectively.

"Remind me why you brought me back again?" Matt asked looking at Chris.

"Who else would we torment? Sarah? She'd beat me within an inch of my life!" Chris laughed.

"I would not," Sarah mumbled as her face flushed red.

"I am quite glad that we managed to revive your friend, but I do have some questions for you both," Ditrina cut in.

"What do you want to know?" Matt asked, confused by her sudden eagerness to speak.

"First tell me everything that happened on the other side, leave nothing out," Ditrina ordered.

"Well I remember casting a spell in the mines, and the next thing I knew I was waking up in a strange empty grey space. A few minutes after I arrived, though it may have been longer because I had no way to measure time, these three blurry men appeared before me and began arguing in a foreign language. I sat there and listened to them until Chris showed up. That's about all that happened really," Matt said.

"That can't possibly be it. Chris, what did he leave out?" Ditrina asked quickly.

"Well after I arrived I spoke to the brothers and they agreed to let Matt keep the book, though grudgingly. After that the books previous owner Ge sent us home," Chris recounted.

"Sent you home how?" Ditrina demanded.

Chris gave a small shrug.

"He just waved his hand in front of our faces and we woke up. I'm not sure what he did specifically," Chris told her.

Ditrina gave a slow moan and ran her hands through her blue hair.

"After all that all you can tell me...is that it was grey?" she asked shrilly. "We just preformed the most important spell in the field of magic since the crisis and all you can say is that it was grey!" Ditrina yelled her voice rising in pitch with every word.

"Calm down Di," Cassy said putting her hand on Ditrina's arm. "I'm sure you'll have plenty of time to talk with them about what happened, Matt did only just wake up after all."

Ditrina gave her a sad look.

"What do you mean? As we were walking in we all heard them saying you're going to leave town soon, how will I be able to ask him anything?" Ditrina asked her face a mask of mourning.

"What are you talking about; you're coming with us, aren't you Di?" Cassy asked slightly confused.

"I'm not part of your company, remember Cas? I helped you all here because we all worked together on the mine contract, but had I known you all were already on the job I wouldn't have come," Ditrina said sadly, but her response was nothing when compared to Cassy's.

"No!" Cassy yelled louder than she intended.

When all eyes turned to her she cleared her throat and said quieter:

"I just thought that, perhaps you would like to travel with us?"

"Why?" Ditrina asked curiously.

"Well, we worked so well together on this last job, it stands to reason that we would be more productive if we joined forces," Cassy said trying to prevail to Ditrina's logical side.

"Though that offer does sound attractive, I doubt your friends would appreciate me just jumping into your group without warning," Ditrina said.

Matt gave a snort.

"Don't worry about that, Sarah tried to kill us and we let her join the very next day," Matt said and Sarah shot him a withering look.

Matt cleared his throat quickly, trying a different approach.

"*Anyway*, you saved our lives in the mines from what I hear, and you saved mine again with your magic. If you want to join our company I'll happily vouch for you," Matt told her and Sarah gave him a small nod, preferring this line of reasoning.

"I agree with Matt, if you want a place with us you can have one," Sarah said firmly. "You can be a permanent partner," she added remembering Ditrina's choice of words when they first met.

"I'm flattered really, but I don't think..." Ditrina began but Chris spoke.

"Ditrina, if you travel with us you'll get a chance to study the artifacts more. Wouldn't you like to see them in action?" he asked trying just as hard as his friends to convince her to sign on with them, eager to learn more about the elf.

Ditrina's black eyes flicked between them as if searching for a trap.

"You all wish for me to travel with you?" Ditrina asked slowly.

She was buried under a wave of:

"Yes!" and "Absolutely!" from the group.

"Very well, I will travel with you for a while, though I will warn you eventually I must return to the elven council to report all I have learned," Ditrina told them.

"No problem, when it's time for your report we'll come with you!" Cassy said. "It would be awesome to see an elven city."

"You are a curious bunch," Ditrina said with a small smile.

"A bunch you'll soon officially be a part of," Chris said with a nod to Matt.

"I'll draw up another contract," Matt said.

Before the sun rose above the horizon Shearcliff and Company gained its fifth member.

CHAPTER ELEVEN

"What do you mean we only made two hundred gold?" Cassy yelled as they rode away from Purevein.

"Well they subtracted the price of all our rooms from our reward, which cut it by nearly half. Even with Ditrina taking a fifth instead of half as she had originally planned each person only made thirty-four gold pieces after the company's share," Matt called from ahead of her.

"I still think I should have received half. I wasn't part of the company at the time of the job," Ditrina grumbled from beside Cassy.

The group rode in pairs, with Chris and Matt in the front, followed by Cassy and Ditrina, and with Sarah bringing up the rear.

"Sorry Ditrina, you should have asked to have been paid before you signed the contract," Chris said with a small laugh.

"I have half a mind to think the only reason you asked me to join was to swindle me out of my money," Ditrina said gloomily.

"Not at all Ditrina, it was at the very most a third of the reason we asked you," Sarah called up to her joining in on Chris's laughter.

As the laughter died down they rode in silence for a time, spirits high, save Ditrina who seemed upset by Sarah's comment. Cassy, who noticed Ditrina's sadness, leaned over from her horse to speak quietly to her.

"Sarah was only making a joke Di, she really doesn't care about the gold. She's just glad you decided to travel with us," Cassy whispered to her.

"*Ohhhhh*," Ditrina said quietly her dark eyes widening.

Without warning she broke out into loud musical laughter startling the other riders.

"Are you alright Ditrina?" Chris called back to her nervously.

"I'm perfectly fine, Cas just explained the joke," Ditrina said and the others exchanged confused looks.

Deciding not to push the matter Chris shrugged and returned to riding.

They continued pressing south until the sun had nearly set, painting the sky a beautiful orange before deciding to make camp. The lands south of Purevein were covered with grassy hills, and they could see for miles around them. The mountain that Chris had grown up beside was now only a faint smudge on the horizon. They made camp atop of a nearby hill within site of the road.

They started a small fire using some of the dry bushes that dotted the landscape for fuel. Cassy set about making a dinner with ingredients she had bought in Purevein while the others busied themselves with the tents and horses. Before long they all sat around the fire with savory bowls of stew in their hands.

Chris looked around at his friends and saw them enjoying themselves. Matt was engrossed within the pages of his newly acquired book while Cassy leaned over to whisper something in Ditrina's ear causing her to giggle. Chris spied Sarah looking at him from across the fire and smiled at her. He couldn't tell because of the firelight but he could have sworn her face turned slightly redder after that. Chris thought about all that had happened in such a short time. Little over a week ago he had been waiting tables back at the Stallion alone save for Mr. Cogwell; now he was camped under the stars surrounded by his new friends on his way towards another adventure.

He felt a twinge of guilt for abandoning Mr. Cogwell without so much as a goodbye but pushed it aside. He had been over this; it had been for the best that nobody knew where he was going so Sorros couldn't link them to him.

"One day I'll return to the old man and give him enough gold he'll never work another day in his drunken life, it's just not safe enough to go back right now," Chris thought to himself.

He decided it would be better not to dwell on the matter any longer and returned to his stew. It was surprisingly good; Cassy's cooking had improved dramatically since she had left home.

"So, Matt, what's the next closest village from here," Chris asked.

The group fell silent awaiting his response.

"Well there are two towns about the same distance from here. Both lay further south of us, with Bleakstar to the east and Torville to the west. Bleakstar is far larger than Torville, in fact it's almost a small city. I suggest we head there first; they're more likely to have work for us," Matt said.

"Bleakstar, isn't that your last name Matt? Are you from there?" Sarah asked him.

"No, but my mom said her grandfather was born there, said he was one of the Baron's bastard sons. I guess that makes me related to the current Baron, though very distantly," Matt said. "I've never actually been there myself; they don't have many temples there so I didn't see any reason to visit."

"I was wondering; what god do you serve Matthew?" Ditrina asked.

Chris braced himself for Matt's outburst knowing this was a sensitive subject for the cleric but to his surprise Matt only sighed.

"I don't have a specific god; none of the temples have accepted me," he said quietly. "I've been to every temple between the capital and Draclige and none of them would take me."

"Why didn't they like you?" Cassy asked, having never actually heard the full story.

"The temple priests liked me just fine, but it's not for them to decide. For a cleric to be accepted the gods themselves must give a sign, either accepting or denying your right to be a cleric. With me they all simply said you're a cleric, just not *my* cleric. So I wandered from place to place doing odd jobs and visiting obscure temples until I decided to travel with Chris," Matt said.

"It's good you don't serve any one god, they are treacherous beings and not to be trusted," Ditrina said simply before returning to her stew.

The others were shocked; all races worshiped the ten gods.

"What do you mean Ditrina, do you not worship the ten?" Sarah asked surprised.

"Of course not, none of the elves worship the gods. Why should we? Humans who wish to use magic must worship the gods, pleading for their power like beggars. The gods grow fat on this worship while you suffer, they are not worthy of their position," Ditrina said darkly.

The others fell silent, unsure of how to react to her claims, while Matt looked to be growing angry at her words. Cassy sensed it would be best if the topic was changed quickly and turned to Matt.

"So you said you've been to the capital? What was that like?" she asked suddenly.

To her relief he answered, successfully distracted from Ditrina's heretical statements.

"The city of Hailguard is big, really big, about three times larger than Draclige to be precise. I was born there actually, but my mother gave me to the temples to train when I was six so my view of the city is different than most others," Matt said.

"How so?" Chris asked, curious of his friends past.

"Well the temples get a lot of respect from everyone, so even though I was just a kid because I was a cleric in training I was treated with almost reverence. Had my mother not given me to the priests my childhood would probably have been very different," Matt told them.

"Why did she give you to the temples?" Sarah asked.

"Well we didn't have very much money and with five brothers we had a lot of mouths to feed. My mom decided it would be better off if she sold me to the temples. They got a set ration of food every week and in exchange I would be trained as a cleric. Everybody wins," Matt explained.

"But you never had any choice in the matter, what about what you wanted to do with your life?!" Sarah asked outraged.

"I was six!" Matt laughed. "I spent my days running through the gutters with the other children; I had no plans at the time. Once I went to the temples I learned how to use magic and speak to the gods. It was a lot more fun than racing through the poor quarter of Hailguard to be sure, and the meals were a lot more regular. I stayed in the city until I was sixteen then I started exploring, traveling from city to city looking for temples to apply to. I spent nearly three years doing that. What a waste," Matt said with a sigh.

"At least you got to explore a bit, I've spent my entire life in Shearcliff working at the inn until I met you in Algeminia," Chris said.

"You said you left home at sixteen Matt?" Cassy asked him.

"Yeah, why?" he asked.

"No reason, that's just the same age I left home at. I know what it's like to be out in the world without anyone to rely on," Cassy told him.

Chris gave a snort.

"You only traveled one village away before you set yourself up as a petty bandit robbing farmers. I'd hardly compare you to Matt, who traveled halfway across Targoth by himself on a holy mission," Chris said with a laugh.

Cassy scowled at him.

"I went farther than you ever did, and I had only been a bandit for a few months when you arrived! I spent the better part of two years exploring the wilderness around the mountain and practicing my archery," Cassy said angrily.

"And why were you practicing your archery sis?" Chris asked innocently.

"So I could be a good bandit!" Cassy yelled before realizing she had fallen for his trap.

Chris and Matt burst out laughing while Ditrina looked confused by the sudden turn in conversation. Sarah grew angry.

"Chris, you never told me you sister was a criminal," Sarah said darkly.

Chris grew worried that their feud would start anew but before he had a chance to defend his sister Cassy spoke.

"True, I was a bandit, but I never killed anyone. I only stole food and supplies. Besides you can't talk, you were serving under that monster Sorros when we found you," Cassy shot back.

Sarah was quiet for a moment and Chris and Matt held in their breath. The women's feud had not been over for long and neither of them fully trusted the truce as of yet. Sarah laughed.

"True enough, I did work for that asshole for a while. Guess that makes me no better than you really," Sarah said and Chris and Matt let out their breaths in a sigh of relief.

"How did you end up serving under Sorros anyway? He doesn't seem like the type of person you'd like to hang around long term," Matt asked her.

"Same reason you ended up taking a job from him I guess, money," Sarah said and stared into the fire. "I've been working as a sell sword since I was twelve years old. I ran away from home when I was little and stumbled across a mercenary band, called themselves the Band of the Boar. One of the members decided it would be useful to have a personal squire and asked me to travel with them, promised I would get fed each day. It sounded like a pretty good deal to me at the time; I had been living as a beggar since I left home, so I agreed. I ended up serving as a squire for one of the knights in the band, Sir Hughes, for about a year. He taught me how to swing a sword so I could look out for myself on the battlefield and as it turned out I was far better with a blade than I was as a squire. When I was thirteen years old I signed on as an actual member of the band. Sir Hughes actually ended up promoted to the leader of our band a few years after I joined. Life was good. We spent the next three years chasing bandits and catching petty thieves in the villages we went to, never saw any actual battles. That changed when we were hired by the crown to deal with barbarians from across the western sea. We were told that it was a small group of raiders set up in a small town. What we found was a small army entrenched into a coastal city; they had turned the place into a fortress. We weren't the only band hired to deal with the raiders as we found out, three other companies were already laying siege to the city gates. When the gates finally fell the Band of the Boar was the first through the breach. We fought as hard as we could but in the end we were cut to pieces, none of us had ever seen a major battle before. Still, when the dust cleared the city was ours. We chased the raiders back to the sea and cut down any that didn't make it to their boats in time, but the Band of the Boar suffered heavy casualties. Nearly three fourths of my comrades had fallen in battle including Sir Hughes, and of those who survived most were wounded. I was one of the few to escape unscathed, most likely on account of my smaller stature at the time. With the Band of the Boar destroyed the surviving members signed on to the other mercenary bands that had fought in the battle as is common practice for sell swords but I couldn't bring myself to do it. With the Band of the Boar gone it didn't feel right just signing onto another band the same day, I felt like it would be a betrayal to the fallen. So I left on my own and headed east. I sold my skills as a body guard and worked for some interesting people doing interesting things. One of those people recommended my services to Governor Sorros, who happened to be looking for a competent swordsman as it turned out. I was twenty at the time, and not knowing any better I applied to be Sorros's sword master. Several others including Droga entered the competition, which was a tournament to test the skills of the applicants. I made it to the final round before losing to an older man named Fenir from the far south. I did succeed in impressing Sorros with my tenacity however, and he offered me a position on his city guard. He offered a job to Droga too. Droga had fought dirty in his match and Sorros seemed to like that. I wasn't interested at first until I heard the amount he was offering, fifty gold pieces every week,"

Chris gave a low whistle upon hearing the sum.

"With that much gold, you'd be able to retire pretty young," Chris said impressed.

"Yeah, that's why I agreed to work for him," Sarah told him. "What he didn't say was that he was subtracting food, lodging, and equipment from my weekly pay. In the end I was making far less than he had actually promised, but by then it was too late, and I didn't exactly have anywhere else to go. So, I served under that foul man for the next two years and earned the title of Captain of the guard, which I shared with that scum Droga. Those weren't the best two years but I was getting paid regularly, even if it was less than I had hoped, and I had half of the city guard under my command so it was worth hanging around," Sarah said.

"Why did you leave if it was worth staying?" Ditrina asked.

Sarah looked at the dirt and mumbled.

"What was that?" Ditrina asked leaning forward, eager to hear more of her story.

Sarah continued to mutter unintelligibly at her feet.

"What Sarah is failing to say is she chased us out of the city before trying to kill us in our sleep. Our kind leader Chris decided to spare her life in exchange for her joining our company," Matt said.

Sarah shot him a murderous look.

"Hey it's true isn't it!" Matt said raising his hands in defense.

Before Sarah could reply Chris jumped into the fray.

"Wait, since when am I the leader?" he asked with surprise.

"What do you mean? You've always been the leader," Cassy laughed.

"Says who?" Chris exclaimed.

"Says all of us," Matt told him. "I agreed to follow you remember? That makes you my leader."

"And do you really think I'd be following around that midget if you weren't here?" Cassy asked him.

"Still that hardly makes me…" Chris began but Sarah cut him off.

"The only reason I'm here is because you spared my life, I follow you and you alone," Sarah said proudly.

"I told you we're even so…" Chris tried to speak but Ditrina drowned him out.

"It seems the group has decided that you will be our official leader, I haven't traveled with you long but if they all deem it wise to follow you, you must be fairly competent. I too shall follow you Christian Shearcliff," Ditrina said formally.

"I really think we should put it to a vote," Chris said in defeat.

"It seems we just did," Cassy said cheerfully.

"What's your problem with being the leader anyway?" Matt asked.

"I've never led anyone before! I have no idea what I'm doing!" Chris said nervously.

"You've been leading us just fine so far, just keep doing what you've been doing," Matt said before drinking the last of his stew with a slurp.

All save Chris laughed, even Ditrina, and they returned to their dinners. When they had finished eating the sun had been replaced by a million stars and the fire burned low. Ditrina cleared her throat.

"Leader," she began.

"Don't call me that," Chris said quickly.

"What is our plan long term?" Ditrina asked.

"What do you mean? We're heading to Bleakstar," Chris replied confused.

"I know that, what after that, what's our goal? Where are we *going*?" Ditrina explained.

Chris thought for a moment.

"Well our current plan is to keep heading south taking jobs as we go and getting the word out about our company. Once we've done enough jobs people will start coming to us with work instead of us having to race from place to place. When that happens, we should probably look into finding a permanent base of operations," Chris told her.

"Understood. Your response indicates you have enough of a plan to lead us for the time being though I suggest you look into finding us a more fixed goal than just heading south," Ditrina said before heading toward the woman's tent without another word.

"Told you, you'll be a great leader!" Cassy said before following after Ditrina.

"Goodnight great leader," Matt said as he stood up.

"Please don't encourage her," Chris said with exasperation.

Matt laughed and walked slowly to their tent leaving Chris alone with Sarah. After some time she spoke.

"You should get some rest Chris; I'll take the first watch," Sarah told him.

Chris started with surprise.

"Do you really think that's necessary?" Chris asked her.

"We're wanted remember? Sorros won't stop looking for you just because you escaped Draclige. Sorros has almost surely received word about Droga and his men by now, he'll be coming for you," Sarah told him. "I told them I was heading after you so that may have bought us some time but when I don't return to the city with a report he'll send more men out to search."

"All the more reason to head further south then, I don't want anything to happen to you guys because of me," Chris told her.

"That's very kind of you but we made our choices willingly, we all joined knowing what it meant," Sarah said reassuringly.

"I don't think Ditrina knows," Chris said uneasily.

"Oh trust me, she does. She and Cassy talked plenty before you woke up," Sarah said. "Everyone here joined on their own free will knowing the risks."

"You didn't," Chris said quietly.

Sarah stood and walked around the fire so she could sit beside him. She placed her arm carefully around his shoulders.

"Chris you gave me a choice few would have. I told you this then and I'll tell you again, I wouldn't have given me that same choice if I was in your position. I'm grateful you did what you did," Sarah told him.

"I know, but I still can't help but feel I dragged you into this. You said it yourself; you had a good life back in Draclige even if you didn't like Sorros much. You were just doing your job and you ended up a wanted criminal because of it. I know the choice I gave you, and I know you swore to travel with us, but I release you from that oath. You signed the contract under duress and I can't ask you to follow me because of that. It's not too late, you can still go back and Sorros will be none the wiser," Chris told her.

Sarah was quiet for a moment.

"Do you not want me around Chris?" she asked quietly.

"No, that's not it at all! You saved my sisters life and you're a fantastic fighter, it's just that I feel awful about how we forced you to come with us," Chris said softly.

"In that case listen to me Christian," Sarah said firmly, locking eyes with him. "I accept your offer, and claim my freedom, so know when I say this it's *my* choice. I will follow you if it means sailing across the western seas to lands unknown. I pledge my loyalty to you and you alone. When you need me I shall be your sword and when you are in danger I will be your shield. I am yours to command," she said formally.

"I thought I told you to stop acting as if you owe me your life," Chris said slightly bemused.

"This has nothing to do with that," Sarah said seriously. "I've spent the last two years of my life serving a monster, before that I wandered aimlessly selling my skills to the highest bidder. No more. I've finally found someone I'm proud to serve. If I had wanted to I could have slipped away any time since we met and been back in Draclige within the week. I'm here because I want to be here, and I serve you because I want to serve you, no other reason," Sarah said determinedly.

Without warning she pulled him into a hug. Surprised, Chris returned the hug awkwardly.

"What was that for?" Chris asked slightly confused as she pulled away from him.

"My thanks for giving me a purpose again," Sarah said brightly before standing up.

As she walked to her horse and began strapping on her armor she said:

"Go get some rest, I'll wake you for your shift in an hour and a half."

Still shocked by her sudden hug Chris stood up slowly.

"Sure thing Sarah," he said still trying to follow the path of their conversation that had led to her hugging him. "I'll see you in a little while."

Chris was not alone in his dreams that night.

"Well hello there mighty leader!" Mi chirped brightly as Chris materialized into the grey world.

"Not you too," Chris groaned.

"Your right, not just him," Matt laughed.

Chris recoiled in shock.

"Matt, what are you doing here!?" he exclaimed.

"Don't you remember Chris?" Ge said as he popped into sight. "Matt will be joining us from now on when we meet as a result of his possession of the book," Ge explained.

"Yeah, I was just chatting with Mi about some of the adventures he got up to when he was still alive, he lived quite an amazing life," Matt said.

"Please, you're making me blush," Mi said happily.

"Well it's true!" Matt laughed.

"I hate to break up the budding romance but where's Al? He's not still mad is he?" Chris asked them.

"Nah, he's alright; Al's just spending some time with his family tonight is all," Mi replied.

"Wait what?" Matt exclaimed.

"What's the problem Matt?" Mi asked him.

"What do you mean he has a family, are there more of you?" Matt asked looking around as if spirits were about to start popping out of thin air.

"More dead people? Of course," Ge replied. "Just as you travel from the physical realm to meet us here, we travel from the astral realm as well. Because none of us are able to cross the boundaries between the living and the dead we meet halfway instead in the space between realms," he explained.

"What did you think they just hung around here waiting for us to show up?" Chris laughed. "They have afterlives to live."

"You sound real official Chris, but don't forget it wasn't so long ago we had this exact conversation with you," Mi taunted.

"Yeah but Matt's a cleric, he should know this stuff," Chris defended.

"Hey, this type of magic is *way* beyond me," Matt cut in. "I haven't the foggiest idea how this enchantment works."

"I could explain it to you if you like," Ge told him.

"Would you? I would really appreciate it," Matt replied gratefully.

"That's all well and good but you spell junkies take this talk elsewhere, too much magic discussion ends up giving me a headache," Mi said with a dismissive wave of his hand.

"Of course brother," Ge replied and gripped Matt's hand, disappearing from sight before Chris had a chance to blink.

"Well, now that their gone we can speak freely lady-killer," Mi said cheerfully.

"What are you talking about?" Chris asked suspiciously.

"Well I'm assuming you don't want your buddy to know *everything* that goes on in your life. It's unavoidable that I'll know what you get up to but we can keep it between us," Mi said tapping his blurry nose.

As an afterthought, he added:

"And Al of course."

"I still don't know what you're talking about," Chris said defensively.

"Don't play dumb Chris, I share your memories remember," Mi said as he slinked over to Chris and slid his arm around his shoulders. "I'm talking about *Sarah*, you twos hug earlier. Nicely done wooing her by the way."

"I'm not *wooing* anyone," Chris said angrily.

"Oh come on Chris, that little speech about her freedom was golden. You worked her like a pro, and that's coming from the master himself," Mi said knowingly.

"I was being serious Mi; I wasn't trying to seduce her or anything!" Chris exclaimed.

"You mean to tell me you haven't noticed the way she's been looking at you since she joined? You haven't noticed how much she blushes when you pay her the slightest bit of attention?" Mi asked innocently.

Chris's next outburst died in his throat. He *had* been noticing how much she seemed to blush but hadn't put much thought into the matter; he had been busy worrying about Sorros, then Matt. Mi saw Chris's hesitation and capitalized on the opportunity.

"You *have* noticed haven't you?" Mi asked, a sly smile creeping onto his face.

"Well I guess, but I really didn't put much weight to it, she's twenty-two and I'm eighteen!" Chris said nervously.

"Not quite eighteen yet," Mi reminded him.

"Exactly! What would she see in me that she wouldn't see in someone her own age?" Chris asked.

"Oh come on Chris, you're not even trying anymore are you?" Mi taunted. "Think, Sarah started fighting at the age of thirteen; saw her first actual battle when she was younger than you. If I've read her correctly, which I can assure you I have; she's the type of person who puts stock in ability, not age."

"Wouldn't she be interested in someone with far more experience then?" Chris asked.

"Well, you had three, now two, of the most powerful artifacts on

Targoth in your possession. Since you two met, in her eyes you've saved her life, fought by her side against a hoard of monsters, and shown her you respect her thoughts and opinions enough to release her from your services entirely. I'm having trouble understanding what you're not seeing here," Mi laughed.

Chris was silent as the pieces fell into place in his head. Now that Mi had put it in the open he fell like a fool for not seeing it himself.

"What should I do Mi?" Chris practically begged him.

Mi stepped away from him and seemed to ponder his request. After letting Chris squirm for a while an evil grin spread across his blurry face.

"I'm just gonna let you take this one on your own," Mi said with the same grin still plastered on his face.

"Not funny Mi, I need help," Chris begged.

"Alright, alright," Mi said raising his hands in surrender "If you're so sure you want my advice, *listen up*. If you wanna impress her just keep doing as you've been doing. So far you've done a good job of securing her interest, why fix what's not broken am I right?" Mi asked. "Just make sure you don't rush things, take it slow and give her some more time to fully fall for you before doing anything rash. Maybe buy her something nice the next time you're in a town or something?"

"That…actually sounds like really good advice," Chris said shocked, after all he had been expecting some sarcastic remark or joke.

"Hey, don't act so surprised, I may have lived fifteen hundred years ago but boy I most certainly *lived*…if you get my meaning," Mi told him.

"Thanks Mi, I really appreciate it," Chris said.

"Ah think nothing of it buddy, I am here for advice after all," Mi said.

Chris went to reply but the world began fading around him.

"Ah, it seems it's your turn to take watch. We'll speak again, though I cannot promise another private moment such as this will come any time soon. Remember what I said, and try not to screw things up too badly!" Mi called after him as Chris awoke to Sarah's face.

"It's your turn to take watch," she told him, and he smiled at her.

CHAPTER TWELVE

After two days of riding, watching the rolling hills evolve into well maintained farmland, they finally saw Bleakstar standing proud on the horizon bathed in the afternoon sunlight. The town, really a small city, sat atop a hill with a castle keep visible rising above the defensive stone walls. Even from a distance the bustle of everyday life could be heard confirming that Bleakstar was alive and thriving. The group rode together through the gates and everywhere they looked they saw happy people, mostly humans but with a few scattered dwarves and the odd orc wandering through the streets shopping and going about their business.

Despite the variety, Cassy and Ditrina quickly attracted attention, with the town's people stopping to gawk at the elf and naga. After enduring this for several blocks Ditrina grew short tempered and pulled her cloak's hood up to hide her face. Cassy had no such relief.

Most of the buildings were wooden and two to three storied, with bright flowers blooming in the windows and fluttering blue and yellow banners depicting a gryphon clutching a shield hanging wherever they looked. Compared to Draclige the streets were narrow, and the few soldiers they saw were cheerful and friendly. Overall the town seemed to pulse with life of its own, bringing Chris joy.

"It's much nicer than Draclige isn't it," Sarah remarked as they rode slowly down the main street taking in the sights.

"Far nicer, even the soldiers seem happy. I don't think I ever met a single nice soldier in Draclige," Matt said.

Sarah gave him a dirty look.

"Present company excluded of course!" Matt added hastily.

"We should probably find an inn to stay at," Ditrina said before their conversation could go any further.

"Good idea Di," Cassy agreed. "Sing out if you see anything!" she called to them.

It wasn't long before they saw what looked like an inn, a three storied building with its sign showing a singing woman with a snake's tail and wings. Engraved above the door were the words:

The Singing Siren

"What do you guys think?" Chris asked as they looked at the establishment, which appeared well maintained from the outside.

"It looks fine to me," Sarah told him and the others agreed.

They tethered the horses outside, Sarah and Chris deciding to keep their swords, and walked in to be greeted by the sound of lively music, drums and a lute, as well as a flute all being played from a stage in the center of the room. A man and a woman sang upon the stage in harmony with the band. The inn's common room was two storied, with the first floor housing the bar as well as tables scattered around the stage. A staircase ran up the left hand wall to a balcony that ringed around the room featuring more tables and a low railing so patrons could still see the stage. Chris assumed the rooms were located on the top floor. The room was packed with people enjoying the music and food, both of which seemed excellent. They stood near the entrance for a time enjoying the music. Before long one of the many servers navigating the tables noticed them and rushed to their side.

"So sorry, we're very busy today. Do you have a reservation for the upper or lower floor?" the boy asked.

He looked to be no older than fifteen and had short brown curly hair and wide eyes. He wore the same outfit as the rest of the servers; black pants with a white long sleeve shirt, over which he wore a black vest.

"Actually, we'd like to buy some rooms if you any are available," Chris replied.

The boy looked confused.

"Rooms? What rooms? This is the Singing Siren," the boy said nervously.

"This is an inn isn't it?" Cassy asked him.

The boy looked up at her with awe, seeming to notice her for the first time.

"What are you?" he asked breathlessly.

"What do you mean?" Cassy replied slightly irritated.

"You've got scales, and claws!" the boy exclaimed excitedly. "Are you a monster?" he asked taking a small step away from her.

Cassy grinned though it did not reach her eyes and leaned her face close to his, showing off her fang filled mouth.

"That depends sweetie, on whether or not you're going to tell me if you have rooms available," Cassy said in a sickeningly sweet voice resting a clawed hand on his shoulder.

"What do you mean? We have no rooms!" the boy squeaked, shaking in fear.

"Is there a problem?" asked a lanky man with a receding gray hairline wearing a white apron over the same uniform the other workers wore, who had suddenly appeared behind the boy.

The boy stepped hastily away from Cassy to the man's side.

"What type of inn is this?" Cassy asked him irritably. "This rude little brat says you don't have any rooms."

"That's because this isn't an inn at all, the Singing Siren is the finest dining hall in Bleakstar, not some common slop house, and I can assure you my staff are well mannered and would never insult a guest," the old man said pompously.

"I wouldn't be so sure of that," Chris told him. "That little shit called my sister a monster just a moment ago," he said darkly staring down at the boy who was doing his best to hide behind the old man.

To Chris's surprise the old man spun quickly and hauled the boy before them by his ear.

"Is this true?" the old man demanded, his voice full of menace.

The boy struggled to escape his vice like grip to no avail. He gave up struggling and turned to look at the man as best as he could.

"Mr. Norton I didn't mean any disrespect I only..." the boy stammered.

"Is it true?!" Mr. Norton bellowed causing the other servers to pause for a second to watch the confrontation.

"Yes," the boy said quietly.

Mr. Norton inhaled sharply through his nose.

"Go to the kitchens and wait for me to arrive. We will discuss this incident further then," Mr. Norton said darkly and the boy scurried off out of site. "I'm so, so sorry about him. Please, let me make this up to you all," he practically begged.

"You could start by telling us where we could find an inn so we can get out of this damn place," Cassy said angrily.

"I'll do better than that; I'll pay for your rooms tonight at the best inn in town, the Gallant Dragon. I'll send one of my staff down to reserve your rooms and bring your horses down. While you wait please enjoy all the Siren has to offer, free of charge," Mr. Norton told them.

Cassy opened her mouth to speak, most likely something foul based on her expression, but Chris was faster.

"We'll happily accept your offer," he said brightly.

"Wonderful," Mr. Norton said with relief. "Allow me to show you to your table," he said and led them up the stairs to a round table large enough sit eight. "Make yourselves comfortable, my staff will take care of your horses and the food will be around shortly," Mr. Norton said before disappearing back down the stairs.

"Why the hell did you accept his offer? I don't want to spend another minute in this miserable place," Cassy said angrily, but Chris detected a hint of misery in her voice.

"What happened downstairs was an accident; the boy had probably never seen a naga before and spoke without thinking," Matt tried to explain but Cassy shot him an evil look.

"I don't care if he's never seen a naga before in his life or if his mother was a naga, there's no excuse for that little brat," Cassy hissed.

"Calm down Cas," Chris said. "I know you don't like it when people look at you like your different but you have to remember that you *are* different, you're six and a half feet tall with razor sharp claws, scales, and a mouth full of fangs."

Cassy looked at him with betrayal written across her face but Chris held up his hand signaling that he wasn't finished.

"What I'm trying to say is that just because you look scary doesn't mean you're a monster. As much as it sucks people are always going to give you strange looks because they don't know any better. That's not what's important though, what's important is that the people who know you and care about you aren't concerned with what you look like," Chris said.

Cassy looked less angry but unconvinced.

"He's right," Sarah spoke up. "When we first met I know we didn't get along."

"That's putting it lightly," Matt muttered but Sarah ignored him.

"As I was saying," Sarah said with a sharp look sent in Matt's direction. "Of all the reasons I had to not to like you the fact that you're a naga wasn't one of them. Who cares whether you have scales or not? You're a wonderful addition to the company and we would be worse off without you," Sarah told her.

Cassy smiled at her.

"Thanks Sarah," Cassy said.

"I've worked with people of almost every species you can imagine, hell I'm fairly sure I'm one of the only people who can say they've worked with an elf," Sarah said with a glance in Ditrina's direction. "I feel that I've learned something in my travels; species means nothing. I've met orc's who were some of the kindest people you'll ever meet, and I've met humans who are some of the foulest monsters to walk across Targoth. It doesn't matter, what you are doesn't make you a monster, who you are does. You're not a monster Cassy," Sarah told her.

Cassy gave a sniffle and nodded, Chris took note of the fact her green eyes were tearing up.

"Besides, many of them may be jealous," Ditrina said suddenly.

"What do you mean?" Cassy asked not understanding.

"I've noticed that many human women spend incredible amounts of time on their looks, applying makeup and painting their nails bright colors in hopes of improving their appearance. Despite this I've yet to see any human who's managed to rival your scales in terms of beauty," Ditrina said running a finger across the scales on Cassy's hand looking at them closely. "Each one reminds me of a little green gem," Ditrina said happily her inspection complete.

Cassy's caramel colored cheeks flushed darker than normal and she seemed at a loss for words. Rather than try to speak Cassy leaned in and kissed Ditrina suddenly. Sarah gave a low whistle while Matt almost fell out of his chair in shock.

"What the hell is *this* about?" he whispered violently in Chris's ear as Ditrina pulled Cassy into an embrace, still kissing her.

"You really aren't observant are you?" Chris replied quietly.

"You mean your sister and Ditrina are a thing?" Matt whispered.

"Shut up and don't ruin their fun," Sarah whispered from Matt's other side. "And you really need to learn how to whisper more quietly," she added as an afterthought.

"How did you miss the fact that they've been getting close? They've been inseparable since the mines," Chris asked him quietly.

"I wasn't in a position to notice if you recall," Matt hissed back at him.

"Still," Sarah whispered "The entire trip here they rode together laughing and talking, and they always sit next to each other at dinner, even now their chairs are right next to each other. I'm lost to how you didn't see this actually," Sarah laughed quietly.

"It's because Matt's about as dumb as his horse," Cassy called from across the table.

The three of them gave a small jump of surprise.

"I've got good hearing remember," Cassy laughed tapping her ear.

Chris recovered first.

"Let's try to be fair to Matt's horse here," Chris said and everyone laughed.

Ditrina seemed to find this especially funny for some reason, and was doubled over in her chair gasping for air as she fell into fits of giggling, causing the rest of them to laugh even harder. They were still laughing when the server arrived a few minutes later. To their surprise it was the boy from before. Their laughter died suddenly and the boy found himself watched by five pairs of unfriendly eyes.

"What is it you want brat?" Cassy asked, irritated by his intrusion.

"Well… I just…" the boy stammered. "I just wanted to say I'm sorry that I asked if you were a monster earlier I shouldn't have said it and I'm very sorry it won't happen again miss," the boy said in a rush.

Cassy just stared at him letting him squirm.

"Yeah yeah, whatever, just bring us our food," Cassy said with a dismissive wave of her hand.

The boy let out a small gasp of happiness.

"You mean it?" he asked.

"Sure, just bring me something to eat before I change my mind," Cassy said with slight irritation.

The boy decided he wouldn't press his luck by hanging around and raced away.

"Well I'm disappointed; I was hoping you'd toss him over the balcony," Sarah said with a chuckle.

"Would you rather I toss you over instead?" Cassy asked raising an eyebrow and sneering at her, the stress of the day finally catching up to her.

"I'd like to see you try," Sarah said growing angry that Cassy snapped at her for making a small joke.

"Ladies, play nice," Matt cautioned but both women shot him withering looks.

"Stay out of this cleric!" they yelled in unison before glaring at one another with renewed hate.

"I thought you two had reached some sort of understanding?" Chris asked nervously looking between the two of them.

"Yeah, but just for today let's see how high your sister bounces when I toss her across the room," Sarah said rising from her seat.

"I'm down for a little sport," Cassy spat as she rose from her own seat flexing her claws at her side.

"Sit down both of you!" Chris yelled at them.

Sarah responded immediately.

"Yes Chris," she said quickly, dropping into her seat like a stone.

Cassy still stood and leered at her.

"When did you become my brother's pet?" she taunted from across the table.

Ditrina reached up and pulled Cassy back into her seat displaying surprising strength in her thin arms.

"Hey, Di what the hell…" Cassy began but Ditrina said something under her breath and Chris felt the presence of magic.

Cassy fell silent, her mouth still moving but with no words coming out. She looked at Ditrina questioningly.

"That is no way to behave at the table; you need to apologize to Sarah," Ditrina said with irritation showing in her black eyes.

Cassy tried to argue but again no sound came out of her mouth. Ditrina merely raised an eyebrow and waited. Realizing she had no way out Cassy lowered her head and nodded. Ditrina muttered something else and the spell was lifted.

"I'm sorry Sarah," Cassy said looking embarrassed.

"Now Sarah, you apologize to Cas," Ditrina said turning her gaze to her.

"Why should I? She's the one who started it after all…" Sarah said trailing off as she noticed what Ditrina was doing.

"I merely believe it would be a wise decision," Ditrina said cheerfully, resting her hand palm up on the table, holding a swirling ball of fire.

"Yeah, sure, of course. Sorry Cassy," Sarah gulped.

Ditrina smiled and the fireball vanished.

"Good, now everyone is friends again! I admire how other the other races instantly repair friendships when there is an apology made, no amount of words can repair an elven feud. They often go on for centuries," Ditrina told them.

"She does know that's not how it works right?" Matt whispered in Chris's ear.

"Shut up! Do you want her to pull the fire back out?" Chris hissed under his breath.

"Right, sorry," Matt whispered.

"Foods here!" called a cheerful serving girl, who was accompanied by several other waiters all caring platters of food and tall mugs of ale.

"About time," Chris said grateful for the distraction.

"By the way, Mr. Norton wanted to know what the inn's reservation should be put under," the girl asked.

"Shearcliff and Company," Chris replied.

"Thanks! I'll let you guys enjoy your meal then," the girl replied and ran off.

The arrival of food served to distract the women from their argument. The group began to dig in.

"I don't think I've eaten this well since Dewbank!" Chris exclaimed, elbowing Matt who was busy stuffing his face with most of a chicken.

"No, this is far better than Dewbank, this is the best food I've ever tasted!" Matt replied once he cleared his mouth.

"I agree; this is really, really, good," Sarah said between large mouthfuls.

"Between you two we're going to run out of food!" Chris laughed.

"You never know when you're going to get another meal like this," Sarah told him. "Enjoy it while it's here," she said before taking a large bite out of a drumstick.

"This is the best human food I've tried so far," Ditrina said.

Unlike the others, she ate in a refined manner, carving off small portions of whatever it was she wanted.

"Still, it's nothing compared to what the elves can make," she added as an afterthought.

"If the elves can cook better than this then I need to visit the elven cities," Matt replied.

"Only one," Ditrina said shaking her head.

"Only one what?" Matt asked confused.

"There's only one elven city, and it's protected by powerful enchantments so you can't just walk into it," Ditrina explained.

"Well you'll just have to bring us there some time then," Cassy told her before taking a drink of her ale.

Her face lit up.

"Chris! You have *got* to try this!" she called to him.

Curious Chris tried his own drink, and found it remarkably good, but very strong.

"Go easy on that Cas, I don't wanna have to carry you out of this place," Chris warned but she waved him off and took another deep drink from her mug.

"Forget that, I'm taking Sarah's advice. Who knows when I'll get to have a drink this nice again," Cassy called then finished her mug. "Hey little brat!" she called spying the boy from before carrying a tray of food to the table.

When she saw she had his attention she held up her mug.

"Don't let me run out of these!" she called cheerfully.

Chris sighed.

The afternoon turned to evening as they enjoyed all the Singing Siren had to offer, drinking and listing to the music. Chris did his best to moderate how much he drank on account of the volume consumed by Sarah and Cassy. Matt seemed to be doing his best to limit what he drank as well, while Ditrina drank water. As they relaxed the lunch rush ended and the common room mostly emptied out. By the time the dinner crowd had arrived and they had eaten their second meal, Cassy was horribly drunk.

"The lights look funny," Cassy slurred as she wobbled in her chair, pointing at the lanterns hanging above them.

"Cassy, I think you need to stop drinking," Matt warned but she waved him away.

"I'm *fiiiiine*," Cassy giggled still swaying side to side.

Matt gave Chris a worried look but Chris shrugged.

"She'll be alright, she just won't be happy in the morning," Chris told him. "How about you Sarah, you holding up alright?" Chris asked her.

"Please, I'm just getting started," Sarah scoffed but Chris detected her words came slightly thicker than normal.

Cassy swayed a little too far to one side and slumped against Ditrina, resting her head on her shoulder.

"Di! You're not drinking!" Cassy pouted still collapsed against her.

Ditrina did her best to return Cassy to her seat.

"That's because I wish to retain enough of my senses to be useful," Ditrina scolded, still trying to set Cassy upright but each time she let go Cassy would crash back against her.

"You don't think I'm useful?" Cassy mumbled, barely intelligible.

"No," Ditrina said kindly. "I just don't think it's wise for you to be so drunk in a strange city," Ditrina explained softly.

Cassy nodded and buried her face in Ditrina's shoulder seeming to fall asleep. Ditrina looked at Chris for help but without warning Cassy shot bolt upright.

"Your hair is so pretty!" Cassy exclaimed running a clawed hand through Ditrina's long blue hair. "It looks soft, but I can't tell," Cassy whined looking at her scaly fingers with dismay.

Seeming to find a solution she slid her chair even closer to Ditrina until they were touching and buried her face in her hair.

"You smell nice" Cassy mumbled through Ditrina's hair.

Ditrina again looked to Chris for advice on how to deal with her but Chris shook his head, glad he wasn't the target of his sister's drunken rambles.

"Is she always so…" Matt began.

"Clingy? Yes," Chris replied shaking his head sadly.

"Oh gods, Chris!" Matt said suddenly shaking his shoulder.

"What is it… Oh no," Chris said with dismay.

Sarah's chair was vacant, and her mug sat freshly emptied.

"Where did she go?" Matt asked looking around.

"I'm not sure, but she's drunk enough she shouldn't be by herself. We can't let her wander around the place at random. I'll look for her," Chris said standing up.

"I'll come with," Matt said but Chris shook his head.

"I need you to help look after my sister, it'll be worse if she gets out and about," Chris told him.

Matt looked at Cassy, who was still firmly attached to Ditrina, who was still struggling to free herself and sighed.

"Yeah I guess, just don't take too long. I'm not sure how long I'll be able to entertain her once she gets bored climbing on Ditrina," Matt said.

"Help," Ditrina mumbled from under Cassy.

"Yeah, yeah I'm coming; it's your fault for encouraging her earlier you know," Matt said and walked around the table to try to pull off Cassy.

Satisfied that the situation here was under control Chris ran down the stairs and looked around for Sarah. Not seeing the redhead anywhere in the Siren he pulled up the hood of his cloak and raced into the street.

"Best I'm not seen running through the streets like a madman before looking for work tomorrow," Chris muttered to himself as he scanned the streets for Sarah. Still seeing no sign of her he picked a direction and ran deeper into the city.

As Chris searched, the last of the evenings dim light was replaced by the glow of small lanterns hung between the buildings on strings. Chris would have stopped to admire the beauty of the town but he was too intent on tracking down Sarah. Usually Sarah would be the last person he would worry about, an accomplished fighter with experience dealing with cities and crowds, but Chris wasn't sure how drunk she had become and couldn't be certain she wouldn't get herself into trouble. With the aid of the cloak Chris went unnoticed by the town folk. He slipped through crowds like a ghost and navigated the streets quickly looking intently for her. Almost half an hour went by with no sign of Sarah. Just when he was preparing to head back to the Siren to try a different street Chris noticed a small offshoot of the main road that squeezed between two tall buildings that he had yet to explore. The faint rasp of metal could be heard from within.

Chris jogged between the buildings and found himself standing in a small courtyard. It seemed the small entrance he had found was the only way in because he was enclosed by the backs of several buildings. Two strings of lanterns hung across the courtyard crossing above the center, lighting the area in a soft glow, and flowers had been planted along the sides of the buildings. A large fountain gurgled quietly in the center of the clearing, spitting a small stream of water into the air that caught the lantern light and sparkled like a million diamonds. Sarah sat on the edge of the fountain, her red hair made an inferno by the light, sharpening her long sword absentmindedly. Chris watched her for a moment, deciding it would be best if he wasn't seen yet before walking forward slowly.

"Isn't your cloak supposed to hide you from me or something? Sarah asked without looking up from her sword.

Chris paused for a moment before continuing his approach.

"Yes, but it has a fatal flaw. If you want to find me more than I want to hide then I'll be found," Chris said before sitting next to her.

"Figures," Sarah said simply as her cheeks flushed red.

They sat quietly for a while; the only sounds the gurgling of the fountain and the rasp of Sarah's sword against the sharpening stone.

"I thought you sharpened your sword back in Purevein?" Chris asked breaking the silence.

"I did, but that was a while ago," Sarah replied without looking up.

"You haven't used the sword since then though," Chris said softly.

Sarah sighed and sheathed the sword.

"I know. I just find it relaxing is all," Sarah told him.

There was another long silence.

"Why did you run off?" Chris asked her quietly.

Sarah did not answer right away.

"I just got tired of watching your sister crawl all over Ditrina, so I decided I should get some fresh air," Sarah told him.

"Are you two going to start fighting again?" Chris asked her.

"No," Sarah sighed loudly. "It's just she really gets under my skin sometimes is all."

Chris laughed.

"Trust me, I grew up with her, I know how she can be," Chris said and they laughed quietly.

"Why did you come after me Chris?" Sarah asked him when they stopped laughing.

"Well, I was worried you were a little too drunk to be out wandering the streets by yourself," Chris told her and she gave a small snort.

"Chris, I've spent most of my life surrounded by soldiers. It takes a lot more booze than that to knock me off my feet," Sarah said.

"I worked at an inn Sarah," Chris told her detecting the slurring of her speech and raised an eyebrow.

"Alright so I'm a little drunk," Sarah admitted.

"Let's head back to the Siren then," Chris told her but she shook her head.

"I told you, I'm not in the mood to watch Cassy grope Ditrina for the rest of the night," Sarah said.

"I thought you said you were raised by soldiers, I figured that type of thing wouldn't bother you," Chris said slightly surprised.

"Usually it wouldn't, but I'm not in the mood tonight," Sarah informed him.

"Is something wrong?" Chris asked her concerned.

"It's nothing, don't worry about it," Sarah said looking at her feet.

"What's the matter?" Chris asked, his voice full of concern. "Let me help you, whatever it is."

"Alright then," Sarah said so softly Chris barely heard her.

She slid along the lip of the fountain until she was pressed against Chris's side. Sarah leaned her head on his shoulder and gave a small sigh of contentment.

"Sarah?" Chris asked quietly.

She didn't reply, but lifted her head and locked her gaze with his. Sarah leaned in and pressed her lips against his. Chris pulled away quickly.

"Sarah, you're drunk, we should head back…" he said nervously but she shook her head and pulled him close again.

"I'm not that drunk," she whispered as she pulled him into another kiss.

This time he didn't resist, and wrapped his arms around her. Chris decided perhaps they didn't have to head back to the Siren quite yet.

CHAPTER THIRTEEN

They walked back to the Siren together. Somewhere along the way Sarah slipped her hand into Chris's, not that he seemed to mind. The streets were almost empty, but the lights still shone bright through the windows of the Singing Siren when it came into view.

"Is it just me or is it much louder now than when I left?" Sarah asked him as they stood outside the door.

She was right, in addition to the usual music and chatter that flowed from the place there was the sound of loud cheering coming from within.

Remembering the state of his sister Chris feared the worst.

"We should hurry," Chris said and they rushed inside.

His fears were well founded.

"Oh no!" Sarah exclaimed as she burst into a fit of laughter.

Chris only sighed.

Cassy was on the stage, dancing along with the band. The crowd loved it; she swayed her hips in tune with the beat and twirled like an acrobat from one side of the stage to the other. The servers seemed nervous, but made no move to remove her due to the crowds overwhelming response. Even the band seemed into it, and they played a quick beat for her to dance along to with their singers moving to Cassy's rhythm.

Matt and Ditrina stood on opposite sides of the stage, frantically doing their best to coax Cassy down, but she ignored them and continued to dance wildly. Matt spied them and rushed through the crowd as fast as he could manage.

"I don't know what happened!" he shouted over the crowd. "We lost sight of her for one second and suddenly she was on the stage. Before we could get her off, the crowd formed and she's been up there ever since!"

"Is the staff angry?" Sarah asked him.

"No, but besides that where did you go running off to?! This happened because Chris went out looking for you!" Matt wailed.

"Well I'm glad he did," Sarah laughed. "This is hilarious."

"I have to agree with Sarah, this is pretty funny," Chris chuckled.

"Ha ha, my sisters dancing like a tramp up on stage and I'm just gonna let the poor cleric deal with it," Matt mocked.

"That about sums it up, it was your job to watch her after all," Chris said.

"Well what the hell should I do?" Matt begged.

"Try collecting donations," Sarah chimed in. "It would be a shame to have her put in all this work for nothing."

"Seriously?!" Matt yelled in outrage.

"Why not? Start working the crowd, we'll give Cas the money from the performance," Chris laughed.

"You two are unbelievable," Matt said and stormed back into the crowd, but Chris noticed he began talking to the people as he passed them and was taking coins.

"I have an idea," Sarah said and pushed her way through the crowd to Ditrina.

Chris saw them whisper for a moment before Ditrina shrugged and Sarah returned.

"What was that about?" Chris asked her.

"Oh nothing, Ditrina's just gonna add a little something to the show is all," Sarah told him. "Come on; let's head back up to our seats," Sarah said before taking his hand and leading him away.

When they arrived at the table they found it taken by two men intently watching the show.

"You're at our table," Sarah warned them.

"So?" one of the men asked.

"There's plenty of room for you two as well," the second man said gesturing to the open seats.

"You misunderstand me," Sarah said with menace in her voice. "Beat it."

The men looked at the very angry woman with a sword on her back and decided the seats weren't worth arguing over.

"Sorry miss," they said meekly and quickly moved on.

Sarah smiled and sat so that she had a good view of the stage, and Chris sat beside her.

As they got comfortable the crowd below them gasped and cheered louder. Chris saw the serpent from the mines, though much smaller this time, twisting and flying above the stage. The crowd ate it up, nearly hysterical at the display of magic. Matt patrolled the crowd taking coins from almost everyone at this point while Ditrina stood a ways away chanting softly. Cassy continued to dance, treating the serpent like an infernal dance partner, twirling within its flaming coils.

"Well isn't that something," Chris said with awe.

"Thought you might like that," Sarah said and leaned her head on his shoulder again.

Chris reached down and entwined his hand with hers, and together they watched the performance.

Later that evening when Cassy had grown tired of dancing she climbed off the stage and curled up asleep atop a nearby table. Chris and Sarah left their seats above and walked down to help her, but Ditrina reached her first. In a surprising display of strength Ditrina scooped Cassy's limp form off the table and carried her over to where Chris and Sarah stood. Matt pushed his way through the crowd and joined them.

"Would you rather I carry her?" Sarah asked Ditrina.

"No, I'm fine, I'm stronger than I look you know," Ditrina told her.

"So you are," Matt said, impressed that Ditrina was able to hold up Cassy without any signs of strain.

"I'll go get directions to the inn," Chris told them and walked off to find Mr. Norton.

After asking a server where to find the old man Chris tracked him down in the kitchens behind the bar.

"Mr. Norton, thank you for your hospitality but we should probably head to the inn now," Chris told him.

"Of course, you will find the Gallant Dragon down the south road, it has a wonderful stone statue of a dragon out front, you can't miss it," Mr. Norton told him.

"I'm sorry we caused such a racket," Chris admitted to the man.

"Don't worry yourself over it, besides the other customers seemed to enjoy it so who am I to complain?" Mr. Norton asked. "Besides, it was my staff who wronged you, I'm just happy we were able to make it up to you," he added.

"The food was excellent, thank you. We'll be sure to stop by the next time we're in Bleakstar," Chris told him.

"Planning on leaving the city soon?" Mr. Norton asked.

"We're looking for work and don't expect to be in town for long," Chris told him.

"May I suggest you head up to the castle and speak with the Baron's steward then? I'm sure he can find a job for a group such as yours," Mr. Norton offered.

"Thanks, we'll be sure to ask him," Chris said brightly before turning to rejoin his companions. "Let's go guys; the inn is just down the road," Chris told them.

They left the Siren, with Ditrina still carrying Cassy, and walked down the street towards the inn. It was late enough that they saw almost nobody on their trip.

"So where did you run off to earlier?" Matt asked Sarah as they walked behind Ditrina, just in case she needed assistance.

Chris led the group.

"Oh nowhere in specific," Sarah replied casually.

"*Why* did you run off then?" Matt asked.

"My, we're full of questions tonight aren't we?" Sarah asked.

"I'm just trying to figure out what the problem was. That wasn't like you," Matt replied.

"Don't worry about it, Chris solved the problem already," Sarah said and quickened her pace until she was beside Chris and slipped her hand into his.

Matt stopped for a moment in shock, and prepared to ask what had happened between them earlier but stopped himself. He shook his head and started walking again; some things were best discussed in private.

"I'm terribly sorry, but we were only able to reserve three rooms for you," the innkeeper told them when they arrived at the Gallant Dragon.

"Well now what?" Matt asked Chris after the innkeeper had given them their room keys.

Chris shrugged.

"I don't see a problem; we'll just pair off, with someone getting a room to themselves," Chris told him.

"I'll share a room with Cassy, after all she's not in the best shape yet and I can use my magic to keep her comfortable," Ditrina volunteered.

"Thanks, Ditrina," Chris told her.

"That leaves us. So which of the three of us will be bunking together?" Matt asked Chris and Sarah.

Sarah gave him a strange look.

"Dibs," she said quickly and slipped her arm around Chris's waist.

"What?" Chris and Matt asked in unison.

"I'm calling dibs on Chris. We'll share a room tonight and you can have the extra room to yourself," Sarah explained to Matt.

"Alright then," Matt said a little surprised.

Chris shot him a worried look, like he was calling for help, but Sarah was already leading him by the arm down the hallway toward their room. Matt allowed himself a small smile and retreated to his own room, chuckling to himself.

Once inside the room Chris stood awkwardly as Sarah tossed her gear into the corner and dropped her weapons haphazardly on the floor as she approached the bed. He watched, unsure of what to do, as Sarah let her hair out of its braid and pulled off her leather traveling clothes leaving her wearing only a thin cotton undershirt and shorts. She sat on the edge of the single bed the room had to offer and yawned, but then seemed to notice Chris had yet to move.

"Is there a problem Chris?" she asked with slight concern.

"No, it's just…" Chris said but Sarah cut him off.

"Good, then hurry up and get undressed, I wanna go to bed," she said and leaned back on the pillows.

Chris pulled off his cloak and hung it behind the door, and set his sword and knife against the wall. He undressed himself quickly and pulled on a pair of soft cotton trousers he had purchased for sleeping back in Purevein. He approached the bed with nervous excitement, and stood beside it unsure of how to proceed.

"Seriously, is something the matter?" Sarah asked sitting up.

"No, it's just I've never…" Chris trailed off awkwardly.

Sarah looked at him blankly for a moment before comprehension flooded onto her face. She laughed softly, and Chris thought it sounded every bit as beautiful as the music back at the Siren.

"Relax Chris, I just want to go to sleep," Sarah reassured him. "Come on, lay down," she cooed as she reached up and tugged on his arm.

Chris slid into the bed next to her and she smiled and blew out the small lantern on the nightstand, plunging the room into darkness. Chris closed his eyes to sleep, but felt Sarah's well-muscled body nestle up against him, resting her head on his chest. Deciding there were defiantly benefits to the life he had chosen Chris drifted off to sleep to the sound of Sarah's even breathing.

"I'm not surprised to see you tonight," Chris said as he suddenly found himself standing before Mi. Unlike their last meeting they were not alone, and Chris saw Al standing beside Mi, as well as Matt and Ge waiting for him.

"You blew it!" Mi wailed and tugged at his hair.

"What are you talking about?" Chris asked baffled at Mi's distress.

"It was perfect, you acted like a real pro every step of the way, but when you finally get her to bed you blew it!" Mi moaned.

"Ignore him, you acted like a gentleman," Al counseled.

This was the first time Chris had seen Al since their fight, but thankfully Al seemed to be back to his usual self.

"I know you two share my memories but can we not talk about this?" Chris asked.

Mi continued to lament Chris's *failure* as he put it while Al smiled.

"Of course, of course, we'll leave the matter be," Al said with a small chuckle.

"They might, but I will agree to no such promises! Gimme details!" Matt said greedily.

Chris laughed.

"There's honestly not that much to tell," Chris told him sheepishly running a hand through his shaggy hair.

"There could have been!" Mi yelled.

"Shut up Mi!" Matt yelled back. "I know you didn't do anything like that Chris, if you had your grin would have split your head in two. I'm asking how long you and Sarah have been together. Is this new?" Matt pried.

"Yeah sort of, I think she's been a little interested in me for a while now, but I didn't really know what to do about it. Mi gave me some advice and one thing led to another and we were kissing by a fountain tonight. I'm not sure what happens next," Chris told him.

"Are you sure you don't have any ideas at all?" Matt asked all too innocently.

"Shut up," Chris said with a laugh and shoved him lightly.

"Listen; if you don't know how it works I can explain it!" Mi said hopefully. "That must be your problem, you just don't know what you're doing, and that means it's not your fault!" Mi rambled making excuses for Chris.

"Mi, I know how sex works," Chris said with irritation, ending his stream of hopeful babble.

"Then why didn't you do anything in there?!" Mi practically screamed.

"Perhaps our friend felt the moment wasn't right," Al suggested.

"What are you talking about? She practically dragged him off to that room! That was the single greatest moment in the history of moments!" Mi shrieked hysterically.

"I'm inclined to agree, Sarah did seem interested in Chris's company," Ge said simply, before falling back into the silence he had kept so far.

"See! Even Ge sees it! Even! Ge!" Mi yelled and returned to ranting incoherently.

"Relax you three. Chris has plenty of time to spend with Sarah. I doubt it'll be long before he has the pleasure of her company, so why rush things?" Matt asked.

"Thanks," Chris said relieved to have backup. "Besides, Sarah was pretty tired, I'd rather she be well rested and full of energy before we try anything," Chris said to Mi.

Mi stopped his ranting and a wolfish grin spread across his blurry face.

"*Ahhhhh* I see," Mi said slyly. "That's more like it, forget my previous outburst, I support this decision entirely," he said and let out an evil chuckle.

"Mi, behave," Al cautioned but Mi's chuckling turned into maniacal laughter.

When it subsided he turned to Chris.

"Our friend here values quality over quantity," Mi said rubbing his hands together. "Chris, like myself you seem to have a taste for the finer things," Mi sighed.

"I think I've had enough of this for tonight," Chris laughed.

"I agree; we've given the poor guy enough shit for one evening. I'm gonna get some rest," Matt laughed.

"You're already sleeping," Ge pointed out.

"Could've fooled me," Matt replied before fading out of sight.

"Send me back please Ge," Chris asked him.

"You can do it yourself, just envision yourself fading into nothingness," Ge told him.

"It's that easy?" Chris asked in shock.

"Of course, I had to design it so that Mi could do it after all," Ge replied.

"Hey!" Mi yelled and Chris sensed another argument brewing.

Chris smiled and saw Mi storming over toward Ge as the world faded around him and cast him into a deep dreamless sleep.

Cassy awoke in a strange place, unsure of how she got there. As she looked around her she realized she was in an inn, most likely the Gallant Dragon if her memory served her correctly. The more she tried to remember the foggier things became. She had kissed Ditrina, she remembered that much, and after that...drinking. Lots and lots of drinking. And something about dancing? She wasn't sure and didn't know if she wanted to remember the details.

"Good morning," Ditrina said.

Cassy shot bolt upright in surprise but wished she hadn't, her head suddenly felt as if someone was hitting her with an axe. She let out a pathetic moan and slumped forward, face in hands. Ditrina sang something softly, and Cassy felt the pain subside until she was able to sit up again.

"Thanks Di; that really helped," Cassy said gratefully.

"Of course Cas," Ditrina said with a smile.

Cassy then realized that Ditrina was sitting tucked into the same bed as her.

"Di, did we..." Cassy began nervously but trailed off unsure how to properly ask her question.

Ditrina cocked her head to the side in the way Cassy found so cute and looked at her with her large black eyes not understanding.

"Did we do what?" Ditrina asked her curiously.

Deciding that nothing too outrageous had happened while she was drunk Cassy smiled at her.

"Nothing Di, thanks for watching over me," Cassy told her.

"Anytime Cas," Ditrina said and gave her a small smile. "You should try to find Matthew, he has the money your performance earned," she added.

"Performance? What performance?" Cassy asked.

"Turns out you are a remarkably good dancer, even while intoxicated," Ditrina remarked.

Cassy groaned.

"At least tell me I kept my clothes on?" Cassy asked hopefully.

"You did, but I don't see how that makes much of a difference, your usual outfit is quite revealing," Ditrina pointed out.

Cassy looked down at herself and saw she was wearing only a long nightgown.

"Speaking of my clothes, where are they?" Cassy asked her.

"Oh, you were quite sweaty after your dance, so I changed you into that before I put you to bed," Ditrina told her.

"You undressed me?" Cassy asked her a little surprised.

Ditrina looked at her blankly with her dark eyes not understanding.

"I said that already, are you ok Cas?" Ditrina asked with slight concern.

Deciding Ditrina wasn't following the same trail of thought that she was Cassy let the matter slide.

"*Anyway...*" Cassy said moving on. "I'm going to track down the others and see about getting my gold," Cassy said as she slipped out of bed.

"Hopefully the next time I'm undressing you you'll be awake so we can enjoy it more," Ditrina called softly as Cassy was opening the door to leave, causing her to stop in her tracks.

"I hope so too," Cassy said blushing furiously before shutting the door behind her.

After taking a moment to collect herself Cassy moved to track down Matt to get her money, and to question her brother as to why he let her dance around like a fool all night.

Chris awoke feeling happier than he had in his entire life, an achievement he attributed to Sarah who was still sleeping beside him. It seemed during the night she had snuggled closer to him and wrapped her arms around his body, holding onto him as she utilized his chest as a pillow. Chris shifted slightly to better see her and Sarah made a small sleepy noise, hugging him tighter, but made no move to awaken.

Chris lay still, enjoying the peaceful moment. He watched Sarah's striking face as she slept, and thought she looked more at peace than he had ever seen her. He stroked the back of her head lightly, feeling the smoothness of her soft hair, which had fanned out across the covers while she slept like a red silken sheet. Sarah smiled slightly in her sleep. They stayed close, enjoying each other's company and the quiet of the morning until the door of their room burst open.

"Chris! What the hell were you thinking having people pay to watch me dance?!" Cassy yelled as she barged in shaking a sizable bag of coins angrily.

She stopped in her tracks as she saw Sarah nestled against Chris. She stood there, mouth agape; green eyes the size of moons as Matt raced into view.

"Wait don't...go... in... there..." Matt trailed off as he saw the damage was done.

Cassy looked between Matt and Chris in shock as Sarah raised her head sleepily off Chris's chest, face hidden behind a curtain of hair. She yawned and tossed her head back, regaining her sight and smiled at Chris, still not noticing their unexpected guests. Seeing that Chris was looking at the door rather than her Sarah glanced in Cassy's direction.

Matt decided it would be best if he removed himself from the situation as fast as possible and disappeared out of sight while Cassy backed away slowly, still unsure of what to do. Sarah slid her arm out from under Chris and reached off the edge of the bed, sitting up suddenly holding one of her thick bladed short swords. In one smooth motion she gave the sword a small toss, griped it by the hilt and hurled it at the doorway.

Cassy yelped and slammed the door shut in the nick of time as Sarah's sword thudded into the space she had just occupied. The sword sunk deep into the back of the door quivering slightly and they heard rapid footsteps retreating down the hall.

"It's rude not to knock," Sarah yawned then snuggled back against Chris's chest, returning to sleep before he could speak.

Two hours later the entirety of Shearcliff and Company stood assembled outside of the inn having eaten breakfast and readied their gear.

"Alright, today we're going to head up to the castle to talk to the steward. Mr. Norton seemed to think he might have work for us. We also need to restock our supplies and pick up some equipment while we're in town," Chris said holding up a small list of things they needed to buy.

"Well I don't see the need for all of us to go to the castle," Ditrina pointed out. "Chris needs to go as our leader, and one other person should probably accompany him, but the rest of us can handle the shopping."

"Any volunteer's to head up to the castle with me?" Chris asked.

Sarah shrugged, Ditrina shook her head, and Cassy seemed to be not paying attention.

"I'll head up with you; I might see a relative of mine," Matt said.

"Sorry, but I've had my fill of castle types," Sarah explained.

Chris nodded his understanding.

"I'm sure he's a fine Baron and all, it's just that dealing with Sorros for so long has put a foul taste in my mouth whenever I talk to someone sitting in a throne," she elaborated.

"I'm kind of surprised you don't wanna tag along Ditrina," Matt said. "I would've thought you would want to meet a human ruler."

"Usually I would agree with you but I have other plans for today," Ditrina told him.

"Really? Do tell," Matt said.

"I'm going to visit the merchant district with Cassy. We'll be able to find most of the things on the list while we're there as well," Ditrina explained.

"Have fun you two," Sarah said with a smile, all traces of her morning fury long forgotten. "I'll pick up everything you guys can't find by myself; I actually have things I need to pick up as well."

"So its decided then. Me and Matt will head up to the castle to talk to the steward or the Baron or whoever we can find, Cassy and Ditrina will head to the merchant district, and Sarah will pick up the odds and ends. Anything anyone wants to say before we head out?" Chris asked.

"Matt and I," Matt said.

"What?" Chris asked.

"You said me and Matt; it should be *Matt and I*," Matt explained. "You need to sound educated in front of the Baron if you want him to take you seriously, I know that may be hard for you," Matt said with a smirk.

"Shut up Matt" Chris sighed.

The castle was far bigger up close. Chris had briefly seen the castle at Draclige, but had done his best to avoid it at the time; as such this was his first time getting to examine one in detail. It was an impressive structure, standing in the center of town like a stone sentinel keeping watch. It seemed impossibly old, with years of wind weathering the stones until they appeared smooth and without seam, like a mountain with doors and windows. Despite its aged appearance the castle seemed to pulse with a life of its own. Bright banners fluttered on the parapets and voices could be heard drifting from within.

"Do you think it's cold in there?" Chris asked as they approached the gates.

"Probably not, it's spring time so it's warm enough outside to keep the temperature comfortable within the walls, and in the winter castles light plenty of fires to ward away the chill," Matt told him.

"Have you spent much time inside castles?" Chris inquired.

"Not really, but truth be told many of the temples in Hailguard are the size of castles so there's not much difference really," Matt explained.

By now they had reached the entrance to the castle and found their path blocked by a pair of armored soldiers with halberds.

"Halt," the older of the two soldiers told them as they lowered their halberds across the gateway forming an X. "What business do you have in the castle?" he asked them.

"We're here to talk to the steward, heard he might have work for adventurers," Chris told them.

"The steward is bedridden with stomach flu; you'll have to come back some other time," the soldier said but his younger companion shook his head.

"Actually, I heard the Baron himself saying he wanted to hire somebody to investigate a problem in Torville earlier, maybe we should let them through?" the younger soldier asked.

"Fine," the older soldier said and lifted his halberd. "Escort them to the throne room and keep them out of trouble," he told his companion.

"Don't worry, we never cause trouble," Matt told them and the older soldier chuckled.

"Well don't start now," he told them.

"Please follow me," the younger soldier told them and led them into the castle.

The castle was abuzz with activity. Servants rushed across their path, darting in and out of rooms and through corridors.

"Where are they heading off to?" Chris asked as they walked.

"Not sure," the young soldier replied. "Some are messengers bringing news from one end of the castle to the other; others are carrying out various duties to ensure life in the castle stays as smooth as possible."

"Where is the throne room?" Chris asked him.

"It's located in the center of the castle, on the first floor," the soldier told him.

Chris nodded and continued to gawk at his surroundings.

"There's an awful lot of banners," Matt remarked.

"Yeah, the Baroness likes decorating. Every couple of months she has the staff move them around. Truth be told I'm glad I answer to the Baron and not her, not that there's anything wrong with the Baroness, don't misunderstand me," the soldier stammered. "It's just that the soldiers under her command end up acting more like servants and less like guards. If I wanted to be a servant I would have been a servant you know?" he said.

"I get you," Matt chuckled. "One of the priestess back in Hailguard was like that. She treated her clergy like her personal slaves, making them do every little thing for her. I'm glad I didn't end up serving under her."

"Which of the ten did she serve?" the soldier asked.

"Hikara, goddess of extravagance," Matt replied with a laugh.

"Makes sense then doesn't it," the soldier said joining in on Matt's laughter.

"Yeah, I guess," Matt said with a relaxed sigh.

"So which of the gods do you serve?" the soldier asked him.

Matt's joy turned to ash.

"I'm, uh well you see…" Matt began.

"My friend here is currently unsworn," Chris said sparing Matt's pride.

"Well if that's the case after you speak with the Baron you should head over to the castle's temple. We keep a small shrine to Yorken if you're interested," the soldier suggested.

"Thanks, but the god of harvest has already rejected me. I doubt he's changed his mind in the past two years," Matt told him.

"That's a shame; we could really use a new priest. Our current one is getting up in his years," the soldier said.

"Try sending a message to the capital, they'll happily arrange to send you a new priest," Matt told him.

"The Baron tried that, but we haven't heard back and it's been almost a year now. It's not like godless clerics are just wandering around aimlessly, now are they?" the soldier asked and Chris gave a small snort of laughter. "In any event, we're here. If you change your mind about the whole priest thing let the Baron know, I'm sure he'll give you a try. You'll find him right through those doors ahead of you," the soldier said pointing to a pair of grand iron bound oaken doors standing at the end of the corridor. "I'll be heading back to my post if that's all you need," the soldier told them.

"Thanks, I think we'll be alright from here," Chris told him and the soldier gave a wave and retreated the way they had come.

When they were alone Matt turned to Chris.

"Unsworn, that has a lot nicer of a ring than godless, doesn't it?" he mused.

"See? I got your back," Chris said with a small laugh. "Come on, let's go meet the Baron."

Chris pushed open the doors.

"Ah hello there, who might you be?" asked an aging bald man who they nearly bumped into as they stepped into the room.

"Oh, my apologies sir, we were just heading in to speak to the Baron is all," Chris told him.

"How fortunate, had you been a few minutes later you would have missed me," the man said.

"Sir?" Chris asked slightly confused.

"How rude of me," the man said. "Allow me to introduce myself; my name is Francis Severt, Baron of Bleakstar."

Chris looked at the small man with shock; he had been expecting a large man wearing expensive flowing robes and jewelry.

Baron Francis was the stark opposite; he was small and wiry, wearing a brown robe of plain make. His only adornment was a small gold wedding band on his hand. Matt hastily dropped to a knee and bowed and Chris followed suit after a moment's confusion.

"So sorry my lord, we didn't know it was you," Matt said nervously.

Baron Francis laughed.

"Stand up my boy, stand up. No need for such tedious formalities," the Baron said.

"Yes, my lord," Matt said as they rose.

"Relax, you're not on trial boys," the Baron said. "And there's no need for the lord this lord that nonsense, just call me Francis."

"Yes my... I mean yes Francis," Matt said.

"That's better. Now, who might you two be?" Francis asked.

"I'm Christian Shearcliff," Chris told him. "You can just call me Chris though."

"I'm Matthew...Bleakstar," Matt said knowing that this opened up a long conversation about his past.

"Bleakstar eh?" Francis said to himself. "You have the look of a cleric, but aside from father Simon over at the temple I don't believe we have any clerics within Bleakstar, let alone one with a name like yours. How did you come to be called Bleakstar?" Francis asked him.

"My mother said her grandfather was the illegitimate son of one of your predecessors. As such my family has used the name Bleakstar for many years now," Matt explained.

"How interesting, and where does your family live?" Francis asked.

"We're from Hailguard," Matt told him.

"Ah the capitol, how exciting. It's been many years since I've paid a visit to the capitol. It may be time for me to drop by wouldn't you agree?" Francis asked.

"Of course," Matt said hastily but Chris shrugged.

"I don't know you, have a wonderful city right here, so why leave? This place is a lot nicer than Draclige anyway. I've never been to the capitol so I can't vouch for it but I'm sure it's not half as nice as this place," Chris told him.

Francis was quiet for a second then burst out laughing.

"Wonderful! It's rare I find someone willing to speak their mind around me. Most just go along blindly with whatever I say in hopes of currying my favor. I find you quite refreshing Chris. Come, walk with an old man," Francis told them and began strolling down the corridor at a rapid pace for a man of his age towards a staircase they had passed on their way through.

They soon found themselves standing atop the ramparts staring out across Bleakstar and the neighboring farms.

"Lovely view," Matt commented.

"Indeed. I like to come up here and look out across my people to remind myself why I'm here. The reason I have my land, my titles, my power, it's all for them. If I'm not trying to help the people charged to me what is it I am doing with my station?" Francis asked them.

"If you didn't put your people first you would be a poor ruler," Chris told him. "Like Sorros," he added and Matt tensed up.

The Baron seemed shocked as well but recovered quickly.

"My you really do say whatever's on your mind don't you? Carful now, while I value that quality many with power do not. Be mindful of who you go saying that in front of," Francis warned. "But between us, yes, that would make me no better than that tyrant Sorros," he said and Matt visibly relaxed.

"We came to you looking for work Francis," Chris said moving the matter to business.

"Really, and what might you be able to do for me?" Francis asked with a curious smile.

"Well that's what I was hoping you could tell us. We represent Shearcliff and Company, adventurers heading south looking for work," Chris explained.

Francis seemed to grow interested.

"How many people are you traveling with by any chance?" Francis asked.

"We're a rather small band, currently we have five members," Chris told him.

"Splendid!" Francis exclaimed. "As it turns out I have a problem that requires dealing with, one that requires a certain amount of discretion preventing me from using my own soldiers."

"Would this problem happen to be in Torville?" Matt asked.

"Why yes, how did you know that?" Francis asked slightly taken back.

"One of your soldier let us into the castle because he thought we could help you with some matter regarding Torville. It seems he was correct," Matt told him.

"Wonderful," the Baron clapped. "So you'll kill the vampire for me?"

"What?!" Chris and Matt exclaimed.

"My apologies, it seems I've gotten ahead of myself. The problem I'm faced with revolves around unsettling rumors we've received from Torville. From what we've heard a vampire has settled in the area and enthralled the villagers. If I send in my soldiers the vampire will just likely lay low and we'll be unable to find them. I need you to go to Torville and investigate discreetly. Find out if there's any merit to these rumors and if so, deal with the monster. I can't have some beast preying upon my people after all," Francis told them. "So I want you to take the contract to slay whatever monster lurks in Torville."

"Sure, we'll handle it," Chris told him while Matt looked horrified.

"Excellent, when the matter is concluded I shall pay you fifteen hundred gold for your time, even if it turns out that there is no vampire. Report back to me when it is settled, and please, make haste," Francis told them and handed Chris a small scroll he had produced from within his robe detailing their contract to kill the monster.

Once Chris and Matt had left the castle Matt rounded on Chris.

"What in the name of the gods were you thinking?" Matt hissed.

"What do you mean?" Chris asked taken back by his anger.

"I'm not even going to start on how you spoke to the Baron, you're lucky he took a liking to you. What were you thinking telling him we can kill a vampire?!" Matt exclaimed.

"It's just another monster right? How hard could it be? We killed like a hundred mimics back in Purevein," Chris said casually.

"Chris do you have any idea what a vampire is?" Matt asked exasperated.

"Of course!" Chris laughed. "It's a person with fangs who drinks blood. They come out at night and die if they get touched by sunlight," Chris told him. "Everyone knows what a vampire is."

"Right, now we've gotten the children's fairytales out of the way let me explain what a vampire is, a *real* vampire, not the country folktale vampire you're prattling on about. Vampires are incredibly powerful monsters. During the day they're nearly impossible to distinguish from a normal person but at night their eyes glow red and they gain incredible powers. Their skin turns as hard as iron and they can run as fast as a horse. While they do have fangs they are small and often difficult to see. It's true they dislike the sun, but it's hardly lethal to them. They can wield magic Chris, powerful magic, and control those around them given enough time. They're not creatures to be taken lightly," Matt warned him.

"You know an awful lot about vampires," Chris commented.

"Part of training as a cleric is learning to fight the creatures of darkness. I'm not talking about the random beasts that stalk the woods like the dire wolves we ran into; I'm talking about the most wicked of beings. They hide among the people and use them as food or fodder in their spells. Doppelgangers, ghouls, ghosts, and worst of all...vampires!" Matt yelled.

"Well if you trained to deal with them this should be easy then," Chris argued.

"Chris, even if I was a regular cleric with all the power that goes along with that I couldn't deal with a vampire by myself. They told us if ever faced with a vampire to call for backup, a minimum of at least eight fully trained clerics, and to expect heavy casualties," Matt told him, trying desperately to make him understand the danger.

"Well lucky for you you're not going to be alone," Chris told him "We'll discuss this more with the others back at the inn."

CHAPTER FOURTEEN

"You agreed to do what?!" Ditrina yelled excitedly.

"We're going to investigate a vampire report, yes," Chris told her again.

"How wonderful, vampires are incredibly rare. I'll get a chance to add this to my report to the elven council!" Ditrina said with enthusiasm.

"You guys aren't getting how much danger we're walking into!" Matt begged them.

"Well we need work, and we don't have the luxury of just taking the easy jobs," Sarah told him. "If we want to start gathering a good reputation for ourselves slaying a vampire is a good place to start."

"See? They get that this is a good idea," Chris told Matt.

"What about you Cassy?" Matt said as he turned to her, imploring her to help his cause.

"Well I'm not a fan of hunting someone just because of what they are," Cassy said looking at her scaled hands. "But if everything you just told me is true vampires are very dangerous, and they feed directly upon the people around them. I say let's take it down."

"I thought some of you would see reason," Matt said and his shoulders slumped.

"Matt, are you saying you're not going to help us?" Chris asked him.

"Of course I'm going to help you!" Matt snapped angrily.

"Good, because if this proves as dangerous as you claim we'll need your magic to survive," Chris told him.

"Agreed, your healing magic shall prove invaluable. I'll handle offense," Ditrina told him.

"Aside from Matt I'm the only one with any armor, and I doubt he'll be getting close to the creature. I'll try to keep it busy," Sarah told them.

"I can keep it from using magic. If it uses magic like you guys do then it has to speak to use spells. I'll put an arrow in its face whenever it opens its mouth; that should keep its mind off magic," Cassy said firmly.

"Remember, our job is recon. There's no guarantee that we'll have to fight anything at all, but if it comes to it I'm sure my sword will finish the creature off," Chris told them all.

"Well at least we have a plan," Matt said gloomily.

"Don't worry Matt, everything will be fine," Chris reassured him.

They left that later that afternoon. Torville was roughly a day's ride away from Bleakstar, so they planned on arriving sometime after noon the next day. As they traveled they grew somber, as the weight of their mission bore down upon them. Their sullen mood was helped little by Matt who had spent the entire ride thus far praying quietly. When asked to stop he simply replied:

"We'll need all the help we can get."

They decided not to press the matter further.

By that evening there was little joy to go around. They made camp in silence with Matt casting a spell that would alert them to intruders he had recently learned from the book so that they didn't need to post a guard. The tone of the camp changed when it came time to pitch the tents.

"Sarah, what are you doing?" Cassy asked as she noticed her digging through her gear while the others were pitching the tents.

"Well you remember I told you earlier I had some things to pick up while we were in Bleakstar?" Sarah replied.

"Yeah?" Cassy asked curiously. "What of it?"

"I was looking for this," Sarah said as she pulled a new tent proudly out from under her other gear.

Cassy looked blankly at the tent for a moment until comprehension flooded onto her face.

"Oh, well that's...nice," she said blushing to the roots of her hair, unsure of what to think of this matter.

"Well I figured you and Ditrina may like some more privacy, and this way Chris and I get to spent some more time together. I thought it was a pretty good idea if I do say so," Sarah said happily.

"Yes, a wonderful idea," Cassy said warming up to the idea realizing she and Ditrina now had a tent to themselves.

"What's the problem?" Chris asked as he walked over.

"Why do you just assume there's a problem?" Cassy asked him.

"Well you two are talking. That usually means a problem either has occurred, or one is about to," Chris told her.

"Sarah was just telling me how she purchased a new tent back in town is all." Cassy explained.

"Why did she buy a new tent?" Chris asked confused.

"Well I assumed you'd like to spend some time together other than the odd night we end up in a town," Sarah explained with exasperation in her voice.

"Of course!" Chris said hastily.

"Well unless you want to share our quality time together with *Matt* you might be interested in sharing this new tent with me," Sarah told him.

"What's this about a new tent?" Matt asked walking over hearing his name.

"Sarah bought a new tent for us," Chris told him.

"Well what was wrong with our old tent? The two of us fit just fine," Matt said confused.

"He means us as me and him, you'll be staying in the old tent," Sarah told Matt slightly irritated.

"Well who the hell am I going to share a tent with now?" Matt asked turning to Chris. "You should just stay in the old tent with me. The men's tent woman's tent system works fine," Matt argued.

"That system doesn't work so well when two of the women are in a relationship," Sarah explained to Matt.

"If that's the case then you should just use the new tent by yourself. Don't steal my bunkmate just because you want someone to keep you warm at night," Matt said irritably.

"Shouldn't Chris decide this matter himself?" Ditrina asked, summoned by the growing debate. "As the leader, it's his job to assign sleeping arrangements anyway, and it is him you're arguing over,"

"Good idea; Chris tell her you're going to stay with me," Matt said turning to his friend.

"It seems you have two choices; you can go on sharing your old tent with Matt, or you can start sleeping with *me* in the new tent," Sarah said putting her hands on her hips.

"Tough choice, tough choice," Chris said miming uncertainty.

He must have been a little too convincing because Matt's face lit up with hope while Sarah's eyes flashed with murderous rage.

"I'm kidding!" he exclaimed quickly holding up his hands.

"So you'll be staying in our tent then?" Matt asked hopefully.

"Sorry buddy," Chris said giving Matt a pat on the shoulder. "I'll gather up my gear from Matt's tent while you pitch the new one," he said turning to Sarah.

Her face lit up with joy, rage forgotten.

"Perfect! It'll only take a moment," Sarah told him and began busying herself with the tent's poles.

Chris walked off to his old tent and began tiding up his things for transfer while Matt stood defeated with Cassy and Ditrina.

"How could he just go and ditch me?" Matt asked quietly.

"Well unlike you Sarah has a vested interest in sleeping with him. Unless you suddenly decide you prefer men I doubt you can compete with that," Cassy said with a shrug.

"Logically it makes sense for Chris to choose Sarah over you," Ditrina told him.

"Well that makes me feel better," Matt spat.

"I'm glad I was able to help," Ditrina said cheerfully and Matt looked at her angrily.

"Di, Matt was being sarcastic, you've pissed him off," Cassy whispered in her ear.

Ditrina gave a small jump of surprise.

"So sorry Matthew, I meant no offense. I was merely alluding to the fact that you and Chris share a special bond, you get to spend the time you are asleep speaking in private giving you access to more of Chris's company than any other person living. Sarah has no such bond, if she wishes to spend time with our leader she must find that time when they are both awake. I figured such things wouldn't need explaining," Ditrina said with a small shrug.

Matt gave a small sigh.

"Yeah I get it; I'm just a little annoyed he chose so quickly is all," Matt told them.

"I'll say it again because it seems you're not getting it; Sarah has a thing for my brother. For reasons I can't begin to understand she see's something in the little dork. Chris hasn't really had much experience with women, at least not in that I saw while we were living together, and I doubt that changed once I moved out. Now he's got a girl crawling all over him, a girl who's pledged her undying loyalty to him at that," Cassy explained.

"Yes that was indeed a touching little speech they had, we probably shouldn't have been listening," Ditrina said without showing the slightest sign of remorse.

"It's not our fault they were talking so loudly, those tents don't keep out much sound," Cassy argued.

"When was this?" Matt asked them surprised.

"A little after we left Purevein," Cassy informed him.

"If you saw this coming why didn't you tell me?" Matt asked her; annoyed that yet again he was the last to know these things. "And why were you so surprised when you walked in on them this morning?" Matt added confused.

"Well I figured you heard their conversation as well as we did. How were we supposed to know you were asleep?" Cassy rationalized. "As for my surprise, I honestly didn't expect Chris to manage to pull it off. I figured he'd blow it somehow and Sarah would end up gutting him."

"So you were just going to wait around until Sarah disemboweled your brother?" Matt asked shocked.

"Well yeah, I figured you'd just put him back together again like you usually do," Cassy said with a shrug.

"That's horrible!" Matt exclaimed.

"What's horrible is you trying to stop your best friend from scoring. You should be all for Chris and Sarah sharing a tent," Cassy scolded.

"That brings me to my next comment, I seriously hope you two remember what you said about those tents and noise, they're just as bad at keeping noise in as they are keeping it out," Matt warned them.

Cassy had the decency to look embarrassed and blushed while Ditrina just nodded.

"I'll be sure to cast the proper muffling spells in the future before we..." Ditrina began.

"That's fine Di! Matt really doesn't need to hear any more," Cassy said now blushing as red as Sarah's hair.

"Noted," Ditrina said simply.

"Shouldn't you be carrying that warning to the lovebirds over there as well?" Cassy asked him moving the subject away from herself.

"While I can put your brother back together if something goes wrong, I doubt a cleric alive could save me if I say that in front of Sarah," Matt said seriously.

Later that night Chris found himself lying awake unable to sleep, Matt's familiar snoring drifting from the tent next to him, the only sound in the inky darkness. He ran through the events of the last couple of days over and over again in his head and felt that perhaps Matt was correct. They had barely survived the hoard of mimics at Purevein, and from everything he had been told a vampire was leagues above such simple creatures. How could they hope to slay such a powerful foe? What if he was leading his friends to their deaths?

"What are you still doing awake?" Sarah muttered sleepily from beside him.

They had pushed their bedrolls next to one another so that they could sleep next to each other.

"Go back to bed," Chris cooed and stroked her head.

Sarah sat up slowly.

"Is something wrong Chris?" she asked softly.

"It's nothing, don't worry yourself over it," Chris told her as he sat up himself.

"Don't be like that," Sarah said softly. "We're together now Chris, I want to be able to help you in ways that don't involve beating our enemies to a pulp, but for me to do that you've got to talk to me," she told him and he felt her press close against him in the darkness.

"I'm just worried about us...all of us," Chris said softly. "Matt may be a strange example of a cleric but he knows his craft. I believe him when he says this is dangerous. How can I make sure none of us get hurt facing this thing? I hardly have any experience with fighting and the only reason I've made it this far is because I have a magic sword, yet somehow they all expect me to lead them to victory," Chris told her. "I'm unfit to be leading Shearcliff and Company," he announced quietly.

Sarah was silent, but held him tighter.

"Chris, you may not be the most experienced man when it comes to fighting but you are without a doubt the only person fit to lead us," Sarah said.

Chris gave a small sad laugh.

"Sarah if anything you should be the one leading us. You've traveled the world and have experience the rest of us lack," Chris told her.

Though he couldn't see her face Chris felt Sarah shaking her head no against his chest.

"Chris I may be a capable warrior but I'm a poor leader. During my stint under Sorros I commanded almost two-hundred men; I wasn't cut out for it. I was overly harsh, and often I felt as if I had to do everything myself. As a result I mismanaged the people I had under my command and put myself in bad situations that could have easily been avoided. For example if I had simply put out an order to bring you in the day you arrived in Draclige it's unlikely you would have escaped like you did," Sarah told him.

"Let's be glad you're a poor leader then," Chris said and lightly kissed the top of her head.

"Besides Chris, a leader doesn't have to be the strongest fighter of the group. You just have to be able to utilize the people under your command effectively," Sarah added.

"I know; I'm just worried that someone will get seriously hurt. We got lucky back in Purevein with Ditrina saving us in the nick of time, then again with me having the one thing on all of Targoth that could have saved Matt. How long can that luck hold?" Chris asked her.

"There's no such thing as luck Chris, or fate. Things happen because someone or something makes them happen, not because there's some invisible plan for us all. If you're in a battle and your friend gets hit by an arrow and you don't it doesn't make you any luckier than him, it just means the archer was aiming for him and not you. While we can't control every little part of our lives in the end we make our own decisions. You just have to trust that that'll be enough to see you safely to the end," Sarah told him.

"That's why I'm so worried in the first place, what if I make a bad decision and someone dies because of me!" Chris exclaimed quietly.

"People make mistakes Chris. Shit happens and sometimes people die. Matt, Cassy, Ditrina, they don't follow you because they think you make them invincible. It's because you're so worried about them that they follow you. They all had their own reasons for joining our band, but the thing that keeps them here is you Chris. They trust that you'll do your best to keep them safe, and that trust is well founded. You're as concerned with their safety as you are with your own, I'd even say more so. That's another reason your better suited to lead than I am. If things get ugly the only one I'm going to worry about protecting is you, but no matter what happens you're always watching over all of them. I admire that about you," Sarah told him. "You just have to trust yourself the way they do."

"What did I do to deserve someone like you?" Chris asked her still holding her tightly.

"Sparing my life was a good start," Sarah said teasingly.

"I thought I told you to forget about that?" Chris asked bemused.

"Did you? Perhaps you should take my mind off it then," Sarah told him as they kissed, pulling him to the ground.

As they broke camp the next morning Matt singled out Chris at the edge of camp, and took the opportunity to speak to him alone.

"You didn't show up to our meeting in the grey until pretty late last night," Matt remarked "By the time you arrived the brothers had already gone home for the evening and I was just about to leave."

"Sorry, Sarah and I were going over strategies to deal with the vampire," Chris lied.

"Are you sure that was all you were doing?" Matt asked with a knowing grin.

"What do you mean? Chris asked feigning ignorance.

"Well Al seemed pretty distracted last night, and at one point Mi started cheering. Mind telling me what that was all about?" Matt asked innocently.

"I don't know what you're talking about," Chris said shaking his head, but he couldn't help the wide grin that spread across his face.

"That's my boy!" Matt exclaimed and clapped Chris on the back. "I knew you had it in you. Tell me, how was it?" Matt asked.

"Leave him alone," Sarah said with a small yawn from behind them carrying an armful of gear. "If you tease him too much I'll have to feed you to the vampire."

Matt nearly jumped out of his skin.

"Gods Sarah, don't sneak up on us like that," Matt said catching his breath.

"How else would I hear your enlightening conversations?" Sarah asked with a hint of malice in her voice.

"You could just ask questions like a normal person!" Matt argued.

"That's less fun though, this way I can remind you that if you piss me off I can kill you without you ever knowing I'm coming," Sarah said cheerfully before walking off to the horses to stow the gear while whistling a happy tune.

"Well she's in a good mood this morning," Matt remarked.

Looking around to ensure no other prying ears were nearby and seeing that Cassy and Ditrina were still taking down their tent on the other side of the camp Chris grinned.

"Well she should be," Chris said giving Matt a small wink.

"That confident in yourself huh?" Matt laughed.

"You're lucky you were talking to the brothers or else we might have woken you up," Chris said his grin widening.

"Yeah, but not all of us have that luxury!" Cassy called angrily from across the clearing.

Chris and Matt spun in terror.

"Good hearing, remember!?" Cassy said pointing to one of her ears.

The ride to Torville was uneventful. Chris ran through the mission one final time to ensure there was no confusion.

"So here's the plan, Cassy and Ditrina will walk around looking at shops, seeing if anything is out of the ordinary. The key is to make sure you're noticed. Two exotic nonhumans walking around a small town like this should give the villagers plenty to gossip about and draw attention away from the rest of us. Sarah and I will try to talk to shopkeepers without raising suspicion, see what they may let slip about the vampire. Matt I want you to sniff around looking for any trace of magic. Anything you find will most likely be our shadow loving friend so if you can track it that will make our jobs much easier. Remember everyone; we don't know who the vampire is, or how many people it may have enthralled so we have to be discreet. At the end of the day we'll meet up outside of town and compare what we've found," Chris told them.

Torville itself was built into a small grove of trees within the hills. It was a newer village and such there was little farmland surrounding the town, it seemed they relied heavily upon Bleakstar for necessities. The buildings were scattered around a wide main street with a few offshoots leading to smaller shops. It seemed that rather than clearing the trees the villagers had simply built their homes around them, and the streets twisted and turned under the dappled forest light. It reminded Chris of home. As they had planned they arrived slightly after noon. They tethered the horses and made camp outside of town, close enough that they could almost hear the voices of the villagers going about their day. They sent Cassy and Ditrina ahead of the group to divert attention. Only a short while later they heard volume of the town's people increase, and they took this as a sign the villagers had taken the bait. Matt was sent next to slip into the crowd while their attention was still fixed upon the women. Chris and Sarah waited half an hour, long enough they determined that the villagers had returned to their normal activities, but not so long that they had pushed the two strange women from their minds. At the end of their wait they prepared to head into the village.

"It might be best if you don't wear your armor," Chris advised Sarah.

"How do you expect me to fight the vampire without my armor?" Sarah replied irritably.

"I don't. Remember this is just a recon run. If we find the vampire we'll pull out and gear up to hit it when we're prepared. As it is if you go stomping in there wearing full combat gear it'll raise suspicion," Chris warned her.

"Fine, but I'm taking my weapons at least," Sarah said but Chris shook his head.

"That would look just as odd. We're trying to blend in remember? We'll stand out if we're armed to the teeth," Chris said.

"We'll you're going to be taking your sword right? Why can't I bring mine?" Sarah asked annoyed.

"In small villages like this it's not customary for women to carry weapons. If I have my sword I'll look like I'm carrying it to protect you, if we both have swords it'll look strange, trust me," Chris told her.

"What makes you the authority on village life?" Sarah asked angrily.

"You grew up with soldiers; I grew up in a place like this. On this matter I reign supreme, *trust me*," Chris told her again.

"Fine," Sarah sighed. "If we're trying to get into character thought we need a cover. If people ask questions we need our answers to match up," Sarah told him.

"That makes sense, have anything in mind?" Chris asked her.

Sarah thought for a minute.

"Ok, how about this. You're my fiancé, and we're traveling from

Draclige on a holiday. I know the area really well so if people ask too many questions I can deal with them," Sarah proposed.

"Not a bad idea, what do I need to do?" Chris asked.

"Just keep your mouth shut if they seem to know anything about Draclige and try your best to look madly in love with me," Sarah told him.

"Shouldn't be too hard," Chris replied with a chuckle.

"The only problem is we're not dressed for the part. Your sword is too finely made for some commoner; even bumpkins like these can see that. Same goes for the big fancy clasps on your cloak, they'll think your some rich merchant or a noble or something," Sarah told him.

"Well what's wrong with that?" Chris asked confused.

"You may be dress for the part but I'm not. All I've got to wear is what you see," Sarah said gesturing to the rugged leather garb she wore to fit under her armor.

While functional Chris agreed it was far from fitting attire for a nobleman's wife.

"Well Ditrina's clothes are too small, so why don't you borrow some of my sister's clothes? She's taller on account of her legs but your bodies are about the same size," Chris told her.

Sarah blushed as red as her hair.

"I didn't sign up to go parading around town dressed like a whore," Sarah said firmly.

"What's wrong with Cas's clothes?" Chris asked with a small smile.

"You've seen them right? I might as well walk through town naked for all those clothes are worth!" Sarah said unamused by his suggestion.

"Well do you have a better idea?" Chris asked her.

Sarah opened her mouth to reply but shut it without making a sound. Chris raised an eyebrow and waited.

"Wait here," Sarah commanded angrily and stormed over to Cassy's tent.

Chris turned around and waited patiently, hearing the sound of Sarah rustling through Cassy's gear and cursing softly to herself. A couple minutes later Sarah reappeared.

"That looks good on you," Chris said with admiration.

Sarah had chosen to wear the same handmade outfit that Cassy had worn when she first joined them, the red of the cloth matching her hair quite well.

"Shut up. When we finish this mission I'm having a long talk with your sister about clothes that cover your stomach. I mean seriously, this is the most concealing outfit she has! How the hell does she expect to survive in a fight dressed like this?" Sarah ranted.

"Well she uses a bow and tries not to get hit," Chris laughed.

"Yeah, we all remember how well that worked out in Purevein," Sarah grumbled.

"Still, that does look really good on you," Chris told her with a genuine smile. "Between your hair and the clothes your blue eyes really stand out," he said trying to calm her down slightly.

It seemed to do the trick.

"Yeah, well, I doubt they'll be staring at my eyes," Sarah said darkly, but Chris noted that she was no longer yelling and counted it as a victory. "Come on Chris, let's try to look like were having a good time and not get killed," Sarah said taking his arm and leading him into the town.

They walked through the streets for almost an hour, browsing from shop to shop. As they walked they scanned the crowd looking for signs of irregularity but saw nothing. Sarah played the part of his betrothed well; she clung to his arm laughing airily at whatever he said. It was a convincing performance, but it felt wrong. The twittering thing Sarah had become wasn't her. For his part he tried his best to look at everything as if it wasn't nearly good enough for him, picking up items far above his price range, looking down his nose at them before returning them to the shelves feigning disgust. Few people spoke to them, and to their pleasure the town was still abuzz with the news of the elf and the naga from that morning. They spotted Cassy and Ditrina once, at the far end of the street, but did their best to avoid them. They began questioning shopkeepers as they wandered.

"The town seems quite stirred up today," Chris said feigning boredom while speaking to the blacksmith after rejecting several high-quality daggers.

"Yeah, word has it some snake woman and an elf showed up! Got the town running scared," the blacksmith replied.

"All riled up over a naga? You must not get many travelers in these parts," Chris said with a yawn.

"There was an elf too!" the blacksmith said eagerly.

"Please, everyone knows elves only exist in fairy tales," Chris scoffed.

"It's true!" the blacksmith said angrily.

Deciding to distract him Chris pointed to another dagger hanging on the wall.

"Show me that one," Chris commanded and the smith handed him a large finely made dagger, serrated along it's back.

Sarah broke character for a moment, eyes lighting up with hunger as she stared at the blade. She recovered quickly and the blacksmith didn't seem to notice.

"This one is some of my best work," the blacksmith said proudly. "It's fifty gold if you want it,"

"Sweetheart why don't you wander back to the tailor's shop across the street, all this talk of weapons must be incredibly boring for you," Chris told Sarah, hoping to avoid another breach of character.

Sarah gave him a quick glance, fast enough that the smith again failed to notice, but Chris got the message. She was furious.

"Of course honey," Sarah said with a sweet smile before walking out of the shop.

"Fine woman," the blacksmith remarked.

"Indeed," Chris told him, relieved Sarah had gone quietly. "I'll give you thirty for the dagger."

"Forty-five," the smith said.

"Forty," Chris shot back.

"Done," the blacksmith replied and they shook hands.

Gold was exchanged and Chris stowed the dagger in his bag.

"It's a shame you don't get many exotic travelers," Chris told the man. "We were hoping to see something rare, something you can't find in the city."

"Well you came to the wrong place then, we've never gotten a nonhuman in town until today," the smith said quickly.

"Never?" Chris asked skeptically.

"That's right, never. Have a nice day," the smith said shooing him out of the shop.

"I hope that was worth it," Sarah told him when he returned, her voice making her displeasure known.

"The smith was hiding something; he said this town has never had a nonhuman visitor," Chris told her.

"That's impossible, this place is remote, sure, but everyone sees the odd dwarf here or there from time to time. Saying that they've never seen any nonhumans before is total bullshit," Sarah said puzzled.

"Let's keep looking around, maybe we'll learn something else," Chris told her and they continued toward the next shop.

The other shopkeepers spun similar stories. They were pleasant enough until the topic of nonhumans was brought up, then they clammed up and shooed them out of their stores. Speaking to the villagers proved equally unrewarding, and they all swore that nonhumans never visited Torville.

"So what do you think?" Chris asked Sarah later that afternoon as they sat on a bench having visited almost all of the shops.

"Something is wrong here, the villagers act like their reading off a script. Each and every one claims that they've never gotten a nonhuman visitor before but we both know that's shit. They're hiding something," Sarah told him.

"My thoughts exactly. We've only got one shop left to go, let's go talk to them and meet back with the others. It's getting late and I really don't wanna be out here after dark," Chris replied.

They approached the last shop. It lay on the edge of town, under the branches of a large oak tree. The shop was two storied but appeared small beneath the ancient tree. A small sign hung over the door declaring the building as the local apothecary. Together they walked inside. The store was dimly lit and covered floor to ceiling in shelves, sporting a wide variety of herbs and powders. A staircase ran up the far wall behind the counter.

"Welcome!" the shopkeeper called to them stepping out from behind the counter.

He was a tall well-built fellow, with dark brown eyes and a friendly face. Despite the warm weather, he wore a scarf. "What can I do for you two today?"

"We're just looking for the moment, though you have a quite the wide variety it seems," Chris told him once again adopting the guise of a nobleman.

"Thank you, good sir, my wife picks most everything you see herself," the man said proudly.

"Does she now, she must really know her herbs," Sarah said feigning intense interest at a jar filled with green powder.

"That powder is used for curing colds, it's quite useful," the man explained.

"Thank you for your expertise Mr...." Sarah trailed off looking at him expectantly.

"So sorry miss, my name is Rob, Rob Tuxon. I'm happy to be of assistance," Rob told them.

"So Rob, you and your wife treat the villager's ailments?" Chris asked.

"Mostly just my wife to be honest, I don't have the skill she does. I just run the shop and watch the kids mostly," Rob said sheepishly.

"Are those your children there?" Sarah asked pointing to two small faces, little mirrors of Robs own, peeking eargly down from the top of the stairs with large brown eyes.

"Boys! What have I told you about bothering the customers?" Rob scolded and the children disappeared giggling. "So sorry about them," Rob told them.

"Don't worry, my fiancé and I simply *adore* children," Sarah said in her airy noblewoman's voice.

"Nevertheless, I can't have them bothering my customers," Rob told her.

"So Rob, do you have anything here that would be of help to a nonhuman? One of my friends happens to be suffering a bout of stomach flu and as it happens he's a dwarf," Chris told him, watching for his response.

"Sorry, we don't see any nonhumans here in Torville, so I can't help you," Rob said angrily.

Chris was surprised by the force of his reply.

"Are you sure? Perhaps we could speak to your wife, you said yourself she knows the herbs better than you," Chris said trying to glean information from Rob.

"I said we don't have any and that means we don't have any! Now if you're just going to insult me get the hell out of my shop!" Rob yelled pointing at the door.

Chris opened his mouth to reply but Rob gave him no chance to speak.

"I said get out!" he bellowed.

Chris and Sarah left quickly.

Once they judged they were a safe distance away from the store they stopped to talk.

"Well that was strange," Sarah said.

"Extremely. The other villagers acted like they were reading off a script, but he seemed outright hostile. Do you think he's the vampire?" Chris asked.

"I don't think so, while you two were talking I was watching his teeth, they looked normal enough. Besides he's got kids, the vampire is supposed to be new to town remember? He's been here for several years based on the children," Sarah told him.

"Still, that was a strange performance," Chris remarked.

"I agree; he was definitely hiding something," Sarah said. "Let's meet back with the others and compare notes."

"So, what did you guys find?" Matt asked them when they reached the camp.

Chris and Sarah were the last to arrive.

"We found out that Chris is an ass when he's acting like a noble," Sarah said giving him a dark look.

"*Oooooooh* what did he do?" Cassy asked eagerly.

"He shooed me out of the blacksmith's shop right after I saw a dagger I liked!" Sarah complained, looking angrily at Chris.

Cassy grinned over at Chris from behind Sarah's back before her face became a mask of outrage.

"How dare he!" Cassy said angrily. "Chris, the least you could have done is bought your girlfriend the weapon she wanted," she said shaking her head in mock disgust.

"I had to chase her out, if she had stayed there much longer she would have tried to buy half the store! We were trying *not* to draw attention to ourselves remember?" Chris defended.

"Still, that was pretty rude," Cassy said delighting in the chance to cause a problem.

Sarah seemed in the mood to agree with his sister so Chris was forced to act fast.

"Well I was going to wait until after the mission to give it to you, some time when we weren't distracted by a bloodsucking monster and all, but if you insist," Chris said, annoyed he was forced to give up the gift early.

He slung his bag off his shoulder and produced the weapon in question from within.

"Here, I felt bad you didn't get a chance to look around the shop so I bought it for you," he said offering her the dagger.

Sarah seemed taken back.

"Oh… thanks Chris," she said embarrassed by her earlier reaction.

Cassy seemed slightly surprised but more annoyed than anything else. Her fun had ended without anyone getting stabbed; she was sure given more time she could have had Sarah cutting Chris's arms off.

"You're no fun," Cassy grumbled wandering back over towards her tent.

She stopped suddenly, sensing another chance for mischief.

"Say Sarah, I almost forgot, why are you wearing my clothes? Did Chris make you dress up for him?" she asked innocently.

"I was meaning to talk to you about that," Sarah growled, her anger now redirected at Cassy. "We are going to have a nice long talk about your choice of attire," Sarah said storming toward her.

Cassy looked around in terror, her plan again falling apart.

"Matt did you find any magic in the town?" Cassy asked quickly as Sarah grabbed her by the arm.

"None at all, have fun!" Matt said with a wave as Sarah dragged Cassy away.

The sounds of shouting could soon be heard from the other side of camp.

"Nice save Chris," Matt said, genuinely impressed.

"Yeah, a couple more seconds and it would be me over there getting chewed out," Chris said with relief.

"What is wrong with Cas's clothes?" Ditrina asked not understanding the reason for the verbal abuse drifting across the camp.

"Sarah disagrees with the amount of skin Cassy's chosen garb shows," Chris explained.

"Sarah didn't strike me as being big on modesty," Matt commented.

"To be honest I think her biggest problem with it is it's functionality as armor," Chris said with a chuckle.

"Typical," Matt said shaking his head.

"Cas uses a bow, what need does she have for armor?" Ditrina asked still confused.

"She doesn't," Chris explained. "Sarah's just mad because she had to wear it for the day and unlike my sister Sarah enjoys the protection armor provides."

"Why did Sarah have to wear Cas's clothes?" Ditrina asked still confused.

"We were impersonating traveling nobles to avoided suspicion. Sarah didn't think her clothes were appropriate dress for a nobleman's wife. Sadly, she didn't think about her other choices when she made that decision and ended up dressed like my sister," Chris told her.

"I see. Perhaps we should intervene?" Ditrina commented pointing a long finger at Cassy, who was currently being violently shaken by Sarah.

"Sarah! I think she got the message, lay off alright?" Chris called across the clearing.

Sarah dropped Cassy to the ground in a heap and walked back to Chris's side.

"Are you sure I can't try out the dagger, just a little bit?" she asked caressing the weapon longingly.

"We don't need any injuries right now," Chris told her.

"But Matt can just fix her right? He could keep putting her back together again and again and I could cut her apart as much as I like," Sarah said as if in a daydream.

"I am not condoning this," Matt said firmly.

"Remember the contract; you're not allowed to harm the other party members," Chris reminded her.

Sarah's face fell.

"Well that's no fun," Sarah said with a sigh but thankfully she put the dagger away.

Cassy had managed to pick herself off the ground and returned to the group, doing her best to stay well out of Sarah's reach.

"So, we know that something strange is going on here, but none of us found any trace of the vampire. How should we proceed Chris?" Matt asked.

"I think we should report back to Baron Francis. It will set us back a day but I believe he'll want to know what we've discovered before we begin interrogating his subjects," Chris told them.

They nodded their agreement and were about to begin preparing to depart when Matt stood straight up suddenly.

"Something just passed through my alarm spell!" Matt yelled startling them.

Chris drew his sword quickly while Sarah pulled out her dagger, her other weapons on the far side of camp. Cassy realized her bow was still with her own gear as well and quickly stepped behind her brother. Sarah and Chris did their best to form a barrier between their friends and the unseen intruder, readying their weapons and hearing the beginnings of spells being muttered behind them. They stood unmoving, waiting for the intruder to show themselves. The seconds turned to minutes.

"Hello? Is anyone there?" asked a soft woman's voice from behind the tents.

"Luminita" Matt muttered and a soft pool of sunlight formed in the center of camp, brushing aside the evening shadows. "Step forward into the light and show yourself," Matt called.

They watched as a slim figure slipped out from behind their tents and walked slowly into the light. Matt relaxed.

"It's alright, she's not the vampire," he told them.

"Are you sure?" Chris asked, sword still at the ready.

"My spell creates sunlight, if she was the vampire she would be screaming by now. She's safe," Matt reassured him.

They lowered their weapons and walked towards her.

"What are you doing sneaking around our camp?" Chris demanded.

"It's like you said, I'm here because of the vampire," the woman said with a tremble in her voice.

She had curly brown hair and large eyes, and seemed to be terrified.

"You know about the vampire?" Sarah asked intrigued.

"Y…yes," the woman stammered. "I was the one who sent word to the Baron about the monster. It's horrible, she's bewitched the entire village!" the woman told them.

"She? You know who it is?" Matt asked eargly.

The woman looked at him with large eyes and nodded.

"Yes, there is a man who lives on the edge of town, his name is Rob. He runs the local apothecary," she told them.

"We met; he raged at us and threw us out of his shop, though he seemed pleasant enough at first," Chris told her.

The woman nodded.

"That's because of the vampire; he's even more ensnared than the others," she said.

"Why?" Chris asked.

"Rob was the first one to fall to the vampire's powers, in fact the vampire has been using his home as its lair," she told him.

"You mean the vampire is…" Sarah began.

"Yes, the vampire has bewitched Rob into thinking it's his wife, and has been using him to feed its vile children,"

"The children are vampires as well?!" Sarah exclaimed in shock.

"Yes, she killed Rob's old wife and has fooled the town into thinking that nothing ever happened and now the entire town is just a huge feeding ground for the three of them," the woman sobbed.

She fell to the ground and began to weep, and Cassy knelt beside her to try to comfort her.

"Chris, we need to return to Bleakstar at once. I had my doubts about handling one vampire, but three? Even if they are young, together they're far more than we can handle by ourselves," Matt said.

"I agree; we need to report this to the Baron and get reinforcements," Sarah told him.

"No!" the woman screamed startling them.

"What's wrong?" Chris asked.

"You can't leave, not now. Tonight's the night she feeds, you have to protect us!" the woman begged. "She won't come out until the sun has fully set, you still have time. If you strike now you'll catch them when they're sleeping. Please help me."

"Damn," Chris cursed.

"What's the plan brother?" Cassy asked him nervously.

Chris was quiet for a moment.

"Matt, Sarah, armor up. Cas grab your bow. We have to move fast if we're going to stop this thing," Chris told them. "Ditrina, we're going to be in the middle of town so try to keep the collateral damage to a minimum, remember our first priority is the safety of the citizens. Everybody move!" Chris barked.

"Thank you, thank you. May the gods bless you," the woman wept.

"What's your name?" Chris asked her.

"Kelti Tuxon. Rob is my brother," Kelti said with a sniffle.

"Don't worry Kelti; we'll make sure your brother is safe," Chris reassured her.

As the others had been talking Ditrina had watched Kelti, the way she talked, the way she cried.

"Is something wrong Di? You were quieter than normal back there," Cassy asked her as they raced to gather their equipment.

Ditrina thought for a moment as they worked.

"I'm not sure," Ditrina said with a frown.

CHAPTER FIFTEEN

It took longer than they had hoped to ready their gear and as they rode through the streets on their horses the sun dipped dangerously low on the horizon. While before they had tried to be discreet they no longer had such a luxury, and as they hurried along dressed for battle they drew the attention of every villager they passed. By the time the apothecary was in sight a large crowd was trailing behind them bringing with them a low roar of curious babble.

They dismounted in front of the house.

"This crowd is going to be a problem," Sarah remarked.

"You're right. Matt, Ditrina, Cas, hold back the crowd but don't hurt anyone," Chris said looking specifically at Ditrina.

"Why are you staring at me?" Ditrina asked him.

"I just wanted to be perfectly clear. Sometimes you misunderstand me and I don't want to have to explain to the Baron how we incinerated his village," Chris replied.

"Very good," Ditrina said. "I won't incinerate anyone."

Chris gave her a nod and approached the door.

"It's locked," Chris said angrily.

"Allow me," Sarah said and walked purposefully up to the door, clad in steel, a short sword in each hand.

She stopped in front of the door, and promptly kicked it off its hinges.

"After you," Sarah said ushering him inside.

Chris raced through the doorway into the shadowy building, sword drawn. He found Rob standing in the center of the room holding a large kitchen knife before him like a sword. It would have been comical if not for the rage written on his face. He wore no scarf now and Chris saw that the sides of his neck were a mess of scars.

"You! What are you doing in my house? I thought I heard a commotion outside and now I find you breaking into my home!" Rob yelled.

"Rob please calm down we're here to help you," Chris told him walking cautiously forward, Sarah close behind him.

"Help me? How could you possibly help me?" Rob asked confused, still holding the knife.

"Your wife isn't what she seems, you've been bewitched," Sarah said slowly, advancing toward him while Chris edged closer to the stairs.

From outside they heard the sounds of the crowd, their curiosity replaced with malice. Chris felt a rush of energy in the air and realized someone outside must have used magic.

"What the hell are you talking about? What do you want with my wife?" Rob asked, pointing the knife at Sarah.

"Rob the thing upstairs isn't your wife, your real wife is dead. You've been deceived by a vampire," Chris told him.

Rob's face grew pale.

"What are you going to do?" he asked quietly.

"We're going to kill that vampire and free you and the rest of the village from her magic," Sarah said firmly. "Now, why don't you hand over the knife and step aside so we can..." Sarah began.

"Ophelia run! Protect the children!" Rob bellowed lunging at Sarah with the knife.

A lifetime of fighting had sharpened Sarah's reflexes to near perfection and she evaded the clumsy blow with ease, and knocked the knife out of Rob's hand with a flick from her sword. As Rob stumbled forward Sarah swept his legs from under him and he fell with a mighty crash to the ground. Rob tried to rise to his feet but felt the point of a sword digging into his throat.

"Chris go! The suns almost set, I'll hold him here," Sarah yelled planting a steel-clad boot on Rob's chest while digging the point of her sword a little deeper into his neck so that droplets of blood could be seen running down to his chest.

Chris sprinted up the stairs, sword in hand, cloak billowing behind him. The crowd had grown louder outside, and Chris could feel their anger crash over him like a wave. Chris found himself staring at a hallway, two doors to the left, two to the right.

At random, Chris decided to try the left hand door first. He pushed it open quickly and found it filled to the ceiling with drying herbs, but devoid of life. Shutting the door quickly Chris turned to the door to his right. Kicking it open quickly, he found himself looking into a small room with two little beds against the far wall. The room was lit by candlelight aided by the last of the sun's glow seen through the window, growing fainter by the moment. Unlike the previous room Chris was not alone.

She stood in the center of the room, and as Chris entered she dropped into a low crouch, her hands extended like claws before her, teeth bared. Chris could see she possessed two razor sharp fangs that gleamed menacingly in the dim light. Her skin was pale, the color of fresh snow, and her eyes were dark blue and puffy, currently streaming tears. Behind her cowered the two children from before, terror etched into every inch of their small faces.

No one spoke, and the only sounds were the shouts of the crowd and the whimpers of the children.

Chris went to raise his sword, expecting it to burst into flames as it did in the presence of monsters, but instead found the blade so heavy he could barely stand to hold it.

"Well? What are you waiting for?" Ophelia asked, voice choked with tears. "The sun still casts its light upon the world, I have no power. End this!" she sobbed.

Again Chris tested the sword and found he was unable to bring it to bear against her. Holding one hand before him he slowly returned the blade to its sheath.

"I believe there's been a misunderstanding," Chris said carefully, still holding up his hands to show he was unarmed.

Ophelia let out another sob.

"What kind of cruel joke is this?" she demanded.

"I'm just as confused as you are trust me," Chris told her. "Just hear me out and let's try to figure what the hell's going on," he said and took a step towards her.

"Stay away from my children!" she screamed preparing to launch herself at him.

"Ophelia," Chris said quickly. "Do you know a woman by the name of Kelti, Rob's sister?" he asked her.

Ophelia gave a low snarl but halted her attack.

"Know her? That horrid woman tried to kill my children! She slipped poison into sweets and gave it to them. They were just babies!" Ophelia hissed. "If Rob and I hadn't acted quickly they would have died, we were lucky enough to have the right herbs to make an antidote."

"Why would she do such a thing?" Chris asked her.

No sooner then he asked the sun finally dipped below the horizon. Chris watched in awe as Ophelia's eyes morphed from dark blue into a glowing red. From behind her Chris saw two sets of small red eyed staring at him in fear.

"Now do you understand?" Ophelia asked him darkly. "She saw us as monsters, and for good reason," she said, her voice having acquired a strange echo.

"So you did do it," Chris said in horror. "You bewitched the village, and replaced Rob's wife."

"Who told you those lies?" Ophelia hissed "I haven't bewitched anyone, and I didn't kill Rob's wife, I am Rob's wife!" she yelled angrily.

"And them?" Chris asked pointing to the children.

"Rob was their father. Vampirism can be passed from parent to child, like any other disease. You can't begin to understand my pain when I saw my babies shared my curse," Ophelia said.

"Ophelia, we need to go talk to your husband and my friends. Right now everyone thinks that I'm trying to kill you," Chris told her.

"I don't understand why you didn't. You caught me powerless and weaponless. Why didn't you do it?" she asked.

"It's a long story," Chris told her. "I'll explain later, but for now we need to stop the fighting downstairs."

"Is Rob hurt?" Ophelia asked nervously.

"Not much, he attacked us with a knife when we came in and my friend had to subdue him," Chris told her.

"We must hurry," Ophelia agreed. "I need you two to be brave for a little while. Mommy will be back soon," she told her children.

"But it's dark!" cried one of them.

Upon inspection Chris realized they were twins.

"I know, but you need to be brave. This will only take a minute," she reassured him.

Chris led her from the room.

"Is he afraid of the dark?" Chris asked puzzled.

"Of course he is, why?" Ophelia replied.

"I just think it's a little strange is all," Chris told her.

"All young children fear the dark, vampire or not," she said with a shake of her head.

They walked quickly down the stairs and saw Sarah still holding Rob to the floor.

"Sarah, let him go, we were deceived!" Chris told her.

"Chris what the hell are you talking about?" Sarah asked nervously looking at Ophelia.

"Trust me, let him up," Chris told her and she obeyed.

Rob rushed to Ophelia's side.

"Are you hurt? Where are the children?" he demanded looking her over.

"I'm fine, and the children are upstairs. There're frightened but they'll be alright," Ophelia told him.

"I'm sorry, but Ophelia the rest of the villagers...they know you're a vampire, right?" Chris asked her.

"Of course they know," she said annoyed.

"In that case please tell them to go home, and I'll call my friends inside. We don't want anyone to accidently get hurt," Chris told her.

"Very well," she agreed. "You call your friends inside and I'll speak to the townspeople," Ophelia told him.

Together they ran outside to a scene of chaos. Ditrina stood chanting with flames crackling in her hands, multiple scorched patches of earth a testament to her willingness to use them, while Matt was attempting to calm the villagers down to no avail. Cassy was engaged in a shouting match with what appeared to be the leader of the mob, staring at him down the shaft of an arrow.

"Shearcliff and Company! Stand down!" Chris yelled.

"It's alright! You can go home! Everything is alright!" Ophelia called to the villagers.

"Chris what the hell is going on? Is that the vampire?!" Matt yelled.

"Everyone inside! Now! I'll explain everything in a moment, for now just go inside," Chris ordered them.

While confused, they obeyed and retreated into the apothecary while Ophelia worked on calming down the mob. Once inside Matt healed Rob's minor wounds at Chris's request while they waited for Ophelia's return. Half an hour later, after many hurried words to his friends, and much crowd control from Ophelia they all stood assembled in the apothecary.

"Chris, explain what's going on," Cassy demanded and the others nodded in agreement.

"I'd like to know the same thing," Rob said angrily.

"Well to put it simply we were hired to kill her," Chris said pointing at Ophelia.

He then launched into the events leading up to the evening, starting with the Baron's contract, their investigation of the village, and their surprise meeting with Kelti. When he was finished all were silent.

"I still don't understand, why didn't you kill me?" Ophelia asked.

"My sword is enchanted. It was created to smite evil, to slay monsters. It can sense what type of person you are and decides whether or not to kill them. If I try to use it against someone with a good heart the sword becomes unusable, too heavy to weild. Against monsters the sword bursts into flames and can cut through the toughest armor. When I tried to use the sword against you it was as if it had turned to stone, I couldn't swing the blade. You're not a monster Ophelia," Chris told her.

"She's not the only one with questions," Matt said. "Ophelia, how did you end up living in this village, and how are the villagers ok with you staying here? You drink blood don't you?" he asked.

"It's a rather long story," Ophelia told them.

"I think you should start talking then," Ditrina said staring at her curiously with large black eyes.

Ophelia sighed.

"Well, five years ago now Rob found me collapsed from hunger beside the road. I had been hunting for some time but it had been weeks since I had last fed. I had been sustaining myself on the blood of lesser creatures for some time but a vampire cannot survive of such poor-quality blood for long I fear," she said.

"Why were you traveling?" Cassy interrupted.

Ophelia looked at her annoyed.

"My old territory was invaded by a group of clerics seeking to set up a church, so rather than risk confrontation I fled in search of a new hunting ground. It didn't go as well as I had hoped and I found myself overexerted and without any food. That was when Rob found me," Ophelia told them.

Rob took over.

"I was gathering lumber at the time, we were building a new shop and needed the wood you see, when I saw her curled up in a ball beneath a tree. At first I thought she was dead, with her being so pale and all but I saw that she was breathing so I rushed her home. I tried feeding her and getting her to drink but I had no such luck so I left her to sleep. She slept clear through the night without so much as a peep but the next morning I was in for a rough surprise," Rob said with a chuckle.

Ophelia looked slightly embarrassed.

"Yes, when I awoke I smelt fresh blood, and I lost control. Normally I would never try to kill another person, I just take the blood I need while they sleep and use magic so that they don't wake up but I was starving, and had lost my sense of rationality. I attacked him," Ophelia said softly.

"I had come in to see if she had woken up yet, but when I tried to rouse her, her eyes snapped open and she lunged for me! She was weak at the time but nevertheless managed to sink her fangs into my neck. I thought I was a goner but as I stumbled backward I crashed into the window and pulled the curtain off the rails, filling the room with the morning sunlight. Ophelia let go right away and fell to the floor, screaming and howling. She actually hadn't gotten me too badly but it still bled a lot you see," Rob told them.

"Usually the sun wouldn't have such an effect on me; it hurts to be sure, and it's true I cannot use my magic during the day, but it's not enough to force me to release my prey when I have them in my clutches. In my weakened state however it was too much for me to bear, and given a few more moments it probably would have killed me," Ophelia admitted.

"How did you survive?" Chris asked her.

"Well this is the part I can't explain. For whatever reason Rob took pity on me. He spared my life," Ophelia said.

The others all looked at Rob in shock.

"You mean to tell me you survived a vampire attack by luck alone, but just when you have the chance to finish her off you just leave her be?" Matt asked bewildered.

"I couldn't leave her there suffering!" Rob exclaimed. "I helped her."

"You did what?!" Matt shouted looking at Ophelia in shock. "I mean no offence, it's just that...well..." he trailed off but Ophelia was quick to come to his aid.

"No no, I understand completely! I was just as surprised then as you are now. I couldn't understand what he was doing," Ophelia told him.

"I couldn't stand to see her in such pain," Rob told them. "She was just lying there on the ground, screaming and thrashing about, it broke my heart. So I hung the curtains back up to hide her from the sun. After that she just laid there shaking. I knew what she was at this point but even so I couldn't stomach seeing her in such pain, people always told me I had too soft a heart and I suppose they were right," he said shamefaced.

They stared at him in disbelief. Rob cleared his throat.

"*Anyway,* once I had her back in the bed I bound her with all the rope I had around the house. I might be softhearted but I'm not stupid. From there I went about bandaging up my neck, but suddenly I had an idea as to what was wrong with her so I let it bleed a while longer as I gathered the blood in a cup. When I had a good amount, I finished dressing my wound, leaving me with these beauties," he said gesturing to the scars on his neck.

"So, you bring a vampire into your home, it tries to kill you, and in return you feed it and it becomes your friend?" Ditrina asked him intently.

Seeing Ditrina's thought process in motion Cassy jumped in.

"I think this was a special case Di, I don't think that's how all vampires work," Cassy said quickly.

"Shame, I was hoping to add this to my report," Ditrina said sadly.

"As I was saying," Rob said with a sharp look to the women, sharing his displeasure of having his story which he seemed to enjoy telling be interrupted. "When I came back in she was struggling against the ropes. I walked up to her and she tried to bite me from the bed! I held the cup out to her and she calmed down quite a bit. I helped her drink it, I wasn't about to go untying her was I, and no sooner had she finished it then she fell right back asleep! She slept straight into the night, and she scared the hell out of me the next morning to be sure!"

"After I drank the blood I rested to regain my strength. Vampires don't need much blood to survive, and Rob had given me several days' worth in that cup. That night I was feeling much more like myself again, and my strength had returned. I snapped the rope without thinking about it and went off to question him as to why he hadn't just killed me outright. I found the fool downstairs dripping his blood into another cup! He almost fainted when I walked down the stairs, but when I questioned him he explained he was trying to give me something to eat for dinner. I was shocked; I honestly didn't know how to respond. I had never met a human so at ease around one of my kind before so I just sat down and waited for him to finish. After I drank the second glass of blood Rob asked me why I had been passed out in the woods, like it was the most normal thing in the world. I decided to tell him why I was traveling, and that I was looking for a new hunting ground. Rob didn't seem to like the last part and asked what I would do when I found it. He liked my next answer even less. Rob went on to ask a bunch of questions about vampires, focusing heavily on the amount of blood we need to sustain ourselves. I didn't know what he was getting at but I decided to humor him and informed him the amount of blood he had given me so far would easily last me a week. It was then Rob gave me a proposal, I could stay in Torville if I wished and feed upon him whenever I desired, on the condition that I announce what I was to the other villagers and swear to never feed upon them without their consent," Ophelia said.

"And the other villagers were ok with that?" Sarah asked in horror.

"We didn't tell them at first, we let them get to know me without the fangs before we told them what I was," Ophelia told her.

"Ophelia here is amazing with plants and herbs; she started working as the town's doctor. She saved a couple children from a fever that swept through the town the winter after she arrived. After that we decided it was the best time to tell them what she was. They were skeptical at first, but I explained our arrangement and pretty soon they decided it wasn't a big deal. She became so vital to our little town's existence with her herbs that we decided that in the event people came hunting for her we would do our best to help her hide," Rob said.

"That's why all the shopkeepers were spewing that bullshit about never having seen a nonhuman before," Sarah said shaking her head.

"It wasn't the best cover we know, but it's rare we get visitors so it sufficed," Rob said.

"So if the villagers like the fact that you're here how does Kelti fit into this?" Chris asked them.

Ophelia's face darkened and Rob looked ashamed.

"Kelti is my sister; she left the village the year before Ophelia arrived to work in Bleakstar. One thing led to another and Ophelia and I ended up having children. We decided to get married and naturally I invited Kelti to the wedding. That's where everything went wrong," Rob said ashen faced.

"I know what happens next, Kelti poisons the children," Chris said with revulsion.

"When she figured out what Ophelia was she freaked out, and when she learned about the children she...well you already said it," Rob said miserably.

"It was on the wedding night, when we arrived home we found them horribly ill. She had used a common but powerful poison. We rushed to make an antidote and for the first time I was grateful they shared my blood. Any normal human child would have died long before we found them. By the time we had made sure the children were safe Kelti had fled the village. But that was four years ago!" Ophelia exclaimed. "Nobody's seen any sign of her since then."

"Baron Francis hired us to investigate a rumor of a vampire preying upon Torville," Chris told them. "In the end, we were ordered to slay whatever monster we found," Chris said disgusted.

"Kelti was the one spreading the rumors, and earlier tonight she confronted us and urged us to act quickly. She said you had bewitched the village, killed Rob's wife, and were planning on feeding tonight," Ditrina told Ophelia. "I noticed something odd earlier when she was talking, I've realized now she was lying to us. In the future, I must be more aware of that," Ditrina said flatly.

"You're an elf aren't you?" Rob asked with awe, seeing Ditrina's face under her hood clearly for the first time.

"Enough time for that later, where is Kelti?" Ophelia asked, her eyes glowing like coals.

"We left her back at our camp, one moment please," Ditrina replied and disappeared with a small pop.

"Where did she go?" Rob asked in amazement.

"Probably going to fetch Kelti," Chris replied.

Sure enough a minute later Ditrina reappeared holding a confused Kelti by the arm.

"What's going on?" Kelti demanded before noticing Ophelia.

She was growling, and creeping closer by the second.

"That's her! That's the vampire, kill it kill it!" Kelti screamed.

"Give it up Kelti, we know what you did," Chris snarled at her.

Kelti whirled at him.

"All I did was try to kill a couple of monsters before they could hurt anyone themselves, I should be rewarded! I was doing the same job you're hired to do right now, so get on with it and kill her!" Kelti screamed pointing at Ophelia.

"It's true the Baron suspected a vampire was the monster plaguing Torville, however he was mistaken. We were hired to investigate and slay whatever monster we found in the town, and I fully intend to carry out that contract," Chris told her menacingly.

He turned to Sarah.

"Take her outside," Chris ordered.

Sarah nodded grimly and dragged a thrashing Kelti into the street outside the shop. Chris followed behind her, drawing his sword.

"What are you going to do?" Rob asked as the others filed outside behind him.

"Hold a trial, pass judgment, and complete the contract," Chris replied darkly.

"What are you doing?!" Kelti yelled in hysterics as he stood before her.

"This sword was made to destroy evil, to smite monsters. It cannot be used against someone with a pure heart," Chris said softly as he knelt next to her. "This sword showed me that Ophelia is no monster, she's just a mother trying to protect her family. I was hired to slay the monster in Torville, and I think I've found it," he whispered to her.

"You're making a mistake!" Kelti wept.

"Perhaps. If you are as innocent as you claim you have nothing to fear from me. We shall soon see," Chris told her.

He stood up.

"Kneel," Chris commanded and Sarah forced Kelti to her knees, pushing her forward.

"Please, I'm begging you don't do this, please!" Kelti whispered, too terrified to cry out.

The only sound as Chris raised his sword high above Kelti's head were her pitiful whimpers.

They halted abruptly and the monster of Torville was slain.

221

CHAPTER SIXTEEN

Two days later Shearcliff and Company approached the throne of Baron Francis and knelt.

They still wore their traveling gear having returned to the Baron as fast as possible. Matt and Sarah wore their armor while Cassy and Ditrina had opted to wear hooded cloaks to hide their faces and avoid unneeded attention. Chris dressed as he normally did, adorned with his grey cloak and wearing his sword proudly. Unlike their previous meeting the Baron was holding court when they had arrived and as such many of the castles lords and ladies were present. Despite this the Baron wore the same plain brown robes, oddly out of place amongst the finely dressed nobles.

"The contract is completed my lord," Chris said from his knee.

"So soon? I thought it would have taken you at least a week to finish your investigation," Baron Francis exclaimed happily.

"We did our best to act with haste, you seemed quite concerned," Chris told him.

"Very good, very good. If you've returned so soon I can safely assume the vampire has been killed?" Francis asked tentatively.

"No my lord, the vampire was not the monster plaguing Torville," Chris replied.

A low murmur of conversation began flowing from the assembled nobles.

"Not a vampire? Strange, the reports we had received all pointed to such a beast. May I ask what manner of monster you killed?" Baron Francis inquired.

"The monster in question was a woman by the name of Kelti Tuxon," Chris said as he stood. "She had been spreading rumors about her sister in law, claiming she was dangerous. Through our investigation we discovered that Kelti had attempted to murder the children of Rob and Ophelia Tuxon, a fact she admitted to us ourselves," Chris explained.

The nobles burst into conversation, drowning out Chris's own thoughts.

"Silence, Silence!" Francis bellowed.

Slowly the nobles returned to their original state.

"Chris, please explain yourself. Why didn't you bring this woman back to me for a proper trial?" the Baron asked curiously.

"My lord, you hired us to kill the monster lurking in Torville, so we did. It just turned out the monster wasn't the vampire as you had originally thought," Chris explained.

The Baron shook his head.

"I can't believe she would spread such a lie like that. And how could she possibly bring herself to harm her own nephews?!" the Baron exclaimed.

Chris looked to his companions and they nodded. Steeling himself Chris spoke.

"My lord, I intend for my report to be as accurate as possible. It was not my intent to mislead you," Chris began.

The Baron grew visibly interested, leaning forward in his throne.

"Don't worry my boy; tell me whatever is bothering you. The threat is gone, as you said. You have nothing to fear from the truth," Francis said kindly.

"While Kelti did attempt to murder her nephews, the rumors she spread about Ophelia Tuxon were true. She is in fact a vampire, though she hasn't harmed any of the villagers of Torville. The villagers are all aware of the fact that she isn't human yet still see her as a valued member of their community. Currently she is wedded to Rob Tuxon, and they have raised a lovely pair of twins who are also vampires. Ophelia poses no threat to anyone and as such we saw it fit to leave her and her children be," Chris said.

The room exploded, with the nobles going mad with questions. Francis managed to calm them eventually, but it took several minutes. Having silenced the nobles yet again he returned his gaze to Chris. It was equal parts confused and curious, and Chris was grateful he saw no anger in the man's eyes.

"Chris, I'm afraid I don't understand. How is it that you left the vampire in the village? You are aware that vampires must drink the blood of humans to survive?" Francis asked.

"I am my lord. Rob Tuxon gives his blood to Ophelia willingly. The children are only half vampires and as such can sustain themselves on normal food, supplemented with the blood of animals on occasion. I spoke for a long time with both Rob and Ophelia and determined that the family wasn't a threat to anyone," Chris told him.

The Baron shook his head.

"I'm afraid we can't be sure of that Chris. A vampire is a vampire after all. Despite what you have told me I can't have a monster living among my people," Francis told him.

Cassy stood abruptly and tossed back her hood. Chris saw her face had gone pale with anger.

"My lord," Cassy said between gritted fangs. "I beg you to reconsider. As a nonhuman myself I can assure you that that woman poses no threat to anyone. Ophelia agreed to have her identity reveled to you in the hopes that you would see her not as a monster, but as a citizen. If for whatever reason you cannot do this know we will do everything in our power to protect her and her family," Cassy hissed, struggling not to raise her voice.

The Baron seemed taken back.

"While the naga aren't the most common on this side of the world I would hardly compare you to monsters," Francis began.

"Many of your subjects think differently *my lord,*" Cassy told him. "When I walk through the streets of your city the people gawk and stare. Many of your citizens are afraid to speak to me, and have no idea what I am. To them I am no different than a vampire myself, just as much a monster in their eyes. Yet you understand that while I am far from normal, I am just another person. You take the time to recognize my people as people, yet you condemn Ophelia simply because of what she is; you don't take the time to recognize her as a person!"

Cassy seethed.

Chris decided it was best to step in before she said something regrettable to the Baron.

"What my sister is alluding to is we think it would be best if you met with Ophelia yourself, we figured you might be skeptical. We discussed this with the villagers before we departed and they have already begun preparing a feast for your arrival," Chris told him.

"You want me to go meet with the vampire?!" Baron Francis asked with shock.

"Yes my lord. We feel it would be best if you met with her and decided for yourself. The villagers were very excited when they heard you might be coming and seriously hope you decide to grace them with your presence. We will act as your personal escort if you like and will guarantee your safety," Chris told him.

The Baron seemed to have had a response ready but paused to consider Chris's proposal.

"You had said you had wanted to travel my lord," Chris prompted.

After a minute of consideration the Baron spoke.

"And you can guarantee the safety of me and my companions…" the Baron began.

"Absolutely my lord, my companions and I will do everything in our power to ensure your safety," Chris assured him.

"Very well," the Baron said slowly. "I will accompany you to Torville and decide the matter for myself. We will leave the day after tomorrow, my companions and I must prepare for travel. I will send a messenger pigeon to Torville announcing the date of my arrival," Francis told them.

"How many people do you think will be accompanying you my lord?" Chris asked him.

"Just a few, we will have to travel light if we are to make it there quickly," Francis replied with a small smile.

"When Baron Francis said he was bringing a small group I expected no more than a half dozen or so," Chris grumbled to Sarah as they rode toward Torville two days later.

Sarah chuckled.

"What made you think that? Besides, this is the lightest I've ever seen someone in his position travel," Sarah told him.

"He must have brought half the castle with him!" Chris argued.

"He probably did," Sarah said. "Station dictates that he brings his retinue of servants along with him to tend to his needs. Because his wife decided to attend this meeting the number of servants is doubled. Then you have to consider the Baron's knights. Many of them are duty bound to follow him to this meeting because of the potential for danger. Each of them will likely have brought his lady along as well as at least one personal servant or squire. This is equal parts mission and holiday Chris. The chance to see something as exotic as a vampire is a rare treat for these people," Sarah explained.

"Still, this is rather extreme," Chris said gesturing to the massive train of riders and carriages extending behind them.

"What? Did you expect the Baron just to hop on his horse and go tearing off to Torville with us?" Sarah mocked. "Maybe he could share a tent with Matt!" she said laughing once again.

Chris, who had been thinking exactly that decided to remain silent.

"I wonder how the others are faring," Chris asked changing the subject.

"Well Matt seemed eager to speak to father Simon or whatever his name was. He's probably rambling on about spellcraft with the geezer in his carriage," Sarah said with a shrug.

"Didn't Ditrina and Cas end up riding with the ladies of the court?" Chris asked.

"That's right, the Baron offered to allow us to ride with the other women in the carriages. The twittering fools snatched up Ditrina and your sister before they could protest. They're probably getting an endless stream of stupid questions right about now," Sarah said with a savage smile.

"You seem a little too happy about that," Chris remarked. "Any reason why?"

"Well I might have let it slip that Ditrina was an elf when the court ladies tried dragging me off to join their little sewing circle or whatever they wanted to do with me. They ran off to see for themselves after that. Just to play it safe I also may have dropped a hint or two that your sister and Ditrina were romantically involved before we departed, just to keep them out of my hair. There's nothing court ladies like more than new gossip," Sarah told him.

Chris shook his head.

"You're evil," he said in disbelief.

"Your sword says differently," Sarah laughed. "Besides, I have my reasons for wanting to ride in the vanguard with you," Sarah told him.

"Oh really? Care to share?" Chris asked.

"Well, you've never seen a large scale battle before. If a group of bandits or something decides to attack I need to be here to ensure you don't get your head loped off," Sarah told him.

"I've got my sword," Chris defended.

"True, true, and that sword will work just fine against the average cutthroat but what if you go up against some desperate farmer trying to feed his family or something? Do you think your magical sword will cut down a man just trying to save his kids from starving?" Sarah asked him.

Chris paused.

"I'd have to say no," Chris admitted.

"Exactly, and while you're struggling to raise your blade he'll run you through with a pitchfork because unlike you he has no magic sword preventing him from fighting. Don't fool yourself into thinking that sword makes you invincible Chris. You've been lucky that it hasn't gotten you killed so far. From how you said your meeting with Ophelia went the only reason your alive is you arrived a few seconds before the sun set and were able to talk her down," Sarah scolded.

"I thought you said there's no such thing as luck?" Chris asked cheekily.

"You know what I mean," Sarah replied seriously.

"Yeah, I know," Chris said. "But what am I supposed to do, use another sword? It's easy to forget but I've never swung a sword without magic guiding my hand. I wouldn't have a clue what to do if you plopped a regular blade in my hands and told me to fight," Chris told her.

Sarah frowned.

"We'll have to work on that. You can't rely on magic forever, and not everyone we'll have to fight will necessarily be *evil* as your sword puts it," Sarah told him. "Until then just stay close to me, I'll handle anything your sword decides it doesn't wanna kill."

"Sounds like a solid plan," Chris replied with a smile.

They arrived in Torville around sunset, and it seemed the town had undergone a metamorphosis. Villagers rushed from place to place and the once sleepy streets had sprung to life with twinkling lanterns hanging from the trees. Brightly colored ribbons crisscrossed from house to house. The villagers had converted the main road into an outdoor banquet hall. A massive table had been constructed with enough room to seat the entire village as well as the Baron's entourage. Chris found the whole set up impressive, and was surprised the villagers had managed to construct such an elaborate display on such short notice.

"Well they certainly didn't hold back," Sarah remarked.

"I know! It looks like they've prepared an entire month's worth of food for us!" Chris said excitedly pointing to feast arrayed upon the massive table.

"How could I have guessed you'd be most excited about the food?" Sarah asked dryly, shaking her head.

"Don't act like you're not eager to try some of that," Chris replied. "You eat almost as much as Matt."

"What can I say? It takes a lot of energy to keep you idiots alive," Sarah told him.

Chris laughed.

"Let's find the Baron, we're still his escort remember?" Chris said.

"Sounds good," Sarah replied and they dismounted. Together they began searching through the convoy for the Baron's carriage. It wasn't hard to find, it was far larger than any other carriage in sight and surrounded by knights. By now they were recognized on sight and the knights admitted them without issue. Chris knocked on the door.

"My lord, we have arrived at Torville," Chris called.

The door slid open.

"Ah good," Francis replied. "I'll give you two a moment to ready your weapons and armor and then we can depart."

"No need my lord," Sarah told him. "We have everything we need already,"

"But Chris isn't wearing any armor!" Francis said in shock, looking between Chris's slim cloaked form and Sarah's bulky spiked armor.

"I was planning on taking off my armor now that we've arrived actually," Sarah said.

"And I actually don't have any armor, not unless you count these," Chris said gesturing to the small leather bracers he wore and his thin vest.

"But what about the vampire?" Francis asked nervously.

"My lord, the sun will be set soon. When it does she'll be able to use magic. Armor won't make a difference so we might as well be comfortable," Sarah told him.

When she saw the Baron was still skeptical she added:

"We'll still have our swords in case we need to protect you."

"Very well," the Baron said slowly. "Let us head into town then."

The Baron sent word with his knights to the rest of the group that it was time to enter the town. The servants rushed ahead to ensure that everything was in place for their masters while the lords and ladies followed behind Baron Francis. Chris finally caught sight of the Baroness when she seemingly appeared out of thin air beside her husband. She had a kind weathered face, and despite her age she moved with surprising grace.

"So, you're the famous adventurer I've heard so much about," the Baroness said when she noticed him walking beside the Baron.

"Yes, my lady," Chris replied as politely as he could manage.

"Splendid! You'll have to regale me with a story from one of your adventures over dinner. I'm sure you have so many fantastic tales to share," she exclaimed.

"I'm sure you'd find my adventures quite boring my lady," Chris said slightly embarrassed as he recalled his mishaps with the dire wolves and the disaster in Purevein.

Sarah sniggered, noticing his discomfort.

"And who have we here?" the Baroness asked spying Sarah walking slightly behind Chris.

"Sarah Morgson my lady," Sarah replied crisply.

"You talk like a soldier my dear, but you're not one of mine. Do you serve my husband? I wasn't aware he had any woman in his ranks," the Baroness asked.

"No my lady, I serve in Shearcliff and Company. I will be acting as an escort for the Baron and yourself tonight as you meet Ophelia," Sarah told her politely.

"Christian you force a woman to travel with your band? My you are quite the rouge, aren't you?" the Baroness scolded.

Chris looked at Sarah in panic unsure of how to respond signaling for her to come to his aid. He immediately wished he hadn't.

"Actually my lady, the majority of Shearcliff and company is made up of woman. We currently only have two men in the entire company," Sarah told her giving Chris an evil smile.

"My word Christian, you've recruited nothing but women! I say, I didn't have you pegged as such a scoundrel!" the Baroness exclaimed.

Sarah and the Baron both smiled as they walked, enjoying Chris's pitiful attempts to defend himself.

"There's been a misunderstanding my lady, there're only five of us in the entire company! One of the women is my sister, and the other two volunteered to travel with us! I swear I'm running an honest adventuring company!" Chris pleaded.

The Baroness seemed unconvinced.

"That may well be true but I see no reason to target women as candidates. Your sister I can understand but how do you expect to explain the other two?" the Baroness asked him.

"Well Sarah is the finest fighter I've ever met, and our company is lucky to have her expertise. We would be far worse off without her," Chris told the Baroness.

"Really? Is that so?" the Baroness asked Sarah.

Chris had hoped he had gained Sarah's favor with his last comment but she still seemed in the mood to torment him.

"Yes my lady. I do anything Christian requires of him. I fight for him, I manage our battle plans, and per his orders I share his tent," Sarah said forcing herself to look embarrassed to hide the evil smile trying to take over her face.

"My goodness!" the Baroness explained and hurried ahead of them.

The Baron looked at Sarah and laughed before following after his wife.

They had reached the head of the table, which was actually a separate circular table pressed against the main one so that many people could speak comfortably. The Baron sat himself at the head of the table as is customary, with his wife taking the seat to his right. Chris sat beside the Baron, with Sarah choosing to sit beside the Baroness. While this meeting was set to be peaceful they wanted to be prepared, just in case. The villagers began filling in along the length of the table and the Baron's companions mingled among them. Chris couldn't see Matt through the crowd but thought he caught sight of Ditrina's blue hair among a group of noble women.

"So where is the vampire?" Baron Francis asked Chris quietly.

Chris looked around and spotted a woman wearing long a long sleeved dress and a large sunhat making her way through the crowd with Rob in tow.

"There my lord, she's coming here now. Chris said gesturing toward Ophelia.

"The woman in the hat? Why is she wearing a hat? It's almost sundown," Francis asked.

"Ask her yourself my lord," Chris told him as Ophelia arrived.

"My lord," Rob said as he bowed.

"It's a pleasure to finally meet you my lord," Ophelia said as she sunk into a curtsy.

"My lady, I take it you're Ophelia?" Francis asked her.

"Yes, my lord," Ophelia said politely as she rose. "May I sit?"

"Of course," Francis replied somewhat taken back by her etiquette.

"Lord Francis was just wondering why you're wearing a hat this evening Ophelia," Chris remarked.

"Well although it is dark there's still enough sun to make it uncomfortable for me. Once the sun goes down I'll remove it but until them I hope you'll forgive my rudeness," Ophelia said to the Baron as she sat herself beside Sarah.

Rob took a seat next to Chris, dividing the table into men and women.

"I'm quite happy you decided to make the trip out to see us my lord, this way you can see for yourself the way things really are around here," Rob told him.

"Of course, and please, call me Francis," Francis told him.

Rob's eyes widened slightly but he nodded.

They fell silent and tension hung thickly over the table.

"Well I should probably introduce myself as well, my name is Gertrude. I'm Francis's wife as I'm sure you've guessed. The lovely woman to my left is Sarah Morgson, and the rouge beside my husband is Christian Shearcliff," Baroness Gertrude told Ophelia, trying to break the silence.

"Yes, I remember them quite well," Ophelia said with a smile.

"My name is Rob Tuxon, I'm Ophelia's husband," Rob said.

"And as I'm sure you all know I'm Ophelia. I'm the reason you're here, and as you suspected I'm a vampire," Ophelia announced.

The Baron seemed shocked by her sudden declaration but the Baroness recovered for him quickly.

"So my dear tell me, how is it you ended up living among the villagers so peacefully? I've never heard of a vampire coexisting so well with humans before," Gertrude asked.

"Dear!" Francis exclaimed.

"Oh quiet. That's the reason we came isn't it? Best to get the questions out of the way so we can enjoy this wonderful dinner the people of Torville have prepared for us," Gertrude scolded.

"Well it's a rather long story, so we may as well start eating," Rob told them. "Could I interest you in anything my lor...I mean Francis?"

"Some chicken my boy, and perhaps some potatoes," Francis told him. They began to pass around the abundant food joining the villagers in the feast.

Once their plates were filled Rob and Ophelia launched into their tale, telling the Baron the same story they had told Chris a few days prior. The sun sank below the horizon as Rob concluded the tale.

"Incredible, and you two have been living here ever since?" the Baron asked in amazement.

"That's right. We hadn't heard anything from Kelti until she showed back up and started causing trouble again. Thankfully Christian put an end to it before any real damage could be done," Ophelia told him.

"So sorry to interrupt, but could I interest in my lord in something to drink?" one of Francis's servants asked holding a pitcher of wine.

"Of course my boy, leave the pitcher and enjoy the feast. No need for you to miss out on the fun," Francis told him taking the pitcher.

"Thank you my lord!" the boy said with a smile as he ran off to find a seat along the crowded table.

"Now, who would like a glass of wine?" Francis asked them holding the pitcher.

All but Ophelia pushed forward their cups.

"Not drinking my dear?" Gertrude asked her.

"Not wine I'm afraid. Rob may I?" Ophelia asked him.

"Of course dear," Rob said as he handed her a flask from within his shirt.

The Baron watched with interest as Ophelia uncapped the flask and poured a stream of blood into her cup. When she seemed satisfied she carefully recapped the flask and handed it to her husband.

"Thank you dear," Ophelia said. "It seems dark enough now; I think I can do without this," Ophelia said as she removed her large hat that until now had shielded most of her face from view.

The Baroness gave a small gasp of surprise.

"My dear, your eyes…" Gertrude began.

"So sorry my lady, they do this at night," Ophelia said quickly gesturing to her glowing red eyes.

Seeking to pass the awkward moment the Baron held up his glass for a toast.

"To new friends of all kinds!" he exclaimed.

The others quickly followed suit.

"Cheers!" they yelled.

"Does this mean you've decided to allow Ophelia to stay?" Sarah asked him.

"I believe so, she's been nothing but charming since I've met her and she has your commendation behind her. I believe we have nothing to fear from her," Francis told Sarah, though he was looking at Ophelia with a smile.

Ophelia smiled and let out a small sob of relief. It was obvious she had spent the dinner in anticipation and was relieved.

"Well that's welcome news; I was worried we were going to have to relocate Ophelia," Chris sighed happily.

"Relocate?" the Baron asked.

"Well I promised Ophelia I would protect her family, and I don't want to have to fight against your men my lord, so if it came to it we would bring Ophelia with us and try to find her a safe place for her and her family," Chris explained.

"How very... noble of you," the Baron replied.

"Thank you, my lord," Chris said with a slight bow of his head.

As the night drew on they talked about things of little consequence and the pitcher of wine was soon replaced with another and soon after that yet another.

"How are you still able to speak?" Chris muttered to himself as he watched Sarah down yet another glass of wine.

"What was that Chris?" the Baron asked.

"Oh nothing," Chris replied quickly shaking his head as Sarah poured herself yet another glass of wine.

The children of the town had long since abandoned the table and now raced around the edges of the feast, elated that they were able to stay up so much later than normal. Chris smiled as he noticed a pair of troublemakers with faintly glowing red eyes leading another group of children in a game of tag. He sighed, and thanked the gods tonight went as planned.

"Chris may I have a word?" Francis asked after the feast had concluded.

Most of the villagers were in the process of clearing the table with the help of the Baron's servants. Sarah had escorted Gertrude back to the tent that had been pitched for the Baron and herself, and the Tuxons had retired in order to put the children to bed leaving Chris and Francis alone.

"Of course my lord, what's on your mind?" Chris asked.

"You impressed me with how you handled the situation here. Of all the possible outcomes I predicted I never once imagined I would be sharing a meal with a vampire when I hired you. You've proven to me you can handle complex missions competently," Francis told him.

"Thank you, my lord, I appreciate the praise," Chris replied, touched the Baron was taking the time to praise his work.

"I offer more than words my boy; you've done well and have more than earned your reward," Francis told him as he produced a lumpy leather bag from within the folds of his brown robe.

He set it on the table with a thump. Chris looked at it with interest and the Baron beckoned him to take it.

"My lord!" Chris gasped as he looked within the bag.

Rather than gold as he had previously thought, the bag was filled with twinkling diamonds, some larger than the one that had adorned the necklace Chris had received from Mi.

"This is worth far more than what we had agreed to my lord, two of these gems alone could easily..." Chris stammered.

"Relax my boy; in the eyes of an old man you've earned a bonus. Besides, I have another favor to ask of you," Francis told him.

Chris's gratitude shifted slightly to suspicion.

"What favor could constitute such a large bonus my lord?" Chris asked him.

"What are your plans going forward my boy?" Francis asked ignoring the question.

Chris decided to play along, looking at the diamonds as if they would suddenly disappear.

"I planned on taking Shearcliff and Company further south, taking contracts as we go as we look for a permanent base of operations," Chris told him.

"Could I convince you to stay in the area for one more job?" Francis asked while sliding the bag closer toward him.

"I'd say you're doing a good job of it so far," Chris gulped still looking at the bag greedily.

"I have…an associate. He has a particular problem that I believe you may be able to assist him with. Please understand whether you decide to aid him or not the diamonds are yours but I would be grateful if you would lend him your aid," Francis explained.

"I'm listening," Chris said with a smile as he slipped the bag under his cloak.

CHAPTER SEVENTEEN

"Chris, explain to me again why we're riding west instead of south? Last I checked we're still well within Sorros's reach here," Matt asked as they headed toward the western mountains.

The Godspine, as the mountain range was called, divided Targoth in half. Travel across the continent was restricted to a couple well known passes, although much of the Godspine remained unexplored leading smugglers to continuously search for new routes through its snowy peaks and wooded base. Until now they had been too far away to see the Godspine properly but now it loomed larger than life on the horizon.

"As I've explained to you three times so far Matt, Baron Francis has a friend who lives up in the Godspine who could use our help," Chris said with exasperation.

They had been riding west for a week and Matt was still unconvinced this was the proper course of action.

"But you told me that we would've gotten the diamonds regardless of whether or not we helped this mystery man out or not, so why are we traveling so far off course?" Matt asked him.

"If we help this person it will only benefit our reputation, making people more likely to hire us. Besides, Francis told me that he's willing to pay us just as well as he did. Are you opposed to more money?" Chris asked him.

Matt felt the weight of his share of the diamonds at his hip and remained silent.

"Matt does have a point you know, were still deep in Sorros's territory right Sarah?" Cassy asked.

"Yeah Sorros controls everything between the eastern desert and the Godspine and his rule extends as far south as the southern passes. Overall, he has one of the largest chunks of Targoth under his thumb," Sarah said.

"So if we're still in his territory why hasn't he sent troops after us? He couldn't have given up on catching us so easily," Cassy said.

"From what you've told me he likely has no idea where we are," Ditrina said. "We haven't spent much time in any one town, and we've helped people everywhere we've visited so it's unlikely they would have reported us to Sorros, and save for Matt and Sarah he doesn't know our faces."

"That's true. I'm sure he put out a bounty for our capture, but without our faces it's pretty much useless," Sarah replied. "And he wouldn't have any reason to suspect that I'm traveling with you. In actuality he probably thinks I'm dead."

"He does know our name though, we announced ourselves at the gates as Shearcliff and Company," Matt reminded her.

"True," Sarah said. "But you have to consider the only people who associate our faces with that name are people we've helped. We may not have much of a reputation yet, but so far, it's a good one. It also helps that Sorros isn't well liked by the people, so it's unlikely that they'll go out of their way to aid him."

"In short, I think were safe from assassins for the time being," Chris summarized. "Don't worry Matt; I don't plan on staying within Sorros's reach longer than we need too. Once we complete this contract we'll head south as quickly as we can. By then we should have enough money we shouldn't even have to stop to take contracts along the way, we can just go," Chris reassured him.

"Alright, I just hope this contract isn't too difficult. The vampire contract was strange at best; we don't need anything too outrageous right now," Matt told him.

"It should be fine, how much could some hermit in the mountains possibly want?" Cassy asked.

"I'm inclined to agree, I think the most difficult part of this entire ordeal is going to be finding the man," Chris said.

"At the foot of the Godspine due west of here you will find a small village. It isn't on any maps and is too small to have a proper name. Once you find the village ask them to show you the hidden pass. That will lead you to my associate. Once you find him do as you will," Ditrina said parroting the Baron's words.

"Right, so now all we got to do is find this mystery village," Sarah sighed.

It took another three days to reach the heavily wooded foot of the Godspine, and an additional two days to locate the village.

They were unprepared for what they found.

"Are you sure we're in the right place?" Matt asked Chris as they broke through the tree line.

Rather than the sleepy hamlet they had expected they found themselves faced with a bustling town built into the side of the mountain. Some of the homes sat atop stilts so that they stood on the slope and some were carved directly into the stone of the mountain. The town hummed with energy, with people of all shapes and sizes, as many nonhumans as humans, bustling through the streets. Nearly everyone carried a weapon of some kind. As they looked they saw the main street continued into a narrow crevice through the mountainside, a hidden pass.

"This must be the place, there's the pass," Sarah said still in awe of the size of the hidden town.

"I thought it was supposed to be a tiny nameless hamlet!" Matt exclaimed in confusion.

"It must have expanded since the last time the Baron was here," Chris replied. "Come on, let's ask around and see if anyone can help us find our man."

As they rode through the streets they felt something was amiss. It was Ditrina who pointed it out.

"Nobody's looking at us," she remarked.

"What?" Chris said not understanding her comment.

"I'm sure you notice it less because you're a human, but when Cas and I ride into a town without our hoods up we draw a lot of attention. So far the people here are just going about their business. Nobody seems to care that we're not human," Ditrina explained.

"Look around Di, I'd say there's as many nonhumans here as humans. We're not that out of place here," Cassy told her.

"Even so, naga are rare on this side of Targoth, and very few have seen elves before. I would expect a slight sign of interest at the very least," Ditrina said.

"I thought you didn't like the extra attention Ditrina?" Matt asked.

"I'm not saying that I do, it's just that I find it strange is all," Ditrina said flatly.

"I'm sure its fine Di, maybe they've just seen an elf before. There are more of you aren't there?" Cassy asked.

"Yes, but we are still fairly rare Cas so it's unlikely that an elf has wound up in this place before," Ditrina said.

"Well you're here, so maybe others have come before you," Sarah told her ending the discussion.

They tethered their horses outside the nearest inn, the only inn by the looks of things, and decided talking to the innkeeper was a good place to start. Experience had taught Chris that they often had access to good information.

"Hello!" a cheerful voice called to them as they entered the building.

The speaker had a singsong accent that was all too familiar to them by now. He had short blue hair, greenish skin, and pointed ears.

Chris couldn't believe his eyes.

"How can I serve you today?" the elf asked brightly from behind the bar.

Chris stood still at a loss for words as Ditrina entered the bar. The elves stared at each other for a moment black eyes blinking in disbelief before they both launched into a hurricane of elfish as they walked quickly towards one another. Chris and the others stood unsure of what to do as the elves spoke quickly. They didn't seem to be angry at one another but they spoke so rapidly it was hard to tell what the intent of the conversation was. Finally, Ditrina smiled and stepped away from the other elf.

To their surprise the other elf bowed deeply to Ditrina before returning his dark gaze to Chris and his companions.

"Chris, allow me to introduce Samasal Gornit Rike," Ditrina said gesturing to the other elf.

"You can just call me Sam, humans have such a hard time with elven names I've found," Sam said with an easy grin as he shook Chris's hand.

"Sure... Sam. Forgive me, it's just I'm a little surprised to meet another elf," Chris told him.

"Ah! And who might these lovely ladies be?" Sam asked walking toward Cassy and Sarah, who seemed equally shocked at his greeting.

"I'm Cassy, and that's Sarah," Cassy told him warily.

"Do you know Ditrina? You bowed just there," Matt asked.

"Well I've never actually spoken to her before but nearly all the Rikes know about the Fire Princess," Sam said.

"Rikes? I thought Rike was part of Di's name? Are you two related?" Cassy asked him.

"No no no, you misunderstand. Rike is a title not a name. It refers to anyone still affected by the curse of the crisis," Sam said waving his hand dismissively. "Come. Sit. Let's talk a while. It's been ages since I've seen another elf," Sam said as he led them back to the bar.

Soon they found themselves atop comfy stools enjoying mugs of ale.

"So Sam, you said something about a Fire Princess?" Chris asked looking at him curiously.

"Yeah, it's an honor to meet her. You're luckier though, getting to travel with her and all," Sam told him.

"Wait you mean Ditrina? She's this Fire Princess?" Sarah asked in disbelief.

"Well yeah. You didn't know?" Sam asked confused.

They looked at Ditrina, who was poking at her ale curiously, as if it was some new bug she had to take note of.

"Our Ditrina. You're sure?" Chris asked not buying the whole Fire Princess bit.

"Ask her yourself," Sam said with a shrug.

"Di, what's this about a Fire Princess?" Cassy asked rousing Ditrina from her observation.

"Well, I obtained the nickname after I gave up soul transmutation. Because I proved so adept at pyromancy my brothers began calling me the Fire Princess to tease me. Somehow it spread beyond the palace and within the century everywhere I went people called me the Fire Princess. It was terribly annoying," Ditrina said with a small sigh.

"I'm so sorry your highness, I meant no offence!" Sam said quickly.

"Your highness!?" Cassy shrieked in shock.

"Oh, that's right; I forgot to tell you all! I'm a member of the royal family. Had I not been born a Rike I would have been third in line for the throne," Ditrina said as easily as if she was telling them the weather.

Cassy sat speechless, a first for her Chris thought, while Matt and Sarah almost choked on their drinks. Chris managed to recover slightly.

"Moving past the fact that you're a Princess, though we will be coming back to that I assure you, what's this Rike business about? Mind explaining this curse?" Chris asked.

"Simply put those who bear the title of Rike are cursed to never have children. I won't bore you with the details but a long time ago the gods cursed the people of Targoth with infertility. So few of the population was able to have children that for a while civilization crumbled. There was nobody left in the cities so they fell to ruin, nobody plowed the fields so the forest reclaimed them. Over time the curse faded and more and more of the population was able to have children. The world recovered, built new cities, made new fields, and life marched on. This event was known as the *crisis* as humans put it. The thing is, the elves have so few children and live for such a long time that the curse still has a firm grip upon our people. In honesty, almost eighty percent of our population is still cursed, the Rikes as we call them. Those who bear the title of Rike are tasked with exploring Targoth. We venture fourth gathering information to benefit elven kind in the hopes of breaking the curse so once again we can be influential in the world. As it is now, many actually consider us to be extinct," Sam told them.

They sat stunned, and turned to Ditrina.

"Di, why didn't you tell us any of this?" Cassy asked slightly hurt.

"It never seemed important. I have been having such a great time adventuring with you all and didn't want to influence your opinions of me by telling you my status. As for the curse, well it just didn't have any relevance to our situation and you never asked. It just never came up," Ditrina said with a shrug.

"Think carefully Ditrina. Is there anything else of equal importance to those two things you haven't told us? Anything at all?" Matt asked.

Ditrina's face scrunched with concentration as she thought for a minute.

"I have an irrational fear of dragons," Ditrina said firmly.

"Seriously!?" Matt said looking at her in disbelief. "You lump that on the same level of importance as you being royalty!?" Matt exclaimed shaking his head.

"I think a fear of dragons is just common sense," Sarah whispered to Chris.

Sam looked at Ditrina with disappointment. While Matt berated her for her answer Sam leaned across the bar to Chris.

"Is she the only elf you've ever met?" Sam asked quietly.

Chris nodded his head slowly.

"Until you? Yeah," Chris replied.

Sam sighed.

"Oh, what you must think of our people," Sam said with genuine despair.

Chris smiled.

"She may be a weirdo but she's *our* weirdo," Chris chuckled.

"I just thought that…because she was an elf…" Sarah trailed off.

"Nope," Sam said shaking his head. "Her actions do not speak for our kind," Sam told them quietly.

"What happened to *your highness*?" Chris asked with a grin.

"I started talking to her," Sam replied despondently.

"I'm just saying the average person statistically has nothing to fear from a dragon attack making my fears totally unfounded!" Ditrina complained loudly to Matt.

"Ditrina I'm not trying to argue about your fear in specific, I'm trying to explain that it's not nearly as important as you being royalty!" Matt shot back.

"And I'm telling you that it's every bit as important, if not more!" Ditrina yelled angrily.

"Settle down you two," Chris warned.

"Yes leader," Ditrina replied.

"Don't call me that," Chris said irritably.

"Sorry leader," Ditrina said.

Chris sighed.

"Anyway Sam, what's an elf like you doing running an inn at a place like this?" Chris asked.

"Yeah didn't you say Rikes were supposed to explore the world and gather information?" Cassy asked.

"Well not all elves are as adapt at destruction as Ditrina. My magic is far better suited to village life rather than adventuring so I set up this inn at the foot of the pass I discovered and decided to let the information come to me. As it turns out smugglers use this pass all the time to avoid paying the king's toll at the registered passes so I ended up getting quite a lot of business, and a ton of good information. As the centuries passed a people set up a little hamlet here, and it's flourished into the town you see before you; the town with no name," Sam said proudly.

"Sam how long have you been here?" Chris asked him.

"Let's see I've been running the Lonely Elf for almost two hundred and fifty years now, with a few trips back home here and there of course. In that time I've managed to develop something of a reputation among the smugglers so business is never slow," Sam replied.

"What I want to know is how this place has remained hidden for so long. It's huge!" Sarah exclaimed.

"Well when it first started out it wasn't an issue, it was just a handful of smugglers hiding out by a tiny pass. As time went on however and more and more people started living here permanently so keeping this place hidden became a real problem. We started spending so much gold on bribes to keep this place off the charts that avoiding the taxes became pointless. Thankfully we had a stroke of luck a few decades ago when a couple of nobles showed up. One of them wanted to lay low for a while and the other offered to help fund this place in order to keep it hidden if we would let the older one stay," Sam told them.

Chris looked at his friends in surprise.

"Sam, we actually came here looking for someone. We were sent by Baron Francis to aid one of his friends living up in the mountains. Does that name mean anything to you?" Chris asked.

"Of course I know Baron Francis! He's the one who pays to keep this place hidden. How's the kid doing?" Sam asked.

"He's well," Chris said surprised that Sam seemed to know the Baron so well and that he would refer to the old man as a kid.

All humans must appear as children to the elves Chris decided.

"That's good. He hasn't paid us a visit in a long while so if you get the chance tell him that everything is going great here, and the old man is still living up the mountain," Sam told him.

"Could you lead us to this man?" Chris asked eargly.

"Sorry, but I gotta stay here and watch the inn. You really don't need a guide though. The smugglers keep the pass pretty free from monsters and the old man isn't exactly hard to find. About three miles up the pass you'll see a small trail leading deeper into the mountains. Follow it and you'll find the old man's home," Sam said.

"Could you tell us the man's name?" Cassy asked him.

"Again I can't help you there. I've only seen him the one time when he arrived and he never offered me his name. The only interaction he has with our village is that about once a month or so he sends a couple of servants down for supplies. If it wasn't for that we wouldn't even know that he's alive honestly," Sam told them.

"Thanks anyway, we'll be sure to stop back here on our way out of town. For now, we gotta go talk to this mystery man," Chris told him.

"Safe travels my friend; consider the drinks a gift on the house," Sam said with a wave as they stood to leave.

Before they reached the door Ditrina turned and said something in elfish to Sam. He replied quickly and bowed slightly. Once outside Cassy turned to Ditrina.

"What was that about Di?" Cassy asked.

"I was merely saying goodbye," Ditrina said curiously. "Did I do something wrong?" she asked nervously.

"Your fine Ditrina," Chris told her. "Come on everyone, let's find go find our man before it gets dark."

They followed Sam's directions and soon found themselves staring at a narrow trail that led further up the mountain. It was partially hidden by massive pine trees and twisted so much it was impossible to tell how far it led. They began to follow the trail, riding their horses slowly in case of a sudden cliff hidden behind the thick trees. They followed the trail for nearly an hour when suddenly they emerged into a massive clearing. Chris shielded his eyes, blinded by the sunlight after so long in the dim trees. As his vision returned he gasped.

"Gods, what is this place?" he asked in awe.

What he had initially thought to be a small clearing had turned out to be a hidden valley, large enough to hold an entire village. Chris saw a great field of grass spackled by spring flowers running right up to the base of the mountain, and noticed a small lake sparkling in the sun by the edge of the cliff fed by snowmelt. It was quiet and peaceful, with the forest and cliffs blocking off all sound from the nearby village. The serene location's only sign of habitation was the continuation of the trail leading further into the valley, ending at the front door of a log cabin, though calling it a simple log cabin was a horrible understatement. The cabin was immense, easily four stories tall, and impossibly wide. Chris saw it had its own stables as well as a wraparound balcony on its third floor. Smoke drifted up from several of its chimneys.

"Seems even in hiding nobles get to live large," Sarah scoffed.

"This place is incredible," Cassy said breathlessly.

"The mountains are filled with tiny valleys like this one, though it's rare to find one so accessible," Ditrina commented.

"I'm with Sarah; this is pretty extreme for someone trying to hide themselves," Matt said with a chuckle.

"Still, if they have access to something like this you know they'll pay well," Chris said with a greedy glint in his eyes. "Come on; let's greet our new wealthy friend."

They rode up to the cabin and found themselves greeted by a pair of servants, maids by their dress, standing by the front doors. They dismounted and approached. As they inspected the maids they realized they were sisters at the very least, possibly twins. They wore the same blank expressions on their faces, wore the same clothes, and had arranged their blond hair in the same tight bun. In every way they looked identical.

"Hello ladies, we're here to speak with your master," Matt said giving the girls a slight bow.

The women looked at him blankly for a moment before one opened the front door and beckoned them inside.

"I will lead you to the waiting room while she attends to your horses," the maid told them as they entered the massive estate.

The huge doors shut behind them with a dull boom. They walked a short distance through the main hall before the maid stopped them in front of a large table.

"I must ask you to surrender your weapons here," she told them in the same polite tone she had used thus far.

Slowly they deposited their assorted weapons on the table, taking far longer than it should on account of Sarah.

"Madam, you must leave *all* your weapons" the maid stressed to Sarah when she had finished putting down her swords.

"What? That's all of them!" Sarah said indignantly.

The maid stared at her unmoving while they all waited. Chris scanned the table and counted three swords, a shield, and a pair of spiked gauntlets on Sarah's part.

"Sarah, give up the dagger," Chris told her impatiently.

"Fine," Sarah sighed as she produced the dagger from under her thigh armor.

The maid still looked at her impatiently.

"What! That's really everything this time, I swear!" Sarah complained.

"Please remove your spiked armor, it looks hazardous," the maid commanded.

"You've got to be kidding me!" Sarah exclaimed angrily but Chris didn't want to cause any more of a scene.

"Sarah! Just do as the maid asks and ditch the armor. We're not here to fight," Chris ordered her.

Sarah rolled her eyes but did as he said. When this was completed the maid led them to a comfortable room filled with several stuffed chairs and a sofa arranged around a table.

"You will remain here until the master is ready to see you. Please refrain from wandering the estate," the maid told them before shutting them into the room.

"I can't believe she made me ditch my armor! What's her problem!?" Sarah ranted.

"Well considering you're just as dangerous in that armor as most are with a sword I don't think she was entirely wrong," Matt told her.

"Besides, if we run into trouble Matt and Ditrina's magic should be more than enough to get us out of here," Chris told her.

"Still…" Sarah began.

"I know, I know, you don't like not having your armor. It'll be alright I promise," Chris told her.

"You didn't have your armor back in Torville for the feast," Cassy remarked.

"That was different; I wore my armor until I got there and took it off once I decided it was safe. I've yet to make that same call here. Until we've spoken with this mystery noble I wouldn't go being too trusting of him," Sarah told her.

"Sarah it'll be fine. Francis told me he was an old friend of his, and that he could use our help. We're here to help him not hurt him," Chris told her.

"Besides, how much could some old hermit ask of us?" Cassy asked from the sofa.

"Well in theory he could ask for quite a lot, for example…" Ditrina said but Matt cut her off.

"It's alright Ditrina, we don't need any examples right now," Matt said hastily hoping to avoid a rambling lecture from the strange elf.

"Very well," Ditrina said as she sat herself beside Cassy on the sofa.

The others took their seats and awaited the return of the maid in silence. Minutes turned to hours as they waited impatiently. Matt began to read his book while Sarah paced behind the sofa. Chris did his best to relax while Cassy and Ditrina napped quietly together. Without warning the door opened suddenly, reveling the maid from earlier.

"The master will see you now," the maid informed them and beckoned them to follow her.

"Are you sure? You're not going to search me before we go any further?" Sarah sneered as she passed the maid.

"I have no idea what you're talking about," the maid said blankly.

"Don't give me that crap!" Sarah yelled. "You made me cough up all my weapons and ditch my armor for no good reason now you act like it never happened?"

"You must have me mistaken with my sister; I'm Flora, not Fiona," Flora told her.

"You're kidding me," Sarah said in disbelief. "Who names twins Flora and Fiona? How does anyone tell you two apart?" Sarah asked angrily.

"I don't understand, I'm Flora, my sister is Fiona, were totally different so what's the issue?" Flora asked.

"You two look exactly the same! You even dress the same!" Sarah ranted.

"Drop it Sarah," Chris ordered. "So sorry Flora, would you be so kind as to take us to your master now?" Chris asked kindly.

"Of course," Flora replied with a small curtsy. "Right this way."

Flora led them through a series of corridors, past large open rooms meant for large gatherings, and up a flight of stairs before stopping them in front of a small wooden door.

"The master is right inside. I ask that you keep your manners in check, he is a very important man," Flora said looking at Sarah.

"Of course Flora," Chris said with a smile before Sarah could do anything rash.

Chris opened the door and stepped inside the room.

The room was mostly empty, with the far wall taken up entirely by a massive window overlooking the valley, and large bookshelves covering the other walls. The only furniture was a large ornate desk set facing toward the door with an impossibly old man sitting behind it, so still he himself looked to part of the furniture. Five chairs had been arranged before the desk in anticipation of their arrival.

"Please, sit," the old man croaked softly. They took their seats and silence fell over the room.

"Sir, we were sent by Baron Francis, he said we would be able to help you with your problem," Chris said after a while.

"Hmmmmm," the old man replied. "So, Francis finally found a suitable group of adventures. I expected more of you,"

"Sir, if you don't mind me asking, who are you and why were we sent here? Francis wasn't very clear with the details," Chris explained.

"Who am I? I'm just an old man with more money than sense. For now that's all you need to know to keep you interested I presume. Why don't you tell me who you all might be?" the old man asked.

Chris studied him, but found his wrinkled face unreadable. He showed no signs of anger nor relief to see them, and Chris was unsure of his motives.

"We are Shearcliff and Company, an adventuring band," Chris told him. "My name is Christian Shearcliff, the leader of the company. The cleric to my left is Matthew Bleakstar, and the women to my right are Sarah Morgson, Cassy Shearcliff, and Ditrina, respectively."

"Interesting, you have an elf in your company, and a naga. How did this come to pass?" the man asked slowly.

"I joined their company after completing a contract alongside them," Ditrina told him. "Afterwards they offered me a place among their ranks so I accepted due to our effectiveness together."

"And you? How is it a lone naga is found adventuring this far west?" the man asked Cassy.

"Well I can't tell you how I ended up this far west, but I'm here because my brother invited me to adventure with him," Cassy told him.

"Your brother? I see no other naga among you," the man said raising a bushy eyebrow.

"I was adopted into Chris's family when I was very young. I've never actually met another naga," Cassy admitted.

"Really? Christian, your family must have been awfully open

minded to accept a naga into your home. Tell me, how did that play out?" the man asked Chris.

"Well at the time we didn't know she was a naga, her scales didn't grow in until she was older, and I was adopted myself you see so Mr. Cogwell, he raised us, didn't mind taking in one more. When Cas grew older the other villagers didn't take kindly to the fact she wasn't human but it never bothered me," Chris told the man.

"And you? What's your story cleric?" the man asked Matt.

"I'm just a wandering cleric sir, not much to tell really," Matt said.

"What god do you serve?" the man asked him.

"I'm unsworn," Matt said sheepishly.

"I see, I see. How very interesting," the man said nodding his head.

"Alright, we've answered your questions. You know who we are, and more about us than you should," Sarah said, giving the others a displeased look for speaking so freely to a stranger. "Now it's your turn. Tell us who you are and what you want with us," Sarah ordered.

"My my. You're certainly a fiery one," the old man chuckled. "Very well, you humored an old man so I suppose I'll tell you who I am. My name is Hal Regar and I would like to hire you to kill Governor Sorros," he said with a smile.

A stunned silence fell over the room.

"You mean *the* Hal Regar, the man who ran Draclige before Sorros? *That* Hal Regar?" Matt asked in disbelief.

"Well it seems no further introduction is necessary. Yes, I'm *that* Hal Regar as you put it, or at least I was the last time I checked," Hal told them.

"Sir, everyone thinks you're dead!" Matt told him in disbelief.

"Well it seems my plan to hide has worked then, kudos to Baron Francis for keeping this place hidden," Hal laughed.

"Hold on a moment, you said you wanted us to kill Governor Sorros?" Sarah asked him still shocked.

"Yes my dear. That tyrant has terrorized the land for far too long and I feel it was time he was replaced," Hal informed her.

"You say it like it will be as easy as waltzing into his castle and lopping off his head! Sorros has dozens of guards around him at all times, with overlapping shifts so that he's never alone. The man's untouchable, and I should know. I used to work for the shit-stain!" Sarah yelled angrily.

"I have to agree with Sarah, this seems a bit out of our skill set," Chris told him. "I'm not sure what Francis promised you but we're not it."

"Baron Francis agreed to send people my way who he deemed capable of completing this mission. After he helped me flee after the insurrection we made a deal that one day I would retake the city with his help. In return Baron Francis would be allowed to appoint a suitable replacement in my stead," Hal told them.

"You don't seek the throne for yourself?" Cassy asked him.

"No no, I'm far too old to be caught up in running a city. Once a suitable new ruler has been appointed I will function as an advisor and assist him or her in the comings and goings of the region until such a time I feel they have a firm grasp of the situation or I pass away. Honestly it will likely be the second of the two. Sadly finding a suitable ruler among the lords and ladies of the court is no small task so I will be forced to act as a temporary governor until we find them," Hal explained.

"You're glossing over the small detail that involves us actually managing to kill the bastard!" Sarah yelled.

"Oh I'm sure you're more than up to the task, or else Francis wouldn't have sent you to me. Not to worry, I will ensure you will be well rewarded for your efforts," Hal told her.

"I doubt you have enough gold," Sarah said with disapproval written across her face. "Seriously, if you want us to take this suicide mission you better start talking numbers here."

"I believe this will be sufficient," Hal said sliding a prewritten contract across the desk to Chris.

Upon reading it Chris's eyes lit up.

"Well? How much is he offering?" Cassy demanded trying to lean across Sarah to read the paper.

Chris gulped and read the paper aloud. It said:

To those who would slay the false Governor Sorros I, Hal Regar on behalf of the city of Draclige, offer the following reward:

1. A full pardon from all previous crimes and wrongdoings within the realm.
2. Knighthood for all participating members of whatever group that kills Sorros.
3. Titles to a plot of land located within the Godspine, referred to as the "Hidden Valley" as well as all ownership of the estate located upon the premises.
4. Lordship over the neighboring town as knights of Draclige.

On behalf of the people of Draclige we thank you for your service and wish you the best of luck in this endeavor.

Chris read the paper allowed once more in disbelief.

"Incredible," he muttered to himself while the others sat stunned.

"Of course if you would prefer gold I'm sure we can arrange something…" Hal began.

"No no no this is more than enough!" Chris said quickly.

"Chris, you can't seriously be considering taking this contract," Sarah warned cautiously.

"A knighthood Sarah, with land and titles!" Chris said breathlessly.

"May I remind you I've been a knight of Draclige before and I can tell you it's not all that it's cracked up to be," Sarah told him angrily.

"That was under Sorros though; we have a chance to make that title mean something now!" Chris argued. "Besides, the land we're being offered is the perfect base for our adventures! This is everything we've been working towards!" Chris told her.

"I thought we were heading south to escape Sorros!" Sarah shot back.

"We won't have to if we take this contract, we can finally stop running and take things a bit slower, really think about the contracts we take instead of rushing to whatever's closest! Think about it Sarah!" Chris said excitedly.

"May I remind you this all hinges on running right back into the jaws of the man you've been fleeing, the most powerful man on this side of the Godspine! Seriously Chris, you're going to get yourself killed! No reward is worth anything if you're dead!" Sarah exclaimed.

"Sarah, you know how the guards work better than anybody. We're the best chance anyone has to take this tyrant down! Together we can make a plan, and find a way to make this work," Chris said.

"Until he flashed that paper in front of your face you were just as against this as I was! Think with your head and not with your coin purse for two seconds and try to see this is a horrible idea!" Sarah pleaded.

"Sarah it'll be fine. We'll work something out," Chris said.

He turned back to Hal.

"Shearcliff and Company accepts your contract; you can leave Sorros to us," Chris promised.

"Wonderful!" Hal exclaimed.

"Well this is going to be fun," Matt grumbled.

CHAPTER EIGHTEEN

Hal gave them rooms to stay in within the mansion while they formulated their plan. That evening they gathered around a large table in one of the unused meeting halls at Sarah's request. Hal hadn't been seen since their meeting earlier that day by anyone, nor had the maids Flora and Fiona.

"Alright listen up everyone, I was against taking this job, but Chris decided to do it anyway," Sarah said giving him a vile look. "With that in mind Shearcliff and Company isn't one to break a contract so now we have to see this job through to the end. If you want to survive this suicide mission you'll need to do exactly what I tell you, and follow my orders to the letter. Chris and I already had a long talk earlier about this and we decided it would be best if I led this operation myself as a temporary commander due to my unique experience in this matter," Sarah told them.

Everyone was already aware of their talk earlier; in fact they were willing to bet the entire valley had heard it. Proof of their *talk* was still evident in the glowing red handprint throbbing on Chris's cheek as well as several other bruises scattered across his body. Matt decided he would have to cast a minor healing spell on Chris later, out of sight of Sarah of course.

"What do you have in mind oh exalted one?" Cassy yawned.

Sarah ignored her sarcasm and laid a large sheet of paper atop the table.

"This is a rough map of the castle in Draclige as best as I can remember. Getting to the castle won't be a problem, getting into it is another matter however. The last they saw of me I went chasing after you lot weeks ago, so they likely think I'm dead by now. If I was to show up and suddenly demand entrance there'll be too many questions so we can't count on my old rank to see us safely inside," Sarah explained.

"Why don't we just fight our way inside? The soldiers I saw when I was in Draclige didn't look so tough," Cassy asked.

"The average soldier in Draclige is no match for any one of us, you're right, but the troops garrisoned inside the castle are a cut above the rest. Sorros has handpicked the most ruthless and effective killers from among his ranks to act as his personal guards. If we go charging in swords drawn we won't last five minutes," Sarah told her.

"Well that's one stroke of good luck," Chris said.

Sarah looked at him quizzically, and Chris feared another *talk* was on the way.

"What I'm trying to say is that if all the guards in the castle are ruthless killers as you put it then I shouldn't have any problems using my sword against them," Chris said hastily.

To his relief Sarah nodded her agreement.

"That's true, we should at least be able to count on your sword aiding us in this battle, though we mustn't forget that it could just as easily decide some random soldier is too *good* and stop working. With that in mind I think it's best if we divide into three teams for this operation. Chris and I will function as the strike team that actually enters the castle, while Matt and Ditrina draw the attention of the majority of the guards with their magic. Cassy will function as the support group and relay information to the other two teams from a rooftop. I spoke to Matt earlier and he says he can cast a spell on Cassy so that we can hear her voice no matter where we are in the city."

"That's a horrifying thought," Chris muttered, earning himself another glare from Sarah. "Sorry," he said meekly.

"As I was saying, we'll be able to hear her but we'll have no way of replying so keep that in mind," Sarah said. "Cassy is uniquely suited to this role due to her specialty in ranged weapons and heightened senses. Matt and Ditrina, for my plan to work I will need you two to bombard the front gates with magic, as much as you can muster. While I need this to be noticeable we have to do everything we can to keep the citizens out of harm's way. I'm looking at you Ditrina," Sarah said sternly.

"Why are you looking at me?" Ditrina asked innocently.

"Because some of the spells I've seen you cast have a tendency to destroy everything around them indiscriminately, and I doubt I've seen you use all your power yet. Try to hold back a little will you?" Sarah asked her.

"Very well," Ditrina nodded.

"Wait a second, why are you just warning Ditrina? Are you saying my magic isn't powerful enough to do collateral damage?" Matt asked indignantly.

"Just do the best you can buddy, I'm counting on you to keep Ditrina up and fighting," Sarah said with a patronizing smile.

"Oh come on I can fight! I seem to remember kicking your ass twice now!" Matt said angrily.

"And neither time did you manage to kill her, in fact she didn't even need healing after either encounter. On the other hand, I've seen Ditrina turn an entire hoard of monsters into ash with a single spell. You're best suited to support and medical aid, don't let your pride distract you from your job Matt," Chris told him.

Sarah nodded her approval of Chris's comment and Matt decided that Chris's wounds could heal on their own.

"While the spell casters are distracting the guards Chris and I will slip in through a side entrance I know about, security should be light because of you two and I'm counting on Cassy to call out targets as she sees them," Sarah said.

"I understand my role but I don't get how it works. I thought the castle was the tallest building in the city, how can I call targets from a roof if I can't see over the walls?" Cassy asked.

"Because you will be standing on top of the main tower, at the center of the castle," Sarah said as if it was the most obvious thing in the world.

"Sarah, I thought the problem was getting inside the castle? How is Cassy going to just magically appear on the tallest tower?" Chris asked.

"Just like you said; magic. For this mission Cassy is going be bowering your fancy cloak and using it to sneak into the castle through the servant entrance," Sarah told him.

"Now wait a second!" Chris protested. "It's not like I can just hand her the cloak and say good luck! The spirit is bound to me and that's what makes the magic work! Besides, if it was that easy to sneak into the castle why don't I just go and stick a sword into Sorros's back while he can't see me?"

"Think for two seconds Chris! The cloak may hide you from those not actively looking for you but once Sorros dies every guard in the room will be actively hunting for the killer. As someone who's seen through the cloak several times now I can honestly tell you that you won't be able to stay hidden once they start searching," Sarah scolded. "This mission isn't worth your life," she added with genuine concern.

"Besides Chris, I think your wrong about the cloak. Remember, before you formally gave me the book I borrowed it several times with your blessing and it worked fine. Who's to say the cloak would be any different?" Matt asked.

"I agree it warrants experimentation," Ditrina agreed.

"So what am I supposed to do for armor during the fight?" Chris asked.

"Your sword should protect you well enough, if it stops working get behind me," Sarah said curtly. "In order for this to work your sister needs the cloak, so stop complaining."

"Fine," Chris conceded reluctantly. "So far we have the spell casters distracting the guards and try to keep them busy while we sneak into the castle under Cassy's watchful eye and take out Sorros. When are we going to carry out this plan?" Chris asked.

"We should leave as soon as possible actually. Right now Sorros's chain of command is weakened. With Droga dead and me out of the picture there's nobody left to convey orders from Fenir and Sorros to the troops forcing them to do so directly, something they loathe to do. Until they replace Droga and myself they're bound to be unorganized."

"Fenir is the sword master right?" Chris asked.

"Yeah, and we have to hope that we don't run into him while we're in the castle. He's far more skilled with a blade than I am, and to make matters worse he's actually a pretty nice guy from what I could tell," Sarah admitted.

"So, I won't be able to use my sword against him," Chris realized.

"Right. If we run into him it's game over for us, making Cassy's job as spotter even more important. Fenir is easy enough to spot; he carries a huge scimitar and has dark black skin. He was the second tallest in the castle after Droga, so you can't miss him," Sarah told them.

"This sounds like a great plan Sarah, what were you worried about?" Chris asked her.

"You can make any plan sound good on paper Chris; the problems arise once the fighting starts. This plan has way too many holes as it is," Sarah said.

"What do you mean?" Matt asked.

"Well what if they see through your distraction? What if Sorros isn't in the castle? On top of that Cassy will only be able to see the courtyards and walls, once we're actually within the castle Chris and I will be blind. I don't like this plan at all," Sarah admitted.

"I don't think they'll be able to ignore me for too long, if they do I'll bring the entire castle down on their heads," Ditrina said dreamily.

"And Cassy will do a great job as field spotter, leaving you two to act as you see fit," Matt chimed in.

"I agree this plan seems solid. You're being too hard on yourself Sarah," Cassy told her.

"You said it yourself, once the fighting starts there's no way of knowing how the plan will work. Until the point when it's obvious the plan has failed we stick to it. You have insight into this situation that nobody else could dream of Sarah, with you we have a chance of pulling this off," Chris told her.

"I appreciate the support, but if things start looking bad it's Cassy's job to call a retreat. If one part of the plan fails the rest of it goes with it;

therefore don't hesitate to call for a withdrawal if you think it's needed. Do you understand?" Sarah asked Cassy.

"Don't worry; I'll make sure things go smoothly," Cassy said flashing her a toothy grin. "You can count on me!"

Despite leaving early the next morning it took almost two weeks to make the return trip to Draclige. They rode as fast as their horses could manage with Hal taking his time following a few days behind them. Once the city fell it was his job to restore order but that wasn't part of their mission so they left it to him. At the pace they traveled Hal would arrive a week after Shearcliff and Company, however their progress was hampered by the spring rains, which had begun in earnest. Until now they had seen almost no rain on their trip having to deal with only the odd storm here or there, never lasting for much more than a day or so. This time however it seemed the rains would last far longer, and as they traveled it showed no sign of relenting. After the eleventh day of unrelenting rain they arrived at Draclige.

"It's good for us that it's still raining," Sarah told them as they looked out over the city.

"How do you figure?" Matt asked.

"Well on a day like today Sorros is bound to be sitting inside the castle twiddling his thumbs. That swine isn't one to go braving the elements unless he absolutely has to. Does everyone remember the plan?" Sarah asked them.

"How could we forget? You repeated it to us every single night on the way here," Cassy grumbled.

"Good then, everyone follow me. I can get us past the gate guard. Don't draw your weapons unless I do so first," Sarah told them and led them toward the city gates.

They rode straight as if they intended to ride directly into the city until one of the gate guards challenged them.

"Who the hell's riding about in this mess!?" the guard shouted as he dragged his bulk out from under the tarp he and his partner had strung up for shelter.

"Don't you recognize one of your commanding officers?" Sarah bellowed as she swung herself off her horse and marched through the mud toward the hapless guard.

"Captain Morgson?" the guard asked in shock. "Where have you been? It's been weeks!" the guard exclaimed.

"I was out perusing traitors under orders from Sorros himself. Stand aside so I can enter the city and give my report," Sarah snarled shoving the guard back.

Chris was surprised, while normally quick to anger this was a level of aggression he hadn't seen in Sarah before. To his utter despair the guard looked confused and held out his arm preventing Sarah from passing.

"Wait a minute Captain, Sorros gave us a little speech telling us he had no idea where you ran off to. Where were you, and who are these blokes with you?" the guard asked suspiciously.

Chris noticed the other guard was edging his hand closer to the horn strung to his belt. A blast from that would signal an attack and ruin their plans before they even began.

"Gods damn it," Sarah cursed and Chris watched as her dagger appeared in her hand as if by magic.

Before the guard could react Sarah plunged the blade up to its hilt into the guard's exposed armpit, where his armor didn't cover. The guard gave a grunt of pain and surprise and slumped forward into Sarah's arms. The other guard reached quickly for his horn but stumbled backward as an arrow sprouted from his throat. He collapsed against the city wall grasping feebly at his neck as Sarah dragged the first guard's body back under the tarp. With a quick slash of her dagger she sliced through the cords holding the tarp, concealing the guard's bodies.

"That won't keep them hidden long; the next shift will find the corpses as soon as they arrive. We need to move," Chris said looking around nervously.

"Shift change isn't for another forty minutes if I'm telling the time correctly. Cassy needs to be in the castle before the alarm is raised," Sarah told them. "Let's move people."

Sarah sheathed her dagger and Cassy slung her bow back over her shoulder and they headed into Draclige once more.

"There's the servant entrance, time to see if the cloak will work," Chris whispered to the others from within the alleyway.

They had made their way across the city under the cover of the storm without incident. Quickly he unclasped the cloak and fashioned it around his sister's shoulders.

"Can you see me?" Cassy whispered eargly.

"We already knew you were there, and we're just as excited as you. I doubt the cloak will hide you from us," Chris told her.

"Oh, right. Matt, are you ready with the spell?" Cassy asked.

"Whenever you guys are," Matt replied.

Cassy gave him the nod and Matt began chanting quietly. After a moment his hands began to glow with a soft yellow light.

"If you'll excuse me," Matt whispered to Cassy, and blushing furiously he traced a glowing circle around her lips that faded quickly.

Matt then turned to each other person and drew a small glowing mark on each of their foreheads, including himself.

"Can you hear me?" Cassy whispered to them, and though she spoke softly they heard her voice loud and clear in their heads.

They gave her the thumbs up.

"Good, I'll be heading out then," Cassy said and prepared to exit the alleyway but Chris caught her arm.

"Be safe Cas, and good luck," he told her as he drew her into a quick hug. "You too brother," Cassy said with a nod before racing toward the servant door, cloak billowing behind her.

They watched in apprehension as she ran right past several busy servants who didn't react in the slightest. Chris let out a sigh of relief.

"Now we wait for Cassy to say she's in position," Sarah told them and they hunkered down in suspense, trusting the storm to help hide their presence.

"I'm surprised that you didn't wish Cassy luck either Ditrina given how close you two are," Matt told her.

"I wasn't aware I needed to do so twice, last night I spoke with Cas in great detail about her safety. In the future should I do so more than once?" Ditrina asked with honest confusion.

Matt sighed.

"So long as you two talked earlier you're probably good, but keep in mind that Cassy may have expected some form of sendoff," Matt cautioned.

"Oh! Is that all? In that case, I'm glad that last night Cas and I…" Ditrina began but Sarah clamped a hand over her mouth.

Ditrina kept speaking, her words coming though as unintelligible mumbles as Sarah signaled for silence. A patrol of guards marched passed the alleyway, steel boots clanging over the sounds of the rain. After they passed Sarah removed her hand and Ditrina kept speaking as if nothing had happened.

"And after that Cas rolled over and we…" she continued.

"What in the god's good name are you thinking!?" Sarah hissed. "Do you want to get us killed?" she demanded.

"What's the problem Sarah?" Ditrina asked tilting her head to the side.

"You just kept rambling off about whatever the hell you did with Cassy the other night, something we couldn't care less about I may add, while guards walked right past us!" Sarah whispered violently.

"I actually care quite a bit," Matt whispered eargly raising his hand but Chris aimed a savage kick at his shin and the hand quickly fell back to his side.

"I still don't understand. I cast a silencing spell while Matt was casting his enchantment earlier, what's the problem?" Ditrina asked.

Sarah paused.

"You did what?" Chris asked.

"I cast a silence spell. Our voices won't carry outside of the alleyway," Ditrina explained.

"I didn't see you cast anything, when were you going to tell us that?" Sarah demanded.

"You didn't hear me over Matt's own spell most likely and I was going to tell you after I finished talking about last night because Matt asked about that first," Ditrina told her.

"Well in that case, please, go on!" Matt urged her earning himself another kick from Chris.

"That's my sister she's talking about!" Chris whispered angrily.

"Sorry, sorry, she just seemed like she wanted to share is all," Matt said with a sheepish grin.

"You don't have to whisper, the spell is still active," Ditrina told them. "Now, as I was saying…"

Once again Ditrina was cut off as Cassy's voice echoed in their heads.

"I'm in position, start the assault," Cassy told them.

"We can talk as we run," Matt said dragging Ditrina from the alley by her arm.

"We'll head inside five minutes after you start the attack!" Sarah called after them.

Chris pulled his sword from its scabbard and Sarah drew her long sword, shifting her shield from her back to her arm in a fluid movement. Despite the spell they waited in silence, anticipation of the coming battle driving idle thoughts from their minds. In the distance they heard a massive explosion.

"Matt and Di have started their attack, and knights are running like crazy toward the gates. So far everything is going as planned," Cassy's disembodied voice told them.

Sarah began counting softly to herself.

"Time to move," Sarah said quietly rising from her crouch exactly five minutes later.

They ran quickly toward the servant door, now abandoned due to its owners fleeing the sounds of battle.

"Watch yourself guys, I'm going to be focusing on Chris and Sarah for a while," Cassy told them. "Once you're through the servant doors take the left, the guards ran to the right."

Chris and Sarah followed Cassy's instructions, and soon found themselves in a walled courtyard.

"Where to now Sarah?" Chris asked.

"It depends on where Cassy tells us the guards are. Sorros isn't foolish enough to leave himself unprotected," Sarah told him.

As if on cue Cassy spoke.

"Ok from here I can actually see you guys, it looks like the courtyards are all connected so if you stick to those I should be able to keep an eye on you as you move about," Cassy told them. "I don't see any guards on your side of the castle; keep moving towards the main tower where I'm at. I think Sorros might be inside."

"That would make sense, Sorros's personal quarters are located inside the tower Cassy's on. He probably fled there because of the attack. I wish I could ask Cassy if she's seen him, but I guess that doesn't matter. Come on Chris," Sarah ordered.

Together they jogged through the courtyards, pausing whenever Cassy said someone was coming, twice having to dive behind bushes or into doorways to avoid guards rushing the way they had come.

"Alright, you two, that's the entrance to the main tower in front of you, once you head inside I won't be able to help you any more so be careful...wait, somebody's coming out of the tower. He's not wearing armor...doesn't look like a normal guard," Cassy warned.

"Shit," Sarah growled.

They had just entered the middle of the courtyard, and had nowhere to hide. The newcomer spotted them instantly and began walking purposefully toward them.

"Chris get back, that's Fenir. I'll hold him off while you take care of Sorros," Sarah said with determination.

"I'm not just going to leave you here Sarah," Chris said angrily.

"Chris, Fenir is as good with a sword as you are with your magic, and your magic won't work against him making you worse than useless. I'll be able to buy you some time then I'll surrender. Fenir isn't the type to kill prisoners so I should be alright," Sarah replied but Chris thought she sounded uncertain.

"Wait I can see him better now, he's got dark skin and a scimitar. I think that's Fenir!" Cassy exclaimed from above them.

"Bit late for that," Sarah grumbled as she approached the sword master.

"Captain Morgson, what a surprise," Fenir said in a rich voice as he recognized her spiked armor. "What brings you back to Draclige, we thought you ran off?" Fenir asked as he drew his sword with a flourish.

Realizing she may yet talk her way out of the situation Sarah lowered her sword and approached casually. Chris watched with every muscle in his body tense. If he made a run for the doors Fenir would attack Sarah without a doubt, but even still he didn't like the manner in which Fenir looked at Sarah. Despite his friendly words his eyes were filled with mistrust and he had already drawn his own sword. The situation did not look good.

"Fenir, have my reports not been reaching you? I went off in pursuit of the cleric Matthew Bleakstar and his companions after he showed up in the city while he was supposed to be exploring Algeminia with Droga. It took several weeks but in the end, I was able to apprehend the traitor. Sadly, he resisted and did not survive," Sarah lied.

"Interesting, did you tell Sorros about this mission?" Fenir asked.

"No, I had to pursue them on short notice and only managed to tell the gate guard about my departure," Sarah told him.

This much was true at least and she hoped that the guards had told the others of her departure as she had ordered them to. To her relief Fenir nodded.

"Yes, we had received such a report, but recently we had assumed you had failed your mission," Fenir told her.

"Why is that sir?" Sarah asked.

"Because as of now Matthew Bleakstar is attacking the main gates with the aid of another spell caster. I'm sorry Sarah but I'm going to have to ask you come with me. I'd like to hear your report again," Fenir told her and leveled his sword at her chest.

Sarah jumped back and readied her own weapons and Chris rushed to her side.

"Chris don't be stupid, run!" Sarah yelled.

"I'm sorry but your friend is going to have to come with us as well," Fenir said and held his fist up in the air.

In response to his signal a dozen armored guards poured out from the tower and formed a wall around them, cutting off hopes of escape.

"Please come quietly Sarah, I don't want this to end in you getting hurt," Fenir told her.

"I notice he didn't say anything about me," Chris muttered as he readied his sword.

Neither Chris nor Sarah made any move to attack, nor did they make an effort to flee. They simply stood silently in the rain waiting.

Fenir sighed.

"Because you insist on making this difficult you leave me no choice. Guards, take them, alive if possible," Fenir ordered and as a unit the guards surged forward.

"Chris, take the guards! I'll deal with Fenir," Sarah yelled as they sprang into action.

"On it!" Chris replied and swung his sword at the first guard to reach him.

To his relief his blade swung true, and he parried the guards thrust with ease. He let the sword take over and began to weave through the crowd of knights with a dancers grace, dealing death to all around him while doing his best to stay close to Sarah. These must have been some of the cutthroats Sorros used as bodyguards Chris decided, because as he fought the sword showed no remorse. He glanced over to Sarah and saw she was having far more trouble than he was.

As the battle began Sarah charged directly at Fenir trusting Chris to protect her back. She thrust at his unarmored chest but he knocked her sword aside with casual distain. Before she had time to raise her long sword once again he launched a blinding series of strikes at her, and it was all she could do to fend them off with her shield. Recovering slightly she changed tactics and attempted an overhead strike, knowing full well he would evade it. Sarah felt Fenir's sword stop her own above his head, and she made her move. Sarah swung her shield toward his stomach, hoping to slice him open with its sharp edge. Fenir was faster than she expected and managed to jump backward only suffering a shallow cut across his gut. He paused and looked at Sarah, as if reevaluating her entirely.

"That's a fine trick Sarah, but I'm afraid it won't save you. Please, stop this nonsense and come quietly. I promise you'll receive fair treatment," Fenir told her.

"I know what Sorros's idea of fair treatment is," Sarah sneered and readied her weapons.

Fenir shook his head sadly.

"Very well. I shall try to make this as painless as possible," Fenir told her.

"Don't insult me," Sarah snarled as she launched once more into the fight.

Chris had almost finished dealing with the guards. Alone not a single one of them would have provided the slightest challenge for his sword but as a group he was forced to fight more defensively. His main priority was protecting Sarah, but as the battle dragged on he found it was growing difficult for him to protect himself properly. Several times he had felt the sword move to intercept a strike he hadn't seen coming and he was well aware he would have been helpless without his magic. The final guard proved slightly more despicable than the rest because as Chris turned to engage him faint flames licked up the edges of his sword, hissing in the rain. The guard backed away slowly, seeking relief from the wicked sword that had cut down his companions so easily, but Chris advanced. In this fight he knew there would be no quarter.

Sarah's breath came in ragged gasps. Her fight with Fenir was going poorly to say the least. Her helmet had been lost long ago, having saved her head from a vacation across the courtyard courtesy of Fenir's scimitar, but shattering in the process. Her shield arm hung bleeding limply at her side, Fenir having scored a deep blow beneath her shoulder plate rendering the limb useless. Fenir himself bore only the thin cut across his stomach for all her trouble and seemed ready to end the fight. He had offered her mercy once but she figured he had no intention of doing so again. Sarah readied her sword as Fenir launched his final attack.

Chris had just finished with the last guard and turned his attention back to Sarah, and saw in horror that she was injured, and on the defensive. Chris realized that while fighting he had moved across the courtyard leaving Sarah on her own. He sprinted toward her but saw Fenir lunge and knew he wouldn't make it in time. By a miracle Sarah managed to block the strike with her sword, though she was knocked to the ground in the process, her sword flying from her grip.

"I'm sorry it has to end this way," Fenir said as he stood over her.

Sarah fumbled with her good hand trying desperately to draw another weapon but Fenir slashed quickly, rendering her other arm useless.

"I'll give you one last chance to surrender," Fenir said quietly, a sliver of mercy glowing in his eyes as he pressed the point of his sword to her neck.

From the corner of her eye Sarah saw Chris sprinting toward her and smiled at him. She knew he would never make it in time.

"Go to hell," Sarah spat at Fenir and watched as the spark of mercy was replaced with cold determination.

Fenir raised his scimitar above his head and paused. He stood unmoving for a full second, then two as Sarah waited for the final blow to fall.

Fenir looked curiously down at his chest, not understanding why an arrowhead now poked through the front of his shirt. Giving a small cough which covered him in blood Fenir fell slowly to his knees before collapsing face down on the rain slicked ground, a pool of crimson rapidly spreading around him. Chris and Sarah both looked in astonishment at the arrow that had transfixed Fenir, rising from his back.

"Are you two alright? You all started fighting and I didn't have a clear shot without risking hitting you two. Good work getting him to stand still Sarah!" Cassy said excitedly, her voice echoing through their heads.

Sarah gave a weak laugh from the ground as Chris reached her.

"Sarah! Are you alright?" Chris asked as he knelt by her side.

He could see quite a bit of blood pooling around her but was unsure of how much was hers and how much was Fenir's.

"That's why you never give your opponent more than one chance to surrender Chris," Sarah groaned before collapsing onto her back.

Chris dropped his sword and cradled her against him, trying to gauge her wounds.

"We need to get you to Matt," he said scooping her off the ground, groaning from the combined weight of her and her armor.

"Don't bother, I'm not about to kick the bucket just yet," Sarah said weakly from his arms.

"So what then!? You want me to just leave you here until after we finish the mission? You're losing too much blood as it is," Chris told her as he took a shaky step toward the main gates where Matt fought.

"I appreciate the effort you're making love but my legs are fine. I just couldn't stand without my arms wearing armor," Sarah said with a weak laugh.

Blushing, Chris set her upright and helped her maintain her balance.

"Is everything ok down there?" Cassy asked them. "What's the problem?"

Remembering his sister, Chris began waving his arms at the tower and pointing franticly at Sarah. Cassy seemed to get the message.

"What, did she dump you or something? Is that why you're upset? You know I'm not going to shoot her for you," Cassy's voice told them.

Sarah laughed until she winced in pain while Chris shoved his face into his hands.

Trying once more he pointed forcefully at the top of the tower then once at his feet.

"Ooooooh got it. I'll be right down," Cassy told them.

Satisfied, Chris returned to Sarah's side and did his best to slow the bleeding coming from her arms.

"How could she think that I dumped you after you fought so hard to help me?" Sarah cooed as he tied a makeshift tourniquet around one of her arms.

"How can you be so calm right now? He nearly cut your arms off!" Chris chided as he went to work on her other arm.

"Please, I've had worse than this Chris. Besides it figures, I was the only one against the mission and *I'm* the one who ends up injured," Sarah laughed.

"I swear to the gods if you bleed to death I won't forgive you," Chris told her as he finished tying her other tourniquet.

Sarah kissed him lightly on the cheek.

"I'm glad you're concerned Chris, I really am, but if you keep pestering me like a mother hen I'm going to shove my shield up your ass," Sarah told him.

"What seems to be the problem?" Cassy asked as she raced into the courtyard.

"How did you get here so fast?" Chris asked in surprise.

"I jumped from balcony to balcony. It wasn't too hard on my legs but I don't recommend you try it," Cassy said dismissively. "So Sarah, I see you decided to let Fenir carve you like a turkey," Cassy mocked looking at her wounds.

"Listen naga, just because my arms don't work don't think I won't turn you into snake skin boots," Sarah warned.

"Oooooh feisty are we?" Cassy said as she danced backward out of skinning range. "Alright Chris what's the plan?" Cassy asked him.

"I need you to get Sarah to Matt as soon as possible. You two need to get her as far from the fighting as possible. Give Ditrina the cloak and send her after me. I'm going after Sorros," Chris told her.

"Alone? He might have more guards," Sarah warned him.

"I'll be fine; if they're anything like the men I just fought I won't have any problems," Chris told her.

"And what if they're men like Fenir?" Sarah demanded.

"I'll improvise," Chris said with a shrug.

"You better not die for this stupid contract," Sarah said with displeasure evident in her voice.

She turned to Cassy.

"I can walk on my own but you need to carry my sword and shield. I literally just replaced them in Purevein and I don't want to have to do it again," she said irritably.

"Wait, you called me down here just to carry your shit!? What the hell!" Cassy yelled. "I'm not a pack mule!"

"That's right, you're an ass. Now grab my kit and let's get going," Sarah said as she began walking back the way they came.

Cassy sighed but picked up the weapons and followed after the injured warrior. Chris heard Cassy's voice bickering to Sarah in his head long after they had left and sighed.

"Time to kill a tyrant, no pressure," Chris said nervously to himself as he ran into the tower.

CHAPTER NINETEEN

Chris walked slowly through the massive tower. It seemed abandoned as he investigated several of the rooms on the lowest floor. Finding no signs of life, Sorros or otherwise, Chris returned to the entry way which featured a large spiral staircase against the far wall. Despite everything that had occurred Chris realized he had no idea what Sorros looked like and had been relying on Sarah to point him out for him. Chris decided that he would know Sorros when he found him, if he looked anything like how he acted he would be a small fat man cowering behind his guards.

Chris pressed onward up the stairs. Each floor of the tower he explored yielded the same results and as he progressed up its levels he began to doubt that Sorros was here at all. That was when Chris heard a faint noise. Drifting quietly from above him was the sound of a piano being played quite skillfully. Quickening his pace Chris followed the music to its source and found it came from behind a door at the very top of the stairs. Chris stood unsure of if he should wait for back up, Ditrina should be on the way after all. It was then that he felt a familiar presence in his mind.

"Chris, I'm so sorry but I must break my promise," Al's voice spoke urgently in his head.

Chris almost dropped his sword in surprise.

"Al, what are you doing? I thought you could only speak to me in my sleep?" Chris asked in his head.

"No, we can speak to you any time we wish but we swore never to interfere in your daily life. Your decisions are meant to be yours alone," Al replied.

"So why break that vow now of all times?" Chris wondered.

"I didn't want to do this, believe me, but I felt I had to tell you something. I sensed something strange when you entered the tower. Ge is with Matt and Mi is with Ditrina so I couldn't speak with them to confirm my suspicions but now you're closer I'm sure," Al told him.

"Sure of what Al? You're not making any sense," Chris thought angrily. "Now's not the time for crazy spirit stuff, I have to find Sorros and end this."

"Chris this is about Sorros! I sense he possess an artifact as well, one with power equivalent to that of the sword. I'm not sure what it is but the spirit residing within it is strong," Al warned him.

"Well what do we do now?" Chris thought franticly.

"Do what you always do, fight. I'll be by your side and together we will prevail over whatever trickery awaits us beyond that door. I just felt you needed to know," Al told him.

"Thanks Al, I appreciate it," Chris thought.

"Please don't tell my brothers I spoke to you, they might get jealous," Al added meekly.

Chris thought about Mi giving him advice as he went through his normal day and shuddered.

"Don't worry, it'll stay between us," Chris assured him.

"Good. Let us advance then my friend, onward to glorious battle!" Al yelled excitedly in Chris's head.

Chris pushed open the door and walked into the room.

"Well, who might you be?" asked a handsome man sitting at the piano.

This appeared to be someone's privet quarters with a large bed as well as an ornate writing desk pushed into the corner. Chris stared at the man not understanding. He looked to be in his early fifties but was as fit as anyone Chris had ever met. He wore a tight fitting white tunic embroidered in gold and carried a fancy rapier on his belt. On his hand wore a large ornate ring bearing a crest of some kind. He was currently smiling at Chris and had made no move to stand.

"I'm looking for Sorros, where is your master hiding?" Chris demanded.

The man looked genuinely panicked.

"I'm so sorry but you seem to have made a mistake. I'm nobody's servant, I *am* Governor Sorros," he said with a smile.

Chris stood in stunned silence; this man couldn't be farther from the Sorros he had pictured in his head.

"I saw your fight, from my balcony," Sorros said, pointing to the window on the far side of the room. "It was very impressive and if I'm not mistaken that was Sarah Morgson fighting alongside you? How very interesting."

Chris brought his thoughts back to the present.

"Sorros, you will answer for your crimes against Draclige and her people!" Chris said leveling his sword at him.

On cue the blade erupted into flames, brighter than it ever had before. Sorros's eyes widened.

"So it was you who found the crypt! When the expedition I sent to Algeminia did not return I decided someone else must have absconded with the treasures, but I never dreamed that they would come all this way to deliver them to me! You see after I found one artifact in my travels I decided I simply *must* possess them all, you could even say it's a secret hobby of mine. That's why I was so excited when through my research I discovered the location of not one, but three more artifacts within my very own territory! You do understand, don't you?" Sorros asked as he stood smoothly and drew his rapier.

Rather than cross the room so that they could fight Sorros simply pointed the tip of his sword at Chris and said:

"Kill."

"Chris brace!" Al bellowed as a bolt of lightning shot from the tip of Sorros's rapier and smashed into the blade of his own sword, which Al had barely raised in time.

Even so Chris skidded backward under the force of the attack and felt his arms go numb.

"Impressive, though I'd expect nothing less from the Blade of Al. I don't see the Book of Ge or the Cloak of Mi on you though. Have you hidden them somewhere? No matter, I'm sure your friends will tell me once I've finished with you," Sorros said cheerfully as he shot another blinding streak of lightning across the room at Chris.

Chris rolled out of the way, though he felt the bolt fly so close that his entire body tingled. The missed shot hit the wall behind him causing it to explode into a million shards of mortar and stone, exposing them to the rain and filling the room with dust and the stink of ozone.

"You'll have to do better than that little trick if you want to win," Chris laughed, and at that moment he wasn't sure if it was him or Al talking.

Screaming a battle cry in a language only Al knew Chris launched himself toward Sorros, his sword carving a flaming arc through the rain. Sorros's sword met Chris's own with a ringing crash and the battle erupted into full swing.

Their blades flew faster than the eye could track, and each time they connected they showered their wielders with sparks. Had Sorros's thin blade been a regular sword it would have been split in two by the sheer force of their impacts but it seemed every bit as durable as Chris's own sword. This battle would be decided by the strength of the wielders alone, Sorros's magic versus Chris's. Both men fought with superhuman speed and strength, seemingly evenly matched.

After a solid minute of trading blows without either man suffering even the smallest scratch Sorros leapt backwards several paces out of the reach of Chris's sword. Sorros smiled and pointed his blade to the sky, shooting a brilliant streak of lightning into the clouds and blasting the roof off the tower in a spectacular display. Flashes of lightning suddenly forked around the tower and Chris found himself under assault from the very sky. Dancing from side to side Chris did his best to avoid the deadly flashes of light. Sorros didn't wait to see if the lightning would do the trick, rather he redoubled his assault on Chris. Now forced to defend from above as well as below Chris found himself being pushed on the defensive. One step at a time Sorros forced him ever closer to the large gaping hole in the wall.

It was then Chris realized he had lost. He had no trick up his sleeve, no alley to rescue him, only the knowledge that he was outclassed.

"We will win. We will smite him. We will win. We will smite him. We will win…" Al said over and over again in Chris's head, driving all other thoughts away.

"I will win!" Chris screamed at Sorros, each word echoed by Al's ancient tongue.

Chris's blade gushed fire, flames rushing around their feet. Sorros stumbled backward as Chris reversed his grip on the sword, ramming it's blade deep into the stone floor.

"I will slay you!" Al's voice screamed, each word echoed by Chris's own as flames swirled around him, encasing him within a swirling sphere of fire.

Sorros shot a lightning bolt at the vortex of fire only to see it dissipate within the blazing coils. The inferno swirled faster and faster around Chris, buffeting Sorros with scorching wind and evaporating the rain before it landed. Sorros fled for the stairs as the flames grew brighter and brighter, becoming a miniature sun, melting the stones around him.

The world became fire.

From outside the castle Sarah spun as she heard a deafening boom. She watched in horror as a miniature lightning storm spun around the top of the tower destroying much of the building.

She looked at Ditrina who was fastening the cloak around her shoulders.

"Do you have something to do with that?" Sarah demanded.

"No, I use fire magic remember?" Ditrina said calmly.

"Is Chris still in there?" Matt asked, horrified by this display of power.

"I don't know, but we have to get over there to get him out if he is," Sarah said testing her newly healed arms.

It was then that the top half of the tower was engulfed in a massive fireball, creating a blast so powerful that it knocked them off their feet and so hot that it flash-dried the rain soaked ground around them.

"What about that? Did you do that?" Sarah roared at Ditrina as they stumbled to their feet.

"No, though I must admire whoever cast that spell's destructive capabilities, quite impressive," Ditrina said nodding her head approvingly.

"Chris was in that tower!" Sarah screamed at Ditrina angrily.

"If he was in that building he is most certainly dead," Ditrina said flatly. "The shockwave alone would have killed anyone inside that building, not even considering the massive fireball," Ditrina said as easily as if listing off her favorite books.

The lower half of the tower which had survived the blast thus far finally crumbled to the ground kicking up a massive dust cloud as it leveled much of the castle.

"And then there's that," Ditrina added, pointing to the carnage.

"Chris," Cassy sobbed as she fell to her knees, tears streaming down her face.

Matt stood in stunned silence as if moving would finalize the death of his friend. Ditrina shook her head sadly.

"Tragic, but at least it was a painless death. At that range he wouldn't have felt..." Ditrina began but Sarah ended her statement with a crushing punch to the nose.

Luckily she had removed her gauntlets before she was healed, but still Ditrina collapsed in a heap on the cobblestones, cradling her bleeding face as Sarah turned, storming off toward the fallen tower.

"Sarah where are you going? We need to stick together!" Matt called after her.

"He's not dead, he can't be dead! You can stay here if you want but I'm going to find Chris," Sarah snarled as she continued to march toward the rubble.

"You saw that explosion, there's no way he could have survived that!" Matt yelled.

"Consider this; if by some miracle Chris survived that he's bound to be injured. If I find him but he dies because you weren't there to heal him do you know what I'll do to you?" Sarah asked menacingly.

Matt gulped.

"I won't do a damn thing. I'll just make sure you know that your best friend died because you were too afraid to look for him for the rest of your life," Sarah told him quietly.

Matt found the prospect of that more horrifying than any other threat Sarah could have dredged up and followed quickly after her, leaving Ditrina crumpled on the ground and Cassy sobbing quietly, mourning her brother's fate.

Despite how close they were to the fallen tower it took considerable time to reach its base. Their progress was obstructed by a thick miasma of dust that hung in the air blinding them and blocking out the feeble rays of sunlight that slipped through the rain. As they searched through the rubble they called for their missing friend.

"Chris! Where are you?" Matt yelled for the hundredth time.

"Chris!" Sarah screamed franticly.

Matt watched uncomfortably as Sarah dug through the rubble with reckless abandon.

"Sarah take it easy, you're not going to find Chris any faster that way," Matt cautioned.

"Chris is somewhere under this mess and your just standing there!" Sarah screamed at him, tears streaming down her dust caked face.

Matt took a step back in shock; he had never seen Sarah so distraught before.

"Calm down Sarah, I want to find Chris as much as you do but randomly digging won't get us anywhere. Look for his sword; it would have survived the blast," Matt told her.

"What good is his sword to us?" Sarah asked angrily.

"Well the sword can't be lost right? If Chris is alive the sword will be somewhere nearby," Matt reasoned.

Sarah nodded her head and wiped a hand across her face, smearing her tears into the dust.

"Your right; find the sword, find Chris. Thanks Matt," Sarah said with a weak smile.

They made their way deeper into the rubble looking for the glint of metal. After a while Matt spotted something shining beneath a large chunk of stone.

"Look!" he yelled as he ran toward the object in question.

"Is it his sword?" Sarah asked eargly.

"It's *a* sword," Matt told her as he tried to pull the rapier out from under the rubble. "I think it's stuck on something," Matt grumbled as he pulled harder.

With a snapping noise the sword lurched free, a charred hand still clutching the hilt.

"Oh gross," Matt gagged as he wrinkled his nose at the severed limb. He prepared to toss it away but Sarah stopped him.

"Matt wait, give that to me," Sarah commanded.

"Why?" Matt asked confused.

"That hand, it's wearing a ring," Sarah told him as she snatched the weapon away from Matt.

She inspected the ring closely and gave a small gasp.

"This is Sorros's signet ring!" she exclaimed.

"Wait you mean…" Matt stammered in disbelief.

"Chris did it, Sorros is dead," Sarah said breathlessly.

While still in her grip the charred hand began to break apart into ash, slowly scattering around their feet. To their shock once the hand had fully dissipated the sword itself shattered into a million shards of glass around them.

"Why'd it do that?" Matt asked her.

"I'm not sure; I've never seen a sword do that before. Maybe because of the explosion?" Sarah asked unsure.

Well whatever it was isn't important right now," Matt told her. "Let's keep looking."

They continued to pour through the destruction, turning over large chunks of rubble and keeping a watchful eye out for the glint of metal. At some point, they weren't sure when, Cassy and Ditrina joined in the search. Nobody mentioned Sarah and Ditrina's fight, they simply searched in silence. It was Cassy who saw it.

"Everyone, come quick! I found something!" she yelled across the field of carnage.

They hurried to her side and looked curiously at what she had discovered.

"What is that?" Sarah asked staring at the strange object.

It appeared to be a large sphere made up of melted stone fragments from the tower that had fused together. The strange sphere was partially buried in the rubble and was still hot enough that the rain sizzled as it landed on it. Ditrina walked up to it and rapped on the side with her knuckles.

"It appears to be hollow," Ditrina informed them.

"Di is your hand ok?" Cassy asked, fearing she had burned herself on the hot stones.

"I'm fine Cas, specializing in pyromancy I long ago stopped fearing fire. It takes much more than that to burn me," Ditrina told her.

She turned to Sarah who saw blood caked across Ditrina's face from when she had hit her.

"Sarah, Cas explained to me what I did wrong. I'm very sorry if what I said came across as cold or uncaring, I was simply stating the reality of the situation. I hope Chris survived as much as you do and if you think he lived I will help you find him," Ditrina told Sarah.

"It's ok Ditrina, and for what it's worth I'm sorry. I shouldn't have hit you," Sarah admitted. "I was just a little worked up is all."

"Given what we have found so far I think it is likely that Chris is inside that orb. I have no idea how he wound up within it but that's the only place he could be if he survived," Ditrina told her.

"Allow me," Matt said stepping forward.

He chanted under his breath for a moment then held his hands out at the sphere incasing it in a faint nimbus of light mirrored by a tiny orb glowing between his hands. Without warning Matt crushed the tiny orb, causing fractures to race across the original. Slowly the sphere split apart like a massive egg reveling Chris's still form.

He knelt; clothes charred and tattered, propped up only by his sword which was embedded in the stones at his feet. They stared in stunned silence, unsure if he was alive until he drew a single ragged breath.

"Chris!" Sarah yelled jumping down into the newly opened sphere.

As she rushed toward him he slumped off the sword and rushed toward the ground only to be caught by Sarah at the last moment.

"Come on Chris, open your eyes. Talk to me!" Sarah pleaded cradling his limp body.

Slowly his eyes opened as if seeing the world for the first time and she gave a gasp of surprise. Chris's once dark brown eyes now glowed red, the color of molten metal. Sarah realized that the rubies set in his sword were also glowing fiercely, matching his eyes.

"Chris?" Sarah asked tenderly, as if he had somehow become a new person.

"Sarka sal, mika lorwin nargut," Chris babbled at her.

Sarah shook her head not understanding.

"Chris what's wrong, I don't understand," Sarah asked her voice sticking in her throat.

"Salem dorem helfrit. Narka rekite!" Chris rambled back.

Sarah began to weep, horrible heart wrenching cries ripped from within her as she cradled Chris close against her. Matt worked his way inside the spear and looked closely at Chris.

"Matt, I don't know what's wrong with him, he looks fine but he just keeps babbling at me," Sarah sobbed.

"I'm not sure he's babbling," Matt said looking intently at Chris.

"What do you mean?" Sarah asked her voice still choked with tears.

"Gar flosa nar besud?" Matt asked him.

Chris's head snapped toward Matt.

"Flosa Ge nar flosa!" Chris pleaded.

Matt frowned and shook his head.

"It's as I suspected. Chris is speaking in the language of the brothers," Matt told her.

"Well why the hell doesn't he speak common?" Sarah demanded.

"I don't think you're talking to Chris. If I had to guess I would say that's Al, the spirit who controls the sword. It's possible he's speaking because Chris is too weak to do so; though I'm just speculating. The language of the brothers was used before the crisis and is considered a dead language by today's standards but as part of my clerical training

I learned it to read some of the older holy texts. I'm not very good at it but I believe Al just asked Ge for help," Matt explained.

"So Al took over Chris's body!?" Sarah asked in alarm.

"Doubtful. While the spirits certainly have the capabilities to do so they were adamant about leaving our daily lives alone and only communicating at night. The fact that Al is in control means that Chris's mind is unable to use his body. Did I get that right?" Matt asked Al.

Chris's body nodded.

"Does he understand us?" Ditrina asked from the edge of the sphere.

Until now she had been listening eargly to Matt's description of the problem. Cassy looked lost but concerned.

"The spirits share our memories and as such they learned our language through us, at least enough to understand us," Matt explained.

"Yes," Al said in Chris's voice.

"You can speak common?!" Sarah exclaimed in outrage.

"Tarlo," Chris replied in Al's voice.

"Wait that didn't sound like Chris, what's happening?" Sarah demanded.

"I…I'm slipping…" Al moaned.

"Sorka nyota," Chris finished for him. "Sarka flosa…flosa…please," Chris gasped speaking common once more.

"Chris!" Sarah exclaimed happily.

Chris smiled up at her before his red eyes rolled up into his head and his body went limp once more. Ditrina carefully approached Chris's unconscious form and fashioned his cloak around his shoulders.

"Sarah, please grab his sword. I think it will let you pick it up for the sake of returning it," Ditrina instructed.

Sarah laid Chris carefully on the ground before approaching the sword. She reached out and found she was able to grasp it by the hilt and with a mighty tug freed the blade from the cracked stones.

"You better not die," Sarah growled as she laid the sword across Chris's chest, folding his hands over its hilt. "Matt, Cassy, go fashion a stretcher. We need to get him out of here. Move it!" Sarah said, ending her orders with a bellow.

Matt and Cassy leapt into motion hurrying away from her sudden rage, though they each thought to themselves that it was a good sign Sarah was back to her normal level of anger. There was something unnerving about seeing her cry, as if they were intruding upon sacred ground.

"You better not die," Sarah said again, much more softly, so that only she could hear.

CHAPTER TWENTY

"Where am I?" Chris wondered to himself.

He seemed to be weightless, floating through a void. He could hear nothing, see nothing.

"What is this, where's my body?" Chris wondered as he drifted.

It was a pleasant sensation, like he was standing in the sun on a warm day. The last thing he remembered he had been fighting Sorros then fire, lots of fire. After that things got hazy but the one thing he remembered clearly was Sarah. Sarah had been ok, and that was enough to make Chris smile if he had had a body to smile with.

"Hello Chris," Al's voice called to him.

"Al, where am I? What's going on?" Chris wondered.

Without a body he could find no way to speak.

"It seems you've found yourself in a similar akin to Matt's own back in Purevein. Your soul has become detached from your body," Al told him.

"So I'm dying then?" Chris wondered.

"Not exactly. In our battle with Sorros we became…tangled for lack of a better term," Al explained.

"What does that mean?" Chris wondered.

"It means I have committed an unforgivable sin against you, and for that I am truly sorry," Al told him. "When we met my soul was

285

tethered to this world by the sword, and bound to you only because the enchantment on the sword recognized you as its owner."

"Are you saying that the sword was destroyed? Are you going away?" Chris wondered in panic.

"No, the only way for an artifact such as the sword too be destroyed is if its owner perishes. If that were the case the sword would have shattered but as far as I can tell both you and the sword are fine. As for what happened, I stepped too far into the physical world, used my powers too much. Because of this I experienced something similar to what happened to Matt simply in reverse, I lost my connection to the astral realm. In order to stop my soul form dissipating completely I anchored myself partially to you," Al told him.

"So now we have two souls inside one body? How does that work?" Chris wondered.

"You can't fit more than one soul inside of a body Chris. In order to save myself I pulled part of your soul from your body and tethered it to the sword. I'm truly sorry," Al said his voice full of shame.

"I don't see a problem Al. That's what happened to Matt and he's perfectly fine," Chris thought.

"This is a bit different Chris. Matt bound his soul to the book that much is true, but Matt also has his body all to himself. We're now sharing this body, and because of that I won't be able to separate my thoughts from your own," Al told him.

"Wait, so I'll think whatever you think?" Chris wondered.

"No, more so I'll be sharing your thoughts around the clock. Before we could simply review your actions at our leisure while enjoying our afterlives and you could speak to us in your sleep, but things are different now. The half of my soul that once resided within the astral realm now lives within you. I've lost my connection to the afterlife and won't be able to go further than the void we've been meeting in," Al said.

"So, you've become just as mortal as me," Chris thought.

"Essentially," Al replied.

"Al, I'm so sorry," Chris thought. "I know you had a family and I wish I had a way to send you back but I don't understand why you're apologizing to me? In essence my life is unchanged," Chris thought.

"Your life isn't what I'm concerned with, more so I worry about your death. Because our souls have fused when you die I fear the small part of me that remains with the sword when combined with the part of you that shares it may prove enough to prevent you from passing on to the afterlife," Al explained. "I fear I've ruined your death."

Chris could think of nothing to respond with and for an unknown amount of time they drifted in silence.

"I don't mind Al," Chris thought eventually.

"But Chris! After you die your soul moves to the astral realm or else you just drift like this for eternity! One day your friends will pass on but you will remain, lingering, never to be reunited," Al said his voice thick with emotion.

"I'll still be bound to the sword so when I die I'll just have to help whoever wields it next. I may never move on to the afterlife but I'm sure I'll find a way to make do. Besides, I can still get to the space between the realms same as you so I'll always be able to talk to Matt and your brothers at least. I won't be lonely," Chris thought.

"You're taking this far better than I expected," Al admitted.

"Well there's got to be benefits to this," Chris thought.

"Like what?" Al asked.

"That thing you did with the sword, what was that?" Chris wondered.

"I used my magic and channeled it through the blade. Magic is linked to the soul so even in death spirits can wield it," Al told him.

"Were you a cleric?" Chris wondered.

"No, why?" Al asked.

"Well you said you can use magic, but humans can't use magic without the gods," Chris thought.

"The world was a very different place when I was alive, before the crisis as you call it all peoples of all races could wield magic," Al explained.

"What happened?" Chris wondered.

"The gods happened. I won't say any more than that right now, it does you no good to worry over events that occurred over fifteen-hundred years ago," Al told him.

"But you and your brothers could use magic without the gods? I had just assumed Ge was a cleric," Chris thought.

"No we were just kings, irresponsible kings perhaps but still kings. We had a single city that we shared and life was good," Al told him.

Al sighed remembering his life.

"I'm asking because you said that you used magic through the sword and to a lesser extent me. Because we've become intertwined is it possible that I'll be able to use your magic?" Chris wondered hopefully.

Al was quiet for a time though it was hard to judge how long. Chris felt like he could have been speaking for minutes or days.

"I think it may be likely, but don't get your hopes too high," Al warned.

"I won't. I'm just excited by the possibility is all," Chris thought.

"As am I. No human has used magic without the assistance of a god in over a thousand years. When we get the chance we shall speak to Ge on this matter," Al told him.

"Why aren't the others here by the way?" Chris wondered.

"We're not in a place that they can reach us, right now we exist solely within your mind. Until you've woken up they won't be able to speak to us at all. The next time you sleep things should return to normal however," Al told him.

"When will I wake up?" Chris wondered.

"Soon now I think. Your body took a longer time to heal than I expected," Al told him. "Using magic in such a fashion will take some getting used to and may prove extremely strenuous at first."

"Where will I be? Not under a mountain of rubble I hope," Chris wondered.

"Don't worry; your friends took good care of you," Al's voice told him. "In fact we should be waking up at any moment now. I'll do my very best to not distract you when we're awake," Al told him as the warmth that surrounded Chris began to fade.

Chris awoke on a large bed in an unfamiliar room. He looked around and saw that it was richly furnished with a full sized mirror, several carved wardrobes, and a sturdy table upon which his sword lay atop his folded cloak. The bed on which he lay on was by far the most comfortable he had ever used, and wider by a half. Upon further inspection he realized that Sarah's weapons could be seen resting on a rack beside the door and he assumed if he were to open one of the wardrobes he would find her clothes and armor. Sunlight crept in through the large window though the blinds were drawn so he could not see outside.

"Where am I?" he asked aloud.

"I would wager this is the house in the Godspine you earned for completing the Sorros contract," Al said in his head, startling Chris.

"Al, I'm sorry but when I'm awake can you stay quiet unless I talk to you first? I may lose my mind if I have two sets of thoughts rattling around my head," Chris thought.

"Of course Chris, I figured you would ask as much," Al replied before falling silent.

That obstacle overcome, Chris attempted to rise from the bed but found his movements stiff and sluggish, his balance nonexistent.

"Where are my clothes?" Chris muttered realizing he was only wearing a pair of underwear.

He started hobbling across the room toward the wardrobe. On the way, he stopped in front of the large mirror and looked at himself, it had been several weeks since he had had a good look at his reflection.

The weeks of fighting and traveling had changed him. His muscles stood our more than before and he looked thinner than he remembered. Someone had cut his hair in the time he had been asleep, however long that was, so now it hung just below his ears though it was just as unkempt as ever. He had grown a layer of stubble across his face and decided it was high time to find a razor rather than continue on looking like some vagabond. Several new scars could be seen scattered across his body, some on account of his battle with Sarah, some from his fight with Sorros, and more still he couldn't remember earning. As he turned to walk away he stopped, noticing something else differing about himself, a detail he had almost missed. His once brown eyes had been replaced by a rich shade of maroon as if they were carved from dark rubies. While he found this unsettling he decided that he would grow accustomed to it and brushed it off as a side effect of his fusion with Al.

Slowly he dressed himself and did his best to recover his balance. Out of habit he strapped his sword across his back and threw his cloak around his shoulders before exiting the room. It was as Al had thought, he was somewhere inside the estate in the hidden valley. He wandered the halls for a while until he heard the faint sound of voices drifting from somewhere across the house.

"It's been two weeks! What spells haven't you tried yet?" he heard Sarah's voice demand.

"Ditrina and I have used every healing spell we know! These things take time!" Matt shot back.

"There's got to be something you can try!" Cassy yelled, presumably at Matt.

"We have been trying, but his body isn't responding as well as we had expected," Ditrina said, her voice strained.

"You need to try harder!" Sarah snarled at them.

Chris rounded the corner and saw his friends standing around a table in the living room. Ditrina noticed him first, her black eyed widening in shock. Before he could speak she disappeared from sight with a pop only to reappear beside him tackling him in a hug.

"You're ok!" Ditrina squealed in delight.

"I'm fine Ditrina, but what's wrong with you? I've never seen you act like this before!" Chris asked, terrified by seeing the normally subdued and awkward elf act with such enthusiasm.

"Cas told me I should act really, really happy to see you when you wake us to make sure you knew I was worried!" Ditrina said still hugging him from the floor.

"You've made your point Ditrina, you can let me go now," Chris told the overly excited elf.

"Of course," Ditrina said removing herself from atop him and returning to Cassy's side, her face once again a blank slate leaving Chris baffled.

"You're developing a really bad habit of passing out after our missions. This is what, the fourth time I've had to wait for you to wake up because you do something stupid?" Matt asked with a smile. "I'm glad you're alright."

"This coming from the man who passed out from casting a light spell," Chris taunted. "You can't count Purevein against me; you were out *way* longer than I was."

"Fair enough, but it saved your ass didn't it?" Matt replied.

"Fair enough," Chris chuckled in agreement.

"If Matt had let you die I don't think I could have forgiven him," Cassy said wiping a tear from the corner of her eye.

"What about Ditrina! She was helping me so if he died it would have been her fault too!" Matt exclaimed.

"Di's not a healer, it's your job to fix us when we're hurt not hers. Don't go trying to pass the buck on this," Cassy scolded.

Perhaps they would have argued further but Sarah took a single step forward silencing the room. Until now she had simply stared at Chris, her face a shifting mask of emotion.

"I'm glad you're alright Sarah," Chris said smiling in relief.

Sarah simply took another step toward him, her face unreadable.

"Sarah?" Chris asked unsure if she wanted to hug him or hit him. Sarah decided to do both.

"What the hell did you do!?" Sarah screamed as she slammed her fist into his stomach.

Chris doubled over in pain.

"What...are...you talking about?" Chris wheezed.

Sarah looked horrified as if she wasn't the one who had put him in this condition in the first place and pulled him into a tight hug.

"I'm so glad you're ok," she mumbled into his shoulder.

"You've got a funny way of showing it," Chris said, still recovering his breath.

"Oh ha ha ha, very funny Chris," Sarah said angrily as she stepped back.

"I hate to break up the reunion but I think if I let this go on any longer Chris will end up unconscious again," Matt said earning himself a glare from Sarah. "Well it's true! He just woke up and you're already trying to kill him!" Matt exclaimed.

"Chris, can you tell us what caused that explosion?" Ditrina asked him.

Chris looked sheepish.

"Well...that would have been me," he admitted.

"What? How?" Matt demanded in surprise.

"Well Al and I temporarily shared my body and he channeled a bunch of magic through my sword and it sort of...exploded," Chris said meekly.

"Wait, the *sword* did that? Why in the gods name do you still have it on you!?" Cassy yelled, looking at the sword like it may explode again at any moment.

"More importantly you said that you used magic? Without a god? How is that possible?" Matt demanded.

"Well Al provided the magic and I channeled it for him into the sword. Al claims that before the crisis all humans and even nonhumans could use magic at will without the gods assistance," Chris explained.

"That is correct," Ditrina said simply.

"Well what the hell changed?" Matt asked angrily.

"Al wouldn't say," Chris admitted.

All eyes looked to Ditrina.

"Yes?" she asked them.

"What do you know about the magic disappearing?" Chris asked with exasperation.

"Well I'm not a scholar but from what I can remember it had something to do with a covenant the peoples of the world made with the gods in return for them lifting the curse. The elves took no part in this deal and therefore retained our magic even though we too were freed from the curse. Not very fair if you think about it," Ditrina said staring off into space as if in a daydream.

Rather than press the issue they turned their attention back to Chris.

"So what did happen inside that tower?" Matt asked him.

Chris launched into the story of his battle with Sorros and its climatic resolution followed by his strange experience with Al.

"So now Al shares my head with me. He's agreed to keep quiet unless I talk to him first for the sake of my sanity and he'll still attend out nightly meetings but he's lost his connection to the astral realm so he's stuck here forever," Chris said, ending his tale.

"Chris you realize what this means right? You'll never be able to transfer over into the afterlife, you'll be stuck drifting in the physical realm once you die!" Matt said in horror.

"Yeah Al was very clear about that, but the way I see it there's no point bitching about things I can't change," Chris told him.

"Admirable, but you still should look for possible ways to fix this," Ditrina advised having returned from her daydream.

"True, but for now I want to simply enjoy our reward. We're going to be knights!" Chris exclaimed eargly.

"Um…about that…" Cassy began.

"What?" Chris asked worried. "Did we do something to botch the contract? Is Sorros still alive!?" Chris asked nervously.

"No, you killed him, and that's part of the problem. You see that little trick with the fireball you pulled destroyed the entire tower and took a large part of the castle with it. The city's in chaos. Hal arrived a few days after the fight and has done a great job of restoring order but because we caused so much damage the city thinks we're terrorists or something. Hal told us for our safety he wouldn't say a word about our identities and because anyone who saw us fighting was killed when the tower fell we're pretty safe on that front but we won't be knighted to avoid undo attention," Cassy explained.

"Oh," Chris said crestfallen.

"Cheer up buddy; we still got the estate and the hidden valley all to ourselves!" Matt said with enthusiasm.

"What about the village?" Chris asked. "We were going to be made the lords of it but if we're not knights I don't see that happening. Is it being added to the maps?"

"Hal said he was getting old and forgot the precise location of the village. Sly bastard doesn't want to sell out the people who helped him for so many years so for now the village will remain uncharted and off the records," Cassy said happily.

"That's actually great news for us; it means we can travel from one side of Targoth to the other without paying the King's taxes," Matt said.

"So Hal and his servants made it to Draclige alright? That's good. I was worried they might have trouble making the journey," Chris said.

"The thing is… not all the servants went with him," Matt told him.

"What the hell does that mean?" Chris demanded as the twins rounded the corner behind him.

"Good, the Master is awake," one of them said without a trace of emotion in her voice.

"Oh no, *no no no no no*, what are you two doing here?" Chris demanded.

"Master Regar's last orders to us were very clear. We are to serve as your maids in compensation for your lack of knighthood. We are honored," the other maid told him looking like she couldn't be any less honored if Hal had ordered her to muck out the stables.

Both maids curtsied.

"Whatever Hal told you; forget it. Go, you don't need to stay here," Chris told them.

"Master Regar was very specific. We are not to leave your service except in the instance of your death in which we are bound to your next of kin," one of the maids explained.

Chris looked to the others for support.

"I kinda like having them around," Cassy admitted. "It's a huge house and they keep things running smoothly. Plus, when we're away on missions they can keep the place tidy for us."

"I already tried getting them to leave, it's no use. I gave up," Sarah said with a sigh.

Chris was stunned; he had never heard those words come out of her mouth before. Recovering he turned to the maids.

"I don't care what Hal promised you, I'm not paying to have two maids living in my house for the rest of my life, and I don't plan on keeping you two as slaves so you need to pack your bags and get going," Chris told them.

"That's not a problem, Master Regar paid in advance. You don't need to worry about a thing," one of the maids told him.

"Listen, Flora…" Chris began.

"I'm Fiona," Fiona corrected quickly.

Chris sighed.

"Of course you are. You can just take your money and go, I don't need any servants!" Chris insisted.

"No thank you, we prefer to live here," Fiona told him with an air of finality, ending their discussion. "Ms. Morgson, I took the liberty of putting your armor away seeing as you won't need it around the estate. I also moved your things out of Master Shearcliff's room *again* seeing as it is improper for an unmarried woman such as yourself to share the quarters of a man," Fiona told her. "Please refrain from returning for the fourth time."

"How many times do I have to tell you little harpies!? I will sleep in whatever room I want with whoever I want and there's not a damn thing you can do about it!" Sarah bellowed storming out of the room to move her things yet again.

"Ms. Morgson I must insist!" Fiona said as she hurried after Sarah.

"I must aid my sister, if you'll excuse me Master," Flora said with a small curtsy as she hurried after the arguing pair.

"Come on Di! This will be funny," Cassy said as she dragged the elf out of the room after them.

Chris went to follow but Matt caught his arm.

"Sarah's been really worried about you you know," Matt told him.

"Why? Like you said it's not the first time I've been incapacitated after a mission," Chris told him.

"This time was different Chris. You woke up in her arms with glowing red eyes babbling in an ancient language. It shook her up pretty bad," Matt told him.

"Seriously?" Chris asked in disbelief. "I didn't think Sarah got flustered that easily," Chris said.

"When the tower exploded she rushed into the rubble before the dust had settled looking for you," Matt told him.

"No way, from your perspective there's no way it could have looked like I survived," Chris said.

"She was weeping Chris, *weeping*. Once we got you back here she stayed by your side for three days without eating until we literally dragged her out of your room, and even then, she slept beside you every night," Matt told him. "I just thought you should know," he added with a shrug.

"Thanks for telling me," Chris said with a nod.

"If you want to thank me then start by not telling her I said anything, I'd rather keep all of my limbs attached thank you very much," Matt said and Chris laughed.

"Sure thing buddy, my lips are sealed," Chris promised clasping his friend on the shoulder. "I need to stop my girlfriend form killing the maids now; I'll talk to you later," Chris said as he hurried back toward his room.

Chris arrived to a scene of chaos. Cassy and Ditrina stood in the doorway laughing as Sarah engaged in tug of war with both of the maids at once, each holding on to a different weapon.

"Flora, Fiona, I order you to let go of those swords!" Chris yelled.

In hindsight those probably weren't the best words to use because as soon as the maids released the swords Sarah flew backward crashing into a wardrobe.

Rising from the splintered remains of what had once been a lovely piece of craftsmanship with a sword in each hand Sarah looked practically murderous. The maids recognized this and hastily departed from the room with Cassy and Ditrina in tow. Sarah took a step to follow but Chris intercepted her.

"Wait," he told her.

"Chris get out of my way, those two need to pay for…" Sarah began.

"Wait," Chris said much more softly, stepping close to her.

"What is it?" Sarah asked confused, the murder draining from her eyes.

Chris pulled her into a kiss, wrapping his arms around her.

Sarah was surprised, Chris wasn't usually this forward but she responded quickly. Her swords hit the floor with a dull thud and for a time they simply stood entwined. Chris finally broke off their kiss to speak.

"I was so worried about you," he whispered his voice sticking in his throat.

"Why? You were the one who went blowing up a castle and scaring me half to death," Sarah said trying to laugh but failing as her eyes filled with tears.

Her false bravado crumpled around her.

"I thought you were dead," she sobbed quietly into his shoulder as she sunk to the floor, bringing Chris with her.

He pulled her close as she cried, stroking her head softly.

"It's alright, everything is going to be ok," he cooed softly.

"I thought you were dead!" Sarah yelled at him again, her voice full of hurt.

"I'm fine Sarah, everything is perfect," he told her still holding her close.

"How can you say something like that after everything that's happened!? Your soul...the spirit in your head...nothing is ok," Sarah sobbed.

"Everything is perfect because I have you here, so long as we're together nothing else matters. I'll never abandon you Sarah; I'll always come back to you," he promised her.

Sarah dried her eyes and smiled.

"And I will follow you wherever you go. We will be together now and forever, until the very end," she promised him.

"I love you," Chris said pulling her in to another kiss.

"I love you too," Sarah told him.

They stood up.

"Oh and Chris?" Sarah began.

"What is it?" Chris asked smiling.

"If you tell any of the others that I was blubbering like that I swear upon the gods that when I'm through slicing you apart all the clerics on Targoth won't be able to put you back together again," Sarah told him.

Chris simply laughed.

"Sounds fair," he said with a grin.

Al whispered a single word into Chris's mind igniting a though he had never considered. As Sarah went to leave his mind raced faster and faster considering the idea, Al spurring him on, until finally he decided.

"Sarah wait!" he called after her.

"What is it?" she asked confused, they had just been through this routine after all.

"Let's get married," Chris told her.

"What!?" Sarah asked completely bewildered.

"Let's get married," Chris repeated. "We practically exchanged vows already so why not? Let's spend the rest of our lives together; we can start a family here in the valley," Chris told her eargly.

Sarah stood speechless.

"Where did this come from so suddenly?" she asked him.

"I listened to my better judgment," Chris told her.

"Well that's a first," Sarah said with a laugh.

Chris stood expectantly, waiting for her answer but none was forthcoming.

"So…is that a yes?" he asked tentatively.

"Of course it's a yes stupid!" Sarah laughed.

Chris let out a pent up breath he hadn't realized he had been holding and joined in her joyous laugher.

"Come on, let's go tell the others the good news" Chris told her and moved toward the door but Sarah put her hand on his chest.

"Now it's my turn, wait," Sarah said with a sly smile.

"What is it?" Chris asked.

"I think we should start with the starting a family part as soon as possible," she told him as she dragged him toward the bed.

Chris decided he had defiantly made the right decision and silently thanked Al a thousand times on the short trip to the bed. He would have thanked him more but as it turned out Sarah proved far more adapt at holding his attention.

They held the wedding the very next day on Sarah's bequest in the valley by the lake. It was a simple affair, with Matt acting as the priest at Chris's request.

Despite the impossibly short notice Flora and Fiona managed

to procure matching gold rings, engraved with intertwining vines. However, also due to the short notice they were unable to find a dress for Sarah, which Chris suspected was her plan all along.

Rather than wear a normal dress she insisted on wearing her armor which she had polished until it gleamed. Chris had the maids freshly iron his clothes to remove any stray wrinkles but otherwise dressed as he normally would, bearing his sword across his back and wearing his cloak as they exchanged the same vows as the day before. The only people in attendance were Ditrina and Cassy, and the maids of course, but Chris preferred it that way. It felt better being surrounded only by his friends, his new family. If he had been surrounded by dozens of people he barely knew he decided he would be far more nervous, but as it was he found the entire wedding fun and enjoyable.

That evening, after they had spent most of the day drinking and celebrating they convened for a final toast.

"To the adventures of Shearcliff and Company!" Chris said as he raised his glass.

Together they drank to the future, to the adventures they had shared, and the ones yet to come.

Printed in the United States
By Bookmasters